FIRST TO FALL

A LOST STORY BOOKSHOP NOVEL
BOOK TWO

JENNY B. JONES

SWEET PEA PRODUCTIONS

For Librarians—
Keep fighting the good fight.
The world needs your voice and advocacy.
May books never be silenced.

CHAPTER

ONE

OLIVIA

On Monday morning I glanced in my rearview mirror, eyeballed my crooked tiara, and thought, not for the first time, that I should be nominated for sainthood. Or at the very least —and preferable best—receive a fat raise from my boss.

"Who is it you're supposed to be?" the teenage girl from the backseat asked.

"Queen Elizabeth." I adjusted my crown and eased into the left lane. I'd like to say this was my first time driving in a full-length gown, but it was not. When your employer encouraged "fun" by way of too-frequent theme days, you got used to driving in all sorts of costume accessories. Last week my car was in the shop, and I had to catch an Uber dressed as Count Dracula. Turns out, you have to tip extra when you wear fangs.

"Alexander, quit hitting your sister." I threw my best *don't-you-dare* look to the backseat, where Alexander Coulson used his fourteen-year-old sister's shoulder as a punching bag.

"Everyone in the sixth grade thinks you stink, Alexander," Katarina taunted. "They told me."

"They do not!" he countered.

"Do too!"

I turned down the audiobook their mom, and my boss, insisted they listen to during our commute. A dulcet British voice narrated a boring classic no one in the car cared a whit about. Heaven forbid Celeste's children listen to something corruptive like popular music or one of my riveting murder podcasts. Last week's auditory punishment had been a tutorial on Latin verb conjugation.

"Ow!" Katarina retaliated by jabbing her pointy salon nails into her little brother's arm.

"Remind me what we're celebrating today?" I called out as I pushed the gas pedal toward the floorboard. Celeste had called with an emergency, begging me to pick up her children at home in Sugar Creek and drive them twenty minutes away to their elite private school in the next town. How could I possibly say no? Never mind that these emergencies happened at least two times a week and occasionally included what I called "add-ons." These might entail—but were not limited to —picking up poster board en route, leaving extra early for Kat's volleyball practice, or getting halfway to their school only to realize someone had left behind a lunch box, homework, or the class hamster, requiring a return home.

"We're celebrating Alexander remembering to wear under-wear." Katarina stuck her tongue out at her brother.

"Are not!" Alexander doled out three more punches, which barely provoked a flinch from his stout sister. "I'm the new robotics club president."

"That's great, Alexander," I said. "I know your mom is thrilled."

Today's "add-on," at Celeste's command, was a celebratory trip to the Starbucks drive-through. I'd purchase the kids' breakfast and iced mochas, using my own hard-earned money but Celeste's rewards card. Why? Because my boss told me to, and I never let the woman down.

"My mom doesn't even remember I'm in the robotics club," Alexander said.

"I'm sure she does." Was that a lie? No. In the PR business we called that framing information. Because Celeste could remember the birthday and favorite drink of every client we'd ever courted, but her ability to recall details of her children's lives was sorely lacking.

"I asked *her* to take us for our celebration Starbucks." Alexander's bottom lip curved downward in a sad pout. "But she had to leave early for the office, just like she always does."

"Mom told you she'd make it up to you." Katarina dropped her usual acidic attitude and bestowed a rare, sympathetic look upon her younger brother. "She has a lot to do to get ready for today's promotion announcement."

"What?" The car lurched toward the left lane, eliciting honks from the truck beside us and squeals from the backseat.

"Are you trying to kill us?" Alexander cried. "I'm too young to die. I have robots to create and a world to take over!"

I bypassed the rearview mirror and stole a quick glance behind me, locking eyes on Katarina. "Did you say *promotion?*"

My boss's daughter didn't bother looking up from her phone. "Maybe."

I turned off the audiobook as I lost all chill. "Tell me everything you know and do not leave out one detail."

Katarina lowered her device for half a second. "What's it worth to you?"

It was all I could do not to reach one hand toward the backseat and yank her up front with me. "I'll get you a double shot of espresso in that mocha."

Katarina didn't even have to think about it. "I don't want the sugar-free version."

"Okay," I agreed.

"And I want whipped cream," said the crop top–wearing negotiator. "Make that *extra* whipped cream."

Celeste would fire me on the spot if she even knew. "Fine, okay. Now start talking."

Katarina's focus went back to her flashing screen. "There's an opening in the New York office. Mom said she's promoting someone from Sugar Creek."

"For what job?"

"I wasn't interested enough to catch that detail," Katarina said.

"I'll make sure the barista throws in extra chocolate sauce and sprinkles."

"A senior brand manager."

Senior brand manager. That was the role I'd been gunning for the last two years. "This is excellent intel, Katarina. Thank you for sharing."

Alexander leaned forward, his salesman face peeking around the seat. "Stop at the bagel place, and I'll share my secret recipe for slime."

Hanging a left turn, I smiled. "Very tempting, but darn, we're short on time."

I was so ready for a new challenge and to prove to Celeste I was future vice president material. This new role would take me straight to the New York office of Flair, but more importantly, it was happening right on schedule.

Look out, world. Olivia Sutton, is on her way!

"Olivia?" Alexander called.

"Yes, sweetie?" *Nothing will get in my path. Nothing can stop me now. Ain't nothin' gonna break my stride!*

"I forgot my science fair project," he said. "We gotta go back home."

I leaned my elbow on my window and sighed. "I'll turn around."

CHAPTER

TWO

OLIVIA

AN HOUR LATER, my voluminous dress and I finally stepped into the offices of Flair, Inc. Prior to getting the taxi demand from my boss, I'd awakened this morning with a sense of curious unease, stretching my arms with an energy that Red Bull wished they could bottle. Something was in the air, and it was more than the shifting winds of September, more than the leaves outside changing into their fall garments of red and gold. Turned out the feeling had been spot-on.

So today Celeste would announce a promotion opportunity at her marketing firm. I hadn't worked sixty-hour weeks for the last three years for nothing. This new job had my name written all over it, and it was more than time. I'd been passed over for the last two promotions, but there was no way my boss wouldn't pick me this go-round. Had I been more than qualified for the other jobs? Yes. But Celeste was my role model, and I *had* benefitted from more time under her wing.

The coffee shop on the first floor of our office building served their drinks hot and their gossip scorching. It was already abuzz with Flair employees looking for that caffeinated high to jump-start their morning.

I practically floated on air as I swished my way to my friend and fellow brand manager, Elton. "Happy morning to you."

Dark eyes narrowed behind black-framed glasses. "Is it?"

I bent down and scratched the chin of his Standard Poodle. "And good morning to you, FeeFee."

Celeste ran Flair much like a trendy Silicon Valley tech office. Pets were allowed daily, each floor contained two nap pods, and at least once a week someone got run over by an indoor scooter. The office boasted an outside playground *for the adults*, and every Friday ended with a five o'clock happy hour. Some days this place was a circus, but I still counted my lucky stars Celeste had plucked me for a college internship years ago and put me to work.

I couldn't contain my secret any longer. "I have news."

He tilted his head and gave my outfit serious consideration. "Is it that you won prom queen?" Elton's hand swooped in my direction. "Honey, what is this?"

"I'm Queen Elizabeth—the early years."

"The sensible pumps are a nice touch."

"Thanks. I like to be authentic." People got PhDs in less time than it had taken me to put together my thematic outfits over the last nearly-seven years. "Why aren't you dressed up?" My friend wore his usual slacks, button-down, and bowtie.

"What are you talking about?" he asked.

I adjusted my drooping puff sleeve. "Hero Day."

Elton gave one of those *bless your heart* smiles. "That's tomorrow."

"What?" But as more employees began to filter into the building, I did notice a very distinct pattern: No one was in costume.

Elton laughed and picked up FeeFee's leash. "Nice dress, though, Elizabeth."

The panic was instantaneous and nausea-inducing. How had I messed this up? I, Olivia Sutton, did not make stupid mistakes. I was a rule-following, detail-worshipping woman who lived and died by her planner. Yet, thanks to my last project at Flair and my marketing work for my sister's book-shop opening, I'd gotten negative five hours of sleep in the last two weeks, and it showed.

Smelling my favorite dark roast, I dug in my Union Jack clutch for my wallet. "I have extra clothes upstairs."

"Of course you do." Elton took a step closer. "Now spill the news."

I glanced about, assuring we didn't have any extra ears nearby. "There's a job opening in the New York office."

Elton's eyes rounded. "I would kill for that, but"—he held up a hand—"you're due."

"Yes," I agreed with a smile. "I am. But don't let that stop you from applying. You know Morgan will throw her hat in."

We both shared a moment of mutual disgust at the name of our fellow coworker.

Elton ran a hand over his dog's curly head. "You have my vote over Ursula the PR Sea Witch any day. Speaking of difficult women, did Celeste put you on chauffeur duty this morning?"

I eyed the line for the coffee kiosk. "You know I don't mind helping out."

"I do know," Elton said. "That's why I worry about you. Celeste runs you ragged."

"She's a busy single mom. She needs help."

"That woman could afford round-the-clock help. She enjoys watching you do her bidding."

We'd had this discussion many times before, and like always, I was quick to shut it down. It felt heretical to talk badly about my boss and hero, the woman to whom I owed my career. "If you need help updating your résumé, let me know," I told Elton. "Is butt-insky spelled with a hyphen or all one word?"

"Olivia," he said, "I'm worried about you. Are you living your own life...or Celeste's?"

"I appreciate the concern, but when I get that promotion, all the sacrifice and servitude will be worth it."

"When's the last time you did something fun?"

"Last week I watched a five-part LinkedIn Learning course on trend predictions."

"I meant the kind that doesn't involve a laptop, billable hours, or praying three times a day to Celeste, the goddess of expensive shoes and cheap overtime."

Good heavens, this dress itched. Had Queen Elizabeth endured these problems? "As a matter of fact, I'm hopping on a plane with my sisters this Friday night." *Ha! Take that, Elton.* I felt some small measure of satisfaction at my friend's shocked face.

"Tell me it's not a work conference," he said.

"It's not." Though Celeste did want me to stop by and connect with a resort owner to pitch one of her marketing ideas. "My sister Hattie got engaged a few weeks ago, and to celebrate and check out a possible venue, she and Miller are taking their wedding party to Las Vegas."

"Would you like me to describe 'fun' so you can hunt for it while you're there?"

"No, I would not. And excuse me for not being in constant search of merriment and tomfoolery."

Elton's phone buzzed, and he checked the screen. "Ugh, I've been summoned. Celeste needs help with her PowerPoint again." He dipped into a curtsy. "See you upstairs, Your Majesty."

With little time to spare, I hopped in line for another coffee as I finished a text to a client.

One minute later, I sensed my coworker Morgan had stepped behind me. Perhaps the brimstone smell tipped me off.

"Are your morning babysitting duties complete?" Morgan glanced at her gold watch. "You're almost late."

"But I'm not late." I didn't even bother with a pleasant face. "And, yes, I safely delivered Celeste's precious cargo to school. What does it say about our boss's regard for me that she trusts me with the loves of her life?"

"That Celeste sees you as a free nanny?"

"If she trusts me with her children, then she can trust me with anything." I tapped a nail to my chin. "Like an elite client or, I dunno, a promotion."

"Sure. Uh-huh." The woman Elton always referred to as various Disney movie villains snarled at my costume. "What's with the pageant dress?"

"Just doing a test run for Hero Day." My crown slid down the side of my long brown hair. "Which is tomorrow, of course." I fixed the lopsided sash across my chest. "And the outfit works. What a productive morning already. But I'll obviously be changing."

"I'd hope."

Morgan looked glamorous as ever. We both adored our boss Celeste and emulated her fashionable style. It was a daily competition between Morgan and me to see who could look the most glam, and today...I had lost.

Morgan was of the tall, slender breed of woman who was never without makeup and surely never got the theme days confused. "Good job on the album release party last night," I told her.

"Thanks." She glanced over my head as if it pained her to

make eye contact with one so inferior. "Sorry you didn't get the account, but I've enjoyed every minute of it."

"I'm sure you have."

"Though the band kept me up late." Her glossy pink lips opened in a small O as she faked a yawn. "Next week is the Coalminers' party in Nashville. I've been invited, of course."

"Great. I'm happy for you."

I was not happy for her.

Morgan had joined the company six months before I had, yet you'd have thought it was a decade. She constantly acted like the elder PR person. "You probably don't know this, Olivia, but...No doubt this is new territory for you, Olivia, but..." So obnoxious. The woman thought she'd invented PR and treated me like an intern.

"I shouldn't tell you this," I said, "but an inside source revealed a promotion announcement could be forthcoming."

Morgan eyed the menu board. "Does this inside source wear braces and make you edit her ninth grade English essays?"

"Of course not." But she had made me listen to her terrible techno rap the entire way to school last week.

"Well, your exciting exclusive isn't news to me." Morgan's triumphant face clearly had been the recent recipient of Botox, as it barely moved. "I've heard whispers. It will probably go to someone experienced. Are you thinking of applying?" She asked this as if she didn't already know the answer, *and* as if I'd be wasting my time if I tried.

"New York would be a great challenge." I would give my left arm and favorite pair of stilettos to beat out Morgan.

"Do you really think you're up for that challenge?" Morgan tossed her hair and dug out her wallet. "Your family's here in Sugar Creek, and you seem so...settled."

"Change requires sacrifice, right?" My smile was just as lethal as hers.

Morgan's phone buzzed with a text. "Oh, looks like the Coalminers want to discuss extending their contract with Flair. Do I bring in the business or what?"

The barista grinned as I stepped to the counter. "Good morning, Ms. Olivia."

"Rudy, how are you?"

"Very well." He passed me a new punch card. "You want your usual?"

"Yes, please."

"Macchiato with double shot of espresso coming right up."

"Perfect." I stuffed a few dollars in the tip jar and gazed out the wall of glass windows.

"Celeste says we'll have a very special guest at our morning meeting." Morgan stepped up to the counter and returned to reading the heavily scripted menu. "I bet I already know who it will be. Rudy, I'll have my usual as well."

Rudy passed a drink to another coworker. "And what is that, ma'am?"

Morgan frowned with annoyance. "A sugar-free caramel mocha, half-soy, half-almond milk, no whip with a dash of cinnamon."

He scurried away, and Morgan's attention snapped back to me. "It's a very big account, I'm told. Giant." She stepped into my space and grabbed some napkins. "The first phase of the Coalminers' campaign is wrapping up, so it's the perfect time for me to take on a new project."

"Right." I thanked Rudy and accepted my drink, letting the warmth of the cup seep into my hand.

"And what is it you're working on?" Morgan barely paused for time to answer. "Oh, yes. Ozark Mountain Dog Food. How was that photo shoot with all the hunting mutts?"

I'd gone home covered in so much dog hair I looked like Sasquatch, and my ears rang all night with the shrill cries of beagles. "Perfectly delightful."

"We all have to be put through our paces, right?" She lifted her cup in a salute. "Your day for the big account will come. Eventually." With that, Morgan—the intrepid, seasoned elder—made her exit, leaving a trail of residual perfume and condescension.

CHAPTER
THREE

OLIVIA

I RACED up the steps to the third floor, not even bothering with the elevator. I had to get this costume off before the meeting. Even with a collection of planners I followed obsessively, it was so hard to keep up with all the events around the office. Pie Day. Tuba Awareness Week. Dress Like a Favorite Martyr Monday. It was exhausting. I didn't need forced efforts to generate fun and camaraderie. All I wanted was function and efficiency in my workplace. And less dog hair.

I'd just made it to my office, rounded my desk, and removed my pearls when Celeste's assistant stuck her head in the door. "Meeting in the green conference room right now."

I pointed at the billowy gown. "But I need to change."

"Celeste's in a mood," Berta warned. "No time for that." Her eyes tracked me as I packed up my laptop and joined her at the door. "Who are you supposed to be?"

"Someone who needs a day off."

"Like you'd ever take one," she muttered.

With coffee in one hand and my laptop in the other, I scurried to the meeting space, dodging two dogs and a Persian cat.

Last week Milo Riggins brought his albino snake, and Celeste had sent them both home. She had her limits on boundless fun.

The green conference room was an ode to sustainability and Mother Earth. It featured walls papered in bamboo, lights powered by a solar panel that rarely worked, and a giant table surrounded by fifteen chairs all constructed from cardboard. The room smelled like compost, and I couldn't wait until the whole design was recycled.

Celeste did a double take as I entered but proceeded to set up her materials for a presentation.

"Celeste looks furious," Elton whispered to me as I sat beside him and FeeFee. "That doesn't bode well."

"Good morning." Celeste waited for the room to quiet, which did not take long. The woman merely had to blink to command attention. My gosh, she was incredible. Her leadership was on par with anyone running a Fortune 500 company. Her ideas were van Gogh levels of art and genius. I'd seen grown men cry in her presence and countless standing ovations in her honor. She resembled Viola Davis with that same captivating blend of elegance and intimidation.

"Before we get to our original agenda for the meeting," Celeste said, "we have something very serious to discuss." She leveled those eyes on every single person in the room, like a mother making good on her threat to pull the car over for a scolding. "This morning at four a.m., Tinesha Drake was arrested for stalking and breaking and entering the home of world-renowned architect—and our client—Tyrone Phillips."

Gasps filled the fragrant room. Exaggerated looks of shock took over faces. Even FeeFee whined in misery.

"As of the time of her booking, Tinesha is no longer an employee of Flair." Celeste tilted her head back, squeezed the bridge of her trim nose, and released a shuddering breath.

"Counting last month's debacle with Brett, this is two Flair scandals in as many months. I will not stand for even one more step out of line. Not one teensy-weensy smidgen of impropriety or drama. Am I clear?"

Last month our marketing specialist, Brett Hargis, had gotten fired for double-billing a client. That client had not only found the embarrassing discrepancy, but he'd also found Brett in the hot tub with said client's wife.

"Word is already out regarding how unstable Flair looks," Celeste all but shouted. "An hour ago I received a call from the folks that handle the HGTV remodel show that films here, and they've terminated our contract. They will be pursuing another marketing company. I have five messages to return from other clients, and I dread those conversations, as I'm sure *Fizzle to Fabulous* won't be the only one to opt out. Our reputation has been nuked. Do I need to remind you that how you conduct yourself reflects heavily on *my* company?" Celeste did not wait for a response. "So now this firm that serves world-class PR needs its own PR. How horribly ironic."

She paced the front of the room as I sat in my ballgown and tried to process it all. I ate, slept, and breathed this company. Stick me, and I bled Flair. If we didn't change our logo every four years, I would've proudly tattooed Flair somewhere on my person. It devastated me to see our company brought so low by the thoughtless indiscretions of others. And it certainly pained me to watch my hero, Celeste, in agony over the fallout.

My boss resumed her tirade. "We are being scrutinized like never before. So for the next year—at least—if even one of you steps out of line and brings negative press to Flair, you will be fired on the spot." She slammed her manicured hands on the table. "Do I make myself clear?"

"Yes, ma'am," we said in vehement harmony.

She let her gaze travel across each of us, searing her threat into our brains one frightened employee at a time. "You keep your personal lives private, and if you have some crazy lurking inside you, I want you to stick it in one of those packing cubes, shove it in a suitcase, and send it far, far away. I do not ever want to know about it."

That would not be a problem for me. I, Olivia Sutton, upholder of the ironclad calendar and ten-year life plan, was as scheduled and straight-laced as it got. And nowhere in that life plan I so carefully crafted would you find "crossing the line with a client" or "getting myself arrested." I detested drama and would never so much as dip a toe in its waters.

Celeste returned to the helm of the table and took a long draw from her dainty teacup as if to cleanse her palate. "Now that you know how easy it is to find yourself unemployed, let us move on to happier topics. I realize the office has been aflutter with speculation the last few weeks. It's time I put some of those rumors to rest." Celeste stood at the head of the oval table, the queen surveying her empire. "You already know that when my sister suggested I start a satellite office in a tiny corner of Arkansas, I thought she had lost her mind."

The room filled with polite laughter. Morgan sat with her chin propped up on her hands, hanging onto Celeste's every word.

Our boss cleared her throat and continued. "But little did I know she'd discovered an unexpected gold mine for our firm. As a result, we've seen exponential growth at Flair here, and our work rivals that of our New York office."

Elton kicked me beneath the table and leaned in to whisper. "Look at Gunnar. He probably thinks this promotion is his."

Gunnar Zapinski, age thirty-two and twice divorced, barely possessed the ability to find his car in the parking lot. He'd been at Flair the longest, but he wasn't any competition. Our eyes met, and Gunnar gave me an excited but discreet thumbs-up.

"The flagship office has grown tremendously as well," Celeste continued, "and we've decided to bring one of you along to fill a role as senior brand manager."

This was it. The moment I'd been waiting for.

I can provide my application in three different fonts, my résumé in two languages, and my portfolio in five different mediums.

Sign. Me. Up.

"I've spoken to a handful of you and know some have zero interest in leaving the work here in Arkansas," Celeste said.

I could feel Morgan's hyperfocus burn into my head, trying to implant her negative thoughts. Of course she wanted the New York job, and of course she thought she'd get it.

The thought of leaving my beloved home in Sugar Creek caused a pain on par with jumping out of a moving car or stepping into a bonfire. My family, my friends, and my sweet downtown apartment were all here. Yet I wanted nothing more than to learn, climb up the PR ladder in my secondhand Louboutin heels, and run my own firm one day. The best way to make that happen was to take on the bigger accounts in New York. The opportunities there were the stuff of my work-obsessed dreams. And knocking Morgan out of the job would be the cherry on top.

"If you're interested in the New York role, I need an email from you declaring your intentions by end of business today." Celeste paused as the room absorbed the fast deadline.

"So we just apply for the job?" Morgan asked. "That's it?"

"That would be too simple, wouldn't it?" Celeste had mastered the art of the ironic smile, and her lips curved upward. Had I practiced that look in the mirror on more than one occasion? I'd never tell. "I will be assigning everyone who applies a brand-new account."

That sounded easy enough.

"Plus," Celeste added, "along with your updated résumé, I'd like a detailed report in which you tell me about the major client that *you* have secured. One you need to find immediately."

"Any type of client?" Elton asked.

Celeste shook her head like *silly little man*. "I want big name, big company, and big pockets. I want an account that will be a jewel in our now-tarnished crown. Do not bring me some small-town business or a low-key individual. I want a name that makes us look amazing. I want *big*."

I absolutely hated soliciting business. Abhorred. But at this point, there was nothing I wouldn't do to land a mega client. Personally pay for their PR? Absolutely. Promise them the moon and stars? Totally—*and* gift them a telescope to view all the glories when we were done. Give my heart, soul, and twenty-two hours of every day? They could have my every breath. Who needed sleep?

"You'll have one week to turn in your report," Celeste added. "Any more questions?" Her voice snapped with a tone that let us know she was done with the topic.

"Next item of business." Celeste smoothed a hand over the waist of her tailored jacket, as if the meeting had unsettled her stomach. "Today we have the distinct privilege of meeting a new potential client. And ladies and gentlemen, this person is the very definition of heavy hitter—the exact level you should aspire to recruit. This individual and his company are moving to Sugar Creek from California, which will be a boon to the economy of Northwest Arkansas. They're in search of good PR, desire someone local, and are interviewing agencies this week. I was lucky enough to secure some time with this dynamic entrepreneur so we could hear about exactly what he needs." Celeste checked her phone and quickly read a text. "Berta's bringing him upstairs right now." She looked upon her team with some hesitation, but also hesitant pride. "Today we could add a new category to our client list—video games."

Yawn. I knew nothing about video games and hoped this meeting wrapped up soon. I wanted nothing more than to exit the room, race to my desk, and begin researching potential clients.

A knock sounded, and Celeste's face lit. "Team, it is with the utmost enthusiasm and honor that I present to you Arkansas's newest resident. He's made millions in a matter of years creating *Mars Wars*, turning the gaming industry on its head. And his company has just gone public." The door opened on cue, and Berta stepped inside, followed by one very tall gentleman.

My heart torpedoed to my stomach.

The man's eyes traveled across the room, then locked on me.

Celeste extended her hand toward our guest. "Flair is elated to introduce the brilliant innovator we can't wait to partner with—Lachlan Hayes."

My two coffees threatened to come right back up.

Dear God.

It can't be.

My college nemesis. The bad boy of Ozark University. A knave among knaves.

Seven years ago, he'd nearly ruined my life until Celeste had saved me. But before I'd left the university, I'd made sure he would suffer in return.

From the stormy look on his face now, I could tell Lachlan Hayes hadn't forgotten.

Or forgiven.

FOUR

OLIVIA

Flair would not be gaining the Lachlan Hayes account.

Celeste would throw an absolute tantrum. The question was: Would Lachlan tell her it was because of me?

"Sorry I'm late." Lachlan wore a wool stocking cap like it was December in Alaska instead of mid-September in Arkansas.

"No apologies!" Celeste rushed to his side and shooed him into a seat. Right across from me. "Welcome! Welcome!"

He eased his large body into the chair, and I instantly had a fantasy of the cardboard beneath him collapsing. The lanky college boy had sure grown. Now he was a giant of a man, with coppery red hair tied into a ponytail and shoulders so broad, he probably had to angle himself to fit through a doorway. His face showed maturity and hints of age, but his eyes still sparked with mischief. No doubt his brain remained crippled by immaturity and a compulsion for shenanigans.

Beside me Elton gaped in unadulterated reverence. "How wonderful you've stopped by to see us, Mr. Hayes," he gushed. "I'm a huge fan of *Mars Wars*. I can't tell you how many times

I've told myself I'm only going to play for a few minutes, and before I know it, three hours have gone by."

"It's a delightful product, and Mr. Hayes is a genius." Celeste's trio of chunky necklaces clanged as she began her ballet of movement around the table, gracefully walking as she proceeded to lay the groundwork for the needs of the account.

"Please, everyone," the genius said in a deep baritone meant for smoky bars and late-night pillow talk, "call me Lachlan."

I could think of a dozen other things to call him.

Of all the marketing firms, why ours? What was Lachlan doing here in my corner of the world? And why on earth would he move his company to Sugar Creek? This was *my* home.

And what was with his outfit? Besides the ridiculous stocking cap *at a business meeting*, he wore a pink plaid flannel shirt under a fuchsia hoodie that looked like it belonged on a high schooler. A fashion-challenged one at that. It was an odd mix of grunge and Barbie. And *still*, Lachlan Hayes bore a presence. Despite the fact he clearly rejected the idea of shaving, I could tell Lachlan's cheekbones were chiseled, his jaw cut at ninety degrees of stunning, and his gaze, arrogant as it was, reflected intelligence and an unfiltered scrutiny.

I couldn't stand the man.

"Nice dress," Lachlan whispered toward me.

"Mr. Hayes," Celeste cooed, "with such short notice of your visit, I haven't had much time to prepare, but I did throw together a little something to bring my intrepid staff up to speed." She clicked a remote and images popped up on the giant screen that dominated half a wall. "Lachlan Hayes created *Mars Wars* when he was only twenty-one. Eight years and seven spin-offs later, his franchise is a multimillion-dollar industry. In November, Vortex Studios will release the film adaptation of *Mars Wars*, starring Oscar winners Naomi Chin and Eduardo Lima. It's expected to be a huge blockbuster with a sequel already in development. And lest you think I'm done, next spring Netflix will debut this glorious man's anime series based on his fabulous games."

Hoo boy. Celeste was really laying it on thick. Lachlan sat in his chair, his posture that of a fatigued teenage boy, with his annoyingly striking green eyes and his falsified visage of humbleness. But I knew the truth. I knew who he really was.

My boss continued in an almost giddy voice. "Lachlan's Star Gazer Corp. not only creates and sells the games, but they do big merchandising business as well. Last Christmas the *Mars Wars* action figures were *the* hot item."

"You have dolls," I whispered to him. "How cute."

His only response was an infuriating smile.

Celeste now stood behind me, her red Halston suit totally on point, and her instincts so *not*. Working with Lachlan Hayes would be a huge mistake for Flair.

"Star Gazer Corp. will soon release their next *Mars Wars* installment, *Mars Wars: Zombie Edition*." Celeste spoke with a reverence reserved for museum antiquities. "And only a few weeks ago, his company went public. These many developments demand Mr. Hayes be in the media spotlight. He wants the best company to make that happen, and I've assured him Flair is the only choice. It's a large commitment with multi-pronged action items, but nobody can do PR work better than this team right here, Mr. Hayes."

"We would love to be here for you. Completely at your disposal." Morgan's vampy smile communicated to our guest she was available to do that and so much more. And she probably *would* take point on this. She was our elder, after all. "My head is already spinning with ideas."

"I'm glad to hear that, Morgan," Celeste said. "We'll need all hands on deck. Mr. Hayes, the team you see here is the best and the brightest. The most gifted and skilled in public relations. Morgan, here, is one of our lead brand strategists."

Morgan loaded her gloating gun and fired a shot my way. "Thank you, Celeste."

Celeste rested a ringed hand on my rigidly taut shoulder. "Our dear Olivia is also one of the best in brand management."

Lachlan's hooded gaze slid to me. "*Dear Olivia* is an old friend." He paused for dramatic effect. "I'm well aware of her... talent for the spin."

I sat in my uncomfortable chair and prayed for an asteroid shower or an easy breezy typhoon. Was a well-timed implosion too much to ask for?

Celeste changed the slide to an architectural rendering of Star Gazer Corp.'s future Sugar Creek headquarters. "Lachlan has requested someone with an expertise in personal brand development, and let me assure you, sir, nobody does it better than Olivia."

A muscle in Lachlan's jaw flexed. "Yes. I've heard she can really alter an image."

My temper triggered a delusional fantasy, and I envisioned a lightning bolt zapping through the window and striking Lachlan right where he sat. And sure, one could survive being struck by lightning, but alas, all that hair would catch fire and up he'd go in a smoky plume of pink plaid and loathsome smirk.

"I know you have high expectations." Celeste preened as she floated near Lachlan. "Flair's PR department can exceed every one of them. We're responsive. We deliver results. Simply put, your wish is our command."

His gaze locked onto mine, and his smug face let me know he had all sorts of ideas for his wish list.

But as Celeste took her seat, Lachlan's smile thinned ten degrees past bored. He nodded as he seemed to consider her pitch. Then, the god of games spoke. "As much as I appreciate how accessible your team would be, it's come to my attention within the last hour that Flair has encountered some recent issues." Lachlan shifted in his seat, his body leaning closer to mine. "I have very high standards."

"Those employees have been fired," Celeste sputtered. "I do not tolerate anything but professionalism. Please know in working with us, your safety will be maintained. You will never endure one moment of anything less than top-notch service."

"Thank you for your time," Lachlan said. "I will take all this into consideration." He cut his eyes to me once more, like a final stab of the knife before he departed. "But I don't think this is the right fit for me or my company."

Celeste's eyes widened. "But—"

"If I change my mind, I'll let you know." And with that, Lachlan, in his lumberjack flannel and skater boy hoodie, stood and made his way to the door. "Have a nice day."

As he exited, we all sat frozen in place by the dangle of the biggest client and the fastest rejection Flair had ever received.

Suddenly, Celeste jumped to her feet and waved her arms like airport ground control. "You know him, Olivia? Then go! Go after him!"

I shook my head in frantic confusion. "Me? Now? Me?" *No! Anything but that!*

"Yes!" Celeste yelled. "Talk to him! Lachlan has to sign with us, and you can fix it! Go!"

I would've rather run through town naked while twirling flaming batons than chase after Lachlan Hayes. But chase I did, sprinting out of the office and down the hall as fast as my heels and cumbersome dress would allow.

That bulking expanse of a man was just slipping into the elevator when I saw him. The doors shushed toward one another, and as his focus tracked me the entire time, I slid through sideways as though I had no fear of death by squashing.

"You could've held the doors." Panting, I crashed against the back of the descending elevator.

"Oh." Lachlan crossed his arms over his chest. "Going down, Olivia?"

For a few seconds, I thought about disobeying Celeste and pretending I'd been too late to catch him. "You know why I'm here."

"Yes," he said, "but I would so love to see you beg."

A vision of my hand strangling that tree trunk of a neck flashed strong and hot in my mind. "The bad press Flair's experienced are merely flukes. We're a good company, Lachlan. The best."

"I don't care," he said. "It was over as soon as I saw you in the conference room, and you know it."

"You're going to punish those employees in there and possibly jeopardize your own PR success because of something that happened in college?" Still panting, I held up a hand before he could spit out a response. "It's not like I want to work with you either. I'll make sure you're partnered with Celeste herself if you'll reconsider."

Lachlan's laugh rumbled in his chest, and his grin stabbed right into my pride. "I'm not mad at you, Olivia. Because of you, I got kicked out of school seven years ago. Six months later I took my first video game online. Six months after that I made my first million. So maybe I should be thanking you."

But we both knew that was the last thing he was going to do.

The elevator whirred as we dropped another floor. "What happened was your own fault."

He shrugged. "Agree to disagree. But either way, I'm not doing business with Flair." The doors pulsed open as if siding with Lachlan and punctuating his finale. The bright lights of the lobby rushed inside. "You can go back and tell your boss it's a hard no."

The jerk. The pompous, immature boil on my memory.

Lachlan slipped car keys from the pocket of his faded jeans and gave them a twirl around his finger. "Maybe now we're even."

Good riddance, I thought. I couldn't wait to see the last of Lachlan. "Thanks for stopping by the office. Have a nice weekend."

"And thank *you* for the warm welcome into town. Always great to see old friends." He gave the edge of his stocking cap a tug as if tipping a hat. "I'll see you around."

"Don't count on it."

Lachlan stepped out of the elevator, only to turn back and leave me with that familiar frat boy grin. "Oh, I'd almost guarantee it."

FIVE

OLIVIA

Of course I saw Lachlan Hayes that next Friday night.

Hands gripping the armrests, I turned in my airplane seat at takeoff and glared. I'd boarded American Airlines flight 2069 with an eight o'clock landing time in Hell and Misery.

"Seriously, Hattie?" I turned to my sister, who had gamely forsaken a seat by her beloved fiancé Miller to fill up a row with me and our youngest sister, Rosie. "You couldn't have mentioned that Miller not only knew Lachlan, but that Lachlan would be joining us for your engagement celebration weekend?"

"It might've slipped my mind." She raised up in her own seat and waggled her fingers toward Miller a few rows back. "You try planning a wedding in five months. Never mind. I know *you* could pull it off in a week. But my brain is nothing but a list of things to buy, things to stress over, and things I plan on doing on my honeymoon."

"That's exactly how I feel about the bookstore grand opening," Rosie said. "Minus the honeymoon business."

Rosie had spent most of the year renovating an old building, turning it into her dream of a bookshop. Upon our return from Vegas, we'd celebrate the grand opening with a party, and we couldn't wait.

The seat leather squeaked as Rosie turned to face me. "What exactly is the big deal, Olivia? You act like Lachlan insulted your family, took all your worldly possessions, and kicked puppies in your presence. Is there more to the story you're not telling us?"

Hold out your cups, ladies, because I'm about to pour some serious tea. "The name *Lachlan Hayes* should sound very familiar to you because I only cursed it out loud every day of my junior year of college. Your husband's BFF back there is the guy who got me kicked out of Ozark University."

Rosie stole another peek behind her. "Him? The incredibly tall guy with the pretty green eyes and so much facial hair he could be a fire hazard?"

"Yes, him. Lachlan." His name left my lips with two syllables, seven letters, and a profusion of loathing.

"I think he's cute," Hattie said. "In a gamer-nerd sort of way. And Miller thinks the world of him."

Clearly my future brother-in-law had terrible instincts because Lachlan was trouble with a capital T. "He was a party boy without one care for anyone else, and he probably still is. Do guys like that ever change? No, I don't think so."

"Everyone can change." Hattie was our resident therapist, but right now I didn't need her sage optimism.

"The wild boys grow into the best romantic heroes," Rosie said.

"Yeah," I snipped. "In the novels we read for book club. Not in real life." Had the altitude gotten to my sisters? "Need I remind you Lachlan stole and wrecked an Italian diplomat's boat, then got all of us in the international program expelled from the university? And to make matters worse, I lost my summer internship with Fitz and Freeman. Only the country's top PR firm."

"That *was* a rough summer." Rosie patted my hand with sisterly sympathy. "But it's water under the bridge."

"Like the waters of Venice, which I didn't get to see because I got kicked out of the country."

"When we get back home, make an appointment with me," said Hattie. "We need to work on this residual bitterness."

I had gotten past bitter. But I'd never gotten over the pulsing urge to wrap my hands around Lachlan's throat and squeeze. "If Celeste hadn't stepped in, offered me another internship, and convinced Wesley University to accept me without the loss of one single credit, there's no telling what would've become of me."

"You would've overachieved somewhere else." Hattie pushed a few buttons on her in-flight media screen until it came to life with a carousel of movie offerings. "Can we just have a nice weekend without you getting arrested for murder? Your ticket for Cirque du Soleil is nonrefundable."

That was really asking a lot. "I can be civil, but if he trashes the hotel room and you have to pick up the tab, don't say I didn't warn you." The plane wobbled and my gag reflex engaged. "He's so obnoxious, and I don't understand why this blast from my past is suddenly living in Sugar Creek and going on our trip. I was looking forward to this weekend getaway."

"No, you weren't." Hattie pulled out her earbuds and plugged them in. "You're completely flipping out about missing work time. Look at her, Rosie. She has the shakes."

I stopped jangling my leg and forced my body to still. "You know I'd happily drop everything for you in a heartbeat." I didn't need to mention that's essentially what I'd done. I couldn't recall the last time I hadn't worked late into the week-end. And maybe I had felt a little jittery at the thought of powering off my phone until the plane landed. But I would survive. Perhaps the time would give me the mental space I needed to come up with a mega client for our firm. I'd already struck out twice with my preliminary ideas, and time was ticking. Just a dream job on the line. No big deal.

Fifteen minutes later, the bell that cleared us to leave our seats had barely dinged before two passengers from the front of the plane ambled our way, each holding a wineglass.

"Hey, sugars." Sylvie Sutton, grandmother of mine and maven of monkey business, paused at our row and rested an elbow on the seat back beside her. "They have free drinkie poos in first class."

"Also the flight attendant is a straight-up Cat-5 hottie." This, from my Aunt Frannie. "Olivia, do you want his number?"

I placed my laptop on my tray, feeling measurably calmer just by opening a file from work. "I do not."

My grandmother grinned as she scanned the rest of the cabin. "He's not wearing a ring."

Where was that drink cart? "I hope that makes some other woman very happy."

"Geez, what a killjoy," Sylvie said. "Kids today. Am I right, Frannie?"

"A generation in need of help. But don't you worry, I'm going to get his number just in case." Frannie lifted her wineglass in a toast for one. "As in, just in case I want it for myself."

The two shared a laugh, and I didn't bother reminding Frannie she had a boyfriend she adored back home.

Sylvie was the matriarch of our family and the life of any party. That party always included Sylvie's best friend and my aunt-by-choice, Frannie. The two were retired CIA, and they'd yet to find much in retirement that was as much fun as meddling in our lives.

My grandmother smoothed a hand over her flawless

blonde bob and took another sip of wine. "Frannie and I gotta get back to first class. We've made friends with the two plastic surgeons beside us, and I'm hoping for a discount."

"Ta-ta!" Frannie waved her fingers, then followed my grandmother up the aisle. "Don't do anything we wouldn't do!"

No chance of that. I returned to the document on my laptop screen and set my fingers to the keyboard, happy to have some peaceful time to work. I could be civil this weekend —for my sister's sake. But I would also do anything I could to completely avoid Lachlan.

Miller appeared in the aisle a half-hour later. "Olivia, could you do me a big favor?"

I looked up from my work and smiled at my future brother-in-law. "Sure."

"Can you go sit next to Lachlan?"

In public relations, the key to fixing a problem was to define it. And my problem was named Lachlan Hayes.

"I hate to interrupt sister time," Miller said, "but I need to discuss an important weekend detail with Hattie." He cast hopeful eyes at me. "Would you mind switching seats for a bit while I talk to her?"

"Your seat?" I twisted my head toward the back. "Next to Lachlan?"

"That's the one," Miller said. "It's very comfortable."

Rosie was mouth-open, conked-out against Hattie, so she certainly wasn't volunteering. "Okay. Sure." I could be adult about this. "But don't take too long. Stick to the highlights. Talk in fragments."

"Lachlan's harmless." Miller stepped back as I stood.

"Yes," agreed Hattie. "But my sister is not."

CHAPTER
SIX
LACHLAN

I'D ONCE CREATED a game character named Bolivia Dutton.

The alien wore a frumpy jogging suit and had snakes for hair, and her elephant-sized butt was a running joke in the *Mars Wars* chat rooms.

I'd gone seven years without seeing Olivia, until I'd walked into Flair on the recommendation of my best friend Miller James. Miller had skipped over one little detail—that the woman who'd been the bane of my existence in college worked in the very PR department I'd hoped to hire.

And now here she came sashaying down the aisle of the plane, anger flashing in her blue eyes and her pert nose still as stuck up in the air as it was back in school.

I wish I could say the last seven years had dulled the edges of her beautiful features, but instead Olivia had the nerve to only look more gorgeous. I might've disliked her with every inch of my six-foot-two body, but I could still admit the woman bearing down on me looking like she wished my seat would self-eject was prettier than ever.

Olivia's chestnut hair still curled in a slight wave at the

ends, and her figure still curved in all the right places. Then there were those eyes blue as that grotto we'd left back in Italy, and bubblegum pink lips that gave a man ideas. Not that I ever had those ideas about Olivia. I was a lot of things back in the day, but a masochist wasn't one of them.

Her gaze not quite landing on my face, Olivia stopped by my seat and gestured to the spot Miller had just vacated. "I guess I'm supposed to sit by you."

"I've been counting the seconds until you arrived." My legs were already folded origami-style with my knees near my chin, so it was no burden to stand up and stretch as Olivia slid past and flopped into her newly assigned seat.

Did I sniff her as she scooted by? I said I disliked her; I didn't say I was dead. Olivia smelled like anger tinged with a faint floral, as if she'd frolicked in a garden of wildflowers prior to boarding.

But Olivia Sutton did not frolic. I doubted she even knew how to have fun.

With a sigh of regret, I resumed my seat and stretched my legs in a space surely made for short children.

"Why aren't you in first class?" Olivia pulled down the seat tray and set a sleek laptop on top of it. Next came a dictionary-thick planner of some sort.

"Because that's a waste of money," I said.

"You and Miller booked your tickets too late."

"That too." I didn't have a full-time assistant in Arkansas yet, as my last one had chosen to stay behind in California. Between running a business, dealing with movie premiere details, and creating another video game, I was barely keeping my head above water. Not for the first time, I gave thanks for my business partner, the CFO of Star Gazer Corp., but it still left a lot on my plate.

I pulled the script out of the seat pocket in front of me and resumed my close reading of the second act. The next movie was still a little rough, and I'd penciled in some suggestions of places that didn't align with the games. *Mars Wars* had a devout following, and if one single legacy detail was off, the fans would mutiny.

Three minutes later, I'd just gotten to the part where a sister planet exploded into flames when I caught the signs of distress beside me. Though I didn't want to, I looked over at Olivia, only to find her fumbling with the air-conditioning vent above her, her breathing oddly loud. A wild look glazed over her normally condescending eyes.

"You okay over there?" I inquired.

"Fine," she said in a tone of *mind your business.*

Type, type, type. She went back to her spreadsheet, stopping occasionally to wipe the thin sheen of sweat from her temple.

"Are you sure you're all right?" I knew CPR, but the last thing I wanted to do was give mouth-to-mouth to Bolivia Dutton.

"I said I'm fine." Now she reached over my head and aimed *my* air vent directly toward her. "Go back to whatever you're reading."

"It's a manuscript." I continued to watch her, studying the curious transition in the normally unruffled woman.

Olivia leaned into my space, still stealing my air-conditioning. "Do these things even work?" she hissed. "I've felt a stronger breeze from a cat's tail."

"The temperature seems okay to me." I held out my bottle of water. "You're flushed."

She shot me her infamous side-eye. "You could move your arm, you know." She nudged my forearm where it rested between us. "You're taking up more than your territory there, Hayes. I get half and you get half. That's how armrests work."

"Is that so?" I made no move to accommodate her pressing arm. "I'm bigger, so I get more square footage. *That's* how armrests work."

"Isn't it so like you to think so." She fanned herself with a hand. "Your legs are also trespassing."

I glanced down at my painfully cramped legs. "Let's be neighbors who share."

"Hi, there." A raven-haired flight attendant stopped at our row and aimed the high beams of her smile right at me. "I like that hoodie." After a blatant hair toss, she gestured toward my chest where the words *Mars Wars* and a character icon shared space. "Are you a fan of the game?"

Olivia's chest rose and fell like she'd just climbed off her Peloton, but she still had enough oxygen to power a withering look between me and Flirty Flight Attendant.

I set the script in my lap and gave the kind woman a grin. "I play every now and then."

"It's addictive, isn't it?" She stepped closer, her perfume promising more than a bag of pretzels.

"Playing while wearing blue-light blocking glasses can reduce some of that addiction," I told her.

"*Mars Wars* is so much more than a game though, right?" The flight attendant rested a hand on the baggage hold above us. "I've met some good friends playing it online, and last month when my boyfriend broke up with me, I just dove into *Mars Wars* the whole weekend instead of crying my eyes out and eating my weight in ice cream."

Beside me, Olivia typed furiously on her laptop, her poor keyboard suffering with every keystroke.

"I'm sorry about the breakup," I said to our flight attendant.

"I'm not," she cooed, playfully swatting my shoulder. "I'll be back to check on you later."

"Looking forward to it." I watched American Airlines' finest walk away then turned to my seatmate. "Did you just roll your eyes?"

More rapid-fire typing ensued. "No."

"You absolutely did."

"If I did," Olivia said, "it was automatic. A hair-trigger response to watching junior high flirtations."

"I've been back in your life less than a week, and you're already jealous?" If looks could kill, I would've been outside, hanging onto a rotating propeller by my fingernails.

"You haven't changed at all since college, have you?" she asked.

It took effort to maintain my carefree smile, but I hadn't spent years working hard to outdistance my youthful bad reputation just to be kneecapped by one snippy comment from Olivia Sutton. "Is making decisions on faulty assumptions how you operate in business as well, Olivia?" I paused just long enough for her to work up a good glare. "What you saw just now was me being nice to someone. You should try it."

Olivia's murderous look darkened, and I knew she was probably calculating how many levers she'd have to pull to open a door and push me out of the plane.

But then she swayed in her chair and gave a small whimper. "These seats are unbearably close." Her rapid blinking spiked my reluctant concern. "I wish we could open a window."

"Very bad idea. The laws of physics tell us that would not end well." I passed her my bottle of water. "Down some of this. In fact, take it all."

"I'm not drinking after you," she said without much rancor. "Who knows where your lips have been."

My voice dipped low. "Wouldn't you like to know?"

"I would not." A bead of sweat trickled a discreet path down her neck.

"Drink the water, Olivia," I said. "You look like you're on the verge of passing out."

"I'm fine." But she grabbed my water bottle anyway, uncapped the top, and drank—my questionable germs be darned. "Is it warm in here to you?" With her free hand she tugged at the neck of her blouse. "Why's it so hot?"

"I can have that effect on the ladies." Okay, enough of this. I stood and held out a hand. "Let's take a little walk."

"I'd rather not."

"A stroll through the aisle and to the galley is exactly what you need." My fingers clasped her clammy hand. "Come on, Olivia. How about you breathe deeply, ignore those adorable tingly feelings of hatred, and channel all that uppity energy into moving."

"Fine," she said as I helped her to her feet. "But I would've done this anyway. Not because you suggested it."

"Whatever you say, Livvy." Her old nickname slipped off my tongue, and I caught Olivia's instant glare. Only I had dared to call her that back in the day, and not because it suited her. Just because I knew it got under her skin.

With her raggedy breathing and a hand to her stomach, Olivia allowed me to lead her straight to the galley. The fake smile she wore looked at odds with her ghostly white face. "My friend here needs some air," I explained to Flirty Flight Attendant.

Olivia shook her head. "That's not true."

"Pardon me," I corrected. "My archenemy, whom I can barely tolerate, needs some air. Is it all right if we stand here for a few minutes?"

"Of course." The woman was back to cooing, and Olivia was back to eye-rolling. "Is there anything I can get you?"

The flight attendant had directed that question to me, but Olivia responded hotly anyway. "I'm fine."

"How about some juice?" I suggested.

Somewhere a bell dinged, and the attendant frowned as she passed a cup of OJ to Olivia. "I'll be right back to check on you guys."

Risking bodily harm, I placed my hand at Olivia's back. "Take some deep breaths."

"If you begin a guided meditation I'm out." She inhaled for three counts and exhaled for four.

I studied Olivia's face and still did not like what I saw. "Do you always react this way on airplanes?"

"Just when I'm sitting by you." She shook her head and lightly touched my arm. "I'm sorry. I don't mean that. I mean, I *do* mean that, but I didn't mean to say it out loud. My mother raised me better than that." Olivia sipped from her cup. "It occasionally happens. Tight spaces make me anxious." Her hand waved up and down in my general direction. "And you're like sitting by a wall. I'll be fine when I get back to my aisle seat."

"Looks like Miller is still head-to-head with Hattie." I poured more juice, relieved Olivia's color was returning. "Remember that time your sorority and my fraternity went to St. Louis for the weekend?" Was it odd to say I felt a thrum of pride at Olivia's immediate smile? Because I did.

"When we packed out Fox Theatre for *Wicked*?" She licked her pink lips. "You sat in front of me, and I couldn't see most of the show. Then you fell asleep."

"I'm sure at the time I took some perverse pleasure in blocking your view. I remember you didn't want to go up in the arch, but your sorority sisters pressured you into it."

"What an embarrassing memory." She visibly shuddered. "It was very, very cramped in there. And the thing swayed."

She'd thrown up as soon as she'd reached the bottom.

"Didn't you plan that whole trip?" The plane dipped, and my hands reached out to steady Olivia. "And the one we took to Padre Island?"

Her free hand now rested on my chest, and she hadn't seemed to notice. No, she had her business face back on. "I'm still a good planner, Lachlan. Details are my thing. You'll find everyone at Flair is just as good or better."

"I'm firm in my decision not to utilize Flair."

Her hand dropped as the plane leveled. "Can I ask who you *are* using?"

"I'm working with McMinn." I'd heard they were Flair's biggest competitor.

"So you're going with an inferior agency just to spite me?"

Well, the brief pause on Olivia's snobby, dismissive personality had been nice, but there she was again—that snooty, snippy woman we all knew and barely tolerated. "That's so like you to think it's about you," I told her.

"That's so like *you* to reduce it to that and make me sound like a self-absorbed brat."

At that, I had to laugh. "If you've aged out of that phase, I congratulate you."

She took a fortifying breath, probably using the time to mentally curse me. "No matter what you think of my personality, I am very good at my job. You won't find a better PR firm for what you need. McMinn and Associates is expensive, but they're not the best. You're paying for empty promises and an old reputation they no longer uphold."

"That's your opinion."

"It's fact." She glanced at the painfully low ceiling as if pulling down a memory. "I seem to recall you have trouble with facts."

Oh, that was rich. "I could say the same for you." Olivia

hadn't caused my expulsion from college, but she'd certainly made sure I took the blame. "I'm not working with Flair. End of story. Is that because of you? Yes. Do I care that I might be sacrificing quality? No." My gaze swept over her face and form again. "Your color's coming back, and you don't look like you're about to hyperventilate. Since you're not gonna die on my watch, my work is done here."

She tossed her hair and stepped past me. "Like I would've given you the satisfaction."

CHAPTER
SEVEN
LACHLAN

TRUE, I'd made a lot of mistakes in my life. But all Saturday I racked my brain trying to pinpoint what crime I could've possibly committed to have earned an entire weekend with Olivia Sutton. Was it for the time in grade school I'd stuck a frog in my teacher's desk? What about when I was fourteen and stole my dad's car and took it for a joy ride that ended in a spectacular crash? Maybe it was for one of my many transgressions in college, like when my fraternity brother and I broke into the admin building at midnight, hung a sign off the fifth floor sharing the president's phone number, then rappelled all the way down. While none of these was something a parent would memorialize in a scrapbook, they were still only minor offenses. Mostly.

So I couldn't think of one thing I'd done to earn two-point-five days with Olivia Sutton.

I'd managed to avoid her at last night's dinner and show, sitting as far away from her as possible. Then today Miller and I had played golf and hit some blackjack tables while the ladies had gone to a spa and checked out a few wedding venues.

Vegas was a city driven by luck, and I knew mine was about to run out. With a party as small as ours, the odds were I couldn't dodge Olivia much longer.

"Have I mentioned I'm really glad you could make it?" Miller James clapped me on the shoulder Saturday evening and smiled.

"At least three times." I tuned back into the moment, standing awkwardly in the lobby of the Bellagio amid a small group of Hattie and Miller's family and friends. Together we waited for instructions for our first "fun" activity.

"I know you're slammed with work," Miller said. "This means a lot to Hattie. And to me." He grinned. "But especially to Hattie."

"You are so whipped, man." I knew Miller well and had witnessed his transformation from Mr. No Commitment to Mr. Besotted and Obnoxiously in Love. The weekend party was all Hattie's idea, overstuffed with to-do items meant to celebrate their impending marriage and give the couple's closest loved ones time to bond. And had they left Olivia at home, I would've happily superglued myself to everyone in attendance.

After Miller and I returned to the hotel, I'd barely had time to shower before Hattie texted an agenda and requested my presence in the lobby for our next activity.

Miller tossed back the last drops from his water bottle. "You know, if you need a date for the movie premiere, I'm available. Though I will require a limo and a rose corsage."

Man, I'd missed this guy. Years ago in California, Miller had recruited me for his think tank. I'd gained a trusted advisor and a best friend who'd become family. "I'm not that hard up," I said, "but thanks."

The premiere of *Mars Wars* would give the press and entertainment executives an opportunity to scrutinize me even more. The thought made me uneasy every time it crossed my mind. Since Star Gazer Corp. had gone public, my name and face frequently accompanied headlines on financial networks. Investment buzz said our stock could quickly turn into the hottest buy since Amazon. But my CFO warned it was time for my frat boy reputation to die once and for all. Between movie studios and investors, I'd never felt more scrutiny and never had more riding on my image.

That's why I needed someone as good as Olivia to fix my brand.

"I read in *Fast Company* you're the headliner at this year's TechieCon." Miller glanced at his phone, then slipped it back into his pocket. "The article said you'd be making an announcement that would turn the gaming industry on its ear."

"Great quote, huh?"

"Brilliant." Miller nodded his approval. "Really building the suspense."

"Might've had one of my designers send a tip to the reporter that a new technology was coming." My board members, including Miller, knew exactly what my team had been working on for the last two years. It had finally passed testing to my standards and would soon go to production.

"I'm pleased with the development." Miller was chairman of the board and had been with me every step of the way of this new technology. "It's going to launch Star Gazer Corp. into the stratosphere."

"But?"

He rested a hand on my shoulder. "But as your friend, I'm concerned."

"Don't be." I wouldn't have to hire a speech writer for the product reveal at TechieCon. I'd be penning that myself. "The announcement is going to be epic." I'd been counting the days, and when I broke the news, everything had to be perfect. I wanted to appear polished, sound professional, and look a certain someone in the eye when I delivered the news.

I'd waited years for this moment. *Years.*

"Party bus is here!" Hattie ran to us and linked her arm through Miller's as our group assembled. "Just to review the itinerary I sent you and the five reminders that followed, we'll do a restaurant walking tour, hitting some of Vegas's top eateries, then it's a citywide scavenger hunt!"

Her excitement was adorable, and had I not been drowning in work, I probably would've been just as enthused. Food? Loved it. A game? Obviously my thing. Once upon a time I would've partied it up and shown this group what fun looked like. But now I tried to recall the last time I'd had a weekend off.

"Let's go!" Hattie called.

As our group shuffled toward the doors, I walked beside Olivia's grandmother. The woman had been watching me all day, and I'd heard enough about her to know she was one to watch. I made short work of introducing myself.

"Well, hello, big fella. Aren't you adorable?" She extended her hand with a sly smile. "I'm Sylvie, grandmother of the Sutton girls. The woman reeking of maturity and sexiness to my right is my best friend, Frannie."

"Nice to meet you, ma'am." I took Frannie's proffered hand.

"Aren't you just a slice of sweet potato pie with a scoop of ice cream on top?" Frannie touched her lengthy nails to her black hair. "I'm newly unsingle, but if anything changes, I'll let you know."

I grinned, liking these two already. "Are you ready for a little friendly competition?"

"Ready?" Sylvie zipped up her fanny pack that matched Frannie's. "Honey, we're gonna mop the floor with you."

"Second place is for losers." Frannie touched up her lipstick with a heavy hand. "We have connections in the Vegas underbelly, and we will use them if we must."

Sylvie unwrapped a piece of gum and popped it in her mouth. "I hear you and Olivia know each other from college."

"That's correct."

She chewed on that for a bit. "So you have a past. A history. Two sordid paths that crossed in your youth and have intersected once again in your prime."

"Very prime." Frannie eyed my left bicep. "Grade A."

"Olivia and I never dated or anything," I informed them.

Sylvie did not look convinced. "Our mid-November selection for book club is *When Hairy Met Sally.*" She eyed my voluminous beard. "It's about a nerdy IT dude by day—"

"Who's an amorous Sasquatch by night." Frannie fanned herself. "He has a heart of gold *and* can fix your Wi-Fi when it's on the fritz."

Sylvie crackled her gum between her teeth. "Sally's a beautiful, type-A woman climbing the career ladder at animal control. They're two wrongs who make a right. Two sexy ships passing in the night. Two opposites who unexpectedly attract." She raised her eyebrows as if trying to send home a message. "Do you know what I'm saying?"

"Not really."

Her voice lowered, and she poked her red nail right into the center of my shirt. "Sometimes love is found when you least expect it."

Frannie gave a firm nod. "And so are fur balls."

"I will take this under consideration," I said as I held back a smile.

Sylvie stepped onto the party bus, then glanced back. "Best of luck to you on the scavenger hunt." She leaned down and delivered a wink and a promise. "You're gonna need it."

Turns out I *was* going to need that luck.

We tumbled out of the Smoky Rib restaurant, our last stop on the food tour and my least favorite. They'd served a nice mocha cheesecake with caramel swirl, but I firmly believed barbeque was a magic left to the true pit sorcerers, people who conjured epicurean magic with the right ratio of smoke, wood chips, and dry rub.

"Okay, guys." Hattie adjusted the small veil her sisters had earlier placed on her head. It matched the sash that said Bride-to-Be. "Scavenger hunt time."

"Bring it!" Frannie shouted. "I'll take *all* you turkeys down."

"We're working in pairs for this one," Hattie said. "Miller's passing out your clue sheet. Take a photo of each location and text it to me. When you're done, report to the Tropical Paradise Club. First team done wins bragging rights and a stay at the new Sugar Creek Bed-and-Breakfast, complete with spa package."

She could keep the B&B stay, but I was all about those bragging rights. Then again, thoroughly trouncing Olivia would be enough win for me.

Speaking of Olivia, she stood as far away from me as she could, which suited me just fine. It made it even harder to notice how she looked beautiful tonight. Unlike me, she'd changed into something nicer for the outing. Her short dress hugged her curves, and her ever-present heels made her calves pop. Hair that she'd eventually tugged into a ponytail on the plane now hung in loose waves.

"Now for the teams," Hattie called. "Frannie, you're with Sylvie."

The two high-fived then did some elaborate hip bump.

47

"Rosie and Miller will be partners," Hattie said. "And I'll be at the bar because I created the game." She mimicked chugging a few drinks. "So sad for me."

No. That left me with...

"Lachlan," Hattie said, "you'll pair with Olivia." Hattie's eyes landed on me. I didn't know her well, but I was pretty certain I caught a flash of calculated mischief pass over that pretty face.

Olivia and I stared at one another, and what I saw on her face reflected the same annoyance I felt.

Okay, I could be a decent sport about this. Maybe not a good sport, but I could manage decent. Polite, even. Then I wouldn't have to see Olivia again until the wedding next year.

There was no way out but in, so I made my way to Olivia, ready to tackle our list of clues and get this over with. "You should know I'm here to win," I told her.

"That makes two of us." Cerulean eyes sliced into me. "Try to keep up."

Oh, was that how it was going to be? "I'm pretty sure I'm about to show you how it's done."

"Like you did in college?" she had the nerve to ask.

I consulted the sheet of clues. "Hey, do you think your raging bitterness can help us solve some of these riddles?"

Olivia opened her mouth to fire back, but one of the teams raced by, and she instantly shifted gears. "You help me win this thing, and I promise not to insult you one more time for the rest of the weekend."

"Nix the dirty looks, and you have a deal."

I could tell that one hurt. Then Olivia saw Miller and Rosie sprinted past us. "I'll take it," she said.

My side pressed against hers as I shared the list of clues, and we both speed-read number one: *Take a photo of a boat that never sinks.*

"Treasure Island," we said in unison.

"Already got us an Uber." I slipped my phone into my pocket and grabbed Olivia's hand. "Let's go, partner."

<hr>

Two hours and ten stops later, with adrenaline pumping through my veins, I kept the pace behind Olivia as she ran inside the Tropical Paradise Club.

I blinked against the darkness and pulsating techno music vibrating the walls. Following instructions, we wove through a mass of partyers and hightailed it to the neon green bar.

Hattie sat in an acrylic barstool sipping a drink straight from a pineapple, happily watching our approach.

"Congratulations, team," Hattie said. "You're the first to successfully complete the tasks and arrive."

I was just about to high-five a grinning Olivia when most of our group burst in.

"No way!" Miller broke through the crowd and yelled over the deafening music. "How did these two beat us?"

Frannie and Sylvie walked over, each carrying a fruity concoction. "Oh, were we supposed to check in?" Sylvie pursed her lips against a glittery straw. "Frannie and I met some mai tais and just had to say hello."

Rosie ran straight to us, holding her side as if it ached. "Don't tell me we came in last!" She paused a moment to catch her breath. "Of course Olivia would win. She probably had a strategy before she got in her Uber."

"Lachlan loved my flowcharts and graphs," Olivia teased back. "Though I did not appreciate his rule of not stopping at bathrooms."

"What's our team motto?" I asked Olivia.

She rolled her eyes. "Tinkles are time-wasters."

"Very impressive work from everyone." Hattie eased off her stool and slipped a medallion over Olivia's head. "I award you the first and only pre-wedding party medal." Hattie had to practically jump to reach my head. "Here's your medal, Lachlan. Now, drinks on us. Let's celebrate!"

Without even thinking, I hooked an arm around Olivia and gave her a quick hug. "Great job, Livvy."

Olivia threw her arms around me and squeezed. "We did it. We beat them all."

High on victory, I spun her around until the world tilted.

Then our eyes met, and reality came crashing back.

The woman in my arms was Olivia Sutton. I didn't like her, and she most certainly didn't like me.

With a delicate cough, Olivia took a step in retreat. "That can't happen again."

She didn't have to tell me twice. "Purely driven by the thrill of the win."

Olivia's hair caressed her shoulder as she glanced behind her at the bustling dance floor. Then back to me. "I'd like to pitch an idea."

I was ten times a fool, but I stepped closer. "I'm listening."

She seemed reluctant to share and delivered her pitch slowly. "We could extend our truce for a few more hours."

I could see some merit in this. "Keep talking."

"We finish out tonight's event," Olivia said, "then tomorrow, we're—"

"Back to being mortal enemies."

She nodded. "Spewing disdain and disregard."

"I like it." As the song changed to one I almost knew, I extended a hand. "Let's go dance and forget we can't stand one another."

Olivia's face lit up as she graced me with a rare laugh, a melodic sound that slid across my senses. She placed her hand in mine and tugged me toward our party already on the floor. "Friends for a few more hours."

"But," I reminded her, "in the morning, everything changes."

At the time—I had no idea how right I was.

CHAPTER

EIGHT

OLIVIA

When I woke up Sunday morning, I became aware of two things:

One, I felt hungover, though I knew I hadn't ordered a drop of liquor.

And two, I was pretty sure I had accidentally married someone.

In terms of major life mistakes, this certainly topped face-planting on the treadmill at the gym. It was even worse than the recent charity basketball game when I had attempted a layup, been clotheslined by Morgan, and fallen straight into Elton's crotch. It even eclipsed this summer's lows, when I'd been dumped by the most perfect boyfriend and discovered Morgan had been given an account that should've been mine. Those travesties were now on par with stepping in gum compared to waking up in Vegas married to a man you had little memory of wedding.

I mentally consulted the Olivia Sutton Life Plan, and unintentional marriage was *nowhere* on it. I couldn't even imagine the ripple effects of this horrendous occurrence.

Besides disjointed flashes and fragments, I had no recollection of last night once we arrived at the club. That was the most frightening thing.

The harsh light of morning streamed through the hotel room window of the Bellagio, and I slapped my hand over my eyes. My tongue felt like wool in my mouth, and I was certain at some point last night I must've used my head as a battering ram. It hurt so badly I wanted to remove it from my body.

My phone on the bedside table read eleven a.m., and I'd been awake for exactly ninety seconds. Plenty of time to catalogue this series of perplexing and cataclysmic observations.

First, an arm was flopped over my stomach. A very male arm.

Next, someone was spooning me. A full-on melding of bodies, like puzzle pieces that fit together a little too well.

Third, as I slowly extricated myself from this guy's too-friendly clench and sat up, I recognized his sleeping face and felt a shock and disgust that would surely follow me all the days of my life.

Finally—and this was the part that took the awfulness to new heights—my left hand sported a gold band that matched my bedmate's. Remnants of a wedding were strewn about the room like clues from a crime scene.

I spied a bottle of champagne and two clearly used plastic cups.

A wilted bouquet of red roses.

A poorly printed wedding proclamation from the Pink Chapel of Love.

Two Polaroids showing a happy couple kissing at an altar.

And a marriage license my bleary eyes could read even from across the room.

This paper united two people by the names of Olivia Sutton and Lachlan Hayes.

"Lachlan?" I hissed, scrambling out of the bed. "Lachlan."

"Hmm?" Without opening his eyes, Lachlan Hayes scrubbed a hand over his burly face. "Ugh...I feel like I walked into oncoming traffic." One vivid green eye popped open. Then another. I could see my old nemesis struggling to focus. "Why are you in my hotel room?"

"I'm not." I blinked back tears as panic began its torment. "You're in mine."

Lachlan's unruly red hair swished across his bare shoulders as he slowly sat up. His brows knit together as he studied me beside the bed, where I now clutched the comforter as if I wore nothing instead of last night's party dress. "I have...weird memories." He lifted a finger and pointed in my general direction. "You...me..."

"Uh-huh." Where was Lachlan's shirt? Did he have pants on under that sheet? *Please, God, tell me there are pants.*

"We did the scavenger hunt." He began to recite the events of the night, pulling them from the cobwebbed catacombs of his memory. "Your sister partnered us up."

"That's right." That's how I remembered it as well. I recalled actually having fun. For a few hours, Lachlan and I had worked together, both fiercely competitive and united in our quest to finish before anyone else. I even remembered laughing a few times.

"We won, didn't we?" He said this with the certainty of one coming out of a ten-year coma.

"I'm pretty sure we did." I swallowed past another wave of panic. "Then our group met back at the Tropical Paradise Club for a celebration." There had been a catered buffet of appetizers, specialty drinks with catchy names, and so much noise.

"Did we all dance?"

"Yes." I pressed my fingertips to my eyelids to stop the

onslaught of images. "You tried some hip-hop stuff. I remember strongly advising you not to."

"Leave my exceptional moves out of this." He rubbed at the shadowed skin beneath his eyes. "Did we get in an argument?"

"Yes."

He slapped a hand over his forehead, as if the sun streaming in was too much. "Why do we always fight?"

It was true we had a history of it. "You told everyone the real reason we got kicked out of college was because I had a fling with an Italian street vendor."

He removed his hand from his face, and one ginger brow shot up. "*That* you can remember?"

"I also recall you brought me a drink." I pulled my attention away from his surprisingly impressive chest and watched his face for signs of guilt or premeditation. "A Waikiki Watoosie." Dumb name. Great flavor.

"Yeah, yeah," he said. "I'm tracking so far."

"It was supposed to be nonalcoholic."

"I swear that's what I ordered. Extra Waikiki, hold the Watoosie."

My voice went shrill with panic. "What does that even mean?"

"I don't know. The bartender said it. I thought he'd throw in a few more pineapples." Lachlan tunneled his hands through his hair as he sat up.

"I don't remember much after that," I said. It was a frightening omission, and I was not comforted by the agreement on Lachlan's face.

He slowly nodded, looking as if the movement pained him. "Beyond that I only have bits and pieces." He gestured toward the bed. "It doesn't appear like anything happened here though, right?"

"I guess, but—"

"I mean...I didn't." Lachlan pointed a finger between us. "You didn't. We didn't...?"

Scraps of memories flitted through my mind, and I blinked them away. "I don't think so." *Most* of the night was completely missing. "I think I was roofied."

Urgency widened Lachlan's eyes. "I swear to you, Olivia, it wasn't me."

There was some small relief in his declaration. Lachlan Hayes had been a lot of things back in the day—wild frat boy, partyer, serial dater, and all-around slacker. But he hadn't been a creep or a criminal. "I think it's likely you were drugged too."

He sat with that idea a moment. "We need to alert the club. Have them pull some footage." Lachlan maneuvered across the bed to sit at the edge.

I saw pants! Glorious pants that presumably had covered his naughty bits all night long.

Lachlan stood, those blessed jeans as rumpled as his hair. Slowly, gently, he picked up the marriage certificate. "Maybe this thing isn't real. Maybe it's just a joke of a piece of paper."

"We're married." I held up my left hand, then reached for his.

Lachlan viewed the gold band on his ring finger with almost comical horror. His mouth opened, then shut, then opened again. "God help us."

"We can quietly pursue who did this to us while we get the marriage annulled." Did Vegas have a drive-through courthouse for the dissolution of unintentional marriages? And if so, did this place also serve lattes and donuts? Because I suddenly needed to drown my anxiety in sugar and caffeine.

"Yeah," Lachlan said distractedly. "We'll get it annulled."

"Nobody has to know." This was perhaps the most important point, one that I felt deserved flashy lights and bolded letters. "No one but us, right?"

Before he could respond, Lachlan's phone buzzed from somewhere beneath the tangle of sheets. Then it rang.

Somehow, some way, I knew it was a harbinger of doom.

Lachlan's hands disappeared beneath the comforter, and he patted down the bed until he found the demanding phone.

When his face whitened and a curse left his thinned lips, I felt yet another wave of despair.

"I have forty-two text messages and seventeen voicemails." Lachlan held up his screen for my consideration. "Does this picture look familiar?"

A blurry photo revealed the two of us at what was clearly a wedding chapel, laughing. Another photo of us hugging. Then a short video of an underfed, poorly coifed Celine Dion impersonator announcing us man and wife.

The evidence was irrefutable.

"Who sent the video?" I asked. "My family? Because I can keep them quiet. I've got dirt on every one of them, and half of them owe me big fat favors."

"The photos are from your sisters," he said.

"Oh. Thank goodness."

"But the video's from ABC News. It's one of many." Lachlan lifted his bloodshot eyes to mine. "Olivia, the whole entire world knows."

CHAPTER
NINE

LACHLAN

IN GAMING TERMS, I'd had a random encounter and had just been nuked.

Married?

Me?

I would've thrown up, but I wasn't sure my head could handle the effort.

To make matters worse, the news had hit every major news outlet. Some onlookers had taken video of our nuptials and posted it all over the internet. Technology had changed my life years ago, and it had just done it again.

I thought of my dad and brothers—could see them having a big laugh as their maid served them breakfast. "Lachlan's done it again," my father would say. "Screws up everything he touches." Then my brothers would smile at one another, thinking of how lucky they were I'd finally left them alone years ago.

No, I wouldn't think of them now. Who cared what they thought? The real problem was my career. Because this was bad. *Very* bad. I couldn't afford a personal misstep, and this was the equivalent of throwing my body on a land mine.

While Olivia continued to walk the floor and mumble to herself in disbelief, anger heated my blood. I would find whoever did this to us and make them pay. In the meantime, I had myself a wife. Olivia Sutton, of all people. If I had to wake up accidentally married to someone, why couldn't it have been Gisele Bündchen?

But no. In this twisted nightmare, my bride was Olivia Sutton, the girl who'd made my life hell in college, spoke sass and sarcasm as fluently as she did English, and loathed me probably more than I disliked her.

My phone buzzed again, and I made the mistake of glancing at it.

Maxwell Barclay. My CFO.

The man had been my best hire three years ago, adding order and strategy to the company while I focused on the creative. "I've got to take this call."

"Now?" Olivia swiveled from her spot at the window, yesterday's makeup still stuck to her face. "I'm only halfway through my freak-out. I haven't even hit my peak yet—and we still need a plan."

"And we will. After this call."

She huffed, and I shut myself in the bathroom and hit redial. "Hey, Max."

"Lachlan, where are you?" Normally calm to the point of monotone, Maxwell's voice hit a panicked pitch.

"I'm still in Las Vegas."

"You need to get out of there."

My reflection in the mirror would've terrified small children. My eyes were puffy, and my hair looked like I'd just auditioned for a Bon Jovi tribute band. "I'm working on it."

"I'll charter you a flight. so you can begin defusing this

bomb." Max was ever the fixer. "Now tell me exactly what happened and why I had to read about it on some deplorable gossip site."

I quickly explained what little I knew. "We were obviously victims of a crime. I'll pursue it with law enforcement."

"But the damage is done," Maxwell said. "It doesn't matter what the truth is when the internet tells a more interesting story. Lachlan, you're at a pivotal point for yourself and Star Gazer Corp. In a matter of months you've got the movie premiere and a very public tech launch."

This conversation was not helping the jackhammer in my head. "I'm aware."

"So this is how you're going to kick off your media blitz? As a man who got sloppy drunk in Vegas, got married, and now needs an annulment? Is this the guy who investors will trust with their money?"

I was not a reckless person anymore and hadn't been for some time. When did I get to drop the mantle of playboy and be taken seriously? I'd worked too hard to be cast as this character once again. "Then I'll rewrite the story."

"What does that mean?"

"The games that succeed are the ones that tell a good story. If the game doesn't work, you tweak the plot."

"I'm a finance and strategy person, Lachlan. The rest is all frippery and fluff to me."

I'd always been an idea guy. I didn't say they were always good ones, but my mind was a veritable solution factory. So when a vague, nebulous notion dropped in my head, the first bloom of hope poked above the muddy surface. It was insane. Absolutely my craziest idea ever. But I had too much on the line to irreparably screw up my entire future because of a disaster not even of my own making. Besides my own fate, I had employees whose livelihoods depended on my success.

I'd come too far to watch it all go up in flames because of a disaster gone viral.

The question was...did I dare?

And would Olivia ever go along with it?

"I'll call you back, Maxwell."

"Lachlan, I'm not through talking to you. We need to discuss—"

"I'm about to rewrite the second act," I told him. "I'll let you know how it goes."

"Lach—"

The door creaked as I slipped out, my nerves humming with that electric feeling of sudden inspiration, the kind that was half-crazy and half-divine. The same feeling I'd felt the last few weeks of creating *Mars Wars*.

Olivia sat on the bed, wringing her hands. Her hair had been brushed out, but her makeup still tracked down her cheeks. "You've been in there forever," she said. "I had to scream into a pillow."

"Sorry I missed that." It had been a mere five minutes. "Important call."

"Your girlfriend?"

"Yes," I said, "but she's willing to share me."

"You probably have ten more to call." Olivia tied her hair into a ponytail with a snap of elastic. "Maybe we can stop by Bobby's House of Booty Shakes on the way back into Sugar Creek, so you can tell them all at once."

"Hate to take a blowtorch to your impression of me, but I've actually been too busy to date. No one will be crying over this development." Wrenching open an elf-sized refrigerator, I grabbed a bottle of water and twisted the top. "And for the record, my last girlfriend was a kindergarten teacher I dated for two years, and we only broke up because she decided she preferred someone else."

"Oh." I saw Olivia wilt a degree and felt some measure of satisfaction. "I almost believe that."

"How about you, Queen Elizabeth? Do you have someone who's going to want to use my face as a punching bag for marrying his girl?"

She grabbed her own water and drank. "No."

At least we didn't have to deal with *that* roadblock. "I have an idea."

Olivia returned to the bed and pressed her back to the headboard. Her pink dress fanned out around her slender legs, daring me to look. "Lachlan, what are we going to do? I have thirty text messages from one sister alone. My parents are going to freak." Relocating a chunk of tangled hair she'd missed, Olivia regarded me warily. "My grandma will probably kill you in some innovative and horrendously painful way."

"I could have our solution—"

"I can't be married," she went on. "We have to make this go away. My boss said she'd fire the next person who brought scandal to her door, so there goes my promotion. I'll have to sell my apartment and live in my car. Or even worse, live with Sylvie. I stayed with her once for a month. She practices fire drills at two a.m. and eats cold SpaghettiOs for breakfast. And don't even get me started on—"

"Olivia."

"She booby-traps her backyard and conducts nuclear attack simulations. She yodels and makes me pledge allegiance to the United States of Sylvie. I cannot live there."

Ms. Uptight was unraveling right in front of me. Couldn't say I blamed her, but still, it was absolutely fascinating to watch. Dress wrinkled and askew, feet bare, and a face that for once didn't say, "I have the answers, and I expect you to like them."

Rubbing my eyes, I stepped over the wedding debris

littered about the room. We had multiple options to fix our predicament, but coffee was crucial to each solution. Making short work of plugging in the room's Keurig, I felt the smallest measure of relief at the first scent of French roast.

One long minute later, I handed a still blabbering Olivia a steaming mug.

"And my boss is going to fire me. Did I mention Celeste will have my walking papers drafted before our plane touches back down in Arkansas?"

"You might've mentioned it once or twice." The coffee slid warm and potent down my throat, and the crashing cymbals in my head reduced to a snare drum's tap.

"She'll probably have me drawn and quartered in the town square. Something very public and humiliating." Olivia hung her head in her hands. "She warned us. Celeste warned us all. 'No more drama,' she said, and what did I do?"

I assumed the question was rhetorical and wasn't in the mood to answer anyway, so I just sipped my coffee and wished it was a better blend.

"I don't think you understand how this will ruin my life," Olivia said.

Good Lord, my own life had just gone DEFCON 1. "That makes two of us."

"Okay." She took my outstretched cup of coffee and inhaled at least twice. "I'm in PR. Damage control is what I do. It's my thing." Leaving the bed again, she paced the room for a full minute before sitting in a chair and staring helplessly at the wall. "I've got nothing! The closest thing to this I've dealt with was helping an influencer who accidentally posted her skinny-dipping frolic with the gardener." She pressed her fists into her eyeballs. "There simply is no precedent. I have no idea how to fix this."

And then the tears started. Plump, tragic droplets slipped

down Olivia's cheeks, and my heart had the nerve to feel a pang of sympathy.

"It's not our fault," I said gently. "Something was in our drinks." It was the only explanation.

The horror of the reality caught her up short. "Who would do such a horrible thing?"

"I'll call the Las Vegas police and my attorney. We'll ask for security footage from the club."

"So that's our angle? We were drugged, and we get an annulment?" Relief softened the tense features of her face. It was a shame I was going to have to pop that balloon of hope.

I scrolled through my phone, clicking and swiping with angry stabs. "This is CBS News." I flashed her the page.

She pulled the phone closer. "Does that say 'Tech Tycoon Picks His Princess'?" Her revulsion was as strong as my coffee. "That's ridiculous."

I clicked and swiped some more. "Here are more reports from TMZ, CNN, *People* magazine, NBC...Need I go on?"

Her head went back into her hands. "I'm begging you not to."

"This has gone viral, Olivia."

"Why did you have to go and get all nerdy-famous?" she wailed.

"Believe me, it wasn't by choice." Kind of like our marriage. "An investigation could take weeks, and who knows if it will even turn up anything. In the meantime, nobody's going to believe we got married because we were drugged."

She glanced at her own phone, her expression defeated. "Probably not. We look pretty cognizant in these photos. But the people in our lives will believe us."

"That's not enough for me. Is that enough to save your job?"

Her finger stilled over a particularly incriminating photo of us kissing in the chapel. "That promotion had my name on it. Corner office. Manhattan apartment. I can smell the dank subway even now. I've worked day and night, with hardly any time off. I've forsaken so many vacations and family get-togethers. And for what? For it all to disappear because some creep slipped something in our drinks, and we can't immediately prove it?"

"This isn't going to blow over, Olivia. But I have a possible solution to see us through the next few months."

"Does it involve magically turning back time and avoiding the Tropical Paradise?"

"Afraid not." I couldn't believe I was going to utter my next words, but desperation was the source of many an invention. "I have a proposal for you."

She gave an indelicate snort. "I'm pretty sure I've already fallen for that once this weekend."

I held my mug of coffee, idly wondering what these hands had touched last night. "What I'm about to say to you is unorthodox and outrageous. It's not what I want to do, but it is a solution that benefits us both."

Olivia chewed on her bottom lip, her gaze wary but intrigued. "Go on."

"I propose we stay married."

CHAPTER

TEN

LACHLAN

"Stay married?" Olivia choked on a sip of coffee, then coughed in a spectacular fit as her crazed eyes sought mine. "Are you out of your mind?"

"Maybe." Doubts dug tunnels beneath my thoughts, but I trod on. "I'm also desperate. I'm just asking for six months." That would be enough time for my business launches to be firmly settled.

"Absolutely not," Olivia said.

"I'm a man with no other options. You live with me for three months in Sugar Creek as my wife. Your last public appearance would be the movie premiere in November. Then, after that big, swanky event, we quietly separate but continue the ruse." I could tell she was at least listening. "Six months in, we file for divorce."

Olivia's laugh was harsh and raw. "Great, within a matter of months I'd have my first marriage and first divorce checked off my life to-do list."

"It's very efficient." My new wife did not find that amusing. "If we don't play this off as intentional, then it looks as if we married on a drunken spree. It's incredibly bad business for me and, as you said, you'll lose your job. But if we stay married and act like we, you know..."

One dark brow arched. "Love each other?"

"I was going for *like* each other, but I appreciate your vision."

"Lachlan—"

"If we show the world our marriage is a choice we made, then I get to prove to investors and production companies that I deserve to be taken seriously. I'm not just some overnight, accidental success who can't be trusted to run a company in the long term."

Shrewd, swollen eyes narrowed. "There's something more you're not telling me."

I'd shared enough, and it would have to suffice. "Six months, Olivia. That's all I'm asking."

"That's *all*? You're asking me to give up my life and bring shame and deceit to my family—and for what? What do I get?"

"Name your price." I'd write her a check for any amount.

She gathered her hair in her hands and adjusted the elastic, binding the wild strands into submission. If only our problems were so easy to subdue. "You know what I want."

I sighed gustily and patted the bicep that hadn't seen a gym in a while. "If it's my body you're after, I'm gonna have to ask you to wait until I've had a full meal and a complete night's sleep. But I get the allure. I do."

I heard her curse beneath her breath. All these years later, and Olivia was still fun to goad.

Her pink painted toes pushed into the carpet as she closed the distance between us, coming to a stop right before me. "You sign with Flair."

A smart man knew his limits, and for the sake of my sanity, I could not work with Olivia Sutton. "No."

"And I take lead on the account."

Didn't she understand I was offering her something better —money? She could afford a year sabbatical to find herself a better job. "That's not a good idea."

"Then no deal," Olivia said.

"I'll give you a suitcase of cash." It was not lost on me that someone had once thought throwing money at a problem would make *me* fall in line.

Olivia's pert chin rose. "I don't want money."

Panic clawed at my insides. "Lots of zeroes."

"Want to know where you can stick those zeroes?" Same old Olivia. Arrogant and stubborn to her own detriment. "But out of morbid curiosity," she said, "let's hear more about this 'plan.' Do share the details."

"I hear that sarcasm and bitterness," I told her. "See, my wife is more of a gentle, soft-spoken woman." It was everything I could do not to laugh at Olivia's outraged face. "My sweet wife would move in with me, and we'd spend the worst fall and winter of our lives convincing everyone that we're married. In exchange for a large sum, you'd attend events with me and occasionally hold my hand in public, and we'd both look like stable, drama-free people."

Olivia crossed her arms over the strapless bodice of her dress.

"Fine." My volume kicked up a notch. "Do you have a better idea?"

"You're the one who benefits here," Olivia countered just as loudly. "*I* will lose my job. What's happened this weekend is still chaos and negative press for Flair. I'm no better than my stupid co-worker who got caught in the hot tub."

"This isn't blowing over, Olivia. I'd say the buzz is just getting started. You've married Silicon's Valley's current golden child, and whether either of us likes it or not, the world is watching."

Slamming coffee pods and mugs, Olivia set about making herself another cup of mediocre coffee. Her back to me, she mumbled to herself while she worked.

"You don't have to make your decision today." It might've been as foolhardy as walking into a bear's den, but I approached her anyway. "But please think about what will happen when you leave this hotel. I can promise you there's a vulturous group of paparazzi out there. You won't be able to take one step outside without being swarmed by their cameras and questions. Your face will continue to be on TV and all over the internet. Get ready to be the latest meme."

Leaving her coffee gurgling as it brewed, Olivia stomped to the dresser and began throwing clothes into a suitcase.

Olivia was even beautiful when she was mad, but that had always been the case. "Or," I said, watching her pause mid-toss of a dress, "we can walk out of this hotel hand in hand, a couple who's ecstatic that they've gotten married. We take charge of the narrative and spin it in our favor. We don't have to be victims of our circumstances." I shrugged as she zipped her carry-on. "Otherwise we both lose our credibility—and a lot more. You only have to live with me three months. Think about it."

She whirled back around, her carry-on swinging from the hand that now wore a wedding ring. "I don't want to think about it. I am not marrying you, Lachlan. My dignity's worth more than money, and that's final."

Two hours later, we exited the hotel.

I'd secured a waiting ride at a service entrance, and when

Olivia and I wheeled our luggage outside, the bright Vegas sun greeted us. As did a dozen reporters.

Lights flashed as photographers surrounded us. Reporters lobbed questions like grenades. I threw my arm around Olivia and tucked her to my side.

"Mr. Hayes, tell us about your new bride!"

"Lachlan, why the quickie marriage? Do you have more than one big announcement this winter?"

"How does it feel to be a victim of another drunken Vegas wedding?"

"Will your wife join you at the movie premiere?"

"Mrs. Hayes, how will this news be received back home in your small town?"

Olivia dug her heels into the pavement and came to a decisive stop. "Give Flair the account," she hissed toward my ear.

"Lachlan," a reporter shouted, "are you resurrecting your old party-boy ways? How does it feel knowing Wall Street is watching?"

I looked at Olivia and nodded my head. "Done," I whispered. "Whatever you want."

"Mrs. Hayes, do you have a comment?" a woman shouted.

With a hair toss, Olivia smiled at the reporters, looking every bit the cool, confident woman I'd once known. "Actually, I do have a statement," she said.

Olivia Sutton slipped her arms around my waist and gazed up at me like I was her own Prince Charming. "Lachlan Hayes and I have been quietly dating. And while our trip to the altar was fast, it wasn't an impulsive mistake. We hope you'll wish us well and give us the space to settle into our blissful newlywed life."

Then. *Oh, then...*

Olivia rose up on tiptoe, glided her hands up my chest until they paused at my face. Her delicate fingers held my jaw, and she pulled my head toward hers. "Kiss me like you mean it," she demanded.

I was a man who knew when to do as I was told.

So I pulled Olivia even closer, smiled as she gasped in surprise, then covered her lips with mine.

CHAPTER

ELEVEN

OLIVIA

IN MY HEAD, I could hear the conversations I'd soon be having loud and clear.

Hi, Sylvie. Yes, it's true I got married and didn't invite you. Please don't put a hit out on my husband.

Hattie, I can explain. I was so overcome with the romance of the weekend and so inspired by the love you and Miller model that I decided to get some of that sweeping love for myself.

Rosie, my sensitive sister, would you believe that I was blinded by the flashing lights of the casinos and accidentally stumbled into the wedding chapel and said "I do"?

Aunt Frannie, I know you're mad, but please put away your taser. No, you cannot fry my new husband's biscuits.

I spent the entire three-hour flight back home to Arkansas reviewing every possible scenario I might endure with my family. My sisters were going to lose their minds, and I couldn't even begin to quantify what my grandmother would do when she got a hold of me.

I'd received at least ten calls and messages from every human being I'd ever met, from extended family to Celeste, to my high school computer science teacher who wanted Lachlan's autograph. Aside from a text to my sisters letting them know I was okay and homebound, I didn't answer any of them. And really, what would I have said? For once in my life, the planner didn't have a plan. It was a dismal state to be in.

Lachlan snoozed most of the way home, seemingly unbothered. Meanwhile I'd written fifteen pages of ideas in a document titled "I Think I Just Ruined My Life."

The plane groaned as the wheels lowered for landing.

"Nice nap?" I asked Lachlan later as we descended the stairs.

"How sweet of you to inquire, wife." His ridiculous *Dungeons & Dragons* sweatshirt tugged across his chest as he yawned. "I do hear that judgmental tone, and for your information, I feel better."

"Great."

"Good." His phone dinged with a text. "Sylvie says they land at seven-thirty and to be prepared for a family meeting at my house at nine." Lachlan took a second look at his screen. "She also says our firstborn must be named after her."

There would be no little Sylvies, and this left us around three hours.

"How does your grandmother have my number?" Lachlan asked.

"She's former CIA. Within seconds of meeting you, she probably had your social security number and underwear size."

"Disturbing."

"You have no idea." But he was about to find out. "I left my car at my apartment. Can you take me home?"

"Home it is." Lachlan grabbed the handle of my suitcase and maneuvered both bags outside. "But don't get too handsy on the drive. We may be newlyweds, but road safety is priority

73

one." He slipped on a pair of black sunglasses and waved at two photographers crouched in the shrubbery.

Forty minutes later, from the passenger seat of Lachlan's SUV, I stared at the massive house toward the back of the Sugar Creek golf course. "I asked you to take me home."

Lachlan clicked the button to raise one of three garage doors. "I did." The SUV ambled over the driveway and into the dimly lit garage. "Welcome home."

Nope. No way. Absolutely not. "I have a very nice apartment downtown."

"Do you want us to live there? I need two bedrooms for my computer monitors alone."

I pressed the back of my head against the leather seat and wished for the millionth time this was all a bad dream. This sort of thing was cute in a rom-com movie, but the reality of waking up married to a man you didn't mean to wed was the pinnacle of awful. "I can't live with you."

He twisted in his seat to face me. "Who's going to believe we're married if we live apart?"

"Couples do it all the time," I said. "Maybe you should move back to the West Coast for authenticity's sake."

"Nope. We live right here. Together." Lachlan pushed his remote again, and the garage door lowered with a clang, closing us in. Like a jail.

In a fog of numbness, I followed Lachlan inside.

The garage led into a kitchen that would've made Ina Garten proud. Ceiling-height cabinets and quartz countertops lived alongside gleaming stainless appliances. The room was almost as big as my entire apartment.

Lachlan went to the restaurant-sized refrigerator and produced two water bottles. "I'd offer you something stronger, but we shouldn't tempt fate again. With our luck, I'd wake up pregnant." He patted his stomach. "I just lost twenty pounds, and I am *not* going back to my fat joggers."

We migrated to a den, a comfortable spot with a TV large enough to transmit images to outer space. I'd seen smaller screens in movie theaters.

"Take a seat." Lachlan gestured to a cozy, overstuffed chair. "We should get our stories straight."

Panic dug sharp, insistent claws into my insides, and I blinked back tears. It was so unfair. Every *single* time I'd ventured off my life plan, disaster had followed. Historically speaking, this sham marriage could not end well for me. "Lachlan, I've been thinking...and I can't do this."

He settled at the end of the couch, his knees inches from mine. "Don't chicken out on me now, Livvy. It's six months. When it's over, we both get what we want."

"And in the end, I can tell my family the truth?"

"After they sign NDAs, sure." But Lachlan didn't sound like he meant it. "Speaking of family, what should I expect when they show up here?"

Finally, a question with an easy answer. "Some interrogation from my sisters. A planting of undetectable surveillance cameras from Frannie. A challenge to a duel from my grandma."

Lachlan took a swig of his water. "Pistols or swords?"

"Knowing Sylvie, just bare hands."

"I was afraid you'd say that." He rubbed the back of his neck and grimaced. "That woman will have me on the ground in seconds. But your grandma's not the only one out for blood. I've already fielded a few death threats from Miller. Your future brother-in-law is very protective of you."

That was sweet. "Hattie's found a good one."

"And you got me."

He didn't need to remind me, though I did note the odd dip

in his self-confidence. "Let's review, shall we?" I dreaded convincing my family of something I could hardly utter myself. "You and I reconnected as soon as you moved back to town, and things escalated quickly."

Leaning back, Lachlan rested his hands on his stomach and crossed his feet at the ankles. "So quickly you didn't have time to tell anyone."

Our foundation was already shaky. "I would never withhold that information."

"Ah," he said, "but I asked you to keep it quiet because of pending business developments. I had to be sure you were 'the one' before our relationship went public."

"That's kind of dumb."

"If you have a better explanation, I haven't heard it." Irritation clipped his words. "One of us here has crisis management experience, and one of us creates a virtual reality with exploding aliens. Excuse me if I'm not operating on my strengths here."

It would have to do. "Fine. That's our story. We've dated the two months you've been in town. You swept me off my feet."

"I like how you say that as if I gave you an incurable rash."

I leaned toward the man. "Let me be really clear that I still don't like you."

"Duly noted and right back at you." Lachlan slapped his hands on his thighs and stood. "Now, your brood will descend shortly. I suggest we use our time to fill in some blanks and create a believable story." He gazed longingly toward the kitchen. "And make sandwiches. Sham marriages make me hungry."

Within the hour, Lachlan had eaten two ham sandwiches and a handful of carrots, while I'd received a partial tour of the house and spiraled further into absolute panic.

"Why can't I see your office?" I asked as we walked back down the stairs and headed back to the living room.

"Because you'll mess up the mojo." Lachlan ran his hand down the metal banister. "It's my sacred workspace."

"In other words, it's where you keep the corpses of your previous wives."

"That, plus it's really messy." He shoved his hands in the back pockets of his faded jeans. "We *are* in agreement your family's not going to believe our story, right?"

"Correct. Not for a second."

"But we can't afford any leaks or any more people in the know till the investigation wraps, so we push the lie anyway."

I swallowed hard, predicting doom. "I guess."

"You mean yes."

"Yes." I leapt from my seat, nerves firing like race car pistons.

Lachlan's hand on my arm stopped me. "I need to know you're in, Olivia."

I was about to affirm my lukewarm commitment when the doorbell rang. "Oh, Lord. They're here." My watch said we still had twenty minutes. "They're early. That is *so* my family."

Lachlan took my shoulders in his hands, his touch firm and warm. His eyes held mine steady. "We can do this."

"They're not going to believe us," I said. "They're going to grill us until we froth at the mouth and spill everything."

"I won't let that happen. Maybe they don't buy any of it, but we stick to the story. It was you, me, and a bunch of disgusting love between us. We followed our hearts right to the altar."

"That sounds so nauseating."

He nodded gravely. "My third sandwich is threatening to come back up any second."

"When did you have a third?"

"Snuck it in when you were sobbing in the bathroom a few minutes ago."

"You caught that, did you?"

"Pretty sure even the neighbors heard it." Lachlan ran his hands up and down my arms. "You have good lungs."

My new husband was so complimentary.

The doorbell rang again, followed by heavy pounding.

"Let me in, Lachlan Hayes!" called my grandmother from the other side. "You scalawag! You despot! You gorgeous rascal of a woman stealer!"

Then Frannie's voice penetrated the wall. "Your intentions are nefarious! Your words are toxic honey! Your buttocks appear nicely firm!"

Lachlan cut his eyes toward me. "Your people are so weird." Then he smiled as he opened the door. "Hello, Sutton Clan. My adorable tush and I would like to welcome you to my home." He hooked his meaty arm around my shoulders. "*Our* home, that is."

CHAPTER

TWELVE

OLIVIA

IF I'D THOUGHT the paparazzi in Vegas had been loud and pushy, they had nothing on my family.

My sisters, grandmother, and aunt tumbled inside the house, tripping over one another, bellowing questions, hollering dismay, and surrounding me like the wounded wolf in the pack who needed protection. If I hadn't been so drunk on stress and regret, I would've found my family's fierce intrusion endearing and sweet.

Instead it only served to activate a throbbing headache.

"Time out!" I yelled fifteen minutes later. I stood before Lachlan, my back plastered to his front, my shaking arms extended as if shielding him from an oncoming truck instead of four sharp-tongued women. "Can we just calm down, take a seat, and talk quietly and rationally about this? I can't hear one of you over the others." I glared at my grandmother. "Sylvie, I'd appreciate it if you could please holster your air horn."

As we moved to the living room, temper and confusion hung in the air so thick I could almost touch it.

"First, I want to apologize, Hattie." I reached toward my

sister and held her hand in mine. "I ruined your engagement celebration weekend, and that was never my intention. I'm so very sorry."

"Blame that on me," Lachlan said, to my surprise. "The wedding was my idea. We thought we could quietly get married, but it didn't go according to plan. Please accept my apology as well."

"It's okay," Hattie said. "A little more plot twist than I was looking for in my weekend, but it's fine. But let me state the obvious—none of this makes sense." Her attention dipped to the phone in her grip. "Lachlan, your official statement to the press was that you two have dated since you moved to Sugar Creek."

He sat next to me on the sleek, unyielding couch, one arm resting over my shoulders. "That's correct. But I've known your sister a long time. Had feelings for her even in college."

Yes. Murderous ones.

Hattie gave us a thoughtful, pensive look, letting the space stretch out in case we wanted to fill it with further confessions. It was a therapy trick as old as time, and I wasn't falling for it. I would stick to our script, though it pained me to lie to my family and put on such a ridiculous ruse.

"Olivia." Hattie's voice softened enough to coax ledge-jumpers to safety. "This isn't like you. At all. You have a ten-year plan, remember?" She flopped a hand toward Lachlan. "He's not on it."

I did not need that painful reminder.

"In fact," Rosie said, "you told us after your last boyfriend you'd never go off the life plan again."

There it was. The arrow of hurt came at me with a pointy stab, and I was not surprised to see it still wounded. But Rosie was correct—I'd vowed the summer of my disastrous semester in Italy not to veer from the Olivia Sutton Ten-Year Plan. Then

I'd recommitted my allegiance last year when my boyfriend moved to New York, taking my heart *and* a job that should've been mine.

"What can I say?" I literally could not think of anything. I tried not to squirm beneath Lachlan's tightening embrace and somehow managed a smile. "Love is so...unpredictable."

"Is that what this is?" Rosie asked. "You two are in love?"

"We have strong feelings for each other," I said.

Lachlan looked down and smiled at his faux-beloved. "Potent, even."

"So you dated him but said nothing to us?" Rosie's hurt look took a seam ripper to the edges of my heart, and I had to turn away. She and Hattie were my sisters, my best friends. "Why would you not tell us? We share everything."

"I take the blame for that as well." Lachlan's deep, rumbly voice vibrated near my shoulder. "As you probably know, I have a lot going on. Many irons in the fire. Because of that, I've been under a lot of scrutiny—and for the sake of my business affairs and pending deals, I asked Olivia to keep our dating life under wraps. I was trying to protect her too. It was hard, but necessary. And she felt terrible hiding it from you." His hand lightly squeezed my shoulder before making comforting circles around my back. Strong fingers swooped and slid in gentle patterns that I tried in vain to ignore. "Olivia cried a lot about it. Wails and wails. Lots of snot." Then the man had the nerve to boop my nose. "But even with her puffy eyes and gloopy nose, she still looked beautiful to me."

Lachlan Hayes was a profoundly terrible liar. And I needed his hands to stop their soothing roam that was anything but calming.

"But now you're certain my granddaughter is the one?" Sylvie turned cold, calculating eyes to Lachlan. This woman had interrogated international criminals for decades, and now she was about to give Lachlan the business.

"Yes," he replied. "Olivia is the one I decided to marry."

Frannie cracked her knuckles. "And what do you love about her?"

Lachlan joined our hands, linking our fingers. His skin felt warm pressed against mine. "I adore Olivia's sharp mind, her passion for her work and her family, her..." His gaze locked on mine, and I could tell he was struggling. "Even her bossiness is adorable. Her need to be right is so cute. Her fuzzy memory of our college days makes me double over and chuckle. *Oomph.*"

"Sorry." I smiled as Lachlan rubbed his side. "My elbow slipped."

It was too much to hope that the CIA Grannies were done. "So, Olivia," Aunt Frannie began, "when did Tall Boy here first declare his love and affection?"

Remember what you rehearsed. "Lachlan declared his undying love for me in Vegas."

Hattie frowned. "Where?"

"Where?" I repeated lamely.

"Yes," Sylvie snapped. "Give us the location. If there is one, that is."

"It was at one of the scavenger hunt stops," I blurted.

My grandmother leaned forward, no doubt analyzing my every intonation, each tiny movement that might expose me for a fraud. "Which one?"

"The wax museum." Oh, gosh. Why had I said that? There had been nothing romantic at *that* location.

Hattie looked even more confused. "That stop was the country music clue. So...you poured your heart out in front of the Reba McEntire wax figure?"

Lachlan took over, his smile letting me know he was more

than enjoying my misery. "Yep, right there with Reba. I said, 'Here's your one shot, Olivia. Don't let me down.'"

Dear God. Was it too much to ask for the floor to open up and swallow me now?

"And Olivia," Sylvie prompted, "you said 'I love you' in return?"

"She did," Lachlan answered. "In fact, and I don't want to embarrass her—"

"Then don't," I whispered.

"Olivia here said she's loved me since college."

"She hated you then," Rosie protested.

"There's such a fine line between love and hate, isn't there?" Lachlan resumed his hold on my hand, his thumb making lazy passes across my skin. "She realized she'd been so wrong about me, and she'd used anger to guard her heart from the deep and abiding love that threatened to consume her."

My jaw hurt as I unclenched it. "Like a communicable disease."

"That is just like in *Lambda Chi Lovebirds*," Frannie said. "Remember that novel we read for Sexy Book Club?" she asked the other women. "The one where the two college enemies are thrown together ten years later and must battle their love and the forces of evil?" Her attention snapped back to Lachlan. "By chance, are you a prince posing as a commoner who's on the run from royal obligations waiting for you in your homeland?"

Lachlan blinked eyes the color of forest moss. "No."

My aunt sighed. "Pity."

"But back to Olivia declaring her love for me in a very loud and public way." Lachlan gave a jovial laugh, full of smarm and low on charm. "Did I get to the part where she sang 'It Had to Be You'?"

"They don't want to hear that." If I gritted my teeth any harder they would disintegrate to dust.

"Yes, we do," Hattie said, now smiling. "Olivia never sings in public."

"She did for me." Lachlan brought my fingers to his lips and gave my knuckles a kiss. "Even had accompanying hand motions. A little bit of step-clap. Kind of stiff and the rhythm was off, but I loved it."

Frannie clutched her chest. "Oh. I can see it. Isn't it *dreamy*?"

"Not really the word I had for it," I muttered, snatching back my hand.

Lachlan ignored me and continued his happy-go-lucky husband routine. "When Olivia and I won the scavenger hunt, she told me the only prize she wanted was to be my wife. Isn't that true, my little honeybunches of neuroses?"

"No, actually—"

"So I made it happen. Because that's what you do when you have someone in your life as beautiful, smart, and lovesick as Olivia Sutton."

"You mean Olivia Hayes." Sylvie watched me with doubtful consideration.

I'd lost so much this weekend—even my last name. Lachlan and I had pushed a snowball of lies up a hill, and now we were watching it grow as it rolled down. I'd never felt more out of control.

"You should've heard the vows Lachlan wrote." I stared intently at my husband, deciding two could play this game. "He said he loved me more than any of his stupid computers, that he'd spent the last several years wishing he could crawl back to me and beg my forgiveness for getting me kicked out of college, and that he would donate twenty thousand dollars to my favorite charity. That would be your therapy program, Hattie."

My sister brightened. "Wow. Thanks."

I grabbed Lachlan's knee and gave it a firm squeeze. "Then Lachlan pledged a vow of chastity for the next six months to prove the depth of his love and the strength of his feelings."

"Already broken that promise," he said quickly. "My wife is too irresistible. Even if she does snore."

"I do not."

He flashed me a toothy grin, and I removed my hold on his knee. "But she also calls out my name when deep in slumber, so what a blessed man I am. She thinks of me even when she's unconscious."

I closed my eyes. "I would so love to be unconscious now."

"So she can dream of me." Lachlan took my hand in his and brought my fingers to his lips. "But I'm right here. By your side. Aren't you lucky?" He barreled on, lest I reply. "We know this is a lot to take in."

Sylvie sucked in her glossy bottom lip. "You could almost say it's...unbelievable."

"And we know it seems very sudden." My husband gazed upon me with eyes brimming with adoration. "But I'm positively crazy about this woman. And we hope you'll give us your blessing."

"A blessing is cheaper than a wedding present, so you've got mine." Frannie turned to Sylvie. "They could've had one of those robo-vacuums."

"I still can't wrap my head around this," Rosie said. "This is more the type of thing I would've done. I'm the romantic, impulsive one. But you, Olivia? You don't do anything unless it's scheduled years in advance."

Why did my sister say that like it was a bad thing? Plans were important. Necessary, even. Schedules and timelines gave me peace and provided a Zen most people needed drugs to achieve.

Lachlan spared me from having to reply. "This is a huge

adjustment for us as well. And since neither of us has ever been married, we have a lot to learn and will need your wise guidance."

Frannie sniffed and rolled her shoulders. "I can give you all sorts of advice. I've been down the aisle three times."

"Two of them are still alive to tell about it." Sylvie shot a pointed look to Lachlan. "The other one just...disappeared."

"These things happen." Frannie pinned Lachlan with her own steely gaze. "Especially when a man doesn't treat a woman right. You know what I mean?"

"I'll take good care of your niece, ma'am." Lachlan sounded sincere, and it was discombobulating. When had anyone ever taken care of me? I'd been Ms. Independence since the day I was born. I'd had three serious boyfriends in my life, and they'd all been completely satisfied to let me take lead. Of course, they'd also all left me for kinder, gentler options.

Hattie stood with a yawn. "Well, I thought I'd be the first to get married between us, but I've decided to be happy for you, Olivia. If this is what you want, then I'll support you." She pulled me into a tight hug, so familiar and comforting it brought a sting of tears to my eyes. "If you need to talk, you call day or night. Okay?"

I could only nod before Rosie joined the sisterly squeeze fest. "I love you, Olivia."

"Love you both," I said against Rosie's shoulder. "We'll talk soon."

Lachlan shook hands and endured Frannie's lengthy embrace. I left him behind to escort my family to the door, torn between needing relief from their scrutiny and begging them not to go.

Frannie and my sisters climbed into Hattie's car, while Sylvie lingered behind with me at the front stoop. Finally, she turned to me and clamped her hands against my cheeks. "Let's get real, girl. Who are you and what have you done with Olivia?"

I was all out of smiles, even for my grandma. "It's me, Sylvie."

"I've seen some weird things in my day." She turned my face to the left, then the right. "Blink twice if you're being held hostage." She waited no more than two seconds. "Blink once if you're still going to buy a wedding cake and I can go with you to taste test." She gave a satisfied nod. "Atta girl."

"I did not blink."

"There was a definite lowering of the lids."

"There was not."

"I saw what I saw, and I agree to donate my icing-sampling expertise." She gave my cheek a smacking kiss. "Sugar, I'm in your corner. Always. I don't know what happened, but I know you're thrown. When you're ready, you'll tell me. But until then, maybe think of this as an adventure. Because my dear, sweet, type-A darling"—her blue eyes twinkled with moon-glow and mischief—"an adventure could be exactly what you need."

THIRTEEN

OLIVIA

My life was, unfortunately, not a Bridget Jones novel.

If it were, last night after we shut the door on my family, Lachlan and I would've bumbled about in his big house, stealing meaningful glances, accidentally brushing arms as we passed one another, and realizing that due to a series of unfortunate and entirely unbelievable circumstances, there was only one bed to be found beneath his roof. Exhausted, we would've reluctantly slipped beneath the sheets, keeping a continent of space between us, only to wake up the next morning, wrapped in one another's arms and a romantic spell of perfect breath and kisses.

But this was my life. And Bridget Jones I was not.

Instead, I waited until midnight, then left Lachlan's house under the cover of night. I drove straight to my apartment, showered until all the travel grime and residual regrets washed down the drain, then fell into my own bed, where I considered my options for a quality mental breakdown. I lay wide awake all night, staring at my ceiling and wondering if going along with Lachlan's plan had been a mistake bigger than I could possibly handle.

By seven a.m. on Monday, I'd washed two loads of laundry, packed three suitcases to transport to Lachlan's, and even completed a spin class at the gym downtown.

When seven-thirty rolled around, I found myself sitting in my car in Flair's parking lot, wondering what fate awaited me inside. My fingers flexed on the door handle, and I was just about to pull the rip cord when my phone dinged.

LACHLAN

Good morning, wife.

Don't call me that. Why are you texting me?

LACHLAN

Because that's what husbands do. I don't want to deprive you of all the romance I'm supposed to deliver.

Feel free to abstain.

LACHLAN

Are you saying I'm not romantic?

The long line of girls you went through in college certainly seemed to think you were.

LACHLAN

We'll never make it to our golden anniversary if you keep bringing up my sordid past. You know you're the only woman for me now.

The very thought kept me awake most of the night.

LACHLAN

Thoughts of me drove you wild? I knew it
wouldn't take long.

> I'm going into the office now. If I survive my
> meeting with Celeste, I will be home late this
> evening. If she chews me up and spits out the
> bones, my remains belong to my family.
> Not you.

LACHLAN

I will remember you fondly. I think we had at
least ten minutes in Vegas that we got along.
I'll hold onto that the rest of my days. Now be
brave, Mrs. Hayes. You can do this. Fake love
and kisses. XXOO.

I THREW MY PHONE INTO MY PURSE AND STARTLED AS I CAUGHT MY reflection in the rearview mirror. Was that...a smile? No. That was absolutely not allowed. Lachlan Hayes would not charm me with morning banter and zippy texts. He was still obnoxious, and I needed to remember he was a temporary problem. Not a permanent husband.

Another car pulled up beside me, and I gave a half-hearted wave to a curious coworker. It was time to get out and face the music. That music being a funeral dirge.

I bypassed the downstairs coffee shop, ignored the chatter that swelled when I breezed by, and aggressively punched the third-floor elevator button like it had done me wrong.

Slipping inside, I sighed with relief when the doors began to close, only to hear, "Hold the elevator!"

With zero care for manners or appearances, I mashed that door-close button as Morgan stuck her willowy arm inside, prying the doors apart like bratty curiosity had made her superhuman.

"Oh, thank goodness." Morgan swooped inside, looking

quite proud of herself. "That was close, huh?"

Her perfume wafted in a hovering cloud, and I covered my Red Bull with a hand to protect it from the toxic off-gassing. She wore a black pantsuit, her jacket tied with a silk sash, and her dark camisole dotted with delicate sequins. She looked sleek and elegant, while I no doubt looked as if I'd just stepped from the wreckage of a downed airplane.

"Olivia!" she exclaimed, as if she'd just now identified my face. "I don't even know what to say!" Condescending shock rounded Morgan's eyes, and she clasped a hand to her buoyant chest. "I mean...you? Lachlan Hayes? Married?" Her airy laugh sounded like the wheeze of a sharp clarinet. "I saw the news, but is this even real? How could it be, right?" More laughter followed as she waited for me to open my mouth and bless her with a logical explanation.

"It's real." I gave my ring hand a wave then stared at the opposite wall.

"Wow." Disbelief and confusion were pretty much everyone's response, but Morgan somehow took to it a snooty, disdainful level. "Celeste is totally freaked out." My least favorite coworker was high on the joy and victory of my scandal, sloshed on giddiness and petty glee. "Yesterday Celeste called me a dozen times asking if I'd heard from you." Morgan shook her head. "I assumed you wouldn't get the New York promotion, but I never guessed you'd go down in flames like this."

"I—" What? What could I possibly have to say? My brain froze. My thoughts flatlined.

The elevator chugged to a stop, and the doors creaked open.

With a cheery smile, Morgan clapped me on the back. "Good luck in there. You're going to need it." And with that, she sashayed to her office, a woman confident in my demise.

The reality of what came next almost had me retreating into a corner of the elevator and riding it back down.

But I couldn't. I'd made a career in facing problems head-on, and I wouldn't run away now.

A trip to the bathroom, one lengthy visit to the staff lounge, two quick walks up and down the halls, plus three prayers later, I finally stood at Celeste's door and knocked.

"Come in." Sitting at her desk, Celeste spared me a quick look over her cat eye glasses. She was Miranda Priestly in *The Devil Wears Prada*, bidding me entrance and rejecting me with a single withering glare.

I stepped inside, an unarmed innocent walking into the battle zone. "Good morning, Celeste."

She put down her phone and raised one perfectly waxed eyebrow. "Shut the door."

The only time Celeste closed her door was on the rare occasion she wanted to yell. I'd never been the recipient of her raised voice...until now.

She crossed her arms over her slender waist, her straight spine pressed into the back of her chair. "You bid me good morning. But is it, Olivia? Is it a good morning?"

Flair Survival Rule Number 27: Never answer Celeste's rhetorical questions. "I can explain."

She held up a hand, her red nails glistening beneath the dangling lights. "You are my sane one, my levelheaded one. All this time I thought you were so like me—my young protégé. But this drama? These are not the actions of a Celeste Coulson."

I wanted so badly to tell Celeste everything. Surely she'd understand if I explained we'd been drugged and were simply trying to make the best of it—for the sake of Lachlan's business *and* Flair.

"I'm sorry I didn't tell you I was getting married," I began. "But please understand—"

"I don't care if someone hijacked the Strip, held you at gunpoint, and forced you to marry Lachlan Hayes." I was surprised Celeste didn't breathe fire. "For the simple fact that it went viral, it does not matter."

There went my plan to gain her sympathy with the truth.

Celeste turned her laptop around so I had a view of her screen. "*People* magazine reports you two had dated for two whopping days."

"That's not accurate," I said. And it *wasn't* true. We hadn't dated at all.

She pushed play on a video. "This is footage of you kissing Hayes, then kissing the minister, then cartwheeling down the aisle, baring your Victoria's Secrets for all to see."

The video continued to play, and my voice could be heard shouting, "Don't tell my boss!" while a sloppy cartwheel took out two chairs and a fern.

"If you had married a no-name individual, I would not have cared what you did in Vegas," Celeste said. "But you married a tech mogul who has millions watching his every move."

"I'm sorry the wedding was so gauche."

"Gauche I could handle." Celeste maximized another photo that showed me face down in the chapel souvenir cake. "All of this just makes you look like a total kook."

I had zero memory of the cake, and right now that seemed like a shame. "I'm aware I look out of control, but—"

"People do not entrust their reputations, brands, and businesses to cartwheeling women who flash their bloomers. They want stability. They want people who do not get married by Cher."

"It was Celine."

"Excuse me?"

"The person who married us." I cleared my throat and wondered if my face looked as hot as it felt. Because it felt like I had it pressed to a porthole of hell. "It was Celine Dion."

Celeste stood up and slapped her hands on her desk. "I don't care if it was Beyoncé herself. This is unacceptable. Shall I quote the fourth paragraph in the *Celebrity Spin* article?"

"I'm begging you not to."

My boss shoved her red bifocals on her nose and proceeded anyway. "Lachlan Hayes's bride is a brand specialist at the marketing firm Flair, based out of New York and Arkansas. The new Mrs. Hayes has spent her career fixing the images of others, and now she has quite an image adjustment of her own to deal with. Was it a drunk dare? A tipsy trip to the altar they now regret? A bender blunder? Or maybe...the two really are in love? Only time will tell." The glasses came off, and without saying a word, Celeste demanded a response.

I blinked back tears, wounded by her disappointment. "I understand the wedding was in poor taste, but after all I've given this company, are you really going to fire me for finding love and getting married?"

"I said in our last staff meeting that I wanted no more drama. So maybe this wedding *is* the best decision you've ever made and you're blissfully in love. What matters *to me* is that I specifically said if any employees of mine caused the tiniest dustup and found themselves on the news, in the news, or even news-*adjacent*, I would fire them immediately. Your wedding is your business, but when that wedding puts you on the homepage of TMZ, it becomes *my* business. Had you gotten married in a cheap chapel without making national news, then I might've used this time today to hand you a gift card to Nordstrom instead of your walking papers."

"If you'd only let me explain—"

"My only recourse is to follow through on my word. Otherwise I will look like a complete fool."

"But Celeste—"

"Olivia, this pains me more than you know. I saw such great things for you. You have incredible potential, and I've always envisioned you racing up the Flair ladder. I wanted you by my side one day here in this very office."

"Then make that happen." When it came to this job, I had zero shame. "Please."

"I'm sorry." Celeste's eyes met mine, and her stern face softened with regret. "I have no choice but to let you go."

"I've given my life to Flair." My volume ramped up with the hurt. "I've sacrificed almost every weekend in the last seven years. I've turned down headhunters offering me higher paid positions."

Her chest rose on an indignant inhale. "Then you should have no problem finding another job."

That was it? After all I'd done for Celeste? Her kids? After all I'd given to this company?

I would not cry in front of her. I didn't cry at work—ever. But the unshed tears stung my eyes anyway. She was my mentor, my hero. I'd worked with her since I was an intern in college. After all that, where was the grace? Where was Celeste's heart? "Okay, then, if there's nothing I can say..."

My hero stood and gestured toward the door. "I'm afraid there isn't one thing you could say to change my mind."

It was time to throw my Hail Mary. "If you let me stay, I can guarantee Lachlan Hayes will hire Flair for his PR."

"Well." Celeste collapsed into her seat and pursed her lips into a wry grin. "I guess I won't be firing anyone today after all."

CHAPTER
FOURTEEN
LACHLAN

Backpack slung over my shoulder, I stood in front of the five-story building on 9200 Castle Drive Monday afternoon and took it all in. The future offices of Star Gazer.

If only my mom could see me now. I blinked back tears I'd deny ever shedding and gave a thoughtful glance toward the heavens. *I made it, Mom.*

This was mine—all of it. The building, the business within it, and the dream. My past self could never have envisioned the future possibilities. Yet here I was—ready to walk inside the empire I'd created.

But alone. Again.

Not to sound pitiful, but it would've been nice to have someone to share this moment with. I mean, I officially had a wife, but asking Olivia to see the office hadn't felt right. She wasn't allowed in my treehouse.

We'd owned the property for two months, and though much work had been done, a significant amount remained. Today was the first day I'd stepped back inside since I'd closed the deal. Sure, I'd driven by it a hundred times, but due to ongoing construction, occupancy had been out of the question. When I'd visited my friend Miller last year, I'd fallen in love with Sugar Creek and knew this was where home would be for the business and for me.

I pushed my hair out of my eyes and set my Converse to the sidewalk, counting how many steps from my car to the front door. Forty-five. Exactly forty-five steps to unlock the next level.

"Yard needs mowing," said a voice behind me.

I twisted the key into the lock and grinned at the welcome addition to my one-man celebration. "Maxwell. What in the world are you doing here?"

"Weekly design meeting," my suit-wearing CFO said, as if I'd forgotten. "Also you mentioned you'd visit the new office today. My plane was delayed, so I hope I'm not late."

I peeled open the creaky door. "Are you telling me you flew all the way from California to attend a meeting you barely tolerate? You do love me."

Smiling, Maxwell followed me inside. "You always say I'm your right-hand man. If I'm moving here to this dusty map dot, I might as well see for myself what I'm getting into." His hand clapped my shoulder. "Let's go check out this office of ours."

Maxwell Barclay was not only my CFO, but a friend. He was more starched than Olivia, though they both shared a love for rules, arrogance, and telling people what to do. These were not characteristics I looked for in a life partner, but in my CFO? Vital. Max had joined me at a point when I was drowning, then whipped my infant company into shape and provided the vision and structure we needed to survive. Without him, I would've been a one-hit wonder. Now I had a thriving enterprise and the capacity to focus on the art while Maxwell took care of details.

Construction crews scurried like busy ants, carrying equipment and tending to noisy tasks. The bottom four floors were barely more than gutted shells, but I'd memorized the blueprints and design mock-ups and saw the space through that finished lens.

I took Maxwell on a don't-touch-anything tour of the bottom floors before we journeyed to what would be the executive level. The fifth floor had received significantly more attention than the rest and looked nearly habitable.

"This is my office." I stuck my head inside a large space filled with windows. "Yours is across the hall."

Maxwell stepped over a pallet of wood flooring in his future part-time office. "Why's my office half the size of yours?"

"I'm twice as large. Plus, I do all the work around here. You're just the pretty face." I punched my friend in the shoulder as we inspected his new space.

"Cool, then I'll send you a few dozen spreadsheets and legal contracts to work on today. Oh, and then there's the HR meeting to discuss staffing needs, the day next week devoted to the forensic accountant, plus I need to hire one more attorney."

"See, you barely work." I'd missed harassing Maxwell. With him here scowling, today almost felt normal. "I could have all that done before second breakfast. Maybe when you start really carrying your weight, we'll discuss office upgrades."

"Says the guy who installed a soda fountain and a video arcade in his last office."

"This disrespectful attitude is all about my high score on *Tetris*, isn't it?" Maxwell worked harder than anyone in the company, and we all knew it. That's why I paid him very, very well. "Man, it's good to see you and that surly face."

"I hope you haven't torched too much in my absence," he said with a haughtiness I knew Maxwell only partially meant.

"Just my personal life."

He paused in his inspection of the green space outside the window. "When you become a public figure, the line between your personal and professional life can easily blur."

"I'm aware."

He turned toward me then, that analytical, killjoy look back on his face. "I guess I should say congratulations on your marriage."

Max was more secure than the vault down at the Sugar Creek Bank and Trust, and I knew I stood in the cone of confidentiality. "Olivia Sutton and I go way back. We've mutually agreed to dislike each other for years."

"She appears to be playing the part of a happy bride."

"Olivia has a lot on the line as well." Would I have stayed married for a promotion? Zero chance. But when Olivia set a goal, she let nothing stop her. "The media uproar seems to have diminished some."

Maxwell rubbed a hand over his doubtful face. "How long will you let this play out?"

"Six months."

He gave a huff of amused disbelief. "Only you would wake up in Vegas married to a beautiful woman you can't stand. And at the worst possible time for the company."

"I'm doing all I can *for* this company." Now it was my turn to get serious. "I've got this under control. But you said you had news from the detective?"

Max rocked back on his heels, a nervous habit he rarely broke out. "The Tropical Paradise Club had one working security camera that night."

"Let me guess: It wasn't in the bar area."

"Parking lot."

"What about cameras from nearby establishments?" I asked.

"He looked at lots of footage, but hundreds of people come and go. Vegas is a tourist mecca. Nobody was wearing a shirt that said, 'I roofie drinks.' The detective and his team interviewed waitstaff, bartenders, and a handful of the regulars. Not one person saw anything, Lachlan. I'm sorry."

"Me too." Someone had irrevocably altered two lives. "It wouldn't have changed much for Olivia and me, but some justice would've been nice."

"You just keep doing what you're doing," Maxwell said. "The more settled and rehabbed our CEO appears, the more it calms stockholders."

This is what my life had come down to. Life decisions for the sake of financial success.

Maxwell looked scornfully at the sawdust that now covered the toes of his dress shoes. "And how is this wife of yours?"

"Olivia's okay," I said. "If you like the vapid, shrewish type."

"She's also quite pretty."

I led us out of Max's office. "Hadn't noticed."

He gave a snort. "Right."

I glanced at my watch. "We have two minutes until the meeting. You know I can't stand to be late." Ignoring Maxwell's eye roll, I escorted my favorite grumpy CFO to a room three doors down. We settled in at a conference table the previous occupants had left and fired up our laptops.

"Thanks again for being here." I clicked a link that would begin our remote meeting. "I don't care what your wife and kids say, Maxwell. You're a nice man. Even moderately tolerable on occasion."

"My family will like me even better when I get out of their hair and work in Arkansas half the year." He pulled a water bottle out of his messenger bag. "Don't get too attached to my face," Maxwell said as he joined the virtual meeting. "I'm headed back to San Francisco this evening."

"There goes my idea for a slumber party." I smiled toward my laptop screen and greeted my design team. "Good morning, God's gift to gaming. Let's get started."

We had a full agenda and wasted no time. I met with each department once a week and made sure my hand was always in the mix. Even though I did very little of the design these days beyond initial plotting and illustration, no detail went to production that wasn't approved by me.

"How's the new game going?" Zinna, one of my senior designers asked me. "How long until we see the concept map?"

"Still noodling on some things," I told her. "The characters are locked in. I'll get those ideas to you soon." Digital characters I understood. Their wants and needs were obvious and so gloriously basic. In *Mars Wars*, Captain Triton aimed to save the world and rescue Princess Serafina. Easy stuff. The good captain should try figuring out *real* people. Now that was where things got difficult.

"Let's shoot for Friday on the concept map," Zinna said.

"Leave him alone," Reggie Benson told her. "Boss in still on his honeymoon."

"Maybe next time you can invite us to the wedding," Kalpesh said. "Or at least the after-party."

"Everything happened very quickly." I stared at the tiles of faces I depended on daily. "And unfortunately, no reception."

"That's a real shame," said Maxwell with zero conviction. "But your team decided to bring the reception to you." Stoic old Max stepped into the hall for a few moments, and when he returned, darned if he wasn't carrying a cake.

"He shipped cake to all of us," said Zinna. "From your favorite bakery in the Valley."

All twenty designers held up a slice of cake. Some donned

party hats while others blew into obnoxious noisemakers that I knew drove Maxwell nuts. "This is amazing, guys. I can't thank you enough. Raises for everyone."

"Really?" Kalpesh asked.

"Definitely not." Maxwell handed me a plate. "But, Lachlan, we wish you and Olivia well."

"To a long and happy marriage!" Reggie shouted.

Maxwell crossed his arms over his suit jacket and found one of his rare grins. "Looks like Captain Triton finally got his princess."

FIFTEEN

OLIVIA

"I SEE YOU'RE ALIVE."

These were the first words that greeted me as I entered Lachlan's kitchen that night. I'd had to repeat our story all day, and after work I'd driven to my apartment on autopilot before realizing that was no longer where I lived. Had I shed a few angry, hot tears on the way to Lachlan's? Only the dark of my car and a box of tissues stuffed in my console knew.

I tossed my keys on the counter and regarded my husband. "Disappointed I've survived to annoy you another day?"

"Not really." He pulled a bottle of wine from the refrigerator. "I wasn't ready to be both a new husband and a widower in the span of forty-eight hours." He retrieved glasses from a cabinet and began to pour. "Though I've been sitting here thinking about all the messy decisions I'd endure as a widower. What would I do with all those high heels? Would I inherit all your personal planners, and should I just throw them away?"

I wanted to grab his silly ponytail and yank. "Touch my planners and die."

"I would've kept some of the stickers." He handed me the glass of white wine. "To remember you by."

"What do I smell?" The heavenly fragrance of garlic and butter permeated my senses.

Lachlan slipped off an apron that demanded I kiss the cook. "Since you've returned unscathed, you're going to need to eat. I kept it warm in the event of our blessed reunion."

Curiosity and hunger getting the best of me, I joined Lachlan at the stove. Surely it was the defeating fatigue that made my heart loosen its belt and let out some of the hatred. "What is this?" I was looking at a restaurant-quality pasta dish.

His green eyes met mine as he shrugged. "Just something I threw together. No big deal."

"A bowl of cereal is throwing something together." I should know because cereal was a mainstay in my own routine. Pardon my bragging, but I could serve up an impressive bowl of Cinnamon Toast Crunch. "This is full-out cooking." I attempted to dip a finger in the sauce, but Lachlan swatted me away.

"I don't know where your hands have been," he said.

"Things said to you many times in college." I tried once more to steal a taste, but Lachlan used his large body to block my path.

"Did your boss forbid you from eating lunch?" Lachlan asked. "Here." He deftly twirled pasta around a fork and brought it to my lips. "Taste."

My eyes narrowed. "Did you spit in it?"

"That's insulting."

I matched his aggravating grin. "So...arsenic?"

Lachlan gave a shrug before his gaze settled on my mouth. "You won't taste a thing."

As I stood there close to Lachlan, a steaming bite of heaven between us, a couple things occurred to me at once.

One, it was certainly an intimate thing to have a man feed you. As Lachlan guided his fork toward my mouth, my hand instinctively covered his. Our eyes met and held, and for a moment, I glimpsed something vulnerable and gentle in Lachlan's gaze before he diverted his attention somewhere in the region of my chin.

Two, I'd never been this close to Lachlan without wanting to do him bodily harm. I waited for that instant flare of revulsion, but it didn't come. Surely my instincts were dulled by the fragrance of a white sauce and the fatigue of the day. Because, I reminded myself, I did not like this man.

I leaned toward Lachlan and took the offered bite. I could feel his eyes on me, watching, waiting, tugging that short thread of tension between us.

Then the flavors hit my tongue, and holy cannoli, the man could cook. "Is this *homemade* Alfredo sauce?"

Lachlan seemed to have a hard time pulling his focus from my lips. "The jar stuff is an insult to taste buds." Then with a shake of his head, he stepped away, only to then produce a Caesar salad from the fridge. "Sit down and let's eat. I'm starving."

It was almost nine o'clock. "You cooked *and* waited for me?"

He shrugged it off and retrieved another fork from the counter. "I thought we might have something to celebrate. Either that or you'd need to eat your feelings."

"I don't do that," I said. "I double up on my spin classes instead."

"Huh." Lachlan ladled out a heaping mound of pasta and handed me the plate. "Then let me show you how it's done."

A few minutes later we settled at the quartz island big

enough to seat half a football team. Despite an entire row of barstools, Lachlan took the one right by mine. Much like on the plane, his legs invaded my space.

Lachlan spun another forkful, then turned those devil-may-care eyes to me. "Since you were gone all day and came home in one piece, I assume Celeste showed you mercy?"

I blotted my lips with a napkin. "Are we really doing this?"

He chewed, and one side of his mouth hitched in a grin. "What?"

"Having a civil conversation."

"Instead of hissing at one another and continuing our hate fest?"

"*Hate* is a strong word." Granted, it was one I'd used many times in reference to Lachlan. "You have to admit you were profoundly terrible to me in college."

His neutral mask returned. "Right back at you."

"What is that supposed to mean?" Did he seriously think my bossiness and micromanaging tendencies could compare to his past misdeeds? "You got me kicked out of college."

Lachlan held up his wineglass and gave a mock toast. "Again, right back at you."

I folded my arms on the bar and leaned into his space. "Have you suffered a head injury since we left school? How on earth do you figure I got *you* kicked out of college?"

Now it was his turn to glower. "You told the university that I, alone, was the mastermind behind our fateful boat ride."

I'd been a junior and Lachlan a senior. Along with ten other students, we'd been selected for a summer term in Italy to pursue our respective studies at the famed Naples School of Business. I'd lined up an internship for the following senior fall semester with a renowned PR agency, and my transcript would've let future employers know I'd studied in an elite program abroad. I'd been poised to be in high demand. The world was my oyster.

Then Lachlan did his Lachlan thing.

Our summer group had become fairly close, and Lachlan had secured a boat to transport us along the coast of Capri to a tourist stop called the Blue Grotto.

"You told us you'd *rented* the boat," I reminded him, because apparently he'd rewritten the story in his head. Then he'd rammed said boat into the dark cave, and we capsized. We'd been lucky to come out unscathed. In the dark of the grotto, I'd swum to a touring boat and sputtered as they pulled me aboard.

"Not one of my finer moments," Lachlan said, "and I do admit to paying for the boat rental. As for the rest, your old boyfriend shares significant blame—which, I recall so clearly, you denied when questioned by the authorities."

Preston Westerfield of the Massachusetts Westerfields. We'd dated for two years, and after the semester in Italy, he'd broken it off and taken up with a cheerleader who liked parties, fast cars, and Boston accents. "After all these years, you still have trouble accepting responsibility."

"I've owned my part."

"But not the part where you took the boat without the owner's permission, we all got in trouble, and had to pay for its repair. The fact that the owner was a very irate Italian dignitary was a nice plot twist, wasn't it?" I held up a hand when Lachlan tried to interrupt. "And let's not forget my absolute favorite part—we got expelled."

Lachlan's nostrils flared as he set down his fork. "Fine. You want an apology?"

"I've only waited years."

"I'll give you an apology." Lachlan stood and tossed his napkin to the counter. "As soon as I get the one you owe me."

CHAPTER
SIXTEEN
LACHLAN

OLIVIA STILL BELIEVED our debacle in Italy was completely my fault. It was water under the bridge—or in our case, the cave—but it still grated. There had been more to the story, and surely she'd known it even then.

"You won't admit to being responsible for everything that happened?" she now asked again.

This woman didn't deserve my Alfredo sauce. "What I admit to," I conceded, "is making a lot of mistakes in my younger days. I earned quite a reputation and often lived up to it. My therapist would say I did the best I could with the tools I had." I could tell I'd shocked her with that revelation. "Accept it—I'm a Renaissance man now."

That almost got a laugh out of her. "You do cook well. I'm totally going to finish this before I call Poison Control."

I should've focused on the lift of her haughty eyebrows, but my gaze snagged on the sight of her pink lips sealing around her fork of noodles, then her lashes lowering as she sighed in contentment. "Let's agree not to talk about college anymore tonight, shall we? I was young and stupid. You were young and—"

"And?" She let the word hang there, a husky dare.

"Like everyone else, you saw what you wanted to see." Remembering one more contribution to the meal, I pulled some French bread from the oven and set it between us. "Now pretend I'm a doting spouse and tell me about your day."

"Why?"

Why, indeed? I should've gone to my office, shut the door, and returned to work. Or opened my laptop and replied to the fifty emails waiting for a response. Instead, I stayed right where I was and watched my pretend wife spread a thin layer of butter on her steaming bread. "I'm acting like a husband. It's practice."

She took a small, dainty bite. "So you truly don't care about my talk with Celeste?"

I faked a yawn. "Boring stuff, Sutton." That wasn't entirely true, and I could tell from her smile she wasn't buying it. It was weirdly nice having someone in the house to talk to, but I'd stab my tongue with the fork tines before admitting that to Olivia.

She relaxed her shoulders and propped her elbow on the counter, her hair falling over her shoulders like a caress. "In that case, Celeste was terrible to me. She had my termination packet ready and told me how disappointed she was—how she'd expected me to be her protégé and I'd let her down, telling me I was nothing like her after all."

"Maybe that's a good thing."

"She let me know my behavior was a total embarrassment to her and Flair, even making her point with the help of visual aids."

"Like a PowerPoint? Interpretive dance?"

"Worse." Olivia shuddered. "I had to rewatch our Vegas

videos." She paused as she chewed a bite of noodles. "New ones have popped up online, by the way."

"Not one person has paid us for all the online content we've provided." I pierced a piece of chicken and brought it to my lips. "Is it because we don't have SAG cards?"

"Celeste claims it wasn't the marriage that's a fireable offense, but the way I handled myself—like a drunken *Bachelorette* contestant."

My fork stilled over my plate. "Did you tell her the truth?" We'd decided we'd keep it quiet until the investigation wrapped up in case the police turned up nothing.

"I almost did."

Panic hooked me by the collar. "But?"

"Instead I told her I'd secured your PR account, and I'd take it somewhere else."

Well, wasn't that a much-needed shot of relief? I gave Olivia a smile. "Mrs. Hayes makes threats."

"Mrs. Hayes is still employed." Her phone dinged for the fourth time since she'd sat down.

"One of your disappointed boyfriends?"

"My sisters." She tapped out a quick reply. "They've now committed to nightly check-ins to make sure you haven't tied me up and thrown me in a closet."

"I would never do something that unoriginal."

"I'm pretty sure they still doubt my sanity—and our story."

"I'll win them over." People liked me. Especially the ladies. I didn't question my superpower; it just was. "Do they play games? I could create them each one. Do you think Rosie seems more like an alien hunter or a fire-breathing warlord?"

"Leave my sisters to me." Olivia pulled an elastic from her wrist and tied up her hair in a movement of hands and tresses that held me spellbound. Everything she did was so efficient, yet elegant. "The less interaction you have with my family, the better," she said. "The last thing I need is for them to get attached to a husband I don't intend to keep."

"So you're saying I'm incredibly charming and need to turn it down?"

A little moan escaped from her lips as she took another bite. "At the risk of giving you a compliment, this pasta is amazing."

"Thank you." I would cook Alfredo every night if she'd make that satisfied noise again. "I'll probably be insufferable for at least twenty-four hours now."

"Sounds like a normal day." She ate in silence for a few moments before resting her fork and regarding me with reluctant interest. "So where did the game mogul learn to cook? Le Cordon Bleu? Personal lessons from your pal Gordon Ramsay? No, no, I've got it—you once employed a hot chef who showed you a thing or two."

I rubbed a napkin across my mouth. "Taught myself." Did I enjoy watching Olivia's doe eyes widen? I did indeed. But did I also enjoy the way her blue irises darkened? No. I hardly noticed.

She pushed aside her plate and leaned back against the upholstered barstool, her posture sliding into a relaxed pose. "Recently?"

"When I was a kid." I could still remember that little apartment in Texas—the peeling Formica kitchen counter, the cracked tile floor, the way smoke would waft in from our Marlboro-puffing neighbors. "It was either that or eat bologna every day. My mom worked two jobs and wasn't home much."

Olivia's forehead wrinkled with a small frown. "Did you have other family to look out for you?"

"No. I was a latchkey kid by the time I turned ten."

"And your dad?"

I sighed, already fatigued by the explanation. "Long story."

She leaned her chin into her palm. "Pretend I have the time to hear it."

This was odd—this temporary truce of ours. "Short version is my bio-dad was a jerk, I have two older half-brothers who are equally awful, and they live miserably ever after in Houston and New York."

"Did you see them much?"

I thought of my last few years of college and felt that familiar resentment. "No." I was done with this topic. It was old and worn-out, and it ushered in memories I didn't feel like revisiting. "You, on the other hand, have a great family. Intrusive and possibly diabolical if crossed, but clearly they adore you."

Olivia smiled, a sight I found myself unexpectedly liking. "They drive me nuts," she said, "but they definitely love me."

"What about your parents?" I'd yet to meet them. I'd expected some gray-headed father to come after me with a shotgun and demand to hear my intentions.

"They now work for Doctors Without Borders. So does my brother Colin. But growing up, my dad had a medical practice here in Sugar Creek, and our family life was very normal. Minus a grandmother in the CIA."

I'd spent most of my life being jealous of normal. I swore I'd grow up to have the white picket fence dream—playing fetch with a dog in the backyard, throwing a football with my kid beneath an oak tree, sitting beside my wife in a church pew on Sundays. And now here I was—trapped in a disposable marriage that meant nothing. The family life just wasn't meant for me.

Olivia gave my kitchen a long, studious inspection. "You have a nice house."

"You say that with zero sincerity."

"I'd rather be at my home, but yours is lovely..."

"And?"

"And it doesn't look like you."

Her impression of me was cast in an ancient mold. We were both different people now. "You don't know me anymore."

Her tired eyes met mine. "I know you, Lachlan Hayes."

"Doubt it, but it's cute you think you do." We'd delved into the past and our families, and now it was time to get down to the real issue. "How about we discuss my needs?"

"If this is where you demand your husbandly rights, I'm packing up another serving of that pasta and heading back to my apartment."

"Interesting that you'd take my innocent words to such a naughty place, but I'll overlook your lack of virtuous intentions." I lifted my napkin to her parted lips and dabbed at a small drop of sauce. "I agreed to give you my PR business," I said. "Now tell me how you'll turn me into a new man."

CHAPTER
SEVENTEEN
LACHLAN

MY WIFE WAS TIRED, and a nicer man would've encouraged her to go upstairs.

So of course I ignored that idea.

Olivia yawned and checked the time on a phone that had just dinged again. "We can start your brand revamp at the office tomorrow."

"I'd rather talk away from listening ears and sit in a seat that doesn't smell like compost."

"I have another project I'm working on tonight and need to finalize those details before I call it a day."

"Your sister's bookshop opening?" I asked.

Her smile lit her eyes. "How did you know?"

"Sugar Creek is talking about little else than the new store. I assumed you were in charge of her marketing."

"Rosie's worked very hard and overcome a lot to start her own business. I suppose I could say the same for you."

"Did you just pay me *another* compliment? I should probably document this."

"Don't get used to it," Olivia said. "Now, if we're going to talk PR, tell me what you have in mind."

A tension worked its way up my chest and into my throat. "I've been in the spotlight some, but mostly I let other people handle the public stuff while I remain in the background. I'm a game designer who somehow became a CEO." I still felt like that kid who wrote code and designed games for fun in his dorm and not like the head of a multimillion dollar company. "Since we have a lot of high-profile events coming up, I'll be even more visible."

"I sent an updated list of ideas to you this afternoon," Olivia said. "Did you want to discuss those?"

"I want to discuss my image first."

She nodded. "Sure. Your brand, the message your work and website convey, the—"

"I mean my *actual* image." I ran a hand down my beard, which was admittedly a bit on the scraggly side. "I can't avoid media events any longer, and in order to be taken seriously as a CEO, I need to act the part."

Olivia banked the fatigue and sat up straight, immediately engaged with the talk of work. "I'm still finalizing your plan, but we'll do national and local television interviews, print media, the most popular podcasts, some charity events, a few well-placed online articles...and that's just to start."

Her list sounded completely overwhelming—yet exactly like what I needed. "I want you to make me into the type of guy who can deftly handle all that *and* look the part."

Her eyes went right to my hair captured in a ponytail, then traveled down to my hoodie, t-shirt, and hole-ridden jeans. "Are you asking me to get you a makeover?"

"I want it all." I stood, trying to ignore the way her faint perfume crooked a finger and beckoned me to inhale. "This is my moment, Olivia. I don't want to mess it up. I'm a gamer nerd, stepping into the sandbox with corporate giants. I know I need help with my image, and if I ever had any doubts, seeing headlines like the 'Grizzly Gamer Gets His Girl' and 'Man-child Mogul Marries' made it crystal clear."

"That is some terrible alliteration."

"I want to see headlines like 'Well-Spoken Coding Wizard Wows Wall Street' or 'Suave Silicon Samurai Slices into Success.'"

She tapped a memo into her phone. "'Dang Delicious Dude Displays Digital Dominance'?"

"You think I'm delicious?"

Olivia's head shot up and her eyes went wide. "It was an example." She waved her hand between us. "I thought we were doing a bit."

"It sounded very sincere. Like it came from the heart."

She returned her attention to her phone. "You are still so annoying."

"You'll grow to appreciate it."

"Probably with the help of prescription medication," she mumbled.

In college I would've said a twenty-page term paper was more enjoyable than Olivia's presence, but even then she'd been fun to spar with. Now her zingers were delivered from the very kissable lips of a beautiful woman, one whose blue eyes flashed restrained smolder and throaty voice could narrate a grocery list and still turn a man on.

Not that *I* was turned on. I wasn't.

"There are so many events." I said this like I'd contracted a new plague. "From a black-tie charity gala to the five hundred calendar items you've sent."

"And you want to look as successful as you are." She slowly nodded. "Are you willing to trim up your hair a bit and trade in your Garanimals for adult clothes?"

"My t-shirt collection and I are offended, but yes. I'm temporarily willing to lose the long hair and gloriously comfy attire."

"I can make that happen." She consulted the calendar on her phone. "I should be able to get you scheduled with my makeover team next month."

"That's too late," I said. "Celeste promised me instant results in our initial meeting. Money is no object."

Olivia's gaze narrowed as she went into solution-genera-tion mode. "I have some favors I can call in," she finally said. "I can't promise anything, but I'll see what I can do."

My PR needs went deeper than a shave and a new wardrobe though. It was more than humbling to have to unfurl some vulnerability before Olivia Sutton of all people. "Also...it's possible a lot of the social rules escape me."

"I do media and etiquette training all the time," she said. "That part's easy."

I hated to tell her, but it would *not* be easy. My father had once tried to make me more socially presentable, but that had backfired spectacularly. Then he'd just given up on the process —and me.

We spent awhile longer discussing strategy and brain-storming ideas. When midnight rolled around, Olivia stood and pressed a hand to her back. "I need a quick break."

"No, we're done for tonight."

"But—"

"The rest can wait. Go to bed. You look dead on your feet, and if I have to hear the phrase *media training* one more time, I'm going to cancel everything and do all my future interviews in biker shorts and tank tops." I watched her face contract in predictable distaste.

"Fine." Olivia's sigh made the tendrils around her face dance. "Oh, one more thing."

"Yes?"

"I guess you should show me to my bedroom."

Her words should not have set off a ripple of awareness along my spine, but it did. Obviously I was tired too. "Follow me, Mrs. Hayes."

"Right behind you, Mr. Sutton."

CHAPTER
EIGHTEEN
OLIVIA

I'D LIKE to say my bedroom was on a separate floor from Lachlan's or at least in a different part of the house.

But nope.

My new husband gestured to the tall white door, ten short steps from the master suite. "Your room is next to mine."

"How many bedrooms does this house have?" I asked, growing more tired and cranky by the minute.

"Five."

"I'd like to pick another one."

"The others aren't furnished yet."

Of course they weren't.

He tightened his grip on my suitcases. "On the bright side, you have a great view of the twelfth green."

My room could have a great view of Channing Tatum's naked chest, and I still would want to move down the hall. (After a lengthy peek, of course.) "Fine. We'll fix this later. Right now, I need a shower and a bed."

Lachlan led the way inside the spacious room, and I could tell a professional decorator had worked some magic. A white duvet covered a king-sized bed whose headboard took up most of a wall. Trendy sconces sprouted over nightstands, which was a welcome sight for this late-night reader. Large canvases of muted colors filled the opposite wall, where a TV sat inside built-in shelves just begging to be weighed down with books.

"I'll get you an office fixed up in one of the spare bedrooms." Lachlan's neon Nike's swished over the rug as he set the bags down. "Bathroom's in here." He pointed to a door on the left. "Closet's on your right." He scratched the back of his neck and glanced about, looking hesitant and as awkward as I felt. "Do you need anything?"

"A time machine to take us back a week?"

"I was thinking more along the lines of a glass of water or dental floss." He gave a weak laugh. "Look, Olivia, I know this is hard. And weird. And stressful."

"Don't forget slightly terrifying and frustrating and loathsome."

Lachlan frowned. "*Loathsome.* Huh. I wouldn't have landed on that particular word, but I will respect your incredibly negative vocab choices."

"I just wish things were different," I said.

"Me too." A dark look stole across his face. "To make things worse, I'm afraid I have bad news on the Vegas criminal investigation."

"Don't say it."

"It's not possible to track down who drugged us." Lachlan went into detail about private investigators, camera access, and other things I barely caught. All I knew was that we were married and there was no backup plan. No big revelations coming to end this charade.

"I'm sorry." Lachlan ran a light hand down my arm. "But we'll get through it. Together." As if realizing what he'd done, that hand fell away.

"I should call it a night," I said, ignoring the unexpected tingle running from shoulder to wrist. I was positively *wrought* with disappointment, anxiety, and a moderate amount of anger, so why on earth was I feeling zips and zings from Lachlan's hands? "I still have work to do for Rosie's bookshop opening."

"Right. See you in the morning."

"Goodnight."

Lachlan walked away, and I had just fallen face-first into the mattress ready to scream into a pillow when he returned.

"Olivia?"

Couldn't a woman trapped in a marriage-of-convenience have five seconds to gracelessly melt down in the house she didn't want to live in while sleeping next door to the man she wished she'd never encountered *again*?

I sat up and smoothed my hair. "Yes?"

Lachlan hovered in the doorway, his giant form casting a shadow on the floor. "Rosie mentioned an ex-boyfriend."

Taylor the Terrible. "So?"

Lachlan must've found my tone of interest because his face softened into a smile. Then he leaned a hip to the doorjamb. "Tell me about this breakup."

I hugged one of the pillows to my chest. "No."

"I bet it was messy. You buttoned up ones always have messy break-ups."

"It wasn't," I lied. "Goodnight."

"Goodnight." But he didn't move. "Although I'd sleep better if I knew the full tale. Think of it as my bedtime story."

"Try a book instead."

"What if this dude sees you married and decides he wants you back? Should I expect him at our front door?"

I thought of Taylor happily settled in New York at Flair's home office. "Highly unlikely."

"Because Sylvie made him disappear?"

"Because he broke up with me, stole my job, and hooked up with a busy waitress who serves pizza in Jersey. He's not coming back to reclaim me."

"Ouch."

I flopped back onto the bed. "That relationship was the second time I swerved from my Ten-Year Plan, and I swore I'd never do it again."

"Then we drank the funny Kool-Aid and got hitched."

"Every time I don't follow my own agenda, disaster follows. It happened in Italy, it happened last year, and it will no doubt happen in the course of our tragic marriage of six months."

Lachlan angled his head and watched me. "Are you over this guy?"

"Yes." But what Taylor had done to my heart had still not mended. "Goodnight."

"A few more questions. Did he—"

"Out!" I stood and pointed to the hall.

"I'm going, I'm going. The tabloids will probably unearth your secrets and twist them into soap-opera levels of scandal, but sure, keep them to yourself. Why should I know about your life, right?"

With that, Lachlan shut the door behind him.

Leaving me with my anger and regrets.

My least favorite bedfellows.

CHAPTER
NINETEEN

OLIVIA

I BELIEVED IN MIRACLES—WATER into wine, divine healings, the return of boy bands. And Paolo of Paolo Giancarlo's Menswear opening his shop for me after closing time on Wednesday night.

Why had the owner of the South's trendiest, most elite men's boutique—one that had a three-month waitlist for appointments—agreed to open his shop for me? Might've been my desperate prayers. Might've been all the exclamation points I'd inserted into my text. Or might've been that I'd known Paolo Giancarlo since the third grade when he went by the name Paul Green. One time in elementary school I'd picked him for my kickball team first instead of last, and the boy had never forgotten it. Celeste always told me to save owed favors for the important times. Lachlan's situation certainly qualified.

I'd worked late, so Lachlan had met me at Paolo's at nine. This after-hours rendezvous also conveniently decreased our chances of attracting reporters.

The chilly evening air blew Lachlan's long hair as he stood

at the entrance of the shop and watched me approach. "Hey," he said.

I took in Lachlan's wardrobe selection and knew Paulo would have a conniption at the baggy jeans, *Minecraft* t-shirt, and hoodie large enough to double as a tent. "I hope I didn't interrupt a game or whatever it is you do in your spare time," I said.

His amused gaze remained steady on my face. "I was composing a list of wifely duties I wanted my old ball and chain to perform."

"Like choking you in your sleep?"

Lachlan held open the door. "Like putting little love notes in my lunch, folding my laundry to my specifications, and bringing me a cigar and slippers when I get home."

"Is this before or after you take an unfortunate tumble down your staircase?"

Lachlan grinned as the September chill followed us inside. "I'm learning you express love through hostility. By golly, it's adorable."

"My pretend husband is *so* not getting pretend lucky tonight." I sauntered past a grinning Lachlan and went to find Paolo.

The shop owner glanced at his gold watch as I approached. "You're late."

"Sorry." I kissed each of Paolo's smooth cheeks. "Celeste asked me to pick up her dry cleaning after work, and one of the kids had a cooking class."

He air-kissed my cheeks in return. "Why are you still working for that shrew?"

"Because I hope to take over her empire one day."

Paolo caught sight of Lachlan, who'd gotten distracted by a display of pink loafers. "Your tardiness gave me time to catch up on the internet gossip." My friend's shrewd gaze roamed up and down Lachlan's form. "Olivia Sutton, what have you gone and done?"

Wasn't that just the question of the year. "Apparently I went and got married."

"Why couldn't you go to Vegas and bring back debt and a Barry Manilow t-shirt like the rest of us?" Paolo's eyes narrowed when Lachlan moved on to inspect a rack of plaid jackets. "One day you simply must tell me the full story."

"One day." I smiled sadly at my friend. "But not today." Lachlan approached, looking completely out of place in a store full of expensive men's fashion. "Paolo, this is my..." Good heavens, would I ever get used to the word? "*Husband.*"

"Is it now?" Paolo shook Lachlan's hand. "How interesting to meet you."

"Thank you for letting us stop by tonight." Lachlan slipped his arm around my shoulders, and I was so tired I nearly leaned into him. After our kitchen conversation, I found little energy to fuel animosity toward Lachlan. I'd lived with a violent dislike for the man for years, so it was a curious shift. I'd barely slept the last few nights, keenly aware that only a wall separated me from my new husband. Perhaps we could blame my lack of scorn on fatigue.

"Oh, my." Paolo walked a circle around Lachlan, clucking and shaking his head. When the revolution was complete, he did it once more. "Olivia, is this what all his clothes are like?"

"No," I said. "He also wears ironically bad concert t-shirts."

Paolo's slender body convulsed on a gag. Then my old friend closed his eyes and placed his hands at his temples. "I'm having a vision."

I shot Lachlan a surreptitious smile. "Paolo is prophetic."

"A free prophecy with my shirts and pants. That is a heck of a deal." Lachlan watched Paulo continue to massage his forehead, as if the vision needed coaxing out. "Has he ever given you the winning Powerball numbers?"

"Not once."

Paulo hummed before he finally spoke. "Yes, the vision is coming to me. I see...a large bonfire. And flames. They're burning hot and reaching toward the sky."

"Is it our marriage license?" A girl could dream.

"No." Paolo's eyes popped open, and his revolted gaze swept over Lachlan once again. "It's your entire wardrobe. Burn it. Every last thread must die."

Lachlan slid me a look. "Sounds wasteful."

"You came here for my help," Paolo said, "and my help I give." He focused on Lachlan and delivered the rest of his verdict. "I see you in tailored slacks and fitted jackets. Your body is a temple, and hoodies are desecrations."

"But they're comfortable." Lachlan looked at his sweatshirt fondly. "And the temple likes to be warm."

"Fashion does not care if you're cold," Paolo said.

Lachlan regarded the man. "Does it let me wear underwear?"

"Boxers—silk and no briefs."

Lachlan's arm returned to my shoulders. "My sweetie here prefers me commando. Don't you, babe?"

I clenched my teeth and glared at my husband. "Paolo, do you still have that cousin who beats people up for a case of Bud Light?"

Paolo walked away with a *tsk*, motioning for us to follow. He picked up a shirt here, a pair of pants there. "For this winter, I'm thinking cashmere sweaters, wool peacoats, and Oxford shirts. Lachlan, your color palette will include the spectrum of browns, as well as gray and navy. How do you feel about V-necks?"

"I've always been an equal opportunity neckline man,"

Lachlan said. "V-necks, turtlenecks, crew neck—I like them all."

"We'll throw in a few hats." Paolo turned to me. "You are getting him a haircut, correct?"

"Tomorrow morning." Securing him an appointment at Ratify Salon had cost me a lifetime of favors and Frannie's cupcakes.

Paolo waved a hand toward Lachlan's upper half. "The shrubbery on his face?"

"That too," I confirmed. "The works."

That seemed to slightly mollify Paolo. "Very good. I won't sell my hats to just any head."

Lachlan frowned. "I think I might be offended."

"Throw in some casual wear," I instructed. "As well as a tux. He has a movie premiere in November."

"*We* have a movie premiere," Lachlan corrected.

Paolo sniffed and regarded me. "I don't do tuxes."

"No, but you're connected to people who do," I said. "If we leave it up to Lachlan, he'll end up at Chuck's Tux Warehouse on Main Street."

Paolo paled. "I'll handle it." He bent low to inspect Lachlan's feet. "Does he always wear Converse?"

"No," I said, "sometimes he wears Air Jordans."

"Good Lord. No more of that. Size thirteen?" Paolo guessed.

Lachlan was smart enough to look impressed. "You're good at this."

"I'm quite aware. How many pairs?" Paolo asked me.

"Let's start with five. A variety."

"Done. Fall and winter accessories?"

I silenced the ever-ringing phone in my hand. "Please."

Lachlan held up a paisley shirt to his chest. "Are earrings included in my accessories? I cannot pull off anything that dangles."

My friend ignored him. "What about your sister's book-shop opening celebration? Do we need something for that?"

Lachlan looked at me, and awkwardness filled the space between us.

"We're having a big party Sunday before Rosie officially opens her doors," I told him. "I might've forgotten to mention it."

"It happens," Lachlan said, "but I can't go. I leave for Los Angeles tomorrow afternoon and won't be back until next week."

When the twinge of disappointment hit, I had to grab a shoe display to steady myself. Where had that feeling come from? Surely it was nothing more than my need to manage all the variables. Lachlan hadn't mentioned a thing about a trip to LA. "When did this come up?"

"Today. The movie studio wants to meet with my enter-tainment attorney about another deal."

"Oh," I said. "That sounds very promising."

Paolo clapped his slender hands. "Focus, people. Do we need luggage? Man bag? Key fobs? New wallet?"

"Not tonight," I told him. "Only a starter kit to take home."

Paolo might've acted offended by Lachlan's lack of style, but I knew a total makeover for a public figure was Paolo's catnip. "Give me an hour."

Given all I still had to do for Rosie's party, that wouldn't do. "I only have thirty minutes."

"You can't rush an artist."

"I'll let you throw in belts."

"I will return shortly." Paolo scurried away, the artist gathering materials for the transformation of his next canvas.

"Paolo seems sweet." Lachlan watched him buzz near a shelf of socks before diving into a table of sweaters. "Very low-key. We probably pulled him away from a Chiefs game, some brats, and his recliner."

I laughed at the very thought. "Paolo is like me—he lives to work. Despite being closed, he probably would've been here anyway."

Lachlan returned a shirt to the nearby rack and tilted his head. "You live to work?"

"Yes. It's my happy place."

Lachlan strolled to another rack of shirts and thumbed through the selection. "How did your last boyfriend feel about it?"

That felt like a trap of a conversation. "It's none of your business."

But Lachlan was nothing if not persistent. "You said he stole your job. What does that mean?"

It meant I'd overshared in a moment of exhaustion. I wasn't about to admit to Lachlan that my history with men was spectacularly awful, with Taylor being the pièce de résistance. That was, until my Vegas wedding.

But Lachlan was a dog with a bone who refused to let go. "Is that why you split up?"

"Please refer to my earlier statement in which I declared this none of your business."

"I shared the reason for my last breakup," he said.

"Yes, what was the reason again? She thought you talked too much?"

His grin broadened. "Ladies adore my chattiness. Now back to you. Tell me why you and this guy called it quits."

"We wanted different things."

Lachlan nodded gravely. "You didn't respect his choice of day planners?"

If only it had been that simple. Thinking I was in love, I'd stupidly given up so much for Taylor. I'd sacrificed my principles, a promotion, and my heart. And for what? So he could stomp on all of it and go find someone else? He'd said my intensity and 'lack of chill' had stressed him out.

Though I had not scheduled marriage in my Life Plan until at least age thirty, I'd ridiculously thought Taylor should be an exception.

Normally my instincts were flawless, but I'd been so wrong.

"You're seriously not going to tell me what happened in your last relationship?" Lachlan asked.

I could only hope Lachlan would be this persistent with our media training lessons. "I'm not, no."

He leaned closer, almost pressing his forehead to mine. "Is there a secret love child out there somewhere?"

"Definitely not." My goodness, he smelled divine. It was like testosterone dipped in sandalwood. "Though sometimes I feel like I'm now married to a child."

Lachlan chuckled. "You know I'm not torching my t-shirt collection, right?"

"I like a good stretch goal." My phone buzzed with a text from Celeste, and I quickly responded. "But do give them a well-earned break."

Lachlan meandered away once again and held up a polka-dotted poncho. "Do guys really wear this? It seems...busy."

I lifted my focus from my phone. "You could pull that off."

"I'm afraid the pattern would make my hips look big." He returned it to the rack and continued to browse. "Does your boss ever leave you alone?" he asked after my phone pinged three more times.

I fired off a response to Celeste, then three to my connection at *Good Morning America*. "It's a very busy time right now. You're not my only client."

"Is that right?"

"I have other big projects."

"Is that your pet name for me?" he asked. "Big Project?"

I turned toward a display of ties so Lachlan wouldn't see my grin.

Lachlan appeared at my side, standing too close for comfort. "Do these other projects also involve shopping for a man's silk unmentionables?"

"*Attenzione*, Lachlan!" Paolo reappeared, his cheeks flushed and his eyes alight with pure, unadulterated joy. "I'm ready for you." He waved his hands toward the back fitting room. "Third door on the right. Try on quickly, then step out and work the three-way mirror like a supermodel."

Lachlan sent me a saucy wink, then lumbered away to do as he was bidden.

"Thank you for squeezing us in," I told Paolo.

"In exchange for membership into the exclusive Sexy Book Club? How could I say no? I've been begging for that golden ticket for two years." He inclined his dark head toward the dressing room as we sat down before the wall of mirrors. "Your Lachlan. I like him."

"He's not your type." I checked my phone again, inwardly groaning at Celeste's latest demand.

"Lachlan might not be for me." Paolo gave me a pointed look. "But he pairs with you nicely."

I hit send on a text. "Don't get too attached."

"Are you giving me advice?" Paolo asked. "Or yourself?"

The dressing room door opened with a graceless bang, and the man of the hour stepped out.

My sharp inhale matched Paolo's, and I couldn't help but blink twice to make sure this was the same man. Gone was the t-shirt and baggy jeans. Though his hair was still a disaster, Lachlan looked like he'd walked off the cover of *GQ*.

"Paolo, you sure do good work," I whispered.

My childhood friend's gaze traveled from Lachlan's head to his toes. "So does the Lord God Almighty."

Lachlan wore snug-fitting pants, an indigo button-down shirt that contrasted brilliantly with his red hair, nubuck loafers that shined, and a belt that probably cost more than my entire outfit. A cardigan dangled from the crook of his finger, while a hesitant smile played at his lips. "A chunky sweater?" he asked. "Are we sure?"

Paulo rested a hand over his heart as he took it all in. "Oh, yeah. We're sure."

It was nerd chic, hipster elegance, and millennial marvelousness all rolled into one.

My heartbeat thudded against my ribcage and goose-bumps skittered across my skin. I was having a hot flash, a temporary moment of insanity, a blip in my well-ordered universe.

The iceberg in my chest dripped, and a piece of permafrost cracked straight off.

Lachlan stood before me, then gave himself a nervous once-over. "Olivia? What do you think?"

With a shrug, I gathered my purse, stood, and gave a curt nod. "I think it'll do."

"I'm having another vision." Paolo pressed his fingers to his head.

Lachlan draped the cardigan over his arm. "Let's hear it."

"Yes, I see it so very clearly. I was uncertain at first, but now I cannot deny the picture in my brilliant and fashion-forward mind." My friend opened his eyes and studied Lachlan one more time before aiming his shrewd gaze pointedly in my direction. "I see two people who will go through much. They'll laugh, they'll cry, they'll even deny what's in their hearts."

"Ugh, please stop," I told him.

Paolo's fingers returned to his temples. "But in the end, Olivia dear, do you know what's left?"

"The ten percent discount you're going to give us for suffering through this performance?"

"A happily ever after." Paolo smiled and nodded his head with certainty. "That's what I see."

TWENTY

OLIVIA

LACHLAN

Let the record show I like my long hair and beard. Lots of people like my beard.

OLIVIA

Like the woodland creatures that occasionally nest there?

LACHLAN

Are you sure it all has to go?

OLIVIA

The world needs to see your face.

LACHLAN

You like my face, don't you, Olivia?

OLIVIA

In college, I used to fantasize about smothering your face.

LACHLAN

> But you didn't. Because you liked it.

ONCE UPON A TIME, if you wanted your hair done in Sugar Creek, you had two choices: Judy's Cut Up and Dye, where you could get fifty-cent sodas so cold they hurt your teeth and gossip so warm you'd tip extra. Or Ronnie Mack's Barbershop, where Ronnie peddled cuts, shaves, and the worst jokes this side of the Mississippi.

Years ago, when the city received a series of grants to spiff up the downtown, Sugar Creek got herself a face-lift, drawing the attention of proprietors who saw an adorable and welcome place to build lives and businesses. Ratify Salon was one of those additions.

The next morning I stepped out of my SUV, smoothed my fitted jacket and wished I were anywhere but here. In the parking spot beside me, Lachlan unfolded his giant body out of his vehicle, and I saw the hesitation on his scraggly face. He wore his old uniform of jeans and a t-shirt, but by now the look had almost grown on me. It suited him. Just not for his role as CEO.

"If it isn't my better half." He zipped up his hoodie as the wind ruffled his hair.

"You are excellent at math." I kept a firm grip on my cup of coffee, taking comfort from the heat.

Lachlan studied the asphalt beneath his feet. "I missed you at breakfast this morning."

I turned his words over in my head, trying to find the sarcasm, but his face looked completely sincere. "I got an early start today."

Lachlan and I had stumbled upon an accidental morning

routine. After we got ready, we'd meet up in the kitchen where he'd have coffee already brewing. While Lachlan whipped up something quick for breakfast, I'd share a few words on personal brand improvement before the conversation turned to more entertaining topics. Yesterday we'd had omelets, fresh squeezed orange juice, and a lively debate on the best movies of the last decade.

"It was frozen bagel day anyway," he said. "You didn't miss much."

But I had. I'd left for work at six-thirty and found myself wondering what our breakfast topic of the day might've been.

We walked toward the salon as the season's first fall leaves cartwheeled by, their crisp, fragile melodies crackling in the air.

"I've got to catch a plane in five hours, so I'm gonna give this salon thirty minutes," Lachlan said.

"You'll need to triple that." I pulled open the door to Ratify. "My stylist gets scissor-happy when she's rushed."

"Olivia!" Blaire Stewart, newest owner of Ratify and best stylist in the tri-county area, embraced me with the polite hug of one who did not want her clothes disturbed. "Only you and anyone else who'd offer me five times my going rate would be allowed in my salon at such late notice. My waitlist is four months long. Didn't hurt that you threw in an invite to your sister's grand opening."

The salon bustled with clientele who paid dearly for their visits. The scents of fruit and mint essential oils brewed in the air, and indie pop sang from the speaker. "I hope we didn't pull you from anything important," I said.

Blaire's smile was as tight as her pants. "Only a two-hour massage on my first day off since spring. No big."

Without thinking, I slipped my arm through Lachlan's.

"This is the man who owes you a fat check and a spa gift card. Blaire, meet Lachlan Hayes."

Lachlan's hand covered mine. "Nice place you have here, Blaire."

"Yes. I know." Then Blaire did the same thing Paolo had—walked a complete circle around Lachlan, wide-eyed and slightly entranced with the starting point. "This is a lot of hair."

"Indeed it is." I was more than a little fascinated by the current of awareness humming through my system. When had my hand in Lachlan's started to feel right? "What are you thinking, Blaire?"

"That I might need landscaping shears."

"I meant...in terms of stylistic specifics?"

"I think we cut much, but leave some length on top," Blaire decided. "Get rid of the Jason Momoa locks."

"Did you hear that, Olivia?" Lachlan slid his arm around my waist and rested his hand on the curve of my hip. "She thinks I look like a studly superhero."

"Let's shave the face." Blaire turned her spiky head this way and that. "All of it must go."

Lachlan held up a hand. "Wait a minute."

"Leave a little scruff," I said.

"Jolie will be in shortly to handle that, as well as brows." Blaire moved in uncomfortably close to Lachlan, a woman inspecting a wonder of science. "My goodness, the brows are like two sheep in need of shearing, like bloated woolly worms, like two overgrown shrubs fighting on your face. Like a pair of—"

"Maybe we could just go ahead and get started?" I suggested.

Lachlan checked out his face in a nearby mirror. "I do get to *keep* my eyebrows, right?"

Blaire shrugged. "Some."

"Like, at least my left one?"

I bit back a smile and gave Lachlan a look of warning. *Do not bait the nice stylist.*

Blaire regarded Lachlan's clothes with the same level of rejection shown to the eyebrows. "Are his clothes staying?"

"My preference is not to be naked for this," Lachlan said.

Good Lord. If that didn't flash an image right to my frontal cortex.

"I mean, surely you're getting him a new wardrobe, right?" Blaire asked me. "Who will notice this man's hair if he's wearing an Atari t-shirt and his dad's cargo pants?"

"We ordered a full wardrobe from Paolo's," I explained. "Lachlan's been fully outfitted."

That seemed to appease Blaire, as she waved a hand toward her station. "Then let's move on to the next phase of Eliza Doolittle's makeover."

"You're in good hands," I told Lachlan. This was my cue to leave, yet I continued to stand. Why was I lingering?

He frowned. "You aren't staying for the appointment?"

"Can't." Lachlan was headed to Los Angeles in a few hours, and for some reason I wanted to say more than just a curt goodbye—but I certainly wouldn't. That was silly. It wasn't like I'd miss him or anything. Nope. Not at all. "I have things to do,' I said. "I trust Blaire and her team implicitly."

"But I don't." Lachlan glanced back at a woman sporting a mohawk and pulling blades from a case. "These people are armed. They're dangerous. Look at all the stabby things and flammables in this room. I need someone kind and gentle to stay by my side." He reached for my hand and reeled me into him. "But I'd even settle for you."

I patted his chest, nice chest that it was, and bid him adieu. "Goodbye, Lachlan."

"Wait." Lachlan's warm fingers gently encircled my wrist. "So I guess I'll see you Monday night. What will you ever do without me?"

"I'll have Rosie's party this weekend." Four days without him. I did not like how this thought was deflating my caffeine buzz? "I'll also use that time to go through your drawers and computer files."

His thumb passed across my wrist, sending tingles of awareness up my arm. "Make sure you open the file titled 'My Wife Cries for Me in Her Sleep.'"

"I'll delete it."

"Don't do that." Another sweep of his thumb.

"Sending it right to the digital trash can."

Lachlan smiled then, a slight curve of the lips beneath all that facial hair. "Tell Rosie congratulations." Bending, Lachlan leaned toward me and pressed a soft, lingering kiss to my cheek. "Don't miss me too much, wife."

Minutes later, I shut myself in my car and took my first deep breath since leaving the house this morning.

Lachlan was trouble.

Charming, charismatic, and dare I say it—fun—trouble.

But trouble wasn't part of my life plan.

And neither was my husband.

———

The Lost Story Bookshop sure was a beauty.

Regal and mysterious, she sat on a street adjacent to downtown, as if she didn't want to rub elbows with the modernized shops off the square. The old building had been reincarnated many times in its hundred-year life, including the first library the town had ever known.

At two o'clock, I opened the large wooden door that led me

into the wonderland that was Lost Story. The scent of books—old and new—hung on the air like perfume. The last detail of the massive remodel had been completed last week, and the shop looked perfect thanks to Rosie's vision and my heavy design input.

A corner of the shop held a coffee bar that featured Frannie's cupcakes and other baked goods. Cozy seating areas of eclectic, overstuffed chairs and vividly colored vintage couches invited lengthy chats and page-turning moments. The interior was a stunning contrast of antique and modern, working with the old structure and the history of the building, yet incorporating comfortably chic decor. It was a reader's paradise.

Especially for its owner.

"Rosie." My high heels tip-tapped against the black-and-white honeycomb tile that had been rescued from the smother of two layers of laminate. "The place looks ready," I said as I found my sister behind the cash register and gave her a hug. "But the question is, are you?"

Rosie pushed up her glasses, her blonde hair dangling like a drape in her eyes. "Oh, Olivia. Tell me it's going to go okay tonight." She hugged me fiercely, and I felt her every anxious trepidation.

Rosie had been through so much in the last year. She'd tragically lost her fiancé, bought a ramshackle store, and with the help of her sisters, built a dream. The Lost Story Bookshop was a labor of love *and* grief, a physical manifestation of my sister's healing. The shop had a heartbeat and personality. It was life and abundance, while grief remained in smaller, less visible places, like the glue of the wallpaper and the hum of the old lights above.

I held Rosie's hands in mine, trying to transfer confidence and encouragement into her limbs. "It's really happening, Rosie, and it's going to be wonderful."

With a slight smile, my sister inhaled deeply and regarded the space around her. "It's so strange to leave the dreaming stage and begin the reality of all the hopes and wishes."

"The reality is going to be even more incredible. You'll make sure of it." I checked the time on my phone. "I only have an hour before my next appointment, but Sylvie asked me to meet her here to handle a catering issue."

"Yeah." Rosie frowned and averted her gaze. "About that..."

"Well, well, well." Sylvie stepped out of the office door with Aunt Frannie behind her. "If it isn't one of my favorite granddaughters. What a coincidence that you're here and so are we."

"You invited me." I'd no more said the words than the front door swung open and Hattie breezed inside.

"Wow, is it chilly today." Hattie shivered inside her jacket. "Did you see those gorgeous orange leaves on Main Street? I ask you, does any town do fall better than Sugar Creek?"

I looked from sister to sister to grandmother to aunt. "I'm not here to solve a catering dilemma, am I?"

"Sugar." Sylvie clasped a hand on my shoulder and gave me that classic, cue-the-hijinks grin. "We have called you here today because we were too lazy to come to you and because your house might not have cupcakes." She nodded her head toward the coffee bar.

Frannie smacked her lips around a bite and lifted a cupcake in a toast. "Olivia, dear...welcome to your intervention."

I did not have time for this. In the last ten minutes I'd received ten texts and three emails from Celeste alone. "An intervention?"

"You got it." Frannie swiped a dollop of icing from her cheek and licked her finger. "Yeah, it's my first one, so I'm not really sure what I'm doing." She turned to Sylvie. "Do we inject her with truth serum now or save that for after the glitter bomb?"

"Don't be silly, we won't need any truth serum," Sylvie said loudly at Hattie's look of dismay. She then turned to Frannie and lowered her voice to a whisper. "I told you that comes later."

"Let's take a seat, shall we?" Rosie grabbed her teacup and gestured toward the two green velvet couches. "We won't keep you long, Olivia."

Frannie popped the remains of the cupcake in her mouth. "The intervention handbook I found online said a minimum of thirty minutes. Unless hitting and yelling ensued, then we would need to break out the blindfold and muzzle. Wait, that might've been my kidnapping manual. Never mind." My aunt rolled a hand, her wrist of bracelets jangling. "Carry on."

"I still have a lot to do to prepare for Sunday's party," I told them, "and Celeste just sent me another five emergency texts."

"That woman needs to chill," Rosie said.

"I totally agree." Sylvie scooted beside me on the couch. "If you're ever interested, we could make that happen."

"The only thing I'm interested in is what I'm doing here."

My grandma rested her hands in her lap and directed that probing stare on me. "We'd like to talk to you about Lachlan."

Great. Couldn't they pick a less complicated topic? Maybe Middle Eastern politics? The chemical composition of Mountain Dew? "What about him?" I asked.

"You married him," Sylvie reminded me.

The truth never got any prettier, did it? "Yes, I did. But I thought we'd established that, so I'm not sure why you need more confirmation."

Hattie slipped into therapist mode, gentling her voice. "What we need to know is that you're okay."

"Of course I am."

"We mean for real," Sylvie added.

"Still okay."

Frannie licked stray icing off her hand. "For really reals."

"You guys, I know it's been a shock." And nobody was shocked more than I was. "But when it's right, it's right." My marriage happened to have been super wrong, but the statement still held truth…in a universal sort of way. "Lachlan and I have known each other a very long time, and when we reconnected, we found deep feelings there." Like anger and disgust. Oh, and let's not forget some nausea and a clammy sweat.

"We just want you to be happy." Rosie looked more than concerned. "Are you happy?"

I hated lying to my family. They were my everything. Lord knew I would lovingly harass any of them who went to Vegas for a party and came back married to a near-stranger. "I have a job I love and a husband who I just spent my lunch break with."

"You don't take a lunch," Rosie said.

"I did today."

"Aw, he's changing our girl already." Sylvie high-fived Frannie. "Next she'll be cutting out of work early—like at eight p.m.—to go home and canoodle her handsome hubby."

I hated that word *hubby*. Was it really that much of a time-saver to not say that extra syllable in *husband*? Who'd rebranded *that* word?

"Things seemed really stressful on that last day in Vegas," Hattie said. "You fled town without us."

I smiled brightly. "Who knew I was marrying a media sensation?"

"I once married a media sensation," Frannie said. "My third husband was the two a.m. host of the knitting show on our local PBS station." She shook her dark head. "He once made me and his hairless cat matching sweaters. When we got divorced, his fan club threw a party and doubled their financial pledges. The hussies."

"Do you need money?" Rosie asked me.

Good heavens. "No."

She tried again. "Health insurance?"

"No."

"The cheat codes to *Mars Wars*?" Frannie noticed our stares. "What? It's a good game. Olivia could've been desperate to unlock a new level."

My grandmother gave a stern eye roll. "If that coding's anything like the Pentagon database, I can hack that game in three seconds. No need for nuptials."

It was time to wrap up this intervention. "Thank you for your concern. I do love you all for it. But I know what I'm doing, and I'm going to be okay. It would mean a lot to me if you'd drop any hostility"—I shot my grandmother a look—"and any surveillance devices—and welcome Lachlan into our family. Our brood can be a little intimidating, especially those of you with concealed carry licenses, so any kindness you show him would be appreciated."

"All right," Rosie said. "We'll play nice."

"Thank you." I rose from my seat and slung my purse over my shoulder.

Hattie walked with me to the door, the others following behind. "If you're happy, then that's all we need to know."

Rosie nodded her agreement. "She does seem happier since we got back from Vegas."

"I wouldn't go that far." Though I had caught myself singing in the shower this morning. And I even smiled at Morgan in the hallway. "I mean, I've always been a moderately happy person. Maybe not in a showy way, but—"

"No, Rosie's right," Frannie said. "There's a change in you already. And I like it."

"He has put a glow on her cheeks," Hattie added. "Reminds me of when I first fell for Miller."

I wasn't falling for my husband. Definitely not.

"I've decided to accept this marriage," Sylvie declared. "All opposed?" She paused for a count of zero. "All who approve, vote with a show of hands."

Four hands raised toward the ceiling.

"It's unanimous." Sylvie took my chin in her hands, her eyes twinkling. "You tell Lachlan welcome to the family."

TWENTY-ONE
OLIVIA

LACHLAN

Do you miss me yet?

OLIVIA

Like poison ivy. Or high-waisted jeans.

LACHLAN

So that's a maybe.

OLIVIA

I do miss your cooking.

LACHLAN

You say cooking, but what I think you mean is my sexy allure.

OLIVIA

How was the manscaping appointment?

LACHLAN

Avoiding a response on whether you miss my sexy self? Duly noted. Manscaping went okay.

OLIVIA

Send me pics.

LACHLAN

Inappropriate ones? Are we already at this stage in our relationship?

OLIVIA

Pics of your face, Lachlan. YOUR FACE.

LACHLAN

Must get back to a meeting. I'll satisfy your unquenchable need for me later.

THREE DAYS LATER, I stood outside the century-old doors of the Lost Story Bookshop, needing a moment to catch my breath.

Tonight was the soft opening celebration of Rosie's store, kicked off with a formal party before exclusively invited guests were allowed to shop.

Outside the stars sparkled in the clear sky and a full moon hung over the downtown store, as if the celestials gave their blessing for my sister's new venture. I'd say it was her new professional venture, but it was her entire life Rosie had relaunched with the shop.

I rubbed my arms in the chilled evening air. The sleeveless, shimmery black dress hugged my curves and showed off my fading summer tan, but a practical jacket would've felt better. I'd been running hot ever since Lachlan had burst back into my life, and I did not know what to do about that.

I'd thought about Lachlan all weekend.

I'd also thought about the fact that I'd *thought* about Lachlan all weekend. It was unsettling to know I picked up my phone more than I should, hoping for a flirty text or some silly meme he'd created just for me. I found myself missing him in the evenings.

While getting ready, I'd borrowed some toothpaste from his bathroom. And yes, maybe I'd lingered in there and cataloged his Dungeons & Dragons toothbrush, the brand of shampoo resting on a shelf in his walk-in shower, and the interesting cotton robe that hung on the back of the bathroom door.

And since I was already trespassing, I'd also taken a tour of Lachlan's closet, running my hands over his t-shirts and hoodies, oddly calmed by the Lachlan scent of his clothes.

Even the mornings had been oddly still. I'd made my own coffee, and it hadn't compared to the brew Lachlan whipped up whenever I joined him in the kitchen. I told myself I truly didn't miss him—that I was simply a bundle of nerves because he was out of my sight amid his PR training. Several days on his own in California could lead to all sorts of blunders without me nearby.

Yes. That was surely the anxious, melancholy feeling I'd experienced. Lachlan was my client, after all, and it was hard to track the man when he was on the other side of the country.

A scatter of leaves danced across my heels, jarring me back to the here and now. It was time to focus on Rosie and the bookshop.

The door creaked as I opened it, and when I stepped inside, I knew I'd just walked into a future memory.

Tears pricked my eyes as a mingled fragrance hung in the air, the scents of new paint, spiced cider, and hardbound leather.

"Olivia, finally you're here." Walking my way, Rosie smoothed her hands over her little black dress, as she tearfully glanced about her store. "Can you tell I'm sweating right through my extra-strength deodorant?"

I sniffed near her. "I only smell success and happiness. I'm so proud of you."

Rosie stepped back and swiped the moisture from her cheeks. "I owe you big for all the work you've done—the painting, the unboxing, and the million and one marketing tasks I could never have handled or even thought of."

"That's my job."

"You're very good at it."

If only Celeste agreed enough to promote me.

"Yoohoo, sugars! Don't start this celebration without your dear grandmother." Holding a wineglass in the air, Sylvie cha-cha'd her way toward us. My grandmother wore a sleek, black, figure-accentuating pantsuit with bold golden jewelry and electric red heels. Frannie, on the other hand, always took a more casual approach.

"Is that a new wig?" I asked Aunt Frannie. The woman had apparently been quite the expert in disguises back in day, and she still had a small obsession with alternative hair.

"Girl, yes." With her glittery manicure she patted her latest acquisition. "It's inspired by that singer Lizzo. What do you think?"

Rosie and I took in the whole picture—from Frannie's long black locks to her fuchsia sequined dress, right down to her... Birkenstocks. The woman loved her creature comforts.

"You look like a Hollywood starlet." I kissed Frannie's rouged cheek. "Adore the whole vibe." I knew her sweetie Ernie probably did too.

"Sorry I'm late!" Our oldest sister Hattie slipped inside, holding Miller's hand. Love looked good on Hattie, and I was happy to see her settled and content. My two sisters and I had put a lot of work into Rosie's shop, bringing us closer than ever. Our brother, Colin, had chipped in some capital, and while his international work made it impossible for him to be present, he promised to visit soon. The Lost Story Bookshop was a family affair, and it felt right that we'd all worked together to make it happen.

Rosie grabbed a glass of bubbly and waved everyone toward her. "Get your champagne and gather round!" Her eyes did a thorough sweep of the store and its guests, as if she was memorizing every detail to jot down later tonight. "I asked you all here early because I wanted a few minutes alone with my favorite people. It's taken so much to bring the store to life, and sometimes I doubted we'd get here. And I wouldn't have were it not for my family. You've annoyed me, you've helped me, and you've made my dream possible. I know Chase would have loved the Lost Story, and I can almost feel him here tonight." She paused as we all nodded in unison. "The Lost Story isn't just my story, but it's yours as well. This is a place of dreams and hopes that go beyond the walls and pages of the books. Thank you for making *my* dream come true. I pray each of you finds your heart's desire as well." With tears free-falling down her cheeks, Rosie raised her glass. "To the Lost Story Bookshop."

I held up my own glass. "To Lost Story!" The first taste of champagne had just passed my lips when I caught sight of my aunt's face. "Frannie, you okay?"

She fanned herself as her mouth formed a silent O. "Holy stud muffins," she said. "I think a romance cover model just walked in."

Sylvie tossed back her drink and stood on tiptoe to get a better look. "Good heavens. Who is that delicious dish?"

"The star of my dreams tonight," Frannie told her.

Suppressing an eye roll, I turned.

And felt my heart unmoor from my chest.

I blinked at the vision, then squeezed my eyes shut and peered again.

There in the doorway stood Lachlan Hayes 2.0.

Lachlan, the made-over version.

Paolo would've been giddy with the way his clothes hung on Lachlan. A steel gray suit hugged his body, and his white shirt set off a contrast that drew attention to the skin exposed by the top three buttons left undone. He wore no tie, but the pocket of his jacket held a square of deep fuchsia, a small pop of color that was as sexy as it was subdued.

But what absolutely transfixed me was Lachlan's face.

I could actually see it.

And it was unexpectedly beautiful. Very much like the moment of impact in a car crash, I had milliseconds to prepare, and the force of the hit sent me tumbling head over heels into confusion and shock.

Lachlan's hair had certainly met a pair of scissors, but Blaire had taken great care to leave a few inches of length— enough to satisfy should a lady desire to walk her hands through the shiny russet strands.

The acreage of facial hair that had occupied the lower half of Lachlan's face had been brush hogged, leaving only a trim shadow that went from one ear, dipped to his chin, and ended at the other lobe. That left a lot of face to be seen, and I had flashbacks to the boy Lachlan had been in college. There were hints of him there, but now the boy had grown into a man. And, my goodness, was that man unexpectedly handsome. His skin looked soft enough to touch, and his unruly brows were now tamed to set off his moss green eyes.

While those piercing eyes might've been the new star of the show, Lachlan's lips deserved a nod as best supporting actor. Without the choke hold of a mustache, his mouth was on display, revealing two full lips, plump, slightly parted in thought, and entirely kissable.

If one was into that sort of thing.

Frannie fanned herself. "Hold your Spanx, girls. Mr. Tall, Ginger, and Gorgeous is walking our way."

Sylvie ran her tongue over her white teeth. "Suck in your guts, stick out your chests, and telepathically convey invitations to dark corners."

"Stop drooling over Olivia's husband," Rosie scolded. "That man is your husband, isn't he, sis?"

He was. Every gorgeous, reformed bit of him.

The four of us stood transfixed, held captive by the new edition of Lachlan Hayes. His walk needed thematic music—a soundtrack to accompany his every confident and dapper step.

He pulled a pair of glasses from the inside of his jacket and slipped them on.

"Not glasses," Rosie whimpered. "Oh, gosh, I'm a sucker for glasses."

As was I. And in those specs, Lachlan looked like he could recite poetry, score a touchdown, and kiss a girl until she forgot her own name. All at the same time.

He was ten long strides away when his pace slowed. Green eyes held mine, and his lips pressed together. Lachlan glanced down at his suit then back to me.

I slowly nodded my approval.

Frannie's smile never wavered. "He looks like he wants to sweep Olivia up in those big strong arms and make out in the travel section."

Lachlan ran a hand over his face, and I wondered if he missed his full beard. It had been his shield, a place for that ruggedly annoying face to hide.

Someone stopped him with a greeting, and Lachlan broke eye contact with me long enough to bid the party guest good evening.

I'd just gotten my erratic heartbeat under control when

Lachlan appeared at my side. "Hello, ladies." His voice—my goodness, I'd missed that voice. "Mind if I crash your party?"

"Don't you look sharp," Sylvie said. "Olivia, doesn't he look sharp?"

"He does." I couldn't believe the transformation. Lachlan certainly hadn't been hard on the eyes before, but now he looked like that CEO he'd wanted to portray. A roguish, press-you-against-the-office-door-and-kiss-you-senseless CEO.

I really needed to skip a month of Sexy Book Club.

"Blaire and Paolo have worked wonders," I told Lachlan. "What do you think, Sylvie?"

"Ten." She answered immediately. "A perfect ten. Frannie?"

"Eleven-point-five."

Sylvie frowned. "Ten's the max."

Frannie lifted her glass in a one-woman toast. "I gave bonus points for the pocket square and that peek of chest hair."

Lachlan frowned and did up a button. "I feel a little ridiculous."

"Honey," said Frannie, "if this is ridiculous, I'll take two and call myself silly." Her attention moved to a friend across the room waving her down. "Lachlan, I'll have to shower you with more inappropriate compliments later. I see some book club friends I must speak to. Come on, Sylvie." The two dove into the crush of people and disappeared.

"It is my party, so I need to mingle." Rosie took a step toward her guests, then doubled back. "Lachlan, appearances are superficial, and I believe it's the inside that counts, but... you look wonderful."

"Thank you, Rosie." Lachlan appeared genuinely touched. "And might I say you look radiantly lovely tonight. Congratulations on your shop." He watched my sister step into the crowd for a moment before turning his bespectacled gaze back to me. "Hi."

Oh, the glasses. They really were a knee-weakening touch. "Hello there, yourself."

"Should I turn a full circle?" Lachlan asked. "Maybe strut a few steps on a catwalk?"

I smiled and let my gaze linger on the final results one more time. "You do clean up nicely, Mr. Hayes."

"I'm glad you approve." His posture seemed to relax, as if he'd gained some measure of comfort. "But are you sure I don't look too...I don't know, fussy?"

"*Fussy* is not the word I would choose." More like *unexpectedly devastating, disturbingly alluring,* and *maddeningly attractive.*

Lachlan ran a hand over his newly shorn cheek. "I'll have to get up an extra hour each day just to maintain all the shaving."

"Beauty is sacrifice."

Eyes round with feigned shock, Lachlan grinned and tilted his head. "Do you think I'm beautiful, Sassy Sutton?"

I took a sip of champagne. "I meant you're camera-ready now."

"Sure. That's what you meant." He gave a dramatic toss of his much shorter locks. "Just try not to objectify me too much."

"I'll rein those urges in."

"I hadn't realized I'd have to not only deal with being a tech giant, but now balance it with my new status as a sex symbol."

"I'm sure Bill Gates can give you some tips." I plucked a drink from a passing waiter and handed it to Lachlan. "I thought you weren't flying home until tomorrow."

"I changed my plans."

"Why?"

He moved closer until the toes of his shoes touched mine.

"Because last night I ate dinner in a hotel by myself and had the strangest realization."

The heady look in Lachlan's eyes rendered me immobile. "What was that?"

He slipped off those glasses, removing one more barrier between us. "I missed my wife."

I couldn't help my intake of breath, a small gasp of equal parts wonder and surprise. "Oh." I was so proud of how calm I sounded. "Are you married?"

"Yeah." Lachlan plucked a cracker off my plate and popped it in his mouth. "My wife's here somewhere, but she won't mind if I flirt with you. She's not one of those jealous types."

"Nope," I assured him. "Not at all."

"More like the overbearing type."

I took a sip of champagne, feeling a bubble or two float to my head. "I hear she's the successful, motivated, doesn't-have-a-hoodie-collection type."

"Yep. But I married her anyway."

I could've stared at Lachlan's newly revealed jawline all night. It was the perfect plane for lips to travel. "Well, as long as we're being honest, I can't flirt with you because my husband's here somewhere."

"That so?"

"Yes," I said. "He's been on a business trip."

"He sounds important."

"He's always thought so."

Lachlan laughed. "I doubt that. Tell me, did you miss this husband?"

I tipped back my flute and drained the contents.

Lachlan took a step, bringing all that intoxicating handsomeness even closer. "Well?"

"Maybe."

His beguiling smile curved ever so slowly. "You did, didn't you?"

I couldn't help it. My fingertips demanded I touch Lachlan's hair. "I had to fix my own breakfast." Yep, his locks were soft, with just the slightest hold of product.

"Tragic," he said.

Now I found myself running a hand over his cheeks, full of wonder at the mix of stubble and smooth skin. "Made coffee all by myself."

With a subtle shift, Lachlan leaned his face into my touch. "Unacceptable."

At least seventy-five people filled the shop, yet I was only aware of one. "I thought so."

Lachlan's hand reached for me, and he linked a few of his fingers with mine. "Did you think about this husband of yours while he was away?"

"I didn't want to," I answered honestly.

Those green eyes held steady as he considered this. Then finally he said, "I bet he thought of you too."

Had he? Was I the silliest nonwife ever to thrill at Lachlan's words? "Why are you here?"

His laugh breezed near my ear. "Not the reception I was hoping for, but I'll take it. I got bored with the meetings in LA."

Probably not "tour your husband's bathroom and get hot and bothered at the thought of using his toothpaste" bored.

"Is that so?" I studied the contrast of my small hand in his large one. Had a simple handhold from my last boyfriend ever made me this light-headed?

Lachlan watched my face, as if waiting for even a blink of rejection. "The bookshop opening is a big deal to you and your family," he said. "I guess I wanted to be here for it." His hand on mine tightened. "To buy books, of course."

"Readers gotta read."

He kissed my hand, a soft, measured imprint of his lips, his eyes never leaving mine. "Something like that."

Oh, gosh. When Lachlan wanted to charm, he pulled out all the stops.

"So, this husband of yours?"

"Yes?" I whispered.

"Has he told you how lovely you look tonight?"

If I were the heroine in a historical romance, I'd have at least considered a good swoon. "We're not really the complimenting types."

"Then let me tell you what he *should* say." Lachlan lowered his head and brushed his mouth against the shell of my ear. "Olivia." His words were a slow, warm drip of honey. "You look stunning tonight." His nose caressed my cheek, the faintest skim against my skin. "You're elegant, beautiful, commanding...and only moderately shrewish."

I bit down on my glossed bottom lip, refusing to laugh. "My husband prefers me that way."

"He probably prays for your dark heart." Lachlan's gaze lifted over my head then returned to my flushed face. "Your family is staring at us."

I suddenly became aware of what they would see. At some point Lachlan's hands had moved to hold me firmly against him. My own traitorous hands had somehow migrated to the front of his very expensive shirt. "Maybe we should move apart. Mingle."

"Or," Lachlan said.

"Yes?"

"We give them something a little more convincing."

At least five scenarios bloomed into vivid images in my mind. I categorized, labeled, and filed them away. "What... what did you have in mind?"

"Well." Lachlan's voice vibrated low in his chest. "If I were a man who missed his wife, I might take her face in my hands —lightly, carefully—and press a hint of a kiss to one cheek." His lips moved to the spot I had applied blush only an hour before. "And then the other." One simple kiss, not even lips to lips, and I was lost, floating above my body watching Lachlan embrace me. "I'm a man of instinct," he murmured against my skin, "and my gut tells me you're a neck girl."

I was. I really was.

One finger drew a path down the column of my throat, like a match across paper. "But that seems a bit too much for tonight's audience."

Darn it!

I meant, *Right. Of course. Too much.*

"A husband wouldn't want to cause a scene," Lachlan said, his eyes searching mine. "So maybe he'd simply cover your lips with his—like a newly wedded man."

How had I gotten here? To the point where if Lachlan didn't kiss me that instant, I might combust into a thousand tiny pieces of glittery want? "For appearance's sake," I heard myself say.

His smile hovered. "Mostly."

Then Lachlan Hayes, the guy I'd once loved to hate, slanted his lips over mine.

Fire, light, and shock.

The contact could've incinerated this whole store. Sorry, books. We're going up in flames.

Part of me had hoped Lachlan would be a bad kisser. That I'd let his limp lips capture mine while I thought of Hollywood hunks and tried to do my part.

But since meeting Lachlan again, nothing had gone as expected, so of course, the man knew how to kiss—too, too well. I drowned in that kiss, sank low, completely submerged, and remained a mind and body unable to break the surface.

The noise of the bookshop faded away, and all I heard were my own airy sighs. My arms moved northward, twining around Lachlan's neck, while my cheeks brushed against the remaining stubble of his face. I tried to take over, to command the lead as was my habit, but my will had vanished in the ephemeral mist around us.

My head felt light in Lachlan's hands, as if airy dreams had filled my brain. My lungs breathed wonder and my heart beat a desperation invitation. No one had ever kissed me like this —as if I were a treasure, a jewel found after a lifetime of search.

If this was pretending, Lachlan was the greatest of deceivers. I could almost believe this was real myself.

My lips followed wherever Lachlan's led. To be well and truly kissed in a bookstore—was there anything better? The Jane Austen novels were jealous. The Harlequins stared on with regret. The Danielle Steele paperbacks no doubt wept with wanting.

I opened my eyes only to find Lachlan watching me right back. The back of his hand glanced down my cheek and his lips began to descend once more.

"Refill those glasses!" I heard Sylvie call out. "Let's raise a toast to Rosie!"

The intoxicating stardust vanished in an instant, and my surroundings returned—the walls, the books, the people. Seconds ago, I had received the most life-shattering kiss, and the world had simply carried on.

Lachlan's arms released me, but his hand rested at the small of my back. Had he been as affected as I was?

Did I *want* him to be?

Sylvie whistled to gain everyone's attention then held her champagne glass high. "To new beginnings, to making peace with where we've been, and..." I swear her eyes sought me out in the crowd. "To embracing glorious plot twists." She sniffed against tears. "To the Lost Story!"

That night as I closed the door on the bedroom next to Lachlan's, I thought of Sylvie's toast.

It had been meant for Rosie.

But what if it could be for me too?

CHAPTER
TWENTY-TWO
OLIVIA

THE NEXT DAY I'd walked in a bewildered trance. Lachlan's kiss was obviously poisonous, a drug that leeched my mind of the ability to complete a thought, holding reasonable, rational sentiments captive while the scene from last night replayed over and over.

I'd considered bringing up the topic as soon as we got home from the party, but Lachlan had given me a friendly goodnight then departed for his bedroom. I'd listened for fifteen minutes while the shower ran, waiting for my opportunity to knock on his door, but minutes after the water shut off, I'd heard the distinct sounds of a man playing video games while loudly chatting with whom I assumed were online opponents. Lachlan had once mentioned he could lose himself in a game for hours, so I knew our talk would have to wait.

And what would I have said anyway?

Hey, I want to make sure we're clear that kiss meant nothing? But also: *Don't ever present me with the world's greatest kiss again.* From a PR perspective, those were not exactly strong persuasive leads.

So I'd lain awake all night, staring at my phone, the ceiling, and the constant replay of Lachlan's mouth possessing mine.

In the kitchen the next morning, Lachlan had acted like nothing had happened. He'd poured a cup of coffee and handed it to me, casually asking about my schedule for the day as if last night had been a figment of my imagination. Did he regret our kiss? Did he wish he could take back every breathless, heart-stopping detail? Or perhaps it hadn't affected him in the least. What if Lachlan had felt absolutely nothing, while my hormones demanded smelling salts and a fainting couch?

By midafternoon, I couldn't recall much about the last six hours of work, other than the fact that I'd forgotten it was National Squirrel Lovers Day. Celeste had arranged for a rehab specialist to bring in a few of the fuzzy creatures and explain their healing processes. That had been all fine and good until one saw his chance for freedom and attempted a dramatic escape. Elton's dog flew into action, hunting the squirrel, who ran all over the green meeting room as Celeste screamed. Chairs tumbled to the floor, people dove for cover, and papers flew like tornado debris. Eventually the rehab specialist collected his fugitive rodent, gathered his things, and left.

Tomorrow was National Alligator Day. I fervently prayed Celeste hadn't invited guests.

I took a break from my ridiculous thoughts and newly acquired wild animal trauma and drove to the Lost Story Bookshop. I circled the street a few times, struggling to find a parking spot, but there were none to be found. Happy customers poured out of the store, carrying bags whose logo I'd designed. I didn't want to jinx anything, but all signs pointed to a smashing grand opening.

Ten minutes later a bell tinkled when I finally pushed open the door and stepped inside. And didn't it do my heart good to see the place buzzing with people? On the air drifted the scents of books and the robust notes of a dark roast coffee. My ears perked at the light music playing overhead and the sounds of book lovers perusing and chatting. People filled every seating area, and a fifteen-person line snaked to the checkout counter, where Rosie and Sylvie rang up sales.

My eyes clouded with a sheen of tears at the sight of Rosie's grin.

"Need this?" A handkerchief appeared before me, and I startled.

Lachlan. The man who had hijacked my thoughts all day.

Our kiss had been a flirty game, and I'd assumed when I saw him next I'd feel nothing.

That was not to be the case. I felt it all—awareness, warmth, and the strange urge to move closer to Lachlan like he was my sun.

Maybe it was like the flu, and it would pass in a few days. Were there some good multivitamins for this? Did this call for extra vitamin C?

I took the paisley cloth. "This is a pocket square from Paolo's collection."

"I thought it was a fancy Kleenex." Lachlan stood so close his arm brushed my shoulder, sending unbidden shock waves through my system. "I noticed it was a little rough on my delicate nose."

"I'll tell Paolo you're enjoying his hankies," I said, admiring Lachlan's dark pants and cashmere sweater. The glasses were back, and so were the unwelcome flutters in my chest.

Lachlan stepped closer and studied my face. "By chance are you crying?"

"No."

"I didn't know your judgy eyes could produce human tears."

I sniffed and blinked a few times, trying to dislodge the

emotion that had come over me, but it couldn't be helped. I was just so happy for Rosie. "I was thinking of my eventual divorce and got weepy at the sheer joy."

When Lachlan didn't volley back a smart retort, I glanced up, only to find him staring at me. A heavy feeling flashed in his eyes, and had I blinked I would've missed it. But it was there—something sad, a glint of loneliness.

But then he lifted his chin and let his gaze travel the shop. "We'll have to throw a joint party. Give our marriage a proper send-off."

Right. "Then never see one another again."

"A dream come true." He nudged me with an elbow. "Back to your brief interlude into humanity. Why the tears?"

A woman passed by carrying a stack of Whitney Nicole books. Our book club was reading one of the author's latest romances this month. "This bookshop means so much to Rosie —to all of us, really. When Rosie announced that she'd bought this building, we thought she was having a grief-fueled nervous breakdown. But she knew what she was doing the entire time. This place represents everything she holds dear— books, community, and—"

"And her family at the center of it."

"Yes," I said. "We wouldn't have it any other way."

Lachlan went quiet for a moment, letting the thoughts move around in that big head of his. "You'll miss them if you go to New York."

That reminder plucked a heartstring with a little too much vigor. "I can't even think about that." Sure, I could FaceTime and call my family daily, but when it came to returning to Sugar Creek for visits, I was a realist. It would be eons before I'd have time to leave work and travel home. "Do you have other family you miss? Cousins? Aunts?" I inhaled his familiar scent. "Maybe a favorite barber you ignore?"

"No." He watched a group of shoppers. "Some friends back in California, but that's it."

Do not feel sorry for him, Olivia Sutton. Do not. It was emotional quicksand, and I did not want to take this small step of empathy and find myself sucked into a pit of regret. But still —how terribly sad to not have any family to care for you, to call you, to stick listening devices in your car and run background checks on all the men you attempted to date. "You can borrow my family for the next six months." My eyes went wide as I realized that offer had come from my own runaway lips.

"Careful, Livvy." Lachlan turned to me then, and a small smile appeared. "I might want to keep them."

He almost sounded like he meant it. "And our marriage will end in a bitter custody battle?"

Lachlan reached out and gave a lock of my hair a gentle tug. "You get Sylvie and her knife collection, but I get Frannie and her amazing cupcakes."

I hated how much I loved Lachlan's playful side. "No, I get full custody of them both, but you can have summers and two weeks in December."

Lachlan's grin lifted those stubbled cheeks and ignited a strange tipsy feeling in my chest. "I guess we can let our attorneys decide." His eyes locked on mine, then his voice went low as he bent his head toward me. "You're looking at me funny today."

"No, I'm not," I said with a little too much gusto. "I'm...I'm definitely not. Same type of looking. Normal. Kind of irritated and slightly nauseous. The usual."

He now stood way too close. "By chance have you been thinking about our kiss from last night?"

I slowly shook my head, wondering what spell Lachlan had cast that made it impossible to look away. "I...forgot all about it."

His fingers captured mine while his lips hovered near my ear. His breath was a caress, sending a shiver down my spine. "Liar."

"Olivia!"

I jolted and whirled toward the familiar voice. "Rosie." Could she hear my heart pounding? My cheeks felt warm. Did they look warm? Were they splotchy? Did my skin say, "Flirting with Lachlan does weird things to my insides, and I'm so confused and need it all to stop right now"?

"I'm so glad you two are here!" Rosie enveloped me in a hug, her scent of roses and vanilla as predictable as her vintage dress and cardigan. "Lachlan, I thought I saw you walk in." Before Lachlan knew what hit him, my sister threw her enthusiastic arms around him as well.

Lachlan's eyes met mine over Rosie's head, and I simply smiled at his discomfort. "Our Rosie's a hugger," I said. "Get used to it."

"That's right." My sister released him and gave his shoulders a squeeze. "Thank you for the flowers, Lachlan. They're lovely."

"You sent my sister flowers?"

"Beautiful pink and white peonies to celebrate the grand opening." Rosie gestured toward the sales counter. "How on earth did you know that's my favorite flower?"

Now Lachlan was the one who blushed. "Just a lucky guess. Roses seemed a little too on the nose."

"They're gorgeous." Rosie waved at a friend browsing the mystery section before returning her happy attention back to me. "What a lucky woman my sister is to have such a thoughtful husband."

"The good fortune is all mine." Eyes as green as an Ozark pine held such sincerity, I had to remind myself it was all for show. "Mrs. Hayes, what are your plans after this?" His hand reached for mine again, interlacing the fingers I used to imagine wrapped around his neck. "Would you like to take a late lunch, share a taco platter, and make out until the other diners complain?"

A memory of last night's kiss flashed before my eyes once again, and I blinked it away. "Tempting as those tacos sound, I'm going to have to pass. I have a meeting at Flair in an hour. Celeste is trying to get more interviews for you during your movie premiere week." I tried to tug my hand loose from Lachlan's, but he was now sliding his thumb back and forth against my palm. I meant to shoot him the same cease and desist look I gave Celeste's kids when they traded punches in the backseat, but found I couldn't recall how.

"Great," Lachlan said. "Can't wait."

"Is that sarcasm?" Rosie asked. "Sounds like sarcasm."

"We've taken care of Lachlan's exterior image." It really was a struggle to focus on shop talk while Lachlan pressed a kiss to the back of my hand. "But we've yet to...start the media training. Once we do, he'll have a totally different attitude."

"I'm more comfortable being the guy behind the computer," Lachlan said. He dropped my hand, and I'd no more had time to examine the oddly bereft feeling than he curved his warm arm around me and tucked me into his side. His fingers found the ends of my hair, sending tingling sensations straight to my head.

Rosie looked between Lachlan and me, taking in every movement, every touch. "Lachlan, will any of your family be joining you for the premiere? I bet they're so proud."

Lachlan stiffened. Nothing dramatic, just the slightest pause of his body for the span of his deep inhale. Had he not been partially wrapped around me like an adoring husband, I wouldn't have even noticed.

"No, my family won't be joining me," he said. "Just Olivia. And my CFO and his wife."

"My sister hasn't really told us much about your family." Rosie had zero gift for subtlety, nor really any care to pursue it. "Do you have siblings? Some parents back in California?"

"No." Lachlan's big hand left its exploration of my hair and now settled at the back of my neck, lightly kneading a knot with just enough pressure to push a contented sigh from my lips.

"No to all of the above?" Rosie asked.

"My father splits his time between Houston and New York, as do two older half-brothers." His smile looked convincing to the casual observer, but a fake wife knew. "We're not close."

Something about Lachlan's clipped tone caught me right in the squishiest part of my heart, and before I could remind myself the former wild child didn't need my sympathies, I wrapped my arm around his waist and leaned in.

"I've made my own family over the years, and"—Lachlan's eyes found mine—"it's always been enough."

"And now you have us." Rosie beamed.

Lachlan's smile dimmed ever so slightly as he consulted the time on his watch. "I should be going."

"Me too." I slipped from his hold and hugged Rosie once more. "I love you, and I'm so proud of you."

"Thank you." She dashed away a few tears and sniffled. "Chase would love this, wouldn't he?"

"He'd have adored it. And adored you living your dream."

More tears slipped down Rosie's cheeks. "Yeah. I think so too. Darn it, I told myself I wouldn't cry today." She extended an arm toward Lachlan. "Bring it in, brother-in-law. You know you want to. Come on."

"I thought you'd never ask." Then he held us both like he was already a Sutton. "I'm proud, too, Rosie." Lachlan kissed

Rosie on the top of her head and sent me a steadfast wink. "So, correct me if I'm wrong, but does this end in butt pats?"

Rosie laughed and swiped at her damp cheeks. "I'll leave that to you two. I see Mrs. Browning three aisles over. She's gonna need help finding historical romance. She likes the stuff that's spicy but has a cover that says otherwise." Rosie blew kisses to me and Lachlan as she backed away. "Love you both!"

"Love you too!" I called, then turned back to Lachlan. He watched Rosie walk away, and the look on his face could only be described as cautiously hopeful. Like a kid who'd found a bike beneath the Christian tree and prayed Santa hadn't meant it for an older sibling.

"Are you okay?" I asked. "My family can be a lot."

Then his gaze pulled back to mine, and he found his devil-may-care smile again. "We might have to add Rosie to the custody agreement."

"You can't afford her book buying habits."

"Your family is so nice." Lachlan reached out and slid a finger down my jawline. "What happened to you?"

I grinned and captured his wayward hand. "I got married."

"You did, didn't you?" His smile was the best going attraction in the shop, a mix of sexy and soft, with just enough lift of the lips to stir something in my wayward imagination. "See you at home tonight?" Lachlan asked this as if the answer mattered.

"I'll be late." Were things different now between Lachlan and me? They felt different. We didn't need them to be different, right? Bad idea. "I have to pick up Celeste's daughter from gymnastics."

His brows lifted in the universal sign of judgment. "Why can't Celeste do that?"

"Because she'll be in a meeting with the top dogs in the New York office." Sure, I minded the errand. But hopefully

Celeste was discussing my promotion with the uppity-ups at Flair Manhattan. "See you later, dearest nerd."

Lachlan rested his hand over his sweater-covered heart. "I'll miss you, my favorite malware."

I waved my fingers in a saucy goodbye, then sashayed through the aisles in the direction of the door. And when I passed the display that had witnessed my kiss with Lachlan only seventeen hours and fifteen minutes ago, I did not pause. No, not me. I kept walking toward the exit, a woman who definitely was not thinking about that staggering kiss. And I certainly was not remembering how it felt to be in Lachlan's arms. No replays going on in *my* head.

But maybe I did glance back.

And I found Lachlan, hands in his pockets, eyes trained on me.

A ghost of a smile on his lips.

CHAPTER

TWENTY-THREE

OLIVIA

I, Olivia Sutton, future recipient of a fabulous promotion, was on the phone with none other than *Good Morning America*. That's right, one of the hottest, longest running morning shows, and I'd just secured Lachlan an interview for their second hour.

"Wait, when?" Sitting in my office Thursday afternoon, I reached for my energy drink, jolted by the realization it was empty. I hadn't had a hit of caffeine in at least five minutes, and my liver would surely be lonely and confused. "Next month?" Red-hot panic doused my excitement over this total coup. "October twenty-fourth?" That was a little over three weeks away. "Are you sure you wouldn't rather see him right before the premiere? Oh, you had a cancellation? I see. Of course." Dread settled in at the talent booker's words. There was only one answer here, wasn't there? I'd be insane not to say yes. "We'll make it work. Mr. Hayes will be thrilled."

I was seconds away from losing all my pretend chill when the booker finally ended the call. Immediately, I whooped and punched a fist to toward the ceiling. But then reality lassoed my joy and wrestled it to the floor. *Oh, crap. Lachlan has an interview on GMA. He's not even close to ready.*

I resumed my seat and thunked my head on the desk so hard it rattled my laptop. So, so much to do.

"Trouble in PR paradise?" Morgan slithered in and hovered around my desk like an evil specter who'd come to haunt.

I shut my laptop lid and braced myself for my daily dose of harassment. "Not at all. In fact, I just got Lachlan a *Good Morning America* profile." I watched her face still as she absorbed that revelation. "I'm hoping Robin Roberts interviews him, but I should know more next week."

"Wow." Morgan checked a text on her phone. "Go, you, eh? How wonderful." Morgan certainly didn't think it was *wonderful.* "When is this blessed event?"

She just had to ask. "Next month."

Her billowy laughter could probably be heard in the office building across the street. "Next month. Oh, girl. Good luck with that." Morgan sauntered to the chair in front of my desk and assumed a lingering, yet haughty stance. It was the posture of her people. "Can I give you a bit of advice?"

"I'm guessing I can't stop you."

"If you send an unprepared client to a national television show, they will never work with you again."

Obviously I wouldn't be sleeping tonight. "Thanks. I'll keep that in mind. But Lachlan will be ready by then." I fixed a smile on my face and stuck in a barb of my own. "Celeste has been offering extra support and coaching where needed, and together, we're taking Lachlan to a new level of visibility."

Morgan's eyes flashed fire at the mention of Celeste's help. And, okay, maybe all the support I'd received was a two-minute pep talk as I shoved her kids in the car when I picked them up for school yesterday morning. But still, quite inspiring.

"Perhaps one day soon you'll be at a level where you don't need those training wheels," Morgan said. "Did I mention the account I'm working on is Elite Matches? Have you heard of it?"

Who hadn't? They only ran ads all over social media. Elite Matches provided one-on-one matchmaking for people who made at least mid–six figures. Lachlan would probably call them the second our divorce was final.

"With my social media campaign and advertising," Morgan said, "they've already seen a fifteen percent jump in membership."

Fifteen percent was phenomenally impressive. The hussy. "Nice."

"Nice? Try *fabulous*." Her viper eyes roamed to the pictures on my desk. "No photos of your new husband? I hope there's not trouble in paradise already."

Note to self: Plaster office with photos of Lachlan and me. "Lachlan and I have been too busy settling in and working on his brand improvements to get much else done."

"How does he feel about the slim possibility of his wife getting a job in New York?"

"He's very supportive and understands it's highly likely."

Morgan slowly stood. "Does he know your ex-boyfriend works in the New York office?"

There it was—that old stab of hurt at the mere mention of Taylor. "I assure you it won't be a problem for Lachlan."

Her eyes widened with faux concern. "But will it be a problem for you?"

"Turn on the Gamer Channel right now!" Celeste sailed inside my office, her heels clicking a frantic beat on the floor. "Open that laptop, Olivia!"

Celeste wore her Crisis Face, so I quickly complied. She

rounded my desk and loomed over my shoulder. Morgan, of course, followed behind her like the queen's handmaiden.

"Gamer Channel?" Elton appeared, and his dog trotted in to join the crowd. "What is that?"

I furiously opened a web browser as anxiety pooled in my stomach.

"They have a live feed." Morgan held up her phone, where a familiar face occupied the screen.

"And a huge viewership." Celeste glared down at me. "Why am I seeing Lachlan Hayes talking to Howie Benson, lead personality of the Gamer Channel?"

"I—I don't know." *Oh geez, oh geez, oh geez.* This could not be happening. My laggy browser finally loaded the Gamer Channel, and an expressionless Lachlan appeared live on my screen.

"Looks like an interview," Elton said, as his dog meandered to Morgan and sniffed her skirt.

"Yes." I couldn't turn away from the catastrophe unfolding on the screen. "He's certainly...attempting that."

"The question is why?" Celeste asked.

"I...I didn't approve this," I stammered. "I knew nothing about it."

Lachlan's wooden smile wobbled as he fielded Howie Benson's next question. Sentences poured from Lachlan's lips like horses leaving the starting gate. His words held no regard for inflection or connection. Lachlan's hands fidgeted in his lap, and he shifted in an office chair, a monstrous contraption squeaking with his every movement.

"His office is a terrible space for an interview," Morgan said, shooing the dog away in vain. "I'm surprised you haven't addressed this already, Olivia."

I pulled my focus from the screen long enough to shoot Morgan a withering glare. *Back off, you suck-up.* "I haven't had a chance. I'm still working on a giant punch list of other things to get Lachlan ready."

Celeste regarded me with a look that would've made a weaker woman burst into tears.

Finally, *finally*, the segment ended, Howie Benson signed off, and a commercial for frozen pizza began.

I closed my eyes and inhaled, wishing Lachlan hadn't gone off plan. "I'll call him right now."

Celeste's hand swooped in a wide flourish before landing on her hip. She was a tableau of attitude and affront. "Lachlan is not to go rogue while under our care. Is that clear?"

"I assumed he knew." I sounded like a meek child prepared to receive my punishment.

"He clearly is *not* aware of the expectations." Celeste held up her phone like a sacrifice to the gods. "For heaven's sake, I've seen multicar pileups tidier than this. Absolute disaster! Let me remind you, Olivia, if Lachlan looks bad, we look bad."

Specifically, *I* looked bad.

"Yikes," Morgan said. I could hear her smirk, the absolute joy she was surely feeling at my dark moment. "You'd think he would've told his *wife* he had an interview. Who knew he would be this bad at it? Maybe you should cancel that appearance on your big morning show. He'll never be ready in time."

"Morning show?" Celeste asked. "Which one?"

I quickly updated her on my phone call.

Celeste rubbed her temples like she had a migraine with Lachlan's name on it. "Morgan's right. Your husband isn't ready."

"He can be," I assured her. "I'll make sure of it." I couldn't give Celeste numerical data like Morgan. I needed *GMA* to stay in the running for the promotion.

"You fix this, Olivia," Celeste demanded. "He's your responsibility. Not even two weeks in, and this is what happens. It cannot happen again, especially on national television."

"It won't," I said. "I assure you."

Morgan pushed FeeFee off of her and dusted the fur from her legs. "Somebody doesn't have control of her client. I could lean in if you wanted, Celeste."

"You will not be leaning anywhere near Lachlan," I warned, ignoring Elton's silent hand clap behind the ladies.

"This is not up to Flair standards at all." Celeste began to pace. "Lachlan was uncomfortable, his face red as a tomato, and he rushed into every question like he was being held at gunpoint. Did you catch how many times he said 'um'?"

"Quite a few." I knew full well it had been exactly twelve times. My internal filler-word calculator never failed me. "We'll work on it."

"I want this dealt with now." Celeste over-enunciated every angry word. "Call the Gamer Channel. Make sure this media is pulled. It will not live in infamy on the internet. Are we clear?"

"Yes, Celeste." I jotted down her command, as if there were even a tiny chance I would forget. No possibility of that. "And I'll begin media coaching. I'll fine-tune my training modules and hit Lachlan with them immediately." I'd have to cancel five meetings and a work session with our digital department.

"Oh, you'll do more than that," Celeste said. "You are now Lachlan Hayes's shadow, do you understand? I don't want him to attend one single function without you mere feet away."

"But—"

"Not one, Olivia. Furthermore, if I hear of a single appearance of his where you are not in attendance, I will pull you as his brand manager, stick you back on the adult diaper account, and delete your name from consideration for the New York office. Am I clear?"

This moment reminded me of videos I'd seen of high-rise buildings imploding by dynamite. I had an instant vision of my career combusting in the same fashion—a trajectory of fire and smoke, until my dream was nothing more than a great propulsion of ash.

I swallowed hard. "You're quite clear."

"Find Hayes." Celeste pointed ominously toward the open door. "*Now.*"

TWENTY-FOUR

LACHLAN

OLIVIA WAS HOME, and Olivia was angry.

She hadn't even walked inside the house yet, so how did I know?

Perhaps it was my keen intuition when it came to the ladies.

Or maybe it was my years as a game designer watching the micromovements of people for the sake of recreating authenticity.

Could've also been the fact that I saw and heard Olivia's SUV screech down our road at breakneck speed, then whip into the driveway like she expected a pit crew to meet her for a tune-up. Then there was the thunderous slam of her car door followed by the inelegant way she bellowed my name like a medieval fishwife.

The door into the house banged shut just as I grabbed my laptop and settled onto the couch, one apple in my hand as if I'd casually been sitting and nothing was amiss. "Oh. Hello, Wife Number One."

Olivia looked like a fury as she stomped into the den. Ah,

my exquisite bride. Eyes wide and hinting at violence. Her hands clenched at her sides as if she'd love nothing more than to introduce her fist to my nose. Her lovely chest rising and falling in labored, angry breaths.

"You." She pointed a pink painted nail right at me. "Do you have any idea what you've done?"

"I'm getting the feeling here that maybe you want to claw my eyes out?" I bit into my apple and chewed, trying not to focus on Olivia's mouth. I'd kissed those lips only four days ago, a memory I had reimagined approximately 250 times now. I'd had three meetings today and been called out for losing my train of thought twice, so deep was I lost in the reenactment in my head. "With that level of anger, I'm guessing I either messed up the alphabetical order you arranged my spice cabinet, or you caught my interview."

Without much care for electronics, Olivia tossed her laptop bag on a chair, exhaled gustily, then sat down beside me. Her nose wrinkled at the sight of my attire. "I see half of you dressed up for the day," she said.

"That's the beauty of remote events." From the look on her face, Olivia clearly was not impressed with my business on top, comfy on the bottom. I wore one of Paolo's shirts, a tie that I was *almost* certain coordinated, and my ever-trusty sweatpants. The tie chafed, but had my sweats ever let me down? Not once. "I take it you don't approve of my outfit?"

"It looks like a tragic Choose Your Fashion Adventure."

"My adventure involves an elastic waistband," I said. "You should try them one day. I think it would really help some of your anger issues."

Olivia rested her head on the back of the couch and stared up at the ceiling, as if she'd lost the will to return the sarcasm. "I saw the interview, Lachlan. My whole team did."

Suddenly I felt like that teenage boy who was desperate to

please my father, but only earned his disappointment and shame no matter how big the effort. "Was it that bad?" I knew my performance hadn't been great, but with this reaction, you'd have thought I'd belched the alphabet on air.

Olivia sighed again then rolled her head to the side to regard me. "It was...informative."

I couldn't help it. I reached my hand behind her head and rubbed that tense spot at the base of her neck that I'd learned she liked. "Is that PR speak for total crap?"

She didn't move from my touch, but instead closed her eyes and relaxed into it. "I can say the information you communicated was quality. If that was your intention."

"But?" The skin beneath her hair felt like silk. Touching Olivia had been a big mistake. Now I just wanted more.

"We need to establish some ground rules," she said.

I braved a gentle walk of the fingers into her hair. "Sounds boring."

Her eyes were less stabby as they met mine. "Lachlan, you signed an agreement with Flair. In that agreement you promised to adhere to our advice and counsel."

"Speak plainly, Olivia. I have another gig with a podcaster in an hour and don't have time to parse this out."

"Cancel your podcast."

She was totally crushing my mellow "let's hang on the couch together and make out" vibe. "I can't," I told her.

"I'm going to insist you do. If you want my help and the help of Flair, you have to trust the process and believe we know what we're doing. You're not ready for interviews yet. We haven't done any media training, set up your virtual interview space, given you proper audio equipment, or decided on clothing options. There's a time and place for that on the PR plan, and we hadn't gotten there."

Olivia did nothing that wasn't scheduled. "So I was terrible. That's what you're saying."

"I'm here to help," she said. "I'm also here to ask that you not get me fired."

I studied my wife, from her slightly mussed hair to the tension bracketing the mouth that now starred in my dreams. "Was that mentioned?"

"Quite loudly," Olivia answered.

"Sorry." I reached for her hand and gave it a small shake. "You wanted to strangle me when you first walked in here, didn't you?"

She watched our joined hands, and I wondered what she was thinking. "Not for the first time."

"Adult Olivia has such restraint." And talent, and beauty, and confidence, and something that hooked me in a way I'd yet to release. I needed to remember that our marriage was a sham, and in a matter of months we would be over. How many times had I let myself get attached only to find myself holding nothing but heartbreak in the end? I certainly wouldn't be that idiot this time.

"I have a lot riding on your success, Lachlan," Olivia said.

"So my success is your success?"

"Probably."

"And my failure is your failure?"

"Most definitely."

I grinned at her desolate tone. "I have such power."

Her hair swished against her fancy shirt as she nodded. "That very thought keeps me up at night."

I leaned toward her, ignoring her scent of vanilla and chaos. Did she also replay our kiss in her mind? "You think about me at night, Olivia?"

"I do," she admitted. "Usually when I have nightmares about my career being taken down by Hurricane Celeste."

"And where am I in this dream?" I asked.

Olivia swayed a few degrees closer. "Bound and gagged in my trunk."

"Savage." There was the Olivia I knew.

Her words became a soft plea. "Don't screw me over, Hayes."

My thoughts returned to our inevitable end and the growing certainty I would be slightly wrecked. "Right back at you, Sutton."

"Lachlan?" Olivia draped her hand on my leg, earning my complete attention.

"Yes?"

She moved toward me, so close our lips were only a breath apart. "Take me to your office."

TWENTY-FIVE

OLIVIA

"Now I can see why you've kept me out of your office." I walked across the threshold of Lachlan's workspace and immediately wanted to start tidying up.

His office wasn't overly stylized, almost as if he'd told his decorator to leave it alone. Framed prints of his video game characters hung on one wall like family photos, while techie gizmos occupied space on the opposite side. In front of a large window sat a mammoth steel desk holding three monitors and a funky looking keyboard probably designed for gamers. But it was the office chair that was the eyesore and unfortunate focal point.

The chair looked like some invention that Sylvie and Frannie might've encountered in a CIA lab. Positioned on a base, the red chair seemed to be a leather recliner with a pox of gadgets sticking up here and there. An enormous metal arm hugged the back and extended overhead, where a curved screen the width of my refrigerator hung. "Is that a footrest?"

Lachlan looked more than proud. "Heated."

This had been where he'd given the interview. "The gaming chair has to go."

Lachlan took a defiant stance, crossing his arms over his Armani shirt. "That gaming chair is a five-thousand-dollar piece of art that massages my back and contours my muscular tush like a cloud."

"When you sat in it for your interview, I thought you were about to get eaten by a Transformer."

"I can get you one, if this is just your jealousy talking."

How did he think taking a video call from this chair was a good idea? "You can't use this for interviews anymore. It swallows you whole, and it forces you to look up at the camera, which is a very odd angle."

"I'm offended on the gaming chair's behalf, but I will concede."

Trying to ignore the scent of Lachlan's citrusy shampoo tickling my nose, I studied the design of the room again. He'd have a lot of remote interviews in the next few months, and we desperately needed to create a decent backdrop. "Is the office where you're most comfortable for interviews?"

"I'm most comfortable submitting my responses by way of email," Lachlan said.

"I'll be sure and tell that to *Good Morning America*."

"Fine. Yes." He sighed. "I guess this is my favorite spot."

"I'll work up a sketch for some changes I'd like to make, but I want to see a bookshelf behind your desk, some photos of actual humans, and maybe some art."

He pointed to the far wall. "How about—"

"Your framed print of Yoda does not count. Let's get started." I walked to a small seating area, removed a *WIRED* magazine from one chair, and sat down. "Let me have the questions the Gamer Channel sent you before your interview."

Lachlan's big body barely fit in the matching barrel chair beside me. "I didn't get any."

"Didn't you ask for them in advance?"

"No."

Good heavens. Was he daft? "Never go on cold. You always want to know what you'll be asked so you can prepare. So *we* can prepare."

"I don't want to sound like I'm reading from a script," he said. "I like to wing it."

"Clipping those wings tonight, Hayes. And from now on, all interview requests come directly to me."

He crossed his legs at the ankles and frowned. "The virtual world is so much easier to navigate."

"Okay, lesson one is body language."

His posture finally relaxed as his eyes met mine. "I'm already very interested."

Had I ever noticed Lachlan's eyes in college? How they held you like you were the most fascinating thing he'd seen? The way the evening light brought out the flecks of gold? He could disarm any interviewer with one steady sweep of his gaze.

"Olivia?"

Focus, Olivia! "Sorry. Just organizing my thoughts." I quickly explained how Lachlan's monitor or laptop would be set up for the next virtual interview. "You need to lean in."

"Lean?"

Standing, I pressed my hand to his shoulder blades and applied the smallest of pressure. "Pitch forward fifteen degrees. Go ahead, give it a try."

He dipped forward like he'd lost all feeling in his upper body. "Like this?"

"No."

Lachlan tried again, this time with a tilt. "This?"

Sometimes this job was way too hands-on, but one did

what one must. "Let me show you." Looming over Lachlan, I settled my hands on his arms and nearly short-circuited.

Good Lord. It was just a guy's arms. And Lachlan's at that. Was I so deprived that touching his sleeve nearly sent me to the floor? It had been a year since I'd been in a relationship, but that shouldn't mean that I was a desperate hoyden, all aflutter by the press of my fingers to what were, admittedly, fabulous forearms.

"Are you copping a feel?" Lachlan's grinning mouth hovered too close to my cheek.

"I'm certainly not." I was. I surely *had* copped a feel. My nerd husband's biceps were quite pleasing and surprisingly solid too. Sinewy even. "Merely trying to demonstrate..." His limbs were stiff and unyielding. "Could you try to be more bendy? It's like rearranging tree trunks here."

What occurred next was akin to a slow-motion scene in a romantic comedy. But a bad one you might catch late at night on an obscure channel when you'd exhausted all other viewing options.

Because in the same moment I shoved on Lachlan's shoulder, he finally leaned. His hands went to their correct location, but unfortunately, my entire body pitched that way too. My legs slipped out from under me, and a yelp escaped my lips. Next thing I knew, Lachlan held me in his arms like a hot fireman carrying me safely from the flames.

But the flames were right here. Between us.

Lachlan looked down, his head the perfect angle for a kiss. "Did that go better in your head?"

"It...did." Lachlan's arm pressed me against his chest, and I had the strongest urge to curl into his warmth.

His voice dipped low and soft. "I think you're pretty when you're mad."

"You've had lots of chances to see me pretty then," I whispered.

He still had that smile that had bedazzled many a sorority sister. "I was remembering the night of the Lost Story's grand opening."

Oh. That. "Such a busy night. I hardly recall it."

Lachlan's head dipped an inch. "Need a reminder?"

No, that kiss replayed vividly in my head every night. "We're separating in November. We shouldn't...complicate things."

He went quiet for a long beat. "You're so sensible."

To a fault. "Lachlan?"

"Yes?"

I licked my dry lips and watched his eyes follow. And let me say, the words I spoke next cost me dearly because I knew in that moment, I could have anything I wanted in Lachlan's arms. "You can release me now."

Regrettably, he did just that, but the air between us remained charged, as if tension imbued the particles.

I resumed my seat, took three deep breaths, and mentally recalled our agenda. "Let's discuss eye contact. If you're speaking to a screen, look at the camera. I'll tape an arrow to your camera before your next interview."

"I can find the camera, Olivia."

"It's easy to forget midconversation." He looked a little testy now, so I moved on. "If you're doing an in-person interview, look at the speaker."

His newly tamed eyebrows pinched in a frown. "Don't look at speaker if virtual, but look at speaker if in person."

"Correct. Imagine I'm the television personality interviewing you. Eyes on me." As soon as Lachlan complied, my pulse quickened and my throat went dry. His steady gaze dared me to look away. There was a depth there I'd never noticed in our college days. All I'd seen then was the haughtiness and condescension. I knew now that it had probably hidden some pain.

"Do I have it?" He asked, his voice deliciously husky and rumbly.

Heat infused my entire body. "You certainly do."

I spent the next hour throwing out more tips than one evening should contain. By ten-thirty Lachlan yawned three times in a row, signaling our session was over. "Let's stop here for the night," I said, feeling the fatigue creep in myself. I still had at least an hour of work for another client.

We walked upstairs together, each of us quiet with our own thoughts. I wondered if this felt like something married folks would do. Lachlan was probably thinking of gaming chairs and finding desk space for more monitors.

"This is your stop." Lachlan paused at my bedroom door, the dim lights of the hall casting shadows on the floor.

I reached for the doorknob and gave it a twist. "Thanks for walking me home." If Lachlan moved one more step in my direction, he'd be within arm's length. There was something about nightfall, two weary bodies, and the close proximity that had me imagining things I shouldn't. "I'll see you in the morning."

"Breakfast is at six-thirty," he said.

Had I noticed how regal Lachlan's chin looked since his makeover? That chin was made for touching.

"You're giving me that look, Olivia." Lachlan did take that one step.

But so did I, retreating smack into the wall. Oh, this was just like the romance novel we'd read in the summer. I'd never been kissed against a wall. Was it better in fiction than reality? In real life it probably pinched the back and stressed the knees.

"I'm looking at you because you're standing so close," I said, quiet as a hush.

"You're right." Lachlan planted one hand on the wall over my head and leaned, the most perfect incline of forty-five degrees that brought his mouth achingly close to mine. "I wanted to tell you..."

"Yes?" That he couldn't get me off his mind? That he wanted to kiss me until the sun came up? That he also felt a pull that defied gravity and any semblance of logic because we were obviously so terribly wrong for one another?

"Thank you for helping me."

I blinked, ridiculously disappointed. "You're welcome." At the risk of being a complainer, this conversation seemed like a waste of a wall. "Anytime."

"Because it's your job," Lachlan said.

It was becoming so much more, and I needed to rein that in pronto. "Because I care if you succeed."

Lachlan watched me in one long, tease of a moment. "Don't care about me too much." He inched closer, then pressed his lips to my cheek. "I hear I'm quite a bit of trouble."

With that declaration, Lachlan retreated to his room and shut the door.

TWENTY-SIX

OLIVIA

LACHLAN

Watched your voice coaching video. Did you make that just for me?

OLIVIA

Yes. At two a.m. this morning. If you don't commit it to memory, my sacrifice of sleep will all be in vain.

LACHLAN

If I understand this right, I shouldn't give an interview in Klingon or the voice of my favorite alien?

OLIVIA

Jokes about media training, your brand development, or speaking engagements are no longer allowed. Keep them to yourself. I give them zero stars.

LACHLAN

Want to talk about why you were awake at two a.m.? Did thoughts of me keep you up?

OLIVIA

They did not. I was thinking about work.

LACHLAN

You keep telling yourself that, Livvy.

OLIVIA

eye roll I guess I should thank you for the flowers you sent to work today. Brilliant idea. Just one more detail that convinces the world we're a real couple.

LACHLAN

...Who says that's why I sent them?

BY MONDAY, my stress levels could best be described as seismic. We weren't talking little tremors, but the kind of energy that could bring an entire town to rubble.

All weekend, I'd done nothing but make Lachlan eat, breathe, and sleep media training. All of this put me in Lachlan's space nonstop.

Which gave *me* thoughts nonstop.

Between wishing Lachlan would kiss me senseless again and responding to Celeste's persistent reminders that we needed to speed up his progress, I was about two tectonic shifts away from catastrophe.

When Rosie let me know tonight was a read-in at the bookstore, I shut my laptop, grabbed a book, and headed to the Lost Story. Did I have time to sit for a few hours and lose myself in a romance novel? No, I did not. But would it make me feel better and push the release valve on some of this pressurized stress? I certainly hoped so.

"Here's the newlywed!" Sylvie called as I stepped inside the shop.

There was already quite a crowd, especially for the event's maiden voyage. Fellow readers, mostly women who looked about as harried as I felt, sat in chairs, couches, and in cozy corners on the floor. Some had even brought blankets and their own beverages.

These were my people.

Spying Hattie quietly chatting to a group that included my grandmother, aunt, and Rosie, I made my way toward the mystery section where they loitered.

Rosie hugged me tightly, her face as happy as I'd seen it in months. "Can you believe all these people?"

Sylvie, an extrovert if there ever was one, gawked about. "Who knew folks would want to be alone—together?"

"I did," Rosie said. "How heavenly is it to just be with fellow book people, sit and read in the quiet, and *not* talk?"

"We can't talk?" Frannie shot Sylvie a look. "You didn't mention that part."

"Because I knew you wouldn't get in the car if I did," Sylvie said.

Frannie fanned herself with a paperback that featured a buxom woman and a shirtless man. "I was made to talk. It's like my oxygen. I feel faint already. Can someone take my vitals?"

"Are you okay?" Hattie asked, and it took a moment before I realized she was talking to me.

"*My* oxygen is fine." Though I was ready to kick off my heels.

"You look a little wired tonight," Hattie said.

"She's always wired," Sylvie told her. "Have you seen how many energy drinks and espressos she downs in a day? I get A-fib just thinking about it. And do you know why Olivia has a drinking problem?"

"I do not have a drinking problem." Good heavens.

"Because that boss of hers runs her ragged," my grandmother continued. "If she doesn't give you the promotion this time, Frannie and I will take care of her ourselves. Right, Frannie?"

My aunt said nothing.

"Right, Frannie?" Sylvie asked again, with no response. "Fran?"

Frannie released her clamped lips. "What? I'm practicing the not talking thing." She walked away grumbling. "I'm already terrible at this."

"Back to you, Olivia." Hattie directed her hazel eyes my way again. "Are you sure you're all right?"

Hattie was a therapist, and if she asked you if you were okay, you worried your answer would somehow earn you a place on her counseling schedule. "Just busy, as usual." I waved at a friend from church. "I've been doubling up on Lachlan's media training."

"Is that what you honeymooners call it these days?" Sylvie cackled like a bridge troll. "Just doing some 'media training'?" Then her eyes narrowed as she studied my face. "Oh. That really is what you meant. How dull."

"But necessary," I said, explaining the *Good Morning America* development and Lachlan's bombed interview. "He's got a possible slot with Anderson Cooper, then there's that podcast with Jason Bateman, and then—"

"We get it," Rosie said. "It's a lot. But Lachlan couldn't be in better hands. And while I don't want you to move, I can't imagine anyone else deserving that job in New York more. I mean, you did all of Celeste's Christmas shopping last year *while* working twelve-hour days." Her attention snapped to a group of women who shuffled inside. "I better go mingle and help customers find spots. Next time I'll need way more chairs. I hope we have enough cupcakes."

"I'm going to sit down." I eyed a place in a far corner of the children's section right under a giant bunny painted on the wall. "I can't stay long. I left Lachlan three videos to watch on nonverbal communication, and I need to get back home to debrief." My hand shot out in the general vicinity of my grandmother. "And no, that's not a euphemism."

"I raised her better than this," Sylvie told Hattie as I left them both to claim my spot.

Ten minutes later, I sat with my back reclined against a wall, my tailbone moderately protesting, and completely transformed to London, 1740. Historical romance was one of my favorite genres, but I knew the reality was not quite so romantic—corsets that could serve as torture devices, no indoor plumbing, and a criminal lack of the Dairy Barn drive-throughs.

I'd waited fifteen chapters for this couple to finally kiss, and the author had made the delay completely worth it. If only dark alcoves hadn't gone out of vogue.

The hero had just re-upped his commitment to the kiss when my mind detoured to another tall, handsome leading male—Lachlan. That thought leapfrogged right to another thought—kissing. More specifically, *our* kissing. Our romantic interlude may have lacked a drafty castle alcove, but wow, it had still been worthy of a novel. That kiss had also set off a confusing spiral I'd thought I could manage—the dissolution of my strong dislike for Lachlan. I rather liked the man now, and just what did I do about that? I guess that meant we could part ways as friends, right? That was something.

But I'd gotten to see his vulnerable side, his kindness, and let's not forget his cooking skills. Lachlan had made me laugh every day since I'd moved into his golf course manor, and how many times had my ex Taylor made me laugh? I could probably count the instances on both hands. When I was with Taylor, I'd always felt a pressure to tone down who I was. For him, I was always too anxious, too ramped up, too serious, too regimented. He once told me he wished he could find my intensity dial and turn it down. Words like that tended to stick with a girl—more than *Taylor* had stuck with a girl...

Capturing my wandering thoughts, I returned my attention to my book.

Two pages in and a shadow darkened my page. Sylvie.

My grandmother, ever elegant in slender black pants, a sparkly sweater, and enough diamonds to require her own security detail, eased down beside me. She peeked over at my book and nodded her approval. "How's married life treating you?" she whispered.

"Do you mind?" I held up my novel. "I think Felicity's about to tell Lord Bradford she loves him."

"I've read that one. Brad's brother kidnaps her first."

Darn it. "Now why'd you go and ruin the plot for me?"

"I didn't," Sylvie said. "That author has plenty more twists coming."

"Well, keep them to yourself." Whitney Nicole was a favorite author of our book club, though her true identity was a bit of a mystery. "No more spoilers."

"Now I've saved you from having to read about fifteen pages," Sylvie said, "and we can use that time to talk."

I glanced toward a beanbag in the next section where Rosie sat with a glass of wine in one hand and her book in the other. Nacho, the Labrador mix she fostered, rested near her feet. Even with hands full, Rosie was able to give me a shushing finger to the lips.

"My marriage is fine," I whispered to Sylvie.

"Honey, oatmeal is fine. Ten dollars off a brow wax is fine.

The first few months of your marriage should be more along the lines of *fabulous, wickedly invigorating,* and *can't wait to get back home to reenact chapter twenty-three of that book.*"

"It's still an adjustment."

"Indeed it is."

Hattie now settled on my other side. "What are we talking about?"

Peace, quiet, and fictional snogging. That's all I'd wanted tonight. "We're *not* talking. We're reading."

Sylvie took a sip of wine. "I was asking for a status report on her marriage."

"Because that's what you do during a read-in." Being denied my book made me a little punchy, but Felicity and Lord Bradford were waiting for me.

Hattie rested her paperback in her lap. "I can't speak for Olivia, but Miller says Lachlan's happier than he's ever seen him."

The words on my page blurred before my eyes as I caught my sister's revelation.

"Well, of course," Sylvie said. "He's a very lucky man to marry our Olivia."

"Did you know his father was emotionally abusive?" Hattie added. "He all but abandoned Lachlan and his mother in Dallas and left her to raise Lachlan by herself. Lachlan had a job at thirteen, washing dishes for the diner where his mom worked."

Thirteen? Washing dishes? "There was a lot about Lachlan I didn't know when we were in college," I said quietly. "I'm not sure he got to have a childhood."

"You're aware his mom had a heart condition, right?" Hattie asked.

"No, I didn't know that." I hadn't delved much into his mother's story.

"According to Miller, she was always sickly. He took care of her a lot, even when he was just a kid."

What a childhood. If I had known where Lachlan had come from, would it have changed how I'd treated him in college? I wanted to think it would've. "Lachlan's worked hard to make a new life for himself," I said.

"And now you're part of that better life." Hattie smiled. "You're the most stable thing to happen to him in years, Olivia."

Lachlan and I were as stable as a two-legged stool.

"He's certainly not Taylor." Sylvie curled her glossed lip, as if his name tasted sour. "But sometimes we take our old wounds into our new relationships."

"I certainly did when I met Miller," Hattie said.

"I know Lachlan isn't Taylor." This conversation scrubbed against my defenses like sandpaper.

Sylvie rested her blonde head on my shoulder. "Sugar, just because Lachlan wasn't on your timeline doesn't mean he didn't show up right on time. Don't be afraid to love with your whole heart again. With the right person, the risk is worth it."

I said nothing. Just returned to my book where I could spend time with a couple who would get their lives figured out by the end of the last chapter. They'd overcome all the obstacles, find their way to each other, and claim their happily ever after.

I didn't need marriage advice from my family because I wasn't in a real marriage. Very soon Lachlan and I would quietly separate, and we'd go live our lives.

And if the thought of Lachlan moving on and finding his happily ever after with someone else made my heart tremble just a bit, I needed to get past it.

Because I certainly wasn't going to fall in love with a man destined to leave me.

I'd done that once, but never again.

After Lachlan and I split, I'd wish him well and get back on my life plan where everything had its time and place.

With no stops for heartbreak.

CHAPTER
TWENTY-SEVEN
OLIVIA

ONE DAY I'd have a job that didn't require more costume changes than a Harry Styles concert.

At eight-thirty the next evening, on this first week of October, I returned home a tired, bone-weary shell of a woman. I'd worked another thirteen-hour day, most of it spent in a witch's costume. Do you want to know why witches were such angry, villainous ladies? Because their uniforms were impractical and uncomfortable. Maybe if they'd worn yoga pants, they wouldn't have felt like turning people into toads.

I stepped into the kitchen and kicked off buckled heels that looked like they'd been stolen from Hester Prynne's closet.

Lachlan entered the room and noted my attire with an arched brow.

My purse slipped from my shoulder and plopped to the ground as I sat my tired body on a barstool. "Not one word about my outfit."

"Wouldn't dream of it."

I'd left at four-thirty in the morning for a spin class and

had missed our daily breakfast time. "Do you have anything to eat? Crackers? Cheese? A porterhouse steak?"

Lachlan removed my wilted hat and set it on the island counter. "First of all, I have a whole kitchen stocked with food, because unlike you, I don't have trouble remembering to eat. But second, why are you dressed like you took a very wrong turn off a yellow brick road?"

Frissons of awareness glimmered across my scalp as Lachlan restored a lock of hair the hat had displaced. "I've..." Where had I been? Oh, yes. Work. "You said you wouldn't remark on my clothing."

"I thought I could stay strong and honor your weary request, but I can't. Don't keep me in suspense any longer, Professor McGonagall."

"We had a Halloween party at Flair. Celeste required costumes, of course."

"This early in the season? Is this a requirement of your work coven?"

I plucked a tissue from my pocket and blew my nose. Seasonal allergies could be grueling in an Arkansas fall. "We did some team building at the haunted house that just opened for the season, and two of the zombies crashed into one another and took me down with them. They didn't mean to. First day on the job."

Lachlan reached out and traced a red, aching spot above my forehead. "Give me names, and I'll beat them up."

My mind went absolutely blank, and my entire body froze. Oxygen suspended in my lungs and my heart paused midbeat. I silently counted backward from five as Lachlan slid his hand over my brow again. My eyes locked on his, and I saw it—that millisecond of recognition and surprise. As if he, too, felt the combustion and had been taken aback.

I wasn't the only one affected. Why did I take some sort of

perverse pleasure in that? This should make it even more satisfying to nip it in the bud.

But it didn't.

Lachlan's hand dropped, and he cleared his throat. "You do have the makings of a bruise there. Need some ice?"

"No." The percussion of my heart returned, though the beat remained drunk and erratic.

"Where is this haunted house?" Lachlan filled a glass with water and handed it to me.

"The Renaissance faire grounds."

"Man, I love a good Ren faire."

Now that I knew Lachlan better, that did not surprise me a bit. "Maybe Sugar Creek is the town for you after all."

"You have doubts that it's not?"

I questioned daily why Lachlan was here, but I didn't want to dive into that tonight. "I believe you texted me about an emergency?" The message had included lots of GIFs, so I knew it wasn't *too* urgent.

"When's the last time you ate, Sassy Sutton?" Lachlan's hands rested on my shoulders and gently massaged.

I closed my eyes as his fingers worked their own magic on my tired muscles. "This morning."

"Do you not believe in eating?"

"It's a practice I support. I just haven't had time."

"Unacceptable."

I bit back a cry of regret as Lachlan removed those wondrous hands and walked to the refrigerator. Hungry as I was, I would've forsaken food for days if he'd continued his spa-worthy massage.

"Do you want some help?" I asked as Lachlan pulled out a stainless skillet and set it on the stove.

"No," he said. "I've had a long day working on permits for the new office, and I need the break.

I rubbed my aching head. "Don't you have an assistant?"

"Yes." He set a carton of eggs on the counter. "But some things are easier to do myself. The permits are something my CFO Maxwell usually hands off to our legal department, but I wanted to look at them."

"But that pulls you away from the creative side of your work."

"I haven't done much creative in the last year. Things exploded, and it was more efficient to hire designers to do what I'd previously done. I'm still executive designer, but the rest, the really fun stuff, is up to a very talented team."

Weighted with fatigue, I rested my chin in my hand as if my neck could no longer be trusted to hold up my head. "I'm sorry."

Lachlan cracked two eggs with finesse into a bowl. "It's the price of success, I guess." He sliced off two pats of butter into a waiting skillet. "Minus a near-concussion, how was work?"

Here we were, discussing our day like a married couple. "I had to take over Celeste's morning carpool, but other than that, it was kind of fun. Morgan tripped over a hay bale, so that was a highlight. How about you?"

From his position at the stove, Lachlan glanced over his shoulder. "Red tape with the permits, talks with a Hollywood producer, hit a few balls with the groundskeeper, and finalized some details for TechieCon."

I thought of what Hattie had said about Lachlan's childhood. How remarkable it was that he'd made it this far. "I bet Ozark University regrets kicking us out."

"The president probably cries in his pillow every night he can't call us alumni."

Lachlan chopped bacon and some veggies, then added them to the pan. His large hands moved with precision and efficiency. I rather liked his hands. They were strong and capable, like Lachlan himself.

"Did I mention I'm flying out tomorrow morning?" Lachlan asked.

Disappointment fell like a snowflake, a faint, delicate thing that melted upon examination. I quickly put on my *that doesn't bother me at all* face. "Going to check in with your parole officer?"

"Paid him off years ago." The frying pan sizzled and snapped. "No, I'm headed to San Francisco for a licensing meeting."

"That sounds very grown-up," I said.

"Way too adulty." Lachlan added a dash of salt, then three shakes of pepper. "I'll be gone for a week."

"I'll use that time to throw wild parties in your pool house." I watched him toss in another handful of bacon, good man that he was. "You know, if this gaming empire doesn't work out, you can definitely find work as a chef."

He added some onion that sizzled in butter. "My mom was a waitress, so I'd hang out at the restaurant a lot. When I was nine, she worked at Champ's All-Night Café. There was a cook there named Bud who helped me with my math homework and taught me some basics in the kitchen. By the time I was ten, I stayed home alone a lot while Mom worked double shifts. I'd cook for us both."

"When we were in college you lived with your dad, though, right?" I thought he'd gone home to Houston every holiday.

Lachlan's large knife sliced down on spinach. "Tried to. I got kicked out at the end of my junior year."

"Then you moved back with your mom?"

"No, she'd passed away by then."

Didn't that feel like a fist to the gut. "I'm sorry." It felt wrong to discuss it from so far away, so I climbed off the stool and stood next to him. "That must've been incredibly hard." My PR antennae began to ping as his underdog story unfolded. "Where did you live after you got kicked out?"

"College was my home," Lachlan said. "My dad took me in for a bit after high school, but I was an unwelcome guest. I was too wild, and I was the kid he and my half-brothers had never asked for. Things were pretty miserable, and as you can attest, finding trouble was my way to cope."

"But you didn't answer my question. Where did you live?"

Lachlan tended to his culinary masterpiece for a few moments before finally answering. "I couch surfed a lot. Spent a few months living in my car the summer of my senior year."

"Lachlan." That was all I could say. A woman who'd built a career on finding the right words had none.

"Please, none of that." Lachlan dragged a chunk of cheese across a grater. He did not skimp on the steps. "No need to pity me. It all turned out okay."

But had it? "And the summer you went to Italy—"

"My dad paid for it, I got in trouble, and then he never talked to me again."

It seemed the most natural thing in the world to rest my hand against Lachlan's back. "Your dad sounds terrible." I couldn't imagine not having a parent to raise me and love me. I was so lucky I had my family. "You never see your father?"

Leaning a hip against the rim of the counter, he brushed cheese off his hands. "Not in years. But he'll be at TechieCon."

"For you?"

"Hardly." Lachlan eased the edges of the omelets with a spatula. "He owns a tech company with interests in the gaming world."

"So that'll be awkward, right?" I studied Lachlan's face, but it revealed nothing.

"I actually look forward to running into him this time." He sprinkled some fresh parsley on his creation.

"Because you're a success." I could understand wanting to stick it to your deadbeat dad.

"I definitely have some updates for him."

"What if we shared some of your 'self-made man' history in your interviews?"

"No." His tone left no room for argument, but I tried anyway.

"You have an incredible story to tell. Raised by a hard-working single mom, basically taking care of yourself, being homeless for a while...*That's* a story people want to hear."

Lachlan speared me a look. "It's not one I'll be telling." Grabbing two plates, Lachlan made short work of loading them with the steaming eggs. "Take a seat."

Tonight he'd forsaken his beloved jeans and tee for a button-down from Paolo's and a pair of pants that rode low on his hips. They suited him almost as much as his slightly maudlin mood did not.

"You seem preoccupied tonight," I said, wondering about the fatigue tugging at Lachlan's eyes. "Is everything all right?"

Lachlan sat beside me and sighed. "I received a dinner invitation from your governor."

I plucked a piece of bacon with my fork, happy Lachlan hadn't skimped on this important food group. "Why is this a problem?"

"Because it's for her yearly tech gathering," he said. "Apparently Governor Hernández invites about five hundred prominent people in the tech space to the capitol for a fancy banquet. She heard I'm moving operations to Sugar Creek and got wind of my plans to invest in STEM initiatives in schools."

"Probably because I sent her a press release," I told him.

"Sounds like a great opportunity to discuss the importance of an issue that means a lot to you."

"Her keynote speaker canceled, and she wants me to fill in."

"Oh." I was familiar with the now yearly event, and it was painfully soon.

"The who's who of industry will be there," Lachlan said. "The CEO of Walmart, the president of Ozark Global Electronics, the head of tech services for every major brand represented in the state."

"With not even three weeks' notice—and just a few days before our *Good Morning America* trip."

"Exactly."

"Okay. We can do this." *Can we do this?*

"It's a formal dinner." He stabbed a bite and chewed.

"This is the part that stresses you out?"

"It'll be froufrou. With cloth napkins and lots of plates. Probably a confusing abundance of forks."

"Fork abundance is not unsurmountable." I was beginning to understand the source of Lachlan's stress.

Reinvigorated by cheesy eggs and a new challenge, I jumped up and rifled through Lachlan's drawers and cabinets. "You're about to get a quick tutorial." In no time I'd gathered a champagne flute, water glasses, three plates of varying sizes, silverware, knives, and a few paper towels that would have to do for cloth napkins.

I pointed to Lachlan's omelet. "Pretend this is a salad."

"But it's not a salad."

"And we give thanks to the Lord for that." I took three more bites, then regretfully put down my fork. "Napkin goes in your lap."

Lachlan complied with my instruction. "See, I always thought you tucked it beneath your chin to catch dribbles of wing sauce." The grin that returned was positively devastating, and I had a feeling he knew it. "Olivia?"

"Yes?"

"You're staring at my lips." Lachlan's eyes steady on mine, he blotted a napkin to his mouth. "Am I wearing the sauce? Pepper in my teeth?"

"There was something there." I met his gaze, refusing to look away despite the fever burning in my cheeks. "But it's definitely gone. Now, let's discuss silverware."

Those forest green eyes remained on me for a long moment before regarding the table setting before him. "Silverware, yes. A riveting topic. Only outdone by the subjects of the Dewey decimal system and corporate tax code."

"Let us begin," I said. "In my right hand I hold a salad fork..."

Half an hour later, I'd wrapped up my demonstration and had nearly rounded home base on my review. "Soup spoon?"

Lachlan held a medium-sized spoon with pride. "Easy one."

"Bonus round. Show me your relish fork."

"Cheeky. I usually save that for the third date, but since you asked..." He produced the tiny pronged instrument with zero hesitation. "You do realize as my wife, you'll be expected to be by my side at the banquet." Lachlan's gaze could melt butter faster than his skillet.

The two of us on a weekend getaway in Little Rock? That sounded like an absolutely terrible idea. "I'm not sure I can get away for this one on such short notice."

"Olivia?" He reached for my hand and threaded our fingers —together, apart, together. "Be my emotional support fake wife."

Why did Lachlan have to be so charming, so handsome?

Why were my defenses so darn weak? "I'll try to clear my schedule."

"I'll take that as a resounding yes." Then Lachlan lifted my hand to his lips and stamped it with warm kiss. "You and me in a hotel room again. What could possibly go wrong?"

CHAPTER
TWENTY-EIGHT
OLIVIA

LACHLAN

Missing me yet, Olivia?

OLIVIA

No. I've taken up with the neighbor in your absence.

LACHLAN

Bernie Haskell? He's got to be at least eighty-five.

OLIVIA

I'm in love, Lachlan. Positively smitten. Has absolutely nothing to do with the fact that Bernie mentioned he has a bad heart, no heirs, and a very healthy pension.

LACHLAN

He shoots forty-eight over par.

OLIVIA

Our love will see us through.

LACHLAN

Besides your roaming eye, everything else okay?

OLIVIA

I ate the last of the leftovers yesterday.

LACHLAN

So...you do miss me.

OLIVIA

Does Bernie cook?

On Thursday I sat in my bedroom in Lachlan's house and returned my attention to the Flair staff meeting playing out on my computer screen. Celeste did not believe in the value of working remotely, but in this case, she had to comply.

"Elton has what?" Celeste asked loudly, as if her voice needed to carry across the miles.

"He's very sick," I said, not feeling so hot myself. I plucked a tissue from the box beside me from the workspace I'd set up in my room. "I spent all day yesterday with him working on the Wagner Ice Cream account." The company had endured a tsunami of backlash when their Keto buttered pecan turned out to be teeming with carbs. "Elton's at the doctor right now, so out of caution, I'm working from home today. Don't want to contaminate anyone if I've caught what Elton has."

Predictably, Celeste rolled her eyes. "Ridiculous." But she continued her meeting, calling on every brand manager to report on their updates.

What was ridiculous was how quiet this house had been without Lachlan. I missed coming home to whatever dinner he'd whipped up and the smell of his special blend of coffee in the morning. I missed hearing the sounds of him rustling in his room at night as I went to sleep. But mostly, I'd wanted more than a few times to pick up the phone and call Lachlan. Just to hear about his day and tell him about mine. How strange that I had adapted to his companionship so fast.

Lachlan would return next Tuesday night, then we'd have about nine days until the governor's banquet. I discovered I didn't dread a weekend away with Lachlan, which concerned me more than the fact that I'd just downed a shot glass of cold medicine.

"Gunnar, how is the pain reliever account going?" Celeste walked the room, and the camera followed her, as if it knew who was the queen.

"Great," Gunnar Zapinski said. "We've created a family-friendly campaign that shows strong favor with our focus groups. America will forget about that bad batch from the summer in no time."

"Wonderful. Morgan, you're up next." Celeste stood behind Morgan, and the two looked like they'd planned their outfits. Both wore variations on a black Halston silk blouse with chunky gold necklaces.

Morgan hit a few keys on her keyboard and shared her screen, presenting a slide that looked handcrafted by one of our graphic artists. "Elite Matches continues to benefit from our social media, Google, and airport digital ads. Our speed dating event was a huge hit and raised ten thousand dollars for charity. That good press led other outlets to pick up the story, and the combined effort pushed sales another eleven percent."

Ugh. It was so cookie-cutter in strategy, but of course, Celeste loved it. "Fantastic!" My boss clasped her hands together. "Simply spectacular."

"Thank you, Celeste." Morgan stared right at the camera, a terrorist sending her audience a message.

"Your turn, Olivia." Celeste stood in the middle of the

conference room, hands on her hips. "Do tell us how your work with Lachlan is progressing."

I threw down my tissue and ignored the sight of my red nose glowing on the screen. "Lachlan's brand reinvention is going better than expected. He looks polished and professional, he's completed most of my rigorous media training, and we have an impressive lineup of interviews and national media appearances."

"Good." Celeste's seal of approval eased the knot in my scratchy throat. "His next event is what?"

"A remote interview with Stock Market Replay network to discuss the rise of Star Gazer, a few majorly ranked celebrity podcasts, then the governor's gala." I might've acted as if Lachlan could face any of those with flawless performances, but the fact was we still had so much work to do.

"Your media lineup is impeccable," Celeste said, and I could hear that *but* coming. "But you're missing a personal angle."

I dabbed at my runny nose. "Lachlan's in everyone's face right now. He'd have to land the cover of *Us Weekly* magazine to be any more visible."

"I'm currently working on that publication for *my* client." Morgan smirked to the camera again.

"We've discussed this many times, Olivia." Celeste resumed her pacing of the conference room, confusing the autofocus cameras. "What really burrows in people's hearts is the *human* side of the individual."

"I've encouraged Lachlan to discuss his makeover process... for burrowing purposes."

"That does not pluck one single heartstring," Celeste snapped. "Dig deeper. What else is behind his young launch to fame? Who was he at age ten? Sixteen? What dark moments has Lachlan overcome?"

Marrying me, for one. "I'll work on that."

"See that you do." Celeste tapped her tablet stylus to her chin. "Find his story and then tell it well."

"Lachlan's very guarded about his private life," I said. "There's so much about his past that he was reluctant to share even with me." He'd made it clear his family history was off-limits. "The odds of him sharing deeply personal revelations are not good."

Celeste pressed her hands to the table and glared. "Don't think like his wife, Olivia. Think like his brand manager."

"But—" A spasm of coughs interrupted whatever profound rebuttal I had.

"I'll be announcing the promotion finalists soon." Celeste gave me a parting, pointed look. "You wouldn't want to mess up your chances."

CHAPTER
TWENTY-NINE
OLIVIA

THIRTY HOURS later I lay in a curled heap in bed, fondly recalling a time when I possessed the will to live.

Oh, dear, sweet, younger Olivia. She had energy. She brushed her teeth. She could stand upright for more than fifteen minutes without dramatically throwing her hand over her own forehead and flailing back to the mattress. Her life goals amounted to more than a fervent wish to be horizontal.

The Plague That Shall Not Be Named had tracked me down and made me its own. I'd thought I was immune. Olivia Sutton did not get sick, but here I was. Prostrate on sheets that could use a good wash, clutching a blanket, and regretting the shards of sunlight that so rudely barged through the outer edges of the blinds.

It was two o'clock on a thrilling Friday afternoon, and I'd done little more than sleep and attempt to watch Netflix. Judging from the credits scrolling on my TV to a show I had zero memory of watching, I'd succeeded at only one of those.

I had to sit up. What I needed was my laptop and to answer the two hundred work emails that certainly waited for me.

Celeste had called a dozen times in the last few days under the guise of checking on me, but in my sickened state, I had no motivation to paint it as anything more than what it was. Celeste called to nudge me back to work.

When the phone rang one more time, I answered without bothering to check the screen. "Yes, Celeste?"

"Why don't you sneak into your office if you get a chance?" she suggested, completely oblivious to my pitiful greeting. "Wear a mask, and I'll tell everyone to stay away from you."

"I'm contagious," I told her. "That's why. The CDC says I need to quarantine."

"Did you personally speak to them?"

My nasal passages had inflated to twice their size, and a thick fog billowed in my head. I did not have the wherewithal to convince my boss that I deserved a few sick days. "If I come into the office, I'll contaminate people, and they'll be mad. Then when I tell them my boss directed me to come in, they'll be angry at you. And sue you. Do you want a lawsuit, Celeste?"

"My goodness, you're dramatic when you're sick," she said. "Nobody's suing anyone. I didn't *demand* you to come in to work. But since you're awake, why not fire up that computer and get to cracking? Whenever I'm sick, I find the best thing for me is not to wallow in it, but to push myself to new limits and dive into work. Mind over matter."

"My matter has a migraine and can only breathe out of one nostril." It was only a mild case, but I still felt ten shades of miserable. "I'd love to talk more, but it's time for me to take my fourth nap."

"Who's going to drive my kids to soccer tomorrow?"

"Their mom?" Someone really needed to dim that sunshine out there.

"I have an early meeting."

"Maybe it's time to stop withholding the fun from Morgan."

Celeste huffed. "I don't trust her with my children."

"But you trust someone with a plague?"

"Do quit whining, Olivia. I guess I'll find someone to take the children. Maybe their nanny can come in early. Or Elton. I could ask him."

"Goodbye, Celeste."

"Did you type up my notes for the *Parenting for Professionals* podcast?"

"Last week. They're in your inbox. Goodbye, Celeste." I felt like a train was trying to barrel through my head.

"Alexander wants to know where you think he put those science flash cards you made him."

"Left pocket of his backpack." I plucked a tissue from the box and blew my sore nose. "Goodbye, Celes—"

"He's asking me to create flash cards for his English test too. I don't know what he wants. If I sent his notes to you, would you be able to make them?"

I meant to agree to her request, but my sinus medication kicked in, and instead I heard myself say, "Figure it out, please. Nighty night. See you next week."

"Next week?!" Celeste squawked.

Click.

Later I would burn with regret over hanging up on my boss.

But right now, in my delusional, fevered state, it felt pretty darn good.

Not as good as having two functional nasal passages. But moderately dandy, indeed.

With a contented sigh, I snuggled into my pillow and closed my eyes. I was just about to fully commit to my next nap when a gentle knock rattled my door.

"Go away," I said. "I'm not making flash cards."

"Livvy?" Three more knocks followed. "Your studly hero has returned." The door cracked and Lachlan stuck his head inside.

That got my attention. I shot to a sitting position and waved him away. "Go away, Lachlan. I'm contagious. I'm a plague carrier. Save yourself. You have a whole life to live. And by life, I mean interviews that you cannot cancel unless dead." My husband didn't move, but instead stood there looking impossibly handsome except for the frown marring his brow. I did not want to be responsible for anyone else getting sick. "Leave or I'll tell the world I'm one of your four wives, and together we make a happy cult called Lachlan's Ladies."

"You know I believe in fake monogamy in my fake marriage. You and I are like penguins. The two of us bonded for eternity."

"Stop it. You're making my head hurt worse."

"Canadian geese. Gray wolves. Shunning all others and shackled together for life." Despite my dire warnings, Lachlan walked to my bedside and rested a hand to my forehead. "Babe, are you okay?"

"Yes." No. "Mostly."

"Define mostly."

"I want someone to remove my head from my neck, blow it out with an air compressor, and return it to my body."

"Sounds very doable."

"What day is it? What year of our Lord?" The cobwebs cleared enough for me to check the date on my phone. "Aren't you back early?" Maybe I had lost some days in a snot-induced coma.

"I came back as soon as you said you were sick."

"That is so sweet." I rubbed a hand across my damp nose. "But I didn't tell you I was sick."

"Yeah, you did. I called last night and you mentioned it." His hand made smooth, even strokes over my hair. "You said, and I quote, 'I'm dying, Lachlan, and I need you to wipe my brow and hand-feed me chocolates. The good kind. Not the ones from the dollar store down the road.'"

Well. Past Olivia sounded drunk. But she did have good taste in candy. "I'm quite all right now. Please get out before my germs destroy us both."

"You sound like there's a pillow lodged in your throat, and you look like—"

I opened one eye. "Careful there."

Lachlan gave a muffled cough. "You look like a supermodel who stars in every man's fantasy."

"Much better." I flopped to my side, letting my cheek rest against the cool pillowcase. "Do I star in your fantasy, Lachlan?" Sick me could ask that. Healthy me would not even recall it.

A beat of silence preceded Lachlan's deep sigh. "Maybe."

I smiled at the very idea. "Maybe I think of you too." My eyes fluttered open when I heard Lachlan loudly call my name from the doorway. "What?" Where was I? Had I fallen back to sleep?

"I asked you if you'd eaten." He leaned against the frame, a man who knew how to fill a space and all my thoughts.

"Not since this morning." My sisters had brought me food daily and left it at my door, but I couldn't recall accomplishing lunch. "I don't know."

"Have you actually taken your temp?" he asked.

"Parts of me are warm."

"Olivia..."

"Fine. I have a fever. But it's gone down to 101."

I heard a subdued curse, then, "Why didn't you call me sooner?"

"I had my sisters."

"But you didn't have your husband."

My wheezy heart swelled a bit at that. "I did miss you."

"Now I *know* you're ill."

"It surprised me too." I ripped another Kleenex from the box and liberally dabbed at my uncooperative nose. How could something so stopped up be so drippy? "I missed talking to you. I missed our morning meetups in the kitchen over coffee, and I missed our nightly dinners. Sylvie cooked for me, but it wasn't the same."

The silence stretched so long, I thought Lachlan had either walked away or I'd fallen back to sleep. But when I opened my eyes, there he was. Still hovering in the doorway, staring at me as if I'd said something sweet. Had I? I couldn't recall.

"I'll make you some soup," Lachlan finally said. "Will you be okay?"

"Yes, Lachlan." I blew my hair out of my face. "I've survived without you for days."

"But you shouldn't have." Then Lachlan Hayes, the man whose last name I carried, gave me a gentle smile. "Call me if you need anything."

I didn't know if a symptom of this plague was finding your fake husband utterly endearing and adorable, but that was a whole different type of fever I needed to bring *way* down. "I'm just gonna rest my eyes."

"Sweet dreams, wife." Lachlan shut the door with a click, and I heard his voice one more time. "Olivia?"

I tugged the covers to my chin, feeling measurably better now that Lachlan was home. "Yes?"

"I missed you too."

CHAPTER
THIRTY
OLIVIA

THE NEXT DAY I woke up and decided I would live after all.

My nose was now at least semifunctional, and a vise no longer squeezed my head in its steely grip. Arms and legs no longer ached, and the sun shining through the slats didn't make me want to rip the blinds off the wall and toss them out the window.

The worst was over. Thanks to meds, more meds, and the soup Lachlan had left at my door, I was on the healing side of sick.

Yesterday afternoon Lachlan had sat outside my door and talked to me for hours. He'd refused to take my soup bowl until I'd eaten at least half. Which hadn't been too much of a burden because his chicken soup had been a dish made of perfection and magic. And also very sweet.

These past few days as the not-so-walking dead had given me time to think about Lachlan. Even in my phlegmatic state, I'd had to admit the truth: Lachlan Hayes was not the same guy I'd known in college. Maybe he wasn't even the same guy then either.

The grown-up version of Lachlan was kind, thoughtful, and quick with a joke or a home-cooked meal. I loved the sound of his rumbly, low-pitched voice, and the way his eyes held mischief as they followed me in a room. He'd been an attentive nurse since he'd returned home, and I'd welcomed the company instead of finding his presence something to tolerate.

And he'd left California early. For me.

Every time I thought about it, I felt like the heroine in a romance novel.

But did I want to be?

Stretching my arms, I reached for the phone. Twelve texts from Celeste. One from each of my family members, inquiring about my condition. Sylvie asked if Dr. Tall and Ginger had been taking good care of me.

Did Lachlan care for me? No, I couldn't think on that today. Too much to do.

No matter how I felt, I had days of quarantine ahead. Now that the fog had dissipated, a familiar ache grew in my stomach over the thought of letting Celeste and my clients down. Plus, Lachlan needed more media training.

After a quick shower, I brushed my teeth, changed into some clean clothes, and crawled back into bed, laptop humming beside me.

"Olivia?" Lachlan's voice passed through the closed door and slipped around my shoulders like a warm hug.

"Yes?"

"I heard the shower," he said. "How are you feeling?"

"Better, but do not come in here. I mean it." Scraps of conversations came back to me in random order. Had I told Lachlan I'd missed him?

I had.

I clapped my hand over my mouth and squeezed my bleary eyes shut. Oh, no.

Another memory floated through my consciousness.

Lachlan had said he'd missed *me*.

What were we supposed to do with that?

"I think I'm going to make it," I called out, wondering if being ill had rattled my brain.

"Are you saying I need to cancel my help wanted ad for a new wife?" he asked.

"Afraid so." I shut my laptop on Celeste's last email. "We both know I'm irreplaceable."

I heard a quiet laugh from the hall, then the jostling of plates. "I made us some breakfast," Lachlan said. "I'm opening the door and pushing your tray in."

"Are you masked?"

"Masked, gloved, and wearing body armor made of made of disinfectant wipes I taped together."

He was none of those things, but Lachlan bravely entered my room, set down a tray, and closed the door.

"Don't go downstairs yet." I got up and padded across the room. "I saw that other plate. Stay and eat with me."

"Feeling lonely in there?" he asked.

I had barely seen anyone in days. "I'm craving friendly, intellectual conversation." And bacon. "But you'll do."

Lachlan laughed, and I could hear him settle onto the floor. "I called your grandma and sisters and let them know you'd slept through the night and seemed better."

I stilled. "How do you know how I slept?"

His fork clanked against a plate. "I checked on you a few times."

"That wasn't necessary."

"I've watched enough true crime to know if the wife dies in the home, the husband is always the prime suspect."

I picked up a still-warm biscuit and took a glorious bite. "Just protecting yourself?"

"Exactly."

"And how many times did you check on me?" I asked.

"Not sure."

"Round up," I said. "Ballpark. General range. Tally the total and carry the one."

He yawned. "Every few hours."

Buttery eggs melted on my tongue as I processed that. He'd checked on me? Who did that? "Aside from the small creep factor of you staring at me through the night, that was very kind. You must be exhausted."

"We creeps don't need sleep. How are those biscuits?"

I took another bite and knew only bliss and nirvana. "Amazing. I'll have to reconnect with my Spanx, but worth it."

"You can borrow mine."

My phone pinged once, then three more times.

"Is that one of your boyfriends texting?" asked Lachlan from the other side. "He sounds needy."

"It's my boss. And she is needy." I rapidly typed back a response. "She can't recall where I dropped off her dry-cleaning last week."

"Are you her personal assistant?"

"Sometimes it feels like it," I admitted. "Last night at midnight she texted me for her own garage code." That one had gone unanswered until now. How many times did I have to tell her it was the year of her daughter's birth?

Lachlan's voice held that sexy morning rasp. "Has Celeste asked how you're faring or checked to see if you need anything?"

I scrolled through text after text, but it was for naught. "Celeste knows if I needed anything I would ask."

"Huh."

I didn't like that *huh*. "As much as I'm enjoying breakfast, I do need to get back to work."

He shifted against the door, and I imagined Lachlan sitting there in his Pac-Man t-shirt, faded jeans, and bare feet. "I called a doctor friend of mine, and he said you need to take it easy for a few more days, even if you're improving. Rest up."

Maybe it was the medication. Could've been the security I felt with the wall between us. But I took a bite of bacon, criss-crossed my legs on the hardwood floor, then pressed the rarely used share button on my heart. "Here's the deal, husband. Whether I want to or not, there's no time to slow down right now. I have a promotion on the line, plus a parade of events for you. Celeste sees rest as weakness."

"That's dumb."

"While that is profound leadership input, I know my boss. I could be in a medically induced coma, and she'd expect me to call in for our daily meeting. Life is not to be rescheduled for frivolities like sickness." I remembered being so thankful the funeral of Rosie's fiancé had been on a Saturday, so I could take half the day off *almost* guilt-free.

"You sound really stressed in there," Lachlan said.

"I have so much on the line." Later I would regret pouring out my worries, but this morning it felt good to have someone to listen. "I have my regular accounts that I maintain. Then there's your rebranding."

"Which is going incredible," Lachlan said, clearly midchew. "I'm smokin' hot now, so... mission accomplished."

I pushed a bite of eggs across my plate. "If only it were that easy." Lachlan was a bit of a wild card. He wanted a more professional image, yet he still had his stubborn limits. "We can't afford to fail."

We ate for a full minute in silence, then, "Have you ever failed, Olivia?"

"College. Junior year. I was studying abroad..."

"That's the only time things didn't work out for you?" Lachlan sounded strangely unimpressed.

"That semester scarred me for life." If I closed my eyes, I was right back in Italy. My parents informing me the university had kicked me out. The PR company emailing to rescind their invitation for my paid internship my senior year. I was adrift. Until Celeste had saved me. "Then there was Taylor. Major disaster."

"Because you broke up?"

I guess my husband could hear the ugly truth. "Over a year ago, Celeste dangled another New York promotion to our team. I was dating Taylor, and we were serious. I thought I was in love." How pathetic that all seemed now. "After college, I had sworn all fealty and allegiance to my life plan. But Taylor started talking marriage and our future, and I fell for it. No ring and no formal announcement, but we had a date, and we'd made plans."

"For a wedding?"

"Yes." How stupid did I feel about that now? I'd even talked to Paisley, my cousin who worked as an event planner, and we'd taken a tour of a few wedding venues and talked ceremony details. "The job opportunity came up, and Taylor told me he had no interest, but he would follow me to New York if I landed it." I could still see that one night so clearly in my head. It was forever imprinted in my memory. "One evening we had dinner at our favorite restaurant, and I spent the entire meal telling him I'd made contact with a potentially big client. I stupidly laid out my entire PR plan, the one that would've secured my promotion."

"I think I hate this Taylor guy already."

"The next Monday he had lunch with the company CEO,

pitched her *my* branding ideas, then won her over. She signed with Flair two days later."

"You knew this because Taylor told you?"

"I knew this because Celeste announced Taylor's promotion at a staff meeting."

Lachlan let out a ragged exhale. "As if staff meetings aren't bad enough."

"The worst." I'd had to stay in the room for the rest of the hour, looking at his satisfied face while a war of shock and confusion waged inside me. "Taylor left for New York after that. I didn't go with him."

"Geez, Livvy."

"Yeah." Going off-plan? Not for me. It had never, ever served me well. I needed to remember that. "So, yes, I've fumbled more than once."

A plate clanked and a fork followed. I wondered if I'd ruined our little breakfast with my tale of a love gone wrong.

"In gaming you fail forward," Lachlan finally said.

"No thank you." That sounded absolutely terrible. "No time for that."

"But it's a good thing. The idea is without the fails, you won't move forward to your destination where the best stuff is —to your real reward. You fail forward, learning how to do it better and better, until you eventually defeat the Big Bad."

Sometimes I wondered if Lachlan was my Big Bad. "I take it that's the enemy?"

"If you think of it as your enemy," he said, "you've already lost. The Big Bad is the challenge. And yeah, maybe it's the evil character you have to defeat, but more than that it's the things within yourself you need to overcome to make that happen."

A butterfly of anxiety flapped inside my chest, and I took a drink of coffee, hoping to numb the flutter. "Maybe I'll look into failing forward next year."

"What if your time is now, Olivia?" I'd never heard his tone so serious. "What if the things you think are catastrophes are really opportunities to take you to a better place?"

That sounded like the inside of a Hallmark card. "Your failing forward might work for games, but it doesn't work in my business."

"What would you do if you knew it was a guaranteed success? Forget about money or fears or Celeste's expectations. What would you try, Olivia?"

Revisit our kiss.

Wait. Where had that idea come from?

Absolutely not.

No more kissing Lachlan. No more *thinking* about kissing Lachlan.

"You still there, Liv?"

Good heavens, I loved his voice.

"There is one idea I've had for a while. It's probably silly." Actually I'd planned it out my senior year of college and hadn't ever shared it with a soul.

"Let's hear it," Lachlan said.

"Years ago I created a business plan for my own PR agency. Sutton and Associates."

"Sassy Sutton's."

I traced the grain of the wood floor with a finger. "Over the years I've edited the plan."

"You'd represent more exotically handsome gamers?"

"I'd ditch the theme days." That would be first on the agenda.

"No more Queen Elizabeth?" Lachlan asked. "I do love a good tiara."

"I'd cut the workweek to no more than forty-five hours, with exceptions." I was so tired of working seven days a week. And just so...tired. "I'd steal my friend Elton away, and he'd be my right-hand man. And together we'd build a business. One that cared about people and kept their best interests in mind but gave world-class public relations services without compromising on our ethics."

"Sassy Sutton's sounds like a solid business idea." Lachlan sipped his coffee with noisy gusto. "I'd hire you. So why don't you do it?"

Like it was that easy. "It takes money I don't have." I thought of the balance on my credit card from investing in a closet of designer clothes. Celeste expected a Gucci appearance, even though my paycheck was more Nordstrom Rack. "And most businesses fail."

"You wouldn't know until you tried."

"Celeste has taken me under her wing and mentored me for years. She's laid out a career path for me that makes sense, and I'd be stupid to walk away from Flair." I was *this* close to achieving that next level. "Besides, I'm happy at Flair."

"Are you?" Lachlan asked.

"I will be when I get my promotion. Then all the long hours and sacrifices will have paid off. Failure might be beneficial when you're playing a game, Lachlan. But it's a huge deterrent in the real world." And when giving your heart away. "One failure can ruin a reputation, a career—a life." Like mine. "I cannot—I *will* not—let that happen. That's why I've stuck out this marriage, right? And it's why I'll make sure you come out of this winter looking like the smartest, savviest CEO to ever dominate a boardroom or walk a Hollywood red carpet."

Plates rattled again, and from the scrapes and thuds, I knew Lachlan had gotten to his feet. "I'll do my best not to let you down," he said. "I've studied your notes on interview skills and practiced like our lives depend on it. But, Olivia, nobody's perfect, right? If we have some losses along the way, it's going to be okay."

"Easy for you to say." Yes, he had stockholders he was accountable to, but Lachlan didn't answer to Celeste or the inner perfectionist screaming in his head. "Have you beaten your Big Bad, Lachlan?"

I heard his soft puff of laughter. "For me, it's not about beating. It's about overcoming challenges and ending up where I need to be."

"Where do you want to be?" I leaned closer to the door to hear his answer. I expected him to say more movies, bigger money, and worldwide notoriety.

"I'm still figuring that out," Lachlan said quietly. "When I get there, I'll let you know."

"Lachlan?" Though I needed to get to work, I was suddenly loath to lose his company. "Thank you for breakfast. And...for everything you've done."

He took his sweet time in responding. "Anything for my beloved bride."

"Meet back here for lunch?" I winced as the impulsive offer slipped off my tongue. Of course Lachlan wouldn't want to have hallway chitchat again, especially now that he was assured I was on the mend. "Never mind. I have—"

"I'll be here at noon," he said. "Holler if you need anything."

I didn't move, didn't breathe until Lachlan's footfalls faded down the hall and echoed down the stairs.

Holler if I need anything?

Well, Lachlan Hayes.

I'm worried I'm beginning to need you.

CHAPTER
THIRTY-ONE
LACHLAN

"You had to know we'd only get one hotel room."

"Sure," Olivia said as she followed me down the hall of the Grand Embassy Hotel. "Of course, I did." Two weeks after I came home from San Francisco, Olivia was well out of quarantine, back to work, and looking as beautiful as my next heartbreak.

I stopped at room 366 and flashed the keycard until the lock clicked. "Then maybe you could turn down the look of horror on your face?"

Olivia leaned against the wall, gorgeous in a black turtleneck sweater and jeans. Her lips pressed together, as if smothering a smile. "It's jet lag."

I turned, the two of us standing in our own little alcove in front of our door, shielded from prying eyes and the stray passersby. "From a four-hour drive?"

"I haven't slept much this week."

I leaned closer and watched the pulse in her neck skitter. "Thinking of me, Livvy?"

She didn't back away and didn't give an inch. Not that I expected her to. Not my Olivia.

She licked her lips, her eyes steady on mine. "I did have a hot dream about you last night."

This sounded interesting. "Oh, yeah?"

"Yes," she said. "We got divorced in Arizona. It's very steamy there."

My new obsession was ruffling Olivia. I no longer lived for food or oxygen, but moments when she was thrown off balance and pulled out of her buttoned-up, control-freak bubble. "I've caught you checking me out," I told her.

She did not find this amusing. "No, you haven't."

"I have. Sometimes I'll find you staring at me in total adoration."

"I think the word you're looking for is *befuddlement*."

"That's French for *lust*, right?" Before Olivia could snark back, I flung open the door, grabbed her hand, and led her inside.

The chilly hotel room was a modern space with a full balcony that looked out over the city. A basket filled with snacks and drinks sat on a desk, stuffed with a welcome card from the governor herself. I shoved our suitcases into a closet before throwing my tired body on the bed and briefly closing my eyes. I'd been awake much of last night prepping for my keynote, and my eyes stung from exhaustion. I could hear Olivia shuffling about the room, slamming drawers, and huffing dramatically. Any hopes of her taking a catnap with me died a quick death.

I opened one eye and found my wife standing over me, one hand on her hip. "Is there a problem, Olivia?"

My wife regarded me like I was a complete moron. "There's only one bed."

"I'm aware." I snuggled deeper into the mattress. "Fortunately, it's a comfortable one."

"You did this on purpose."

Now both eyes popped open. "Did what?"

"Got a room with only one bed. I've read a few thousand romance novels, so I know this plot device very well."

"I didn't make the hotel arrangements. The governor's office did." I sat up, weary to the bone. "You do know everyone thinks we're *really* married, right? Your family might doubt us, but the rest of the world does not. Thus, one bed would not be considered abnormal."

Rubbing her arms, she stomped to the thermostat, then punched a few buttons. "Most hotel rooms have two beds."

"This one doesn't." The plush mattress squeaked as I got up. "You can sleep here tonight. I'll take the couch."

Olivia eyed a green couch that looked like it would hold exactly a third of my body. "So you can claim the right to complain and make me feel guilty? I don't think so. I'll be the one taking the couch."

That thing looked as comfortable as an army cot. "You'll take the bed, and that's final." She looked worn out too. "That way you'll have more energy to insult me on the way home."

We spent the next two hours with our laptops, quietly working. It was a companionable silence, one I didn't feel a need to fill with conversation. I watched Olivia typing furiously, then grabbing her phone for a text. Every so often her forehead would wrinkle as she frowned, and her lips would pucker in pouty consideration. Her hyperfocus was commendable and so like Olivia. Meanwhile, I could hardly stay attentive to my emails with her five feet away. Her scent wrapped around me and made me want to do nothing more than seek out the exact spot she'd sprayed that perfume. Would I find it at the base of her neck? In that sensitive spot beneath her ear?

She'd kicked off her shoes, and her pink-painted toes wiggled into the comforter as if to gain warmth. My wife, who'd thrown her hair into a loose ponytail, occasionally mumbled to herself, and I found it distracting in the most ridiculously adorable way.

Her gaze drifted over her keyboard...and met mine.

I didn't want to watch Olivia.

But she made it hard to look away.

A small, reluctant smile curved those full lips, and the impact reminded me of the time I got hit in the sternum with a fast-pitch baseball. My heartbeat kicked up a notch, and all I could think about was capturing that smart mouth with my own. What would Olivia taste like today? What would she feel like in my arms right now? Would she kiss with all that frenetic energy that vibrated around her? Would she opt for a slow kiss, completely in opposition to her driven, get-it-done-now personality? Or maybe an urgent meeting of the lips, passionate and quick?

"Something on your mind, Lachlan?"

I dragged my focus from Olivia's mouth to her eyes. "Just plotting a new video game. Working on the storyline."

"Oh." She slowly nodded, a piece of her hair tumbling from its knot. "How does it end?"

"I'm not sure yet." I locked eyes with my wife once again. "But I'm dying to find out."

I'D HAD MY SHARE OF PRETTY DATES, BUT THE WOMAN ON MY ARM tonight beat them all.

Olivia's heels made loud clicks against the sidewalk as we exited the limo and walked to the capitol building. She wore stilettos that brought her height almost to my shoulder and a floor-length red gown with a slit that gave a man ideas. Her hair hung in loose waves, reminding me of the leading ladies from those black-and-white noir movies my mom made me watch on her rare Saturday nights off.

Stars twinkled in the inky sky above us as the late-October wind turned cool and warned us winter waited in the wings. Olivia shivered into her coat at a chilly gust, and I curved my arm around her and nestled her into my side for warmth.

Two men in tuxedos and name tags stood in the near distance as the entrance came in sight.

"Lachlan. Wait." Olivia stepped off the sidewalk so another couple could pass.

"Yes?"

"I..." Her bottom lip held between her teeth, she reached for my tie and gave it a slight tug to the left, then brushed away any lint that dared to linger on my coat. Her hands against my chest had me sucking in a breath and counting backward from ten.

"Everything okay?" Because if she kept touching me, I was not going to be okay.

Finally her eyes met mine. "I just wanted to tell you that you're ready for this. You've practiced, you've prepared, and you're the man of the hour. These people are here to see you."

Now why did she have to go and be nice? Where had that come from? "I think most of them are here for a free meal."

"No, I've been tracking the event's social media pages, and you've been the talk all week. I want you to remember that you've worked hard to be the person so many of these attendees look up to. You not only deserve to sit at their table, but you're now the executive at the head of the table."

It was like my every insecurity had scrolled across my forehead and Olivia had read each one. "Thank you."

"When you give your keynote, remember to let your eyes

sweep the left, right, and middle of the room. Don't rush it, and don't be afraid to glance down at your notecards."

"I was supposed to bring those notecards?" At her stricken face, I pulled them from my inside pocket. "Oh, these."

Olivia's hands clasped my arms, and she squeezed as if transferring all her expert communicator superpowers. "If you get nervous, remember I'm right there in the audience cheering you on."

"That doesn't sound like something my sworn enemy would say."

"She has the night off." Olivia's smile was slow and hesitant. "Your fill-in wife and PR coach is here instead."

"I'm glad you are here." Our eyes met and held, a fragile moment that seemed to halt the clock. Defenses down, vulnerability peeking through, I would've been content to watch Olivia all night.

But then she dropped her hold and took a step back. "Let's go in there and talk broadband, chip advancements, artificial intelligence, and all that other techie crap I won't understand." Olivia added a final surprise, lacing her fingers with mine as we walked through the doors hand in hand.

Almost as if we were married.

CHAPTER

THIRTY-TWO

OLIVIA

HAD the dinner been a baseball game, Lachlan's speech would've been a grand slam.

Was his keynote perfect? No. But it was pretty darn good.

Feeling about ten pounds lighter, I resumed my seat as his standing ovation trailed to a close and returned my napkin to my lap.

"Your husband is quite impressive." Governor Hernández dragged her plate of chocolate cheesecake toward her.

"Thank you," I said. "He was a bit nervous about tonight."

"He shouldn't have been." The governor nodded to an attendee passing the table. "Lachlan's a legend in the gaming world. Isn't that right, honey?"

Governor Hernández's husband, Stuart, swallowed his bite of cheesecake and nodded. "Can't tell you how many times *Mars Wars* has gotten me in trouble. I sit down to play for a few minutes, and the next thing I know half the day has passed. Do you play it, Mrs. Hayes?"

"I don't. Work keeps me pretty busy." A few weeks ago this admission wouldn't have registered on my emotional seismograph. But tonight, the needle left jagged pitches, measuring the force of my unexpected guilt. *Mars Wars* was Lachlan's opus, the work that changed his life. And I hadn't even laid eyes on it. I needed to add that to my hefty to-do list.

"You have to try the original game," Mr. Hernández said. "It's genius."

"And addictive," the governor added. "Stuart even has me playing. I'm partial to the phone app version myself. Gives me something to do during boring budget sessions."

"Hey." Lachlan pulled out his seat and settled in, his cheeks flushed a faint pink. "I think I sweat through my tux."

"You did great." I patted his hand. When Lachlan's arm slipped around the back of my chair, it felt like the most natural thing in the world to lean into his side. He was so sturdy, a solid wall of warmth and comfort. Sometimes being with him was easy—too easy. "Everyone loved it," I told him. "You added that funny Comic Con story and didn't even tell me."

"Did the joke land?"

"You couldn't hear everyone laughing?"

"The roaring in my ears was too loud."

I smiled at Lachlan's sweet discomfort. "It will get easier. I promise."

"A toast." The governor lifted her wineglass. "What a dynamic speech. Hopefully it will inspire all the tech and corporate leaders here to do as you have and invest in their communities and schools. To Lachlan."

"To Lachlan." I clinked my glass to Lachlan's and took a sip, sharing a smile with my husband.

"Now." The governor set down her drink and put her business face on. "Let's talk about what I can do to get more entrepreneurs to relocate to our fine state."

I DIDN'T WANT TO NOTICE HOW MY FAKE HUSBAND CUT A DASHING figure tonight, but it would be like not noticing the Empire State Building was tall or that the Pacific Ocean was wet. Ignoring him wouldn't change the fact anyway—Lachlan looked disarmingly attractive. Male models would weep in jealousy. Hollywood actors should emulate his style, his face, his smolder.

Maybe it was just because I had a thing for men in tuxes, but the sight of Lachlan in formal wear made my skin heat and put my senses in near-meltdown mode. Paolo had selected Lachlan's suit, picking one that fit his personality. My designer friend had eschewed tradition and instead paired Lachlan's black pants and white shirt with a cranberry velvet tuxedo jacket. On some men it might've looked silly, but it was perfect for a quirky game designer. Even with the pop of color, Lachlan stood regal and intimidating, a man to be emulated and observed. And observe I did. Too much. I committed Lachlan's appearance to memory, right down to the faint stubble along his jaw and the Pac-Man socks he'd sneaked and probably thought I hadn't noticed.

But I caught every detail about Lachlan.

This was not good. Not good at all.

Traces of shame still lingered when I thought back to how I'd mooned over Taylor. I became a student of his every nuance as well, until I was so in love I couldn't see that things had changed, and I was being used. I'd been so blind. But never again, right? I'd attempt love once more, but this time according to my timeline. And that plan clearly stated a life-altering romance couldn't happen for a few more years.

"You two should get out there and dance." Governor

Hernández waved a hand toward the dance floor as a band played a familiar John Legend song.

"No, we can't," I blurted.

Dance? As in voluntarily wrap myself in Lachlan's arms and pretend like I loved him? My recent illness had left a side effect not noted by too many medical journals—a strong affection for one's fake husband. Admittedly, a rare lingering symptom. I was probably going to be contacted any day for some clinical trials.

"I mean, it might get in the way of some networking Lachlan wants to do," I added with a little more confidence.

"Oh, I don't know." Lachlan leveled those green eyes right at me. "I think I've talked to everyone I need to."

"Come on." The governor turned toward her husband. "Stuart and I used to dance all the time as newlyweds. Remember that, Stuart?"

"I do indeed," Stuart said. "Hated every minute of it."

Governor Hernández took another swig of wine. "Seriously, I'll probably have to hike taxes for how much I spent on that band. Go enjoy them."

"Lachlan doesn't like to dance." I patted Lachlan's arm. "Right, sweetie?"

"It's true, I don't." He extended his open hand, his large fingers unfurling one at a time. "I love it."

"But he has two left feet," I protested.

"Yep," he said. "And they know how to tear up a dance floor. Let's go."

"Aw, aren't they precious, Stuart?" Governor Hernández rested her head on her husband's shoulder.

"Adorbs."

"Don't they remind you of us?"

"Yes," Mr. Hernández said, "except they look like they like each other."

"Oh, knock it off. All I said was you could've unloaded the dishwasher. It's not like I asked you to sleep in the backyard again."

With little choice, I slipped my hand into Lachlan's and let him lead me to the floor. The lights had dimmed and the band transitioned to a slow song about unrequited love. I personally didn't relate to that topic. Where were the love songs about ice cream and tacos? Those were some power ballads a person could sink her soul into.

"I hadn't even finished my cheesecake," I said as Lachlan's right hand palmed my back and drew me toward him. "If you press me any closer, we'll look indecent."

"The closer we are, the more we appear happily wed."

His warm body aligned with mine as he shifted us slowly across the floor. I tried to ignore the tingles along my skin and the giddy waves of nerves in my stomach. But when Lachlan reached out and drew his finger along the edge of my cheek, my hormones strapped on jetpacks and blasted off.

"What are you doing?" I whispered.

"Acting like I adore my wife," Lachlan told me. "We have three cameras trained on us right now, and the guy in the gray suit standing by the coffee service is a reporter from *Tech Gazette*. Lots of eyes watching." His gaze dropped to mine. "Permission granted to let your hands roam."

"I wasn't going to ask."

"I saw the question in your haughty, yet lust-filled eyes."

This man. "The only thing I'm lusting for is my half-eaten dessert back at the table."

Lachlan spun me out, only to reel me back in. My hand landed with a thud against his chest, and for some reason I couldn't find the will to remove it. Beneath my fingers was a firm wall of muscle and a heart that beat steady. I caught the scent of Lachlan's aftershave, the notes of cedar and spice daring me to lean in.

"Did you just sniff me, Sutton?"

I startled and shook my head. "No. Don't be silly."

"It's okay." Lachlan's hand made a slow, lingering climb up my back to settle at my nape. "I think about your perfume all the time." Green eyes searched my face, and his lips curved. "It's so faint sometimes it's just a whisper in the air. But I love the hint of flowers and oranges. A little sweet and a little tart." He angled us away from another couple, his voice for my ears only. "I'm still not used to your scent in the house. Sometimes you leave for work before I get up, and when I go down to the kitchen, I can smell your perfume there. Like a secret message just for me." His thumb made featherlight sweeps against the back of my neck. "Olivia was here."

It was probably my line next, but my brain locked up, and all I could do was hold tighter to Lachlan and wish everyone else would disappear.

Lachlan swayed against me. "But that perfume of yours really wreaks havoc on me in the evening," he said. "When it's just a ghost of a fragrance, when I have to work to catch it— that's when it drives me wild."

I was a puddle in a dress. A melting pool of awareness and heat. "Lachlan..." That was it. That was my complete sentence. A hundred impressions and feelings, yet words couldn't capture one of them.

"I like to look at you at night." His arms tightened around me. "Did you know that?"

Not quite as sexy, but also not a deal-breaker. "Like when I'm sleeping?"

Lachlan's lips twitched before sliding into a smile. "Like when you're sitting on the couch before bed. Your eyes are a little tired, that rod straight posture relaxes into the cushion, and you always put your hair up in some wild concoction. You've got a novel in your hand, and you're totally engrossed and in another world. When you read your mouth parts a little." His finger stroked across my lips. "Your eyes slide across the page, back and forth. I hear you sigh or watch you smile, and I wonder what's happening in that book that has you so transfixed. But then I realize I'm the one who's transfixed because I'm staring at you and can't turn away."

No man had ever looked at me like this. Like he wanted to pick me up and carry me back upstairs. "Cowboys," I heard myself say.

"What?"

"My current book is about a cowboy."

"Is that your thing, Olivia? Cowboys?"

"No." Right now a video game creator was my thing, and I didn't know what to do with that. Surely it was the ruse we'd created or the intimacy of the evening. Because Lachlan was not my type. And I was not his. "Work is my thing." I wanted to cut off the source of this magnetic pull. "Work is my crush, my obsession. It's what keeps me up at night and occupies all my thoughts."

"All of them?" The back of Lachlan's hand trailed a light path from my temple to the curve of my jaw. "I'm calling your bluff on that one."

Did I dare tell him how I felt? Did I admit it was a powerful, yet undefined feeling that kept me up at night? "Sometimes I think about..."

The way he looked at my mouth was a scandal. "Yes?"

No, I had to stay focused. "The books you see me reading."

"And?"

That look on his face, an open invitation to something he knew we both wanted. "And carbs," I lamely told him. "I miss them. I think of them often and wonder if they miss me too."

Lachlan curled his arm around my shoulders, and his lips whispered against my ear. "Little liar."

If his mouth moved even one inch south it would graze my neck, and it had to be that one glass of wine I'd drunk because there was no other explanation for hoping Lachlan would do just that. The hand he held on my hip tightened, and as he pulled me so close a good intention couldn't fit between us, his eyebrow rose in a question.

"I don't want to like you, Olivia," Lachlan said.

"Then don't." Because I couldn't take it. It was leading to dangerous territory and giving me thoughts I had no business entertaining. "Please don't like me."

"I think it's too late."

The dancing stopped.

My heart stopped.

Had it not been for the flash of a camera, I would've thought the world had even pressed pause.

"Someone just took a picture of us," I whispered.

"Then let's give them some quality content." Hands now framing my face, Lachlan sealed his lips to mine, cutting off my next PR directive.

Brand management could wait.

Because Lachlan was kissing me again.

In romance novels, kisses were so often described in terms of fireworks and other combustibles. But on immediate contact, Lachlan's kiss felt like a thousand heart emojis bubbling up in my chest. Warmth, light, and giddy joy—that was the triple geyser of feelings shooting through my system now. So much desire and need, but beyond that a safe kinship that wrapped around my shoulders and whispered to my heart it would be tended well.

Lachlan's fingers tipped up my chin as his mouth seared over mine. In shushed tones he called me beautiful and sweet, and I wanted to melt into the floor and take him with me. My lips craved more, and I began my own pursuit, taking lead as I was prone to do. But oh, the reward. Lachlan laughed into our kiss and—

My cell phone buzzed.

Lachlan's nose grazed my cheek as I automatically turned my head to locate the interruption. A knee-jerk reaction, born of years of repetition.

"Did you seriously bring a phone?" he asked.

"Yes. My dress has pockets." He was not the least bit impressed. "Isn't that handy?"

"Let it go," Lachlan said.

"I can't." The phone vibrated again, and I fished it from the slit in my skirt. "It's probably—"

"Celeste."

"Yes." Tearing my eyes from Lachlan, I checked the screen. "I have to take the call."

Lachlan released a ragged breath as he dragged his hand through his hair. "Your boss can give you one night off. Whatever debt you owed has to be long since paid, Olivia."

The call went to voicemail as the band played Adele. "I'll decide that."

Lachlan guided us to the side of the room, away from the dancing. "I hate watching the way she takes advantage of you."

I'd heard this from my sisters, and to hear it from him was a match-drop in kerosene. "I think what you meant to say, Lachlan, is that Celeste appreciates and depends on my work ethic and reliability. I'm not swimming in wealth like you. If I don't prove myself irreplaceable, then I'm easily fired."

He gave a dismissive shrug. "Then you find another job with a firm that respects your time and treats you well."

"You make that sound as easy as playing a video game." My words caused an instant snarl on Lachlan's face.

"Is that all you think I do?"

"No, it's not all. But I do think play time is more acceptable in your world than in mine."

Lachlan set his jaw, his gaze stormy as an Ozark spring. "Are you running to Celeste or running away from how you feel?"

A maelstrom of emotions swirled in my chest, and I suddenly found it difficult to breathe. Between Lachlan's kiss and his thorn-covered questions, my entire system was on the verge of overheating.

When my phone buzzed again, I was almost relieved for the intrusion.

Of course it was Celeste.

"I'm going to take this call," I said. "Feel free to use this time to network like we practiced."

"Olivia—"

But I pasted on my Happy Wife smile and walked away. I had some work to do—which included putting some much-needed space between my temporary husband and me.

THIRTY-THREE

OLIVIA

BEING A FAKE WIFE WAS HARD.

We needed a support group. A secret handshake. A lifetime supply of liquor and cookies.

Two hours later I walked beside Lachlan back to the hotel room. My feet hurt and so did my bruised feelings. I'd said things I shouldn't have—things I didn't even mean. But had I apologized yet? Nope.

Because the surly, silent man who called himself my husband hadn't spoken ten words to me since I'd returned after my call with Celeste. But that was okay. I'd danced with Governor Hernández's husband, then some man who'd quizzed me about Lachlan's announcement at TechieCon, which I assured him was top secret even to me. While Lachlan had networked with two other prominent CEOs, I'd spoken to three reporters about Lachlan's movie and philanthropic deeds.

Inside our dim room, Lachlan threw his keycard on the dresser and tugged his tie loose. "Did you get Celeste's problem taken care of?"

"Yes." I'd spent quite a while with her on the phone, then returned to the ballroom to discover my husband had decided to ignore me. "My call was very important." She'd needed me to register her son for a LEGO camp because she couldn't recall his social security number. "Very impactful for Flair." Why did it feel like an Alaskan winter in this room?

"Glad you could help." Lachlan's voice was bland as a rice cake and just as crisp. "I'm sure the business would've toppled to rubble overnight had you not intervened."

Someone had his silk boxers in a knot. "Then you'd be without a PR firm, and Larry from McMinn and Associates would have to take care of you. Larry has bad breath and hits on half his clients, from what I hear." I let my gaze conduct a meaningful sweep of Lachlan. "You're totally Larry's type."

"What type is that? The kind who doesn't leave his date alone for forty-five minutes while she walks her boss through how to register her own kid for a summer activity?"

Kicking off one spiteful, toe-pinching shoe, I gasped. "Were you eavesdropping on me?"

"At the twenty-minute mark I got worried you'd been abducted and needed rescue, so I went out to check on you. I think that was about the time you were instructing Celeste on which room in the house would most likely contain her daughter."

"Why are you acting like the jealous, possessive husband?"

"I'm not." With jerky movements, Lachlan yanked off his jacket. "I'm acting like a guy who worries you're in a two-person cult."

I removed a heavy, dangling earring. "Take that back."

"Not happening."

"Do you have any idea what I could've been doing tonight?"

He threw his tie on the nightstand. "Picking up Celeste's son from band practice?"

"Working on other projects that are falling behind. Or spending time with my sisters." I consulted the thermostat and found it dark and lifeless. "But instead I've given up my weekend to play the part of your wife and overserve in my role as your PR representative."

"Larry probably would've joined me."

"Larry smells like Asiago and mothballs." I grabbed my pajamas and slammed my suitcase shut. Meanwhile Lachlan chose the moment to unbutton his shirt. *Penalty flag on the field!* How could I participate in an intelligent argument when I had to look at *that*? "By the way, Celeste called to say you landed an interview with NPR."

"Great," he declared loudly.

"Good!" I bellowed right back.

Lachlan stood there angrily aiming the remote at the TV and looking like the cover model for the last romance novel I'd read. All he needed was a wind machine to blow his hair and a pirate ship floating behind him.

He dropped the remote onto the bed. "I see you ogling my irresistible form, and I'm going to have to ask you to stop."

"You're totally flexing right now. But I love how you always think I'm checking you out." I dug back into my suitcase with a fury, desperately searching for other pajamas than the ones in my hand. I'd been so overextended, I'd taken Sylvie up on her offer to pack for me, and of course, she'd included one nightie made of nothing but lace and air, which I'd never seen in my life, and another from the back of my drawer that didn't need a public showing for entirely different reasons. "For your information, I barely notice you at all, Lachlan."

That's right. I barely noticed the unexpectedly rippled stomach, the contours of his chest, or the splattering of russet hair. And I certainly did not notice the way his muscles contracted every time he moved or the way his tie dangled loose over his collarbone, as if daring me to grab the ends and pull him flush against me.

"You know what I think you're really mad about?" Lachlan asked.

"Being married to a man who harasses me?" I grabbed my curse of pajamas and took three steps toward the bathroom.

Lachlan stepped into my path. "The fact that you enjoyed our kiss."

This called for complete and total denial. "*That* kiss? The one in the ballroom?"

"Yeah." He made no effort to move but stepped closer. "The one that lit your world on fire."

I laughed at that, a big, loud chuckle forced from the pit of my despairing stomach. "I have zero interest in kissing you. I thought you were playing your role of a romantic husband, and I was doing my part."

"You keep telling yourself that, Mrs. Hayes."

How dare he be right! The unmitigated gall of the man. I would not tolerate this rudeness one more second. "I'm going to take a shower. It'll give you and your arrogance a little time alone."

"Gonna try and wash off your attraction to me?" Lachlan called after me. "Good luck in there."

I clutched my cosmetics bag. "I *was* going to apologize for the mean things I said to you, you know what? Never mind."

"I don't need your apology."

"Fabulous. Because you're not getting one." I all but floated to the bathroom on a cloud of fury, only to turn back in the doorway. "And by the way the thermostat seems to be broken, and if you could fix it, that would be great. Thank you."

I took my time showering, monopolizing the bathroom for

as long as possible. By the time I stepped out, a fog covered the mirror, my skin looked pruned, and I'd steamed every porous surface in the room. Even the tissue hung limp in its box. I wanted so badly to call my sisters and get their advice. How did I handle a husband? Kiss him? Strangle him? It was a toss-up.

When I'd checked every text, outlined Lachlan's *Good Morning America* prep plan, and even taken an online quiz to determine which pizza best fit my personality, I opened the bathroom door and tiptoed back into the room, praying Lachlan was asleep.

He was not.

Lachlan, of the unbuttoned shirt, grabbed a pillow from the bed, tossed it on the floor, then ransacked the closet until he found a thin blanket.

"What are you doing?" Hadn't we already settled the sleeping arrangements?

He threw the blanket on top of the pillow. "That couch is made for toddlers. I'll sleep on the floor, but if you step on me in the middle of the night, I'll know you did it on purpose."

He wouldn't sleep a wink down there. "You can't sleep on the floor."

"Why?"

"Because it's cold and hard and..."

"And?"

"And we're two adults who can share a bed." My anger would keep us warm.

He slipped his wallet from his back pocket and placed it on the dresser. "I'm worried you're going to smother me with a pillow in my sleep."

"Not tonight," I countered. "I'll wait until I'm not the one and only suspect available."

One eyebrow cocked. "What if you try to put the moves on me?"

"You wish." My cheeks warm, I regretfully took off my fluffy leopard robe and laid it at the end of the bed. "I'll put a wall of pillows between us if you think that will protect your virtue." When no zippy retort came my way, I glanced at Lachlan to find him staring at me in wide-eyed bewilderment.

"What is that?" He pointed toward me, the action revealing even more man chest as his shirt pulled away.

My mind struggled to form any words besides *hot husband* and *my hands would like to meet your pectorals.*

I cleared my throat and tugged my long sleeve to my wrist. "Are you referring to what I'm wearing?"

"Yes...What is it?"

"It's a nightgown."

"From your great-grandma's collection?" With a grin that made me immediately regret ever asking Sylvie for help, Lachlan inspected my flannel-clad self from the tips of my toes to the ruffle around my neck.

My hands went to my collar, where my fingers twined in a ribbon. Why couldn't Sylvie have grabbed my cute matching pajama sets? "It's my gown."

"From when you lived in a little house on a prairie?" Lachlan abandoned his pallet in the floor and walked toward me on bare feet.

I retreated one step, then bumped against the desk. "What's wrong with it?"

"Nothing, if it was 1820." He pointed to the collar that came to my throat. "Are you so afraid to show skin, you think the sight of your neck will push me over the edge?"

"I'm cold natured, for your information, and hotels are always frigid. Like ours."

"Our heater is broken, by the way."

251

"See." I threw up a hand. "Who's the weird one now?"

"Still you." Lachlan's grin was straight George Clooney circa 2007, with the twitching lips and eyes backlit by humor and the sheer burden of being gorgeous. "They can't fix it until tomorrow, and there aren't any more vacant rooms."

"Great. That means I'll be adding socks to my sexy ensemble. Can't wait to hear your commentary on that."

That grin deepened as Lachlan reached out and ran his finger along the ribbon. "I feel sorry for the poor Amish woman you stole this from."

Chills erupted beneath my flannel, and I meant to slap his hand away. But forgot. "My grandmother packed for me."

"Is she mad at you?" Now Lachlan's thumb trailed across the lace inset covering my red plaid shoulder. "If Celeste could see you now."

"Laugh all you want, but these gowns are soft and warm." Flickers of desire sparked and reignited, but I mentally doused them with sheer will. "If you must know, every night I stand in front of my closet and spend twenty minutes planning my outfit for the next day, agonizing over each detail. I shop online consignment stores for designer labels like it's a part-time job, and I diet and work out daily so I can fit into what I buy. I try to strike the perfect balance between not out-dressing Celeste and never letting Morgan's attire look better. It's exhausting."

Lachlan rested one hand behind me on the desk, and his hip bumped mine. "I'm tired just hearing about it."

"But these?" I gestured to the voluminous flannel fabric covering my legs. "These pajamas require zero thought. They're like curling up in a blanket. They're reliable and something I can depend on."

"You're more complicated than I thought, Olivia Sutton." Lachlan ran his hand down my sleeve. "I've always loved a good puzzle."

One page of a hotel Bible couldn't fit between us, and every time my chest rose and fell, it brushed against the buttons of Lachlan's shirt. "There's nothing to decipher here."

"Oh, I think there is." His gaze dipped to my lips and lingered. "Maybe the granny nightgown is a metaphor for the softer, gentler life you really want."

Was Lachlan going to kiss me again or just make me suffer with the thought? "Maybe it's just pajamas."

His fingers clasped my hand for two pounds of my heart, his skin hot on mine, impressing a message I wasn't sure I understood.

Then Lachlan simply stepped away, a hint of a smile about his lips. "I think your pajama choice shows all kind of personality."

My throat tightened as I worked to breathe again. "Thank you."

"But if you break out a muumuu for the ride home, I'm finding someone else to marry."

I gave what I hoped was a chummy smile in return. "You promise?"

THREE CHAPTERS INTO MY BOOK CLUB NOVEL LATER, THE BED DIPPED as a freshly showered Lachlan slipped beneath the covers on his side. He wore a shirt that said "Gamers Push All the Right Buttons" and a pair of hot pink boxers.

"Night," I said as I turned and flicked off the lamp beside me, tugging the comforter to my cold chin.

Lachlan doused his light, and the entire bed dipped as he turned over. "Olivia?"

"Yes?"

He took his sweet time, and I'd just about decided Lachlan

had fallen asleep when he said, "Fancy events and being in a room of rich people makes me edgy."

"You are rich people." My teeth chattered with every word.

"I'll never be one of them." When I didn't respond, he added, "I'm sorry I snapped at you. Your job is your business."

I knew I owed him an apology as well, painful as it might be. "I'm sorry for what I said. Your job is important, and you work hard."

"And?" He drew the word out, an extension of syllables and forgiveness.

"And I shouldn't have deserted you for so long. Celeste does intrude on my time, but she means well." My husband-of-convenience shifted closer, and the shadows of his face begged to be traced with a soft hand. "I love what I do, Lachlan."

"As long as you're happy."

"I am." Wasn't I? I mean, of course I wasn't thrilled with the pace Celeste demanded or the tasks she always assigned me. And, yes, maybe she was a little codependent. But I owed her, and I knew she could take my career to places I couldn't on my own.

"Olivia?" Lachlan's voice sounded sleepy and deep, another caress to my overactive imagination. "I'm glad you were with me tonight."

I smiled in the dark. "Me too." I reached for his hand and held it for a brave moment. "I was proud to be by your side."

Then Lachlan leaned over me.

This was it. He was going to take me in his arms and kiss me senseless. His mouth would slant over mine and brand me his for the night.

But just as I reached for my burly, stout husband, Lachlan pressed his lips to my forehead, a lingering sigh of breath and gentle pressure. Goodnight, wife." Then he oh-so slowly lifted his head. "Are you shivering?"

"Ignore that."

He sat up. "I can't. You're shaking."

I was still stuck on the fact that my fake husband apparently had no intention of ravishing me tonight. "Maybe a little."

"It's not that cold, Olivia."

"An Antarctic avalanche could only be colder."

"Here then." Lying back down, Lachlan threw an arm around my trembling body and gathered me to his front. Warmth radiated from his body, and I couldn't help but snuggle closer. I also couldn't help but notice I fit against him as if he were my missing piece.

"Thank you," I said, feeling my limbs begin to thaw.

"Can't have hypothermia set in." Lachlan kissed the top of my head, his breathing low and steady above me.

"Lachlan?" I spoke directly to his shirt-covered chest.

"Yes?"

"Are we getting complicated?"

"We're not tonight."

Drat. "Lachlan?"

"Olivia, you're playing with fire here." He stilled one of my roaming cold hands and clasped it in his large one. "Go to sleep."

"But Lachlan—"

"Seriously, do not move one more muscle."

"Lachlan, my gown's stuck beneath your leg."

With an exasperated sigh, he pulled the fabric free. "I'm sleeping with a Golden Girl." Then my husband tucked the comforter back over us, curved his arm around my waist, and held me like I was someone he might not want to let go of.

I smiled into my pillow and closed my eyes. Warm at last.

THIRTY-FOUR

LACHLAN

Saturday morning I'd awakened in the hotel with my wife in my arms.

That was nothing of consequence for most married dudes, but most married dudes didn't acquire their beloveds by way of roofied drinks and a scheming, deceptive cover-up.

When I'd done a full inventory of the placement of my arms, legs, and any other meaningful body parts, I'd discovered Olivia snuggled into my chest, her head tucked beneath my chin. She had one leg thrown over mine, and that ridiculous, fire-hazard of a nightgown wrapped around my lower body, pinning her to me. I'd discarded my t-shirt in the night, and Olivia's cold hands pressed against my chest, either pursuing warmth or on a mission to drive me mad. She'd achieved both.

So I lay there, oddly content in my discomfort, contemplating our situation. Why had my heart softened at the look of her sleeping face? Why had I thought the curve of her neck was so beautiful I'd wanted to explore it with my mouth and see what made her hum in response? I should've felt nothing for Olivia except relief we were one day closer to the end of our arrangement.

I'd despised this woman in college. Despised as in devoted time best spent studying to fantasizing about creative ways to knock her off that high horse. Yet now that I was getting to know her, she was unraveling all my carefully bound ideas of who she was.

Admittedly, on Saturday morning I'd wanted nothing more than to wake her up with a kiss and claim her as mine.

Then she'd yawned, stretched, first one blue eye popping open, then the other. "What are we doing?" she'd asked.

Lady, I have no idea.

She'd untangled from me, the bed, and that gown that could serve as rope if we needed to scale down the six stories of the hotel in an emergency. Then muttering apologies, Olivia had raced to the bathroom, mumbling something about "this never ends well in romance novels."

By Monday evening, I sat behind the wheel of my SUV navigating the pocked roads of Sugar Creek. One hand gripped the steering wheel while the other rested against Olivia's on the console between us. What would she do if I just grabbed her hand and held it? Did she feel as off-kilter and confused as I did after our weekend in Little Rock?

"Yes, Celeste," Olivia said into the phone pressed against her cheek. "I have it all lined up. Lachlan's chartered a plane, and we'll land in New York at five-thirty and leave immediately for the *GMA* studio." She sent me a pleased smile. "I'll send you video from his gala keynote, but I do think he's ready for Wednesday."

Didn't that just warm the pixels of my heart? I'd spent years purposely not caring if I had anyone else's approval, but to have Olivia's meant everything.

"What's that?" Olivia pulled up a calendar on her iPad.

"No, I'm not interested in taking Katarina and her friends to a K-pop concert." Her eyes squinted shut, and she pulled a face. "Sure, I'll be glad to check. I have your son's band concert on next Tuesday, not this week. I did order those dress pants for him. Right, see you tomorrow." The call over, Olivia let her head fall against the seat. "I need a vacation."

"Isn't that what every day married to me is?" Olivia bit down on a smile, but I saw it. "Tell me again what we're doing at the Lost Story tonight?" All I knew was that my wife had invited me, and I'd looked for any excuse to spend time with her since we'd returned from the gala. On Saturday evening, we'd gone to dinner downtown, laughing and talking as we walked in and out of quaint shops while the scent of fall hung in the air. Sunday, Olivia had talked me into church and family lunch at Sylvie's, where I'd dined on fried chicken and Frannie and Sylvie's gossip. Both had been quite satisfying.

"We're decorating," Olivia said as I turned onto Main Street. "Downtown Sugar Creek's Halloween candy crawl is tomorrow night, and I promised I'd help Rosie at the bookshop."

"Is this some small-town cuteness I shouldn't miss?"

"The kids trick-or-treat from all the local shops. But you'll have to catch it next year because you and I will be flying back from your slam dunk of a *GMA* interview." She returned her iPad to her purse and regarded me thoughtfully. "I bet you were all about some Halloween and dressing up when you were a kid."

"Actually no." Funny how I could still remember the want. "My mom worked most nights. When I was little, I'd go to the restaurant with her in the evenings, then when I was older, she was often sick."

"You've never gone trick-or-treating?"

I shrugged away her unwelcome pity. "It's not a big deal."

Her hand slid up and down my arm in comforting strokes. "Young Lachlan missed out on a lot."

Yes, he had, but at that moment, current Lachlan just wanted Olivia to keep up her sweet ministrations. "I'm glad to pitch in," I said. "Are we going with a Freddy Kreuger theme or maybe a Texas Chainsaw Massacre motif?"

"Something a little tamer. I'm afraid this evening will be boring for you."

"I happen to have it on good authority that when decorating, a tall person comes in handy."

"So does a ladder."

I turned off the car and faced my wife. "I tell better jokes."

She tilted her head and regarded me with a wry smile. "Do you?"

I hugged her to me, a move that reminded me of our shared bed in Little Rock. "You need me, and you know it."

"Maybe I do, Lachlan." She lingered in my arms for just a moment before wiggling out and opening her car door. "But I'll get over it."

WITHIN TWO HOURS OF ARRIVING AT THE LOST STORY BOOKSHOP, THE place looked like a Halloween wonderland. That was the magic of Olivia. With a polite kiss on my cheek for the sake of onlookers, she'd left me as soon as we stepped inside, then went to work. Watching her was like watching a five-star general. She arrived with a list of tasks, assigned jobs, and not only oversaw the work, but decorated sections of the bookshop herself.

My job was hanging fake cobwebs from light fixtures and tall shelving. Olivia had only grabbed a step stool three times and moved my web placement. I bet Spiderman's girlfriend didn't go behind him and rearrange his work.

"Hey there, hot stuff."

I hung one final web on a bookshelf and found Frannie standing within pinching distance. "Hi, Ms. Frannie."

Sylvie joined her, carrying three red Solo cups. "Y'all taste this Spooktacular Punch."

I dusted some residual glitter from my hands and took a cup. Then immediately winced. "Is there vodka in here?"

"Wards off vampires."

Rosie happened to be walking by at that moment, her arms full of a box of small pumpkins. "Sylvie, you're supposed to be perfecting your punch recipe for the *children*."

Frannie took another long swig. "I'd say it's pretty perfect to me."

Sylvie inspected my handiwork then let her gaze do an obvious drift toward Olivia. "How's married life, Mr. Tall, Dark, and Wealthy?"

I bit back a grin and thought of my confusing overnighter in Little Rock. I could still smell her hair in my face. Still recall the feel of her hands on my skin. "Great. The best. Should've done it sooner."

"That is exactly what I said about my bunion surgery." Frannie rattled the ice in her dry cup. "You know this morning we saw photos online of your gala with the governor. Very swanky."

"It was," I agreed. "Not my usual scene."

"Next time," Frannie said, "I need you to take samples of my cupcakes to hand out to the dignitaries."

I thought of Olivia's meticulous PR work. "I'm sure that would go over well with my wife."

Sylvie took a step closer, like a woman about to impart a secret. "Do you care?"

I had to be careful with these two ladies. They could be my

best allies or they could make me disappear to parts uninhabitable, unknown, and very painful. "I do care."

Frannie propped her hand on her hip. "So you like our girl, eh?"

"I'm married to her. I would hope that implies I like her." This was thin ice—this odd space where I didn't want to lie, yet I had a ruse to maintain.

"You two looked perfect together at the gala," Frannie said, a proud aunt.

"Except for those photos of them fighting." Sylvie slipped her phone from her pocket and pulled up a picture. "Scroll through there. Quite a gallery of less than flattering shots."

Sure enough. There were multiple pictures of Olivia and me nose-to-nose and wearing our angry faces.

"You didn't know?" Frannie asked.

"I'm not much for internet gossip."

"Me neither," Sylvie said. "I mean from the looks of the photos, you'd think you two were trying to fake a marriage and publicly cracking at the seams." She lifted her cup and watched me over the rim. "But we know that wasn't it at all, right?"

"Right." I swiped to another photo Sylvie had pulled from TMZ.

"Probably just bad camera angles," Sylvie added.

"Yeah." I handed her back her phone. "I should go find Olivia and—"

"But let's say a couple was in that situation." Sylvie stepped in my path and gave me a weighty stare. "Not you, of course. A hypothetical couple."

"Like Willa and Romero in our latest book club romance." Frannie downed the remaining droplets from her cup and fanned herself. "I'm only halfway through the book, but they're in a marriage of convenience that just turned lava hot. Isn't that right, Sylvie?"

Sylvie's red lips curved. "We're talking scorch-the-earth and leave no remains."

Frannie added to the intel like she knew the fictional couple. "They started out as enemies, then woke up married, thanks to the magic of an angry Irish leprechaun."

"I hate it when that happens." Where was Olivia? I needed to extract myself from this conversation.

"To get out of the marriage would totally ruffle some shamrocks, you know what I mean?" Frannie asked.

"I'm not a big romance novel reader."

"But put yourself in their shoes." Sylvie rested a hand on my forearm. "Because when people started to doubt the validity of their marriage, Willa and Max improved the optics."

I didn't want to hang fake cobwebs anymore. I wanted to go back home to the safety of my office, fire up a game, and shoot some things. "What are you saying?"

"Like more dates, public kissing, tush grabs," Frannie answered. "Would you like for me to demonstrate?"

"No." Lord, no. "That won't be necessary."

Frannie shrugged. "I'm a taken woman, but some tutorial role-play could be useful. For the sake of education."

"I think I'm following." Apparently Olivia and I needed to up our game.

"Do you truly get it?" Sylvie asked.

"Yes." I caught sight of Olivia across the room, laughing at something Rosie said. I'd grown to love seeing these moments where she was happy. "And if I ever find myself in a situation in which I personally need this advice, I'll know who to call."

"For convenience, I have a few different numbers," Frannie hollered as I walked in the direction of Olivia. "Some burner phones! I'm very easy to reach!"

Olivia put down a garland of witch's hats as I approached. "You look like you're on a mission."

"I think it's time we updated my social media."

"Okay." She frowned. "We can do that when we get home."

"I was thinking now." I handed my phone to Rosie. "Would you mind taking our picture?"

She grinned, already enjoying the task. "Just tell me when."

I stepped into Olivia, took her surprised face in my hands, then pressed my mouth to hers. "I think now is just about right."

CHAPTER
THIRTY-FIVE
LACHLAN

NEW YORK CITY NEVER SLEPT, and it seemed neither did I.

Last night I'd been so stressed about my television interview, I'd stayed up until three a.m. tweaking a new game idea. The last thing we needed was another game right now, but my other option had been to wake up Olivia and pour out my soul until I felt better. I'd decided that was a terrible notion, but man, I'd wanted to. I'd wanted to tell her how nervous I was for this *Good Morning America* interview and how worried I was about screwing up. Even more, I wanted Olivia to be proud. I wanted her to see me do it right. To see her eyes light up and her smile—not that professional smile, but the real one she only broke out for special occasions. I wanted to be worthy of her approval. Actually, I wanted to be worthy of a whole lot more.

And that was a problem.

Historically speaking, people in my life didn't stick around, and I had to remember, had to brand it on my brain, that Olivia was only passing through.

The woman I couldn't get off my mind sat beside me on the

chartered plane and gave my hand a squeeze when we came to a stop. "We're here. Are you ready?"

"Ready as I'll ever be." I clasped her fingers, feeling a measure of comfort as her skin pressed against mine. We had indeed upped our public affection output, and I wasn't sure how the press liked it, but I sure did.

Almost two hours later, we sat in the greenroom, ignoring all the snacks I wanted but Olivia forbade me from eating. Something about dairy jacking up the vocal clarity and other tips I barely heard. I personally thought a glazed donut could super charge my speaking skills.

A production assistant stuck his head in the doorway. "Ready in five, Mr. Hayes."

"Lachlan." Olivia turned toward me. "Take some deep breaths like I showed you."

I complied, eyeing the cheese tray on the table beside us. "Let's just get this over with." We'd do a quick lunch afterward, then fly back home. I missed Sugar Creek already.

Olivia stood, and I followed her to the door. She wore an off-the-shoulder blouse that made me want to trace the curve right to her collar bone and a skirt that made these sexy shh-shh sounds when she walked. With Olivia in my line of sight, it was hard to recall my own name, let alone the three talking points we'd rehearsed.

"Are you nervous?" she asked.

"Only ninety percent chance of my throwing up."

Her pink lips curved. "Then that's a ten percent chance you're going to be just fine." Her hands rested on my chest, a calming, warm pressure. "I believe in you, Lachlan Hayes. You've worked hard for this, and you've scored an interview opportunity coveted by top celebrities. And do you know why?"

"Because God is punishing me?" Was it a bad sign that I was already sweating?

"Because *you're* top level. People want to hear what you have to say. You're an inspiration and a dream realized." Olivia patted my left pec. "And you're very mediagenic."

"What does that mean?"

Her hesitation was adorable. "You film nicely," she said.

I gave her the head tilt. "You think I'm handsome."

"I didn't say that."

I took a step closer. "I think you did."

"It was an objective statement from a professional perspective."

"I love it when you get all uppity."

"What I am"— Olivia smoothed a wrinkled spot on my chest— "is proud of you. So is my entire family."

That touching revelation added voltage to the anxiety. "They're watching today, aren't they?"

"Sylvie and Frannie threw a watch party."

Good Lord, the pressure. "I did not need to know that. They really go all-out in supporting you."

"Their party isn't for me," Olivia said. "It's for you."

I coughed to get past the lump now firmly lodged in my throat. Man, I loved those people.

Olivia took a deep breath and motioned for me to do the same. "Don't forget, eye contact, warm smile, and pivot to the movie if the topic strays into unwelcome territory. You've got this." Olivia rose up on tiptoe and kissed my stubbled cheek. "I'm right here with you."

I'm right here with you.

I'd pretty much waited a lifetime for those words.

The fact that they came from Olivia was problematic.

But... did it have to be?

"Interesting pick for lunch." Four hours later, Olivia lowered her menu at the Lambs Club, an older dining establishment in Midtown.

"It's very New York." I scanned the room, still amped up from the interview. "I'm buying, of course."

"You bet you are." She tapped a price on the menu. "Celeste doesn't pay me enough to eat here."

"If you get the promotion," I said around a waiter filling our water glasses, "this will be right in your backyard."

Olivia didn't look too thrilled at the idea. "I don't want to talk about that today." Breaking one of her own rules, she propped her elbows on the table, laced her fingers, and gave me her full attention. "Let's talk about how you just killed an interview on *Good Morning America*."

"Killed it, huh?" I did love the smell of unexpected success in the afternoon. "Is that your professional analysis or your friendly take as my wife?"

"Both." Olivia placed her cloth napkin in her lap. "Lachlan, you were charming and charismatic, and you made both your movie and your company sound phenomenal. The vice president of marketing at Vortex Studios called me herself, and she could not stop singing your praises."

I was just glad the interview was over. That was the longest four minutes and forty-five seconds of my life, and I needed to express my relief by way of food consumption. "Wouldn't have pulled it off without you."

Olivia lifted her water glass. "To many years of success for you and Star Gazer."

"And to happiness." I touched my goblet to hers. "May we both find it and let it lead us where we need to go."

"That's from *Mars Wars*," she said. "The planetary motto, I believe?"

"Has Olivia Sutton been playing video games?"

"No." She rested her napkin in her lap and smiled. "But I did some research."

"I'll convert you yet."

"We'll see about that." Olivia set her fork to her left, her expression steady and serious again. "I know you're being modest, but you have to be proud of your performance today, right?"

Was I? Had I ever allowed myself that luxury? I'd spent my entire life just trying to prove myself and rarely had time to sit back and absorb the win. "As long as I don't have to do that again for a while, I'm happy."

"You absolutely deserve a break." Olivia took a delicate sip of her water. "At least until next week, when you do the *Bella Porter Morning Show*." She held up her phone where a text screamed the news. "Celeste just forwarded the invitation. Face it, Lachlan. You're a big deal."

"That's two national morning news programs for you in a matter of weeks," I said, enjoying the radiant glow on Olivia's face. "Is Celeste showering you in praise yet?"

"She's certainly riding high on the coup for Flair, but I just learned Morgan's client will be included in a Netflix documentary on modern-day matchmaking, so no coasting for me. I need to level up even more."

That Morgan was no match for my Livvy. "I could try to schedule one of those rich dude space flights."

"No."

"Challenge Morgan's client to a lightsaber duel?"

"Also no," Olivia said.

"Find a cure for cancer and stop global warming?"

"Perfect." Olivia consulted her menu, but not before gifting me with a smile. "If you could accomplish both by end of business next week, that would be fabulous."

"Anything for you, babe."

This newly minted big deal and his wife ordered from the limited menu. I decided on the New York strip, and Olivia tried the salmon. Ten minutes into our meal, we'd shared them both like an old married couple. Conversation turned to Olivia's woes with another account she managed, my renovation of the corporate office for Star Gazer, and her grandmother's latest antics, which had been questionable on the legal spectrum—if one respected that sort of thing.

Olivia had just rehashed the highlight reel of my interview, capped off by a round of praise for my dining manners when I saw him.

The man who'd once made my life a living hell.

The man who would now lose the most when my company released its new technology.

I couldn't wait to watch him go under.

CHAPTER
THIRTY-SIX
LACHLAN

"Hello, Hayes."

I set down my fork before my fantasy of throwing it like a ninja star took over. Benjamin Emmerich, seventy-one with shoulders like a linebacker, possessed a crop of thick white hair on his large, angry head, and wore shoes so shiny he could look down and see his own scowl reflected. And the man seized every chance to look down.

"Eight million people in this town, and I have the pleasure of running into you." I wadded up my napkin before tossing it on the table with a little too much gusto. "Olivia, this is Benjamin Emmerich, current CEO of Emmerich Technologies."

"Nice to meet you," she told him with a satisfying amount of reservation.

"Benji, I'd offer to pick up your tab," I said, "but I don't want to."

The old man had a trio of deep creases in his forehead from decades of frowning, and he put them to work now. "Still running that smart mouth, I see. Some things never change, do they?"

270

I gave the man a dismissive once-over. "No, they clearly don't."

Benjamin Emmerich had the nerve to look pointedly at my wife again. "Congratulations on your many achievements," he told me. "Nothing like the tabloids running your wedding photos. I think *Town & Country* published mine."

"Was that the wedding to wife number five or six?" I inquired.

Benjamin smiled, revealing those high-dollar veneers that always looked too big for his mouth. "I hear you're really talking up your big announcement for TechieCon."

Now this I almost enjoyed. "You scared?"

"Of you?" Benjamin opened those ugly teeth and laughed. "You may be having a moment, but you have to know how to run a business to actually maintain that success. When your star fades, I'll still be here."

"Sorry to interrupt," Olivia said in a voice that communicated she was anything but sorry, "but you must not know my husband very well." She wore the perfect ice queen, intimidate-the-peasants expression. "*TIME* called him a genius three months ago. Did you get that issue? I can send you a copy if you'd like."

Benjamin would be skipping that read. "Quite unnecessary," he said.

"So is your treatment of Lachlan," Olivia clapped back. "My innovative, visionary of a husband has worked incredibly hard and is now reaping the benefits of that work."

I conducted a brief survey of the room. Had anyone else heard angels sing?

I wanted to pull this woman in my lap and kiss her until the world faded away. Nobody had ever said nicer things about me, ever. And while I didn't need defending to the likes of a Benjamin Emmerich, I still held out my hands and let Olivia's words drop into them. I'd keep her sentiments tucked into the craggy crevices of my heart until I was too old to remember my own name.

"Lachlan is lucky," Benjamin told Olivia with his hazel eyes on me. "No matter what trouble he stirred up, he always landed on his feet somehow—by luck, not by doing the right thing."

I was just about to open my mouth when Olivia beat me to it. "He has a blockbuster series of games, a movie franchise, and his company's stock has doubled since it went public." Her glare would wither most mortal men. "What is it *you* do, sir?"

Benjamin ran a pale, liver-spotted hand over his navy tie. "I buy and sell companies like your husband's."

"Benjamin also makes sound cards used in gaming," I told her, then took a drink of water. My throat ached with all the words I still wouldn't say. "Tinkers in tech."

Benjamin didn't appreciate that. "What Lachlan fails to mention is my company is the leading innovator and manufacturer of the E-97 sound card, the best sound option available by far. Even the military uses our card for their simulation systems. I once gave your husband a job, among other opportunities, and he screwed it up." Benjamin rested his hands on a chairback and leered in my direction. "You've got some money in your pocket now, but we both know it doesn't change who you are."

A fireball of rage exploded in my head, and were it not for Olivia's hand coming to rest on mine, I would've lunged across the table. Instead, I schooled my features, as I'd always done when dealing with Benjamin, and stared him dead in the eye. "You're right—money didn't change me at all. Hard work and growing up did. It's a shame you didn't have the same results."

"It's one thing to sketch some characters and throw

together a game," Benjamin said. "But it's another to run a million-dollar company."

"Multimillion," I corrected. "And I'm smart enough to hire the best to do what I can't."

"Which is not a lot because Lachlan can do just about anything," Olivia interjected. Her eyes full of venom, she pointed right at me. "This guy. Right here. He's brilliant."

My lips curved in a smile. "Thanks, sweetheart."

She nodded once. "You got it, babe."

"I don't wish you failure, Lachlan," Benjamin said, liar that he was. "I'd just hate to see you playing in a sandbox you're not ready for."

"Let me ease your mind." I tugged on Olivia's hand as I stood, tossing cash on the table. "I'll play in whatever sandbox I want to. I decide where I belong, and I don't need your fake concern or your warnings. What you should be worrying about is your own company. You're a one-trick pony with no diversification, which I recall mentioning to you during my brief employment. One day someone more innovative than you will come along and create what you never could. I'm looking forward to that day, Benjamin. It can't get here soon enough. Come on, Olivia. We're done."

"Goodbye, Mr. Emmerich." Olivia gave him one final parting glare. "Oh, if you ever need any PR help, please give my company a call. That's McMinn and Associates." She plucked her purse from the table and slung the strap over her shoulder. "Ask for Larry."

The afternoon sunshine hit my blazing skin when we stepped outside. Olivia's heels clicked quickly beside me in that comfortingly familiar staccato. November would charge in soon, and fall barely held winter at bay. Olivia tied the belt of her black coat but didn't look at me until we hit the next block.

"Who was that?" she finally asked.

"The owner of Emmerich Technologies." I had no idea where I was going. I just needed to walk. As soon as I cooled down, I would call an Uber.

Olivia tugged on my hand as she slowed her pace. "Why was he so angry?"

"Because he's a miserable guy. My success bothers him." When I could tell Olivia wasn't going to let it go, I gave her a bit more. "He's mad because I succeeded despite him."

"Mr. Emmerich must've been a terrible boss."

I gave a mirthless laugh at the memory. "He was an even more terrible father."

I had to give her credit. Olivia had a heck of a poker face. She didn't even react. "That was your dad?"

"Biologically speaking, yes."

"The guy who left you to fend for yourself after your mother's death?"

I shrugged, used to the dull ache that always accompanied any thought of my dad. "He probably didn't have time to read any parenting magazines." Feeling like I'd put enough distance between my past and present, I found an empty park bench and sat. Gray clouds gathered in the western sky, and the game designer in me thought it was a fitting addition to the setting.

I just needed a moment to calm my mind and flaring temper before I let Emmerich ruin what should have been a stellar day. Olivia eased down beside me, and the two of us people-watched in companionable silence for a while.

Needing the comfort that was only Olivia, I wrapped my arm around her and pulled her into my side. "Once upon a time I was supposed to spend an entire summer in Italy," I finally said.

Olivia looked up at me, her head now resting against my shoulder. "What a coincidence. Me too."

I cleared my throat and took another deep breath. "We'd

all decided to take a boat ride, and I'd agreed to pay for the rental. This rich guy named Preston said he'd handle the details. Remember him?"

She nodded at the mention of her pretentious college boyfriend.

"I gave him the money, and he showed up with a boat. I had no idea he'd stolen it." I pressed my finger to Olivia's lips before she could speak. "If your next question is why didn't I say anything, it's because no one would've believed me." I jerked my head toward the direction of the restaurant. "Benjamin certainly didn't."

"Lachlan." She closed her blue eyes for a heartbeat. "And then I was so mad at you I reported a few other infractions you'd committed."

"All passed along to Benjamin Emmerich. After that I decided I didn't want to be who people thought I was. I've worked my tail off to change my life and my reputation." I watched a jogger trot by, the woman lost in the world beyond the music in her ears.

"Your dad was wrong to not believe you, and so was I," Olivia said. "I'm sorry."

I ran my knuckles across her cold cheek. "Old stuff, right?" Or should've been. Seeing my dad always brought a rush of bad memories. "I lived in my car for three months at twenty-one, then couldn't afford to get back into college. When I asked for help one last time, Benjamin sent his chauffeur to hand me a hundred bucks and a message to never contact him again."

Pity and disbelief darkened Olivia's pretty face, and I welcomed it and hated it all at the same time. "You needed someone to be there for you. How could he do that to you?"

"Benny boy felt like my mom had trapped him, as if getting pregnant was a one-person job. He never forgave her—or me. He eventually married a lady who was kind enough to invite me to stay after my mom died, but that, of course, went south too. Then after the debacle in Italy, he was done." Enough with the maudlin, poor-me story. I hadn't rolled out those tales in ages. "Anyway, that was a long time ago."

"You knew Benjamin would be there, didn't you?" she asked.

I shrugged. "Ben's a man of habit. He eats there at least twice a week, so I knew there'd be a chance." The wind picked up, and I smelled rain on the breeze. We needed to leave, but I didn't want to lose a second of Olivia in my arms.

"You're a grown man who has nothing to do with him," Olivia said as crowds of New Yorkers scurried by. "Why would Emmerich still be so angry?"

"Because he's scared." I watched in fascination as the wind made Olivia's hair dance. "Lots of tech companies are. At the conference, Star Gazer's new product will render others obsolete."

My Olivia had her fair share of instinct and brain cells, and she knew the next part of this story. "You're going to put your father out of business, aren't you?"

"Yes."

"For the sake of revenge?"

"I'd be lying if I said I wasn't going to enjoy that by-product, but this is business. It's always a race to create the next thing, and you can't worry about hurting people's feelings if you knock them off their thrones." Did I completely believe that? I wasn't sure, but my therapist back in California didn't seem to approve when I'd said I was out for blood.

Olivia thought about this for a moment, her eyes averting as she went to that place in her head where strategy reassembled all the pieces until it suited her.

"What I've just told you is confidential information," I warned. "Only a select group of people know. If you leak this information, you'll be one more person upon whom I'll have to exact revenge, which, frankly, is just exhausting."

She barely heard me. "After the product announcement, we'll have comms go out immediately. We paint a picture of a Lachlan who overcame great obstacles, practically raised himself, and succeeded despite it all."

"Benjamin is old tech. He has deep pockets and knows everyone in the industry. He'll have a smear campaign ready to discredit me and my company."

"Not if we portray him as the emotionally abusive, absentee father first."

"No," I said. "He and I have never claimed one another publicly, and I won't start now. The last thing I need is my DNA tied to his and people thinking I got where I am because of family influence."

"They won't if we tell the correct story," Olivia argued. "It doesn't even require spin. In this case, it only requires truth."

"I said no." I'd been an obedient client with all of Olivia's ideas and instructions, but this was a hard pass. "I want no connection to Emmerich. It's the one thing he and I have always implicitly agreed on. We don't share a last name, and my birth records thankfully leave him out." Standing, I leveled a heavy stare at Olivia, needing her to understand the gravity of the situation. "Nobody finds out he's my father. Are we clear?"

As horns blared with passing cards, Olivia nibbled on her bottom lip. "If that's how you want it."

"It is."

"What if it's our Hail Mary?"

"I can handle anything Emmerich throws at me after the conference." I pulled her to me and kissed her forehead. "Especially with the greatest PR help by my side."

THIRTY-SEVEN
OLIVIA

LACHLAN

Where is it you're going today?

OLIVIA

An amusement park.

LACHLAN

If fun is what you're after, I could think of a few things.

OLIVIA

Keep your hands to yourself.

LACHLAN

Gaming, Olivia. I meant gaming. But if you had other ideas...

"WHERE HAVE YOU BEEN?" Elton glanced down at his watch at five o'clock on a stormy Friday evening, his dog panting beside him.

"Nice legs." I cast an appreciative glance at his skinny knees, which protruded from a grass skirt. Then I waved at coworkers at the coffee kiosk. I could use a double espresso. Or three.

"It's Beach Party Day, and you have been noticeably absent," Elton said.

"My coconut bra was at the dry cleaners." Closing my drippy umbrella, I walked with him through the lobby and toward the elevator. "I got volun-*told* to chaperone Katarina's field trip in Branson."

"Ew." Elton took a step back like I reeked of funnel cake and pork rinds. Which I did. "You *could* tell Celeste no every once in a while."

"And I will. *After* the promotion." I could not wait for that moment. *Sorry, I can't take your kid to the orthodontist because I'm in New York.*

"Well, obedient one, Celeste's called an emergency meeting," Elton said. "Didn't you get the text? Lots of exclamation points."

Shoot. Of course something would happen while I was off gallivanting with a busload of angsty teenagers. "I've been at Silver Dollar City. Before the storm hit, my phone fell in the water on the log ride and went dead to the world." I nearly cried just thinking about it.

"Oh, gosh," Elton said. "Olivia without her precious cell? How are you holding up?"

Not well. "I've developed a twitch, and I feel a little faint. So these exclamation points," I said, guiding the conversation back to the potential crisis. "How many are we talking?"

"Five."

My tired eyes widened. That was serious. Three exclamations points meant she needed a favor or had lost a file. Four usually meant a serious announcement or an incorrect coffee order. Five or more was a straight-up Flair emergency...or it meant her replacement coffee order had *also* been wrong.

Elton reached out and attempted to fluff my hair. "Grab some lipstick or something. You look like you went down that log ride headfirst."

"With the exorbitantly expensive photos to prove it." I'd left at five that morning and had gone nonstop at the Missouri tourist attraction ever since. I'd driven like a Formula One racer on the infamously curvy roads back to Arkansas, and I had the queasy stomach for the effort. I was cold, damp, exhausted, and after this meeting, I still had Sexy Book Club to attend when all I wanted to do was go home, tell Lachlan about my day, and crash with him on the couch. He'd curve his arm around me because it was now habit, while I'd snuggle in and try not to think of our separation date closing in. Totally normal behavior for two people who never wanted to be married.

Elton steered me toward the elevator. "By the way, your hot husband did a great job on *GMA*. Dude's come a long way in a short amount of time."

"Thanks, Elton." I pushed the up button, and the doors whooshed open as if anxiously waiting for us. "I'm very happy for him." I'd had some time in the last couple of days to think on Lachlan's run-in with his dad. It boggled the mind to think tech billionaire Benjamin Emmerich was Lachlan's dad. I'd tried to get Lachlan to talk about it on the plane ride home, but he'd brushed it off. I'd been raised in a nurturing family who'd been at my every school function and lovingly hovered as I went to college. I couldn't imagine the rejection Lachlan had experienced.

Benjamin Emmerich had no idea what a smart, kind, selfless son he'd missed out on. Between Lachlan's childhood with an overworked single mother, her early death, and his father's emotional abuse, it was no wonder my husband had maintained that brat persona in college. He must've been hurting so much beneath all that bluster and rebellion. If only I'd known the truth then.

Elton grabbed my elbow and ushered us inside. "Ugh. Don't look now, but Cruella de PR is right behind us."

"I know you see me, Elton Chen!" Running on enviably gorgeous Stuart Weitzman heels, Morgan click-clacked her way into the elevator, a vision of freshness and style. She hadn't spent the entire day chasing after a petulant teenager in between occasional rain and water-soaking rides, then driven the two hours home listening to a slow-moving murder podcast and binge-eating Silver Dollar City taffy.

"Nice dress, Morgan." I pushed the button for the third floor as my least favorite person settled inside the elevator, resting one manicured hand against the rail.

"So very kind of you to say." She smoothed her other hand over the belted waist of her tropical print dress, the A-line silhouette cut from silk, and the panel-slit skirt revealing look-at-me legs. "It cost me half a paycheck, but it'll be a fun piece to take to New York when I get the job."

Elton's eyes narrowed, and he released some of the slack on FeeFee's leash. The dog immediately went to sniffing the closest victim—Morgan.

The three of us swayed with the gentle force of the elevator chugging upward.

Morgan's lengthy eyelashes fluttered up and down as she perused my dirt-spotted jeans and wilted sweatshirt. "Rough day at the theme park?"

I shoved a limp piece of hair off my cheek. "One of the most delightful workdays I've had in ages." If I never got on another roller coaster, it would still be too soon.

Elton chimed in. "Olivia was just telling me that hanging

out with Celeste's daughter and her classmates was like a nonstop party—except a good one. Not one in which the music is techno and you spend the entire two hours petting the host's Labradoodle." He shot me a side eye. "Not that this describes my previous Saturday night. Anyway, I wish I were Celeste's favorite and got handpicked for special assignments with her kids once in a while."

God bless Elton. He wished for that about as much as one wished for smallpox.

"Yes, you're so special," Morgan said as I brushed smudges of confectioners' sugar off my blouse. Then her reptile gaze slid my way and lingered. "Do you have big plans for your husband's birthday on Monday?"

I stared unblinkingly at Morgan. "What?"

"Your husband's birthday. On Halloween? Surely you have that on your calendar. I saw it when I Googled him a few weeks ago."

"Olivia, tell her about the big party you're throwing him." Elton inspected his nails and flashed me an indulgent smile. "I got my invite a few days ago. Cannot. Wait."

"Yes," I finally managed. "It'll be a very big throwdown." Oh, good heavens. I could taste the panic in my mouth. It was a bitter blend of *holy crap* and *what am I going to do?*

"Morgan, maybe your invitation got lost in the mail," Elton said. "These things happen."

Morgan opened her mouth, but I was blessedly spared further inquisition when the elevator doors swished open.

"Out we go." Elton tugged on FeeFee's leash. "Last one to the conference room's a bad batch of Botox." And with that, he grabbed my arm and rushed us down the hall.

Monday is Lachlan's birthday.

That was the thought blaring in my aching head two minutes later as Celeste stood at the head of the conference room table, hands pressed to the hard surface. She let her gaze fall on each one of us. "Kids...I have news."

A real wife would celebrate Lachlan's birthday. So I needed to think like a real wife. I could take him out to dinner—just the two of us. That would be good for a photo op. We could even take the photo ourselves and post it online. To curate our own image.

Or I could just pick up dinner and bring it home. With a gift. What did one get a multimillionaire? A gaming chair that didn't look like a prop hijacked from a *Star Wars* movie?

Or.

I could throw Lachlan a party. Invite my family and give them another opportunity to see us together. But what could I arrange in three days?

"...And that is why I've gathered us back here tonight."

Oh, no. Celeste was talking. And looking at me meaningfully.

Now she cruised around the table, running her hands across the backs of our corrugated chairs, like a grown-up version of duck-duck-goose. "After much thought I have decided to narrow the candidate list for the New York office position."

That sobered me right up. I straightened in my uncomfortable seat and ran my tongue over my taffy-glazed teeth. My laptop flashed a calendar invite, but I slapped the lid down and gave Celeste my adoring, undivided attention. I wanted to be fully in the moment. Zen. Focused. Smelling of corn dogs.

Celeste paused at the opposite end of the table, her hand on Gunnar's shoulder. "Kids, I've watched two candidates shine in the last week. Their midpoint goals have been met or exceeded. They've brought honor and praise to Flair. And they have demonstrated a commitment to their work and this company that sets them apart."

I did eighty percent of your son's science fair project. I grew mold in petri dishes for your second born.

If that wasn't promotion-worthy commitment, then I'd like to know what was.

Celeste patted her dark hair as her red glossy lips eased into a rare smile. "While everyone here at Flair is a winner, these two are the best of the best, and this company wouldn't be the same without them. I'd like to introduce the two finalists for the Manhattan office—Olivia Sutton—"

Yes! It's me. I'm in! All that babysitting and taxi driving. All the weekends and nights and holidays I've worked. All the calls I've taken from Celeste during weddings, funerals, and dates. All the sleep I've lost and the tears I would've cried if I weren't made of robot parts—all worth it. Celeste loves me. She values me. She said I was the best of the best. I'm going to New York, and nobody can stop me now.

"And Morgan Sanderson," Celeste said.

Morgan.

Like a balloon popped midflight, the air left my body. My limbs slowly deflated as my spin in the celebratory clouds came to a halt, and I crashed back to reality.

Of course there were two of us.

And *of course* the other person would be Morgan. But had Morgan bought Katarina her first training bra? No. Had she taught Alexander how to ask a girl to the middle school dance? No, she had not. *I* had.

I also had the one thing Morgan did not: Lachlan.

Tech titan. One of *Newsweek's* 100 Entrepreneurs to Watch.

Next month he would attend his Hollywood premiere, and I would certainly accept my new promotion.

After a few minor announcements, Celeste dismissed the room, and I was soon surrounded by the well-wishes of my coworkers.

Elton high-fived me, then pulled me in for a hug. "I knew you could do it. New York City, here she comes."

"Thank you." I grinned like a woman who was weeks away from having it all.

"Group hug!" Morgan shuffled our way and threw her lanky arms around us. She held us like hugging was as difficult as assembling a piece of IKEA furniture. Did this piece go here? Did this have to take so long? Were there supposed to be extra parts?

I stepped out of the embrace and shook my competition's hand. "Congratulations, Morgan. No matter who's selected, she will be a winner."

"Yes." Morgan lifted her chin and set her shoulders. "I certainly will."

CHAPTER

THIRTY-EIGHT

OLIVIA

To know Sexy Book Club was to love Sexy Book Club.

The literature-loving group had been started by my grand-mother and Frannie when all their other efforts to find a hobby had failed catastrophically. (Do not ask about gator wrestling or naked trapshooting.) Everyone in my family loved books, so my sisters and I were faithful to attend—whether we wanted to or not.

Did the book club involve immersive women's fiction with intellectual talking points and plotlines so tight Reese Witherspoon had already snatched up the movie rights? It did not.

Did it include classics, *New York Times* bestsellers, or that thriller on everyone's nightstand? Don't be ridiculous.

What it did involve was romance novels—and for Sylvie and Frannie, the steamier the better. Always character driven, and bonus points for a quirky plot. The ladies were fans of tropes, and the food continued the theme. Last month we'd read a cowboy romance, so Frannie showed off her pistols. Rosie was appalled and informed our aunt the Lost Story had a strict policy against weapons. Especially ones holstered in brassieres.

My heart lifted at the sight of the Lost Story tonight. Would I ever get over the love and pride I felt for Rosie's dream come true? Exhausted but still high on Celeste's announcement, I opened the doors and made my way inside. It was like coming home.

Paolo greeted me, wearing a chartreuse blazer that I knew he saved for special events. "Hello, darling." He kissed the air near my left cheek. "Thank you for securing my invite."

"Anything for you." I waved at some family on the other side of the store. "Have you met everyone?"

Paolo fanned himself with his paperback. "Mercy, yes. Your Aunt Frannie and Grandma Sylvie have already invited me to be their side piece at senior citizen night at the Cherokee Casino."

I laughed. "I'm sorry. Ignore them."

"Ignore them? I cleared my calendar and offered to drive." Paolo glanced behind him as if making sure ears weren't listening. "How are my clothes being treated?"

"Very well." *So* well. Lachlan was too handsome to ignore, and every day I was losing my resolve to try. "You'd be proud."

My friend looked pleased. "And you? How are you being treated?"

I thought of the feeling of being in Lachlan's arms at the governor's gala, our last kiss, and my relentless desire to hang out with him on the couch tonight. "Also very well."

Paolo considered me for a moment before nodding. "I'm glad to hear it. Now stop monopolizing me, Olivia Sutton. I want to talk to Bitsy Carmichael and get the number of her pool boy."

"You don't have a pool."

"This is not a relevant detail." Paolo waved as he departed, happily leaving me to search out Bitsy near the tray of cucumber sandwiches.

"Olivia!" Hattie hugged me first, followed by Rosie.

Sylvie stuck a carrot in her mouth and took a crisp bite. "Well, well. If it isn't the newlywed. You look like you've been up all night."

Aunt Frannie handed me one of her famous cupcakes. "Are your evenings as hot as Rochelle's in chapter fourteen of *The Amnesiac Princess's Royal Bodyguard*?"

Hardly. "I've been at an amusement park all day. But...I have news."

Sylvie cupped her hand over her mouth and bellowed to the group. "Olivia's pregnant!"

"No!" I yelled over the delighted gasps. "I certainly am not." The faces of thirty-five women and one man fell in disappointment. "Celeste narrowed the candidate list down for the promotion. I'm a finalist!"

"That's great, sugar." Sylvie hugged me again and patted my back. "A little anticlimactic, but still stellar news."

"Congratulations, sis." Hattie handed me a cup of punch served in a bone china teacup. "Your boss would be crazy to pick anyone but you."

"Darn right." My grandmother got that glint in her eye and stepped closer. She was a woman who'd made a career on instinct and her ability to read people (plus an uncanny knack for making things explode). "Olivia Sutton, something else is on your mind. Out with it so I can successfully micromanage the situation before moving on to our book."

The rest of the club had migrated back to the food tables, leaving just my nosy family. "Monday is Lachlan's birthday," I told them. "On Halloween."

Hattie blinked.

Rosie frowned.

"Sounds like a good excuse to eat cake," Frannie said.

"With work being so crazy, the date, um, slipped my mind." I sounded like a total moron. "I just...I have nothing prepared." And there was so little time to throw anything together.

"You've planned a hundred events for us," Rosie said. "You threw the best grand opening celebration."

"And don't forget the birthday party you arranged for Miller's niece," Hattie added. "She still talks about the massive slip-and-slides."

"I do have an idea." It had come to me on the ride over, somewhere between Main Street and Pecan Lane. "My guess is Lachlan didn't celebrate much growing up, so I'd love to recruit your help."

"I have access to some leftover fireworks from the last Olympics." Sylvie looked quite proud of herself. "They're one step below dynamite. Guaranteed to light up your world."

"A little more low-key," I said.

"When you get your idea sorted out, tell us what you need." Hattie's calm demeanor provided a balm to the hectic energy vibrating in my system. "We'll all be happy to help."

"Glad we got that settled." Sylvie reached for her book, stuck two fingers between her teeth, and gave a shrill whistle. "Everyone grab your yummies and take a seat."

As we shuffled to the seating area, my anxiety lessened over Lachlan's birthday. I wasn't sure I could pull off my plan, but with my family's help, it was possible. How had Lachlan managed without a family's support? It hurt my heart to even think about.

Sylvie poured white wine into her teacup and took a fortifying sip. "Now don't forget, next week Rosie's hosting author Jane Montgomery. Jane will sign copies of her novel *The Pescatarian Space Alien Who Loved Me*." She settled into a royal blue chair that sported more character than cushion. "Let's chat about our latest read. How about that limo scene?"

Frannie stood and raised her hand. "I would like to do a dramatic reading."

Oh, geez. If she picked page 285 I was leaving.

"Read page 285!" yelled my grandma.

Rosie sat down beside me and shot me a covert eye roll. "She does the worst British accent."

Frannie gave a solemn nod and cleared her throat. "Rochelle found it hard to remember her own name, but she'd never forget that bodyguard. His dark hair glistened and—"

A pounding on the door interrupted the performance.

"Keep going!" Pastor Mary Higgins demanded.

But the knocking grew louder and more insistent.

"I'll see who it is." Rosie set down her book and scurried to the front of the store.

"It had better not be my cat sitter again." Nadine Simpkins, custodian of the elementary school, shook her white head. "I told Mr. Whiskers and Patty Pitter-Pat that mommy needed her night off."

Rosie unlocked the antique doors with a trio of clicks. "It's Lachlan."

Lachlan? What was he doing here?

"Does he know you're pregnant?" yelled Marge Beaumont.

Lachlan stepped inside and froze. His gaze scanned the room before settling on me.

"Turn up your hearing aids, Marge." I squeezed the elderly woman's shoulder as I passed by. I could feel the curious stares of everyone in the store following me straight to Lachlan.

"Sorry to interrupt the party," Lachlan said to the ladies before turning his attention back to me. "I need a word with my wife."

Frannie sank her lips into a cupcake. "Is that code for heavy petting?"

"Y'all can talk in my office." Rosie shot me a wink. "Just know the security cameras catch *everything*."

"And she'll use the footage to blackmail you into stocking shelves," Hattie said. "Or so I hear."

Lachlan took my hand and led me toward the back, past the memoir section and beyond the display of locally crafted bookmarks. Paolo gave a nod of approval as we passed by, blessing Lachlan's attire. Tonight my husband-of-inconvenience wore dark jeans, a sweater the color of chestnuts, and a frown that put me on alert.

"Whose baby are you having?" Lachlan asked as we walked past the cozy mysteries.

"Chris Hemsworth's," I told him. We were out of view of the book club gang, and I could easily slip my hand out of Lachlan's. But I didn't.

"Which Chris is he?"

"Thor."

"Can't compete with that." Lachlan grimaced as he pulled me into the office. "I think I could hold my own with that Captain America guy, but not a Hemsworth." He inspected a framed photo on a shelf for a long moment. "I feel stupid being here."

Something was definitely bothering my husband tonight. "Why *are* you here?"

"I've been calling you for hours." Standing by my sister's desk, he ran a hand through his slightly disheveled hair, mussing it in a way that only made him cuter.

"My phone got waterlogged. Not sure if it's fixable." If not, I would certainly be getting another one first thing tomorrow morning. I felt like someone had removed one of my organs. "Are you all right?" Lachlan's cheeks tinged red, and his thumb

291

brushed my palm. My breath instantly went shallow, and I suddenly wondered if this was how Princess Rochelle felt when she first woke up from her coma. "Lachlan?"

"I thought something had happened to you. You said you'd be back from Branson around four. Those roads are terrible."

"How do you know that?"

"Miller told me. On the fifth time I called him. He said you always had your phone. When you didn't come home and didn't answer, I got worried." He gave a mirthless laugh. "Look at me being the overly protective husband, right?"

I was trying very hard not to melt like s'more chocolate at his concern. "I'm sorry. Celeste scheduled a late meeting, then I came straight here."

"I'm..." His throat moved as he swallowed. "I'm glad you're okay." Lachlan's chest beneath that high-dollar sweater rose and fell as his breath whooshed from his lips. He planted his hands on his hips. Nodded twice.

Then he hugged me.

Full-on—body grab, big arms wrapped around me tight, his head resting against mine—hug.

Gosh, he smelled like cedar and autumn nights and exactly the place I wanted to be. "Can't breathe here, husband." But I could feel his rapid heartbeat beneath my cheek. And maybe I did nestle in just a bit. Only because it was chilly. We were simply victims of an old and drafty office.

"Do not read into this," he said against my hair.

"Wouldn't dream of it."

"I didn't fear for your life." One hand slid up and down my back. "I wasn't imagining every single terrible scenario."

I bit my lip on a smile. "No?"

"No. I have a podcast interview with Anderson Cooper next week and didn't want to have to find another wife to help."

I wasn't sure when my hands had wrapped around Lach-

Ian's waist, but there they were. And they didn't seem inclined to move. "You'd never find another willing lady by next week."

"I'd need two weeks at least."

"Lachlan?"

"Yeah?"

"I'm sorry I didn't call you. I'm not used to checking in with someone."

He went quiet for the space of three even breaths. "I'm not used to caring."

I closed my eyes against those words and the feather stroke of tenderness behind them.

Lachlan's hands slipped from my back, and he retreated one step. Scowling, he massaged the side of his neck. "That came out a little sweeter than I meant it to."

"You can take it back if you want." Why was I looking at Lachlan's lips? I needed to stop. *Look away. Break contact. Rebuke the lips.*

Still. That mouth had kissed mine. My face remembered it and leaned in for a reunion.

Then Lachlan leaned. His hands reached for me again and—

"Oh, Olivia, sugar!" My grandmother's voice broke through the heady fog billowing behind my eyes, and in one turn of a page, she peeked into the office. "There you two are. I hate to break up this lovefest, but Frannie has wrapped up her theatrical interpretation, and if you don't come back and help the discussion, I fear dear Fran will pick another selection."

What I wanted was to shut the door and get kissed senseless by my husband. But my grandmother wouldn't leave us alone until I returned to book club. "I'll be right there."

I escorted Lachlan back to the front of the shop. If I walked a little closer to him than usual, it was simply the fatigue. And if I looked up at his face and took in that profile more than once, it was just for the sake of our audience.

I opened the door, and Lachlan stepped outside into the night. And didn't he look like the most desirable hero with the wind in his hair and the stars twinkling in the inky sky above?

He'd only taken two steps when he turned back around. "Olivia?"

When had I grown to love what the evening hours did to that voice? "Yes?"

Lachlan's hand went to my cheek, and he pressed a soft, lingering kiss against my lips. "I don't want to take it back."

THIRTY-NINE

LACHLAN

Dearest husband,

For your birthday, I've decided to be nice to you.

Don't get used to it.

Meet me back here at five.

If you're game.

Love,

Your favorite wife

ON MONDAY NIGHT I reread the note from Olivia and smiled. I'd found it on the kitchen counter this morning, right by the coffeepot. While that was a nice surprise, the greater shock was Olivia standing at the stove, spatula in hand, her bottom lip captured between her teeth.

"What are you doing?" I asked.

"Making pancakes." She slid two onto a plate, where five more formed a leaning tower. "Do you have time to eat breakfast?"

Was *Dungeons & Dragons* the best RPG ever created? Did Mario burn for Princess Peach? "I always have time for pancakes."

Olivia wore her hair up, and tendrils framed her face. She rose on tiptoe in those hot pink heels I loved and pulled two more plates from the cabinet. "Grab your coffee and sit."

Was this a dream? Surely Olivia Sutton was not only cooking, but cooking for *me*? "What's going on here?" I asked. "Should I trust you at the stove?"

"Happy birthday, Lachlan." She set down a plate of steaming pancakes at my usual spot at the island, then went back to fill her own plate.

"You're eating with me?" I checked the clock on the microwave. "You're usually at work by now."

Olivia shrugged and served us each two slices of bacon. Then she climbed onto the stool right beside me, her leg pressed against mine. "Work can wait."

A feeling settled in my chest, one I tucked away to unfold and examine later.

My wife picked up her fork and cut one small bite of pancake. Like a desperate man, I watched that bite slip between her lips and disappear.

"In my family," she said, "we have a tradition of a big breakfast on birthdays. And normally since it's your day, you'd get to pick what you want to eat." Her mouth bare of lipstick lifted in an uncertain smile. "I didn't know what you preferred, so I just went with pancakes."

I knew I liked her a lot.

I could admit that, but the revelation came with its share of trouble. I wasn't supposed to like my wife. We were pedal to the floor, speeding straight for Splitsville.

"How'd you know it was my birthday?" I asked.

Olivia pierced another bite with her fork. "I know a lot about you, Lachlan Hayes."

I smiled and tried to ignore the floral scent of her perfume that would haunt my kitchen after she left. "Oh, yeah? How old am I today?"

Her knee bumped mine, and she didn't seem inclined to move. "Fifty."

No hour was too early for sarcasm for my Olivia. "Nice try. Do you have a thing for older men?"

"No, I just fantasize about the senior discount at the Dairy Barn."

"Maybe your next husband will get you half-price shakes."

Then she changed the topic and caught me off guard. "Do you miss your mom on days like today?"

The question instantly irritated, like a cactus needle to the skin. "Birthdays are just another day, Olivia."

She had taken a sip of coffee, her eyes watching me over the steaming mug. "It's okay if you do miss her. You should've been surrounded by loved ones on every single birthday."

I'd had birthdays where I'd dug myself a pit and wallowed in it for days. Not one birthday passed that I didn't think of my mom and wish she could be there to celebrate with me. Then that usually led to thoughts of my dad, and from there the world turned dark and stormy. "I'm a big boy. I don't need anyone to throw me a party."

She chewed her bacon thoughtfully for a moment. "Everyone needs a birthday party. And you didn't answer my question."

"I believe I did."

"I would miss my family if I couldn't be with them on my birthday."

"But you might not be with them next year."

A glimmer of sadness dimmed her eyes. "True. But they'll be with me in spirit." One more drink of coffee, then Olivia poured another round of syrup onto her plate.

"What are we doing at five o'clock?" I asked a few pancakes later, more than intrigued.

"It's a surprise." Her smile turned mischievous and entirely kissable as she stacked our empty plates. "Don't be late."

"You're not going to drive me to a secluded forest and make sure I'm never heard from again, are you?"

"Don't be ridiculous. We have a fake baby to raise."

"Nope," I'd told her as I stood. "That's between you and Hemsworth. I can't love a baby who's genetically guaranteed to be too beautiful to be mortal."

"You're not too hard on the eyes yourself." And with that, my ever-serious wife swatted me on the backside and whistled a happy tune as she left for work.

THE TIME WAS FIVE MINUTES TILL FIVE, AND I STOOD IN THE KITCHEN that evening, rereading the note, thinking poetic thoughts about the swoop and curve of Olivia's handwriting. It was strong and elegant—like her.

The door from the garage opened, and in she walked, a garment bag slung over her shoulder and the day's stress still fresh on her face.

"Hey," Olivia said.

"Hey, yourself."

She draped her bag over a barstool and tossed car keys on the counter. "Did you have a good birthday?" she asked.

"It might've peaked with the pancakes." I'd thought about our breakfast pretty much all day. Replayed our every move, every word spoken. Analyzed Olivia's unexpected act of kindness and wondered what it meant.

Maybe she'd just needed an excuse to eat pancakes.

Or maybe...she had feelings. Warm, maple syrup–covered feelings.

"Are you ready for the next event?" She chewed on her bottom lip, giving me a rare sighting of uncertainty.

"I'm not sure," I said.

"Trust me." Her heels clicked against tile as she walked to the garment bag and handed it to me. "I'd like you to wear what's in this bag tonight."

I looked at it, feeling the weight of foreboding. "If it's booty shorts, you should know I left all my crop tops in California."

She plucked off one dangling gold earring, then another. "Meet me back here in fifteen." Then she kicked off her heels. My neat, no-mess Olivia toed off those pink stilettos right in our kitchen.

My pulse stuttered. "If you're on your way to getting naked, I can be ready in five."

Olivia's laugh echoed as she headed toward the stairs. "You're wasting precious time, Lachlan." When she glanced back over her shoulder, I felt the impact straight to my solar plexus. "You won't want to miss this."

"I'll be here, Olivia." I watched my wife walk away, wondering when she'd become my next addiction. "I'll be right here."

FORTY
LACHLAN

"I LOOK RIDICULOUS." I sat in the passenger side of Olivia's SUV, wishing I had more legroom. Also wishing my legs weren't encased in tights. If anyone doubted how far I'd go for the crush that was my wife, they needed only look at tonight's attire.

Lips pressed together at an impish angle, Olivia shot me a furtive glance and made a right turn. "Stop complaining. You said you'd trust me."

"To buy me dinner." I tugged at my scratchy collar. "At worst I was thinking one of those Mexican restaurants where they stick a sombrero on your head and a mariachi band belts out happy birthday."

"Not for my husband," she said. "That's too unoriginal. Besides, I think the tunic and leggings look striking."

"I look like an overgrown elf." But I grinned despite myself as Olivia's car slowed, and I watched lines of children march in costume to houses, ready to collect their candy. "I can't believe you're taking me trick-or-treating."

"Believe it."

When I'd gone upstairs and opened up the garment bag, I'd found a Halloween costume inside. Had Olivia gone with a classic costume like a vampire or a ghost? No. Had she taken a modern approach and turned me into Superman or another manly hero? Unfortunately not.

No, I would be spending Halloween night dressed as a knight of the realm. One whose tunic barely covered his tuchus and whose tights were so snug, I was about to scare some children. Meanwhile, Olivia was Queen Guinevere, wearing a shimmering, flowy gown, those ever-present heels, and hair cascading in loose waves threaded with gold. She looked ethereal, like she'd walked out of the medieval mist. She was Lady of the Lake, while I was Man Who Likes to Wear Pantyhose.

"And what knight of the realm wears a lacy shirt?" The hideous garment would've gotten a man drawn and quartered.

"Pickings were slim at the party store," she said with zero conviction. "I think it's a bold mix of poetic gentleman on top and fierce warrior below."

"My *below* is trapped like sausage casing. Maybe we should just go home and watch some slasher movies instead. Who's going to give candy to a twenty-nine-year-old man?"

"This is Sugar Creek," Olivia said, adjusting the jeweled necklace resting over her chest. "I can promise you the good citizens will not be stingy with the treats." The car slowed, and she parked on a neighborhood street between a Jeep and a minivan. "Except for Homer Jenkins. He and the Mrs. give out those nasty orange and black peanut wads nobody wants."

Olivia got out and I followed suit. "Maybe we should've stolen a kid and brought him with us," I said. "We'd look more authentic."

"I tried." She smoothed her hands over what she called her empire waist dress. I had no idea what that meant, but I knew I liked it. "I couldn't find any child willing to hand over the loot at the end of the night."

"Kids today are so disrespectful."

"Come on, Mr. Hayes." Olivia reached for my hand and tugged me toward the sidewalk. "I'm about to show you how it's done."

In October, Arkansas could be hot as summer or cool as a winter day. Minus my obscene wedgie, tonight felt about perfect. The dimming sky showed off, painting a colorful canvas with a sunset streaked in hues of pink and purple. With all the advances made in digital graphics—even advances I'd created myself—I could never capture pigments like that. Nature would not be outdone.

The slight chill in the air meant a sweater was preferable, but a frilly tunic would suffice. The wind puffed, rattling leaves of orange, rust, and gold. That same breeze lifted Olivia's hair, making it dance free and wild. I watched her move—graceful and confident, wearing a smile that read friendly to passersby, yet flirtatiously evocative to me. I knew pieces of her would find themselves in a future game iteration, but this time in a more positive semblance. Maybe it would be the wave of her hair tonight. Maybe it would be the ocean blue eyes that saw every detail. Pieces of her would also stay permanently stored in my memory—her scent, her face, the gift that was tonight.

Her fingers tightened around mine, and she took a left on the next street like she was in a race for gold. "Step lively, Lancelot. I see little Timmy Johnson, and that kid grabs extra handfuls when he thinks no one's looking."

But Olivia knew.

You couldn't get a thing past my wife.

Like many of the neighborhoods in Sugar Creek, this one was a collection of Victorian homes painted in shades of sherbet and variations on white. The beauties had stories to tell, and their character and style made me regret my modern home on the edge of town. My house had afforded me the privacy and security my life required, but it had been a sterile place from the onset. Since Olivia had moved in, my house felt homey and warm. I didn't notice the emptiness or hear that nagging echo from the cold floors and lifeless walls.

In two shakes of an oak leaf, we climbed the steps of a mint green Queen Anne.

"Ring the bell," Olivia said.

"I'm not totally ignorant on the process," I told her. I pressed my gloved finger to the bell, praying the homeowner wouldn't see two adults and go to yelling.

"Do it again. The lady in there is practically deaf and refuses to wear her hearing aids."

I obliged, trying to be a sport.

"Are you clear on what you say when the door is opened?" Olivia asked.

"Bring me your wallet and no one gets hurt?"

Olivia's pink lips curved as we waited. "Don't forget I like sour candy."

I looked down at my wife, who was in a curiously playful mood tonight. "Is that a hint I'm supposed to choose your needs over mine?"

She turned back to the door. "I think that was in our vows."

A woman finally appeared, her hair as red as fruit punch. "Well, hello there! Don't you two look precious?"

I turned to Olivia. "She called me precious."

"It's a compliment." Olivia held out her plastic pumpkin. "Trick or treat, Marge." My wife gave a small incline of the head. "Do you have something to say, Lachlan?"

"Trick or treat, ma'am."

Marge tossed back her head and cackled. "Aren't you polite." Her commitment to volume was as commendable as it was painful. "Say, what are you two supposed to be? A lovely princess and her lace-loving stable boy?"

"Marge"—Olivia rested her hand on my arm—"this is my husband. You probably saw him at book club."

"I did indeed." The woman's gaze dipped southward. "Nice pants."

I moved my candy bag over the treasures of my kingdom. "Thanks."

Marge leaned against the doorjamb, seemingly oblivious to the line of kids forming behind us. "Do you read romance novels, young man?"

"I'm more of a nonfiction reader." Was I supposed to hold out the bag or wait for her to make the first move? This trick-or-treating stuff was as tricky as high school dating.

"Speak up, you tall, handsome thing." Olivia's friend tapped the side of her head. "Worked at the Daisy BB gun factory for forty years. Lost my hearing and my first husband to that place."

When Olivia's elbow dug into my side, I stifled a laugh. "I, um, I like books on programming, coding." Was I shouting? I was pretty sure I was. "Occasionally a biography."

"Hmph." Marge should've been impressed but was not. "Well, there's a lot to be learned from romance novels."

"I'll take your word for that."

She aligned her pointer finger inches from my nose. "You better treat this girl right, you hear me?"

I was pretty sure the entire block could hear her. "Yes, Ms. Marge."

"Okay, here you go." She tossed two handfuls of miniature candy bars into my bag. "Don't eat all that tonight. Sugar rots the teeth."

"Thanks, Marge." Olivia grabbed a few candy bars herself. "Happy Halloween." A Barbie and two PJ Masks took our spot as Olivia pulled me off the porch and down the sidewalk. "On to Cherry Lane."

Olivia had procured knee-high boots for me, and they loudly clicked against the concrete like ladies' heels. The bright side was if I ran out of room in my candy bag, I supposed my boots could store the overflow.

A robin's-egg blue Victorian was our next stop, and Olivia filled me in on the owner's longtime membership to Sylvie and Frannie's book club.

"Do not take any pamphlets from this lady," she said, climbing the steps to a cozy wraparound porch. "She has baked goods in that house, and we won't accept holy tracts in their place."

It occurred to me that Olivia would've made an excellent war general.

I knocked on the door and a smiling woman holding a giant bowl of popcorn balls appeared. She wore her dark hair in a crooked bun and a silver cross around her neck. "Happy Fall Appreciation Day," she said, then cut brown eyes to me. "I want you to know I do not support evil traditions. They are of the devil."

"The devil, huh?" I turned to my wife. "Is that who you borrowed my pants from?"

Olivia rolled her eyes and stepped between us. "Lachlan, this is Lupe García. Her husband pastors one of the many churches in Sugar Creek."

"The best church in Sugar Creek." Lupe leaned forward and spoke low. "You come see us. We don't serve that weak grape juice for communion, okay?"

I suspected Mrs. García had sampled the communion juice tonight. "I hear you're a proud member of Olivia's book club."

"I read the books three times each." She waggled her salt-and-pepper eyebrows. "For literary annotation purposes. Now,

Lachlan, being a newlywed, would you like to know the secret to a happy marriage?"

Olivia, who had been about to pop a Jolly Rancher in her mouth, dropped the candy back into her bag. "No, he doesn't."

But Mrs. García had her own pulpit to tend. "The secret to a happy marriage is lots of—"

"Don't say it, Lupe," Olivia warned.

"Cuddle time." Mrs. García peeked inside my candy bag and helped herself to an Almond Joy. "That's all I was going to say."

I grinned, enjoying the annoyance on Olivia's face. "I'll keep that in mind."

Lupe wasn't done. "Of course cuddle time always leads to something else, if you know what I mean."

"He does," Olivia said. "And he doesn't want to hear it.

"I so want to hear it."

Olivia ignored me. "What Lachlan wants is one of those popcorn balls you have right there."

Lupe kept her attention trained right on me. "If you need any marital advice, you come visit. Do you have a home church, Lachlan?"

"Not yet. I haven't been in Sugar Creek long."

Lupe tossed three cellophane-wrapped popcorn balls into my bag. "How are you at the handbells?"

"Not as good as I'd like."

She doled out a single popcorn ball to Olivia. "Pipe organ?"

"More of a keytar man myself."

"That is a shame." The woman dusted off her hands and gave an absent wave. "Well, good to meet you. And congratulations on your marriage." Then her wrinkled face split into an ornery grin. "Our Olivia is a treasure."

I looked at my wife. "I would agree."

Lupe shooed us off her porch. "Bye now. You two go eat popcorn balls and...cuddle."

Two blocks later we arrived at a single-story cream puff whose covered porch invited me to sit on its vintage metal glider. "Want to take a break and make out?"

"There are no breaks in trick-or-treating." Olivia inspected a row of mums and a garden flag that declared the owner to be a Hufflepuff. "Her doorbell's broken, so you'll need to knock."

"For the record, my make out idea was a sound one." I set my knuckles to the door. "This one won't yell at me like Marge, right?"

Olivia laughed. "Quite the opposite."

The screen door creaked open, and a young woman wearing an orange cardigan and a wholesome floral dress greeted us. She pushed up her glasses with a finger.

"Hi," I said.

"Hi?" The woman repeated, studying me over her glasses. "That's not what you say. Olivia, didn't you coach him?"

Olivia tsk-tsked. "Use your big boy words, Lachlan."

The current Mrs. Hayes was enjoying my discomfort a little too much, but somehow I would get her back.

I stuck out my candy bag and recited my line with more energy. "Trick or treat."

"There you go," Olivia said. "You're getting it. Lachlan, this is Tillie Smyth. She's a children's librarian at the Sugar Creek library. Tillie, this is Lachlan Hayes."

"Our patrons love the graphic novels based on your games, Mr. Hayes."

I shouldn't admit it, but I was mighty proud of the books. I donated them by the truckload every month, hoping they might inspire wayward, lonely kids like I'd been. "It's Lachlan."

"Tonight it's Sir Lachlan the Brave," Olivia corrected.

"I think she means Sir Lachlan Whose Pants Are So Tight

He's Losing Circulation." They did not want me to get into the topic of chafing. "And thank you, Tillie."

"You'll have to come by and speak to our teens sometime," the librarian said. "We have a gaming club."

"I'd be glad to."

Satisfied, Tillie threw two Sugar Creek Library bookmarks in the bag. "Those bookmarks include instructions for getting your own library card." Then she added two king-sized bags of M&M's. "Easy sign-up online. Come on down, and we'll find you the perfect book."

"Thank you."

"He'd like to donate some gaming systems and copies of autographed *Mars Wars* books," Olivia said.

"Get out!" Tillie clasped a hand over her mouth. "That would be amazing."

"Happy Halloween, Tillie!" Olivia took my hand and led me down the steps. "We need to keep moving. We have a schedule to keep, and I've yet to score any Sour Patch Kids."

"See you at book club, Olivia!" the librarian called.

We visited more houses, but after about twenty stops, I lost count. I carried a bag so full of candy, I'd need to upgrade to a wheelbarrow if we added more.

"One final house," Olivia told me. "Let's drive for this one."

The sun had long set, and now the moon kept us company as we walked toward Olivia's SUV. Families shuffled by, with excited children leading the way. Streetlights flickered above, casting luminous shadows of Olivia and me onto the pavement.

Even with the occasional moments of awkwardness, I'd had a blast tonight. Olivia and I had laughed as we'd journeyed through the neighborhood. She'd regaled me with tales of everyone we met, leaving no gossipy detail unshared.

I'd awakened this morning with my usual birthday dread,

but my unexpected wife had turned it all around. She'd made the day into something I enjoyed. I mean, sure, the candy was great, but being with Olivia tonight almost felt like home.

Were we just getting that good at faking it?

Or had we stumbled into something real?

It seemed like the most natural thing in the world to reach for her hand as we strolled. She didn't pull away, didn't even flinch. Olivia just slid me a look in the dark, her smile something I'd remember when I was white-headed and overcome with years. Then she held my hand all the way to the car, as if we were a couple.

As if we were in love.

CHAPTER

FORTY-ONE

LACHLAN

Five minutes later Olivia stopped the car, this time parking right in the driveway.

"Last one," she said. "Get your grabby hands ready."

She opened her door, but I reached for her arm, halting her departure. "Olivia?"

"Yes?" A cacophony of children's voices swelled outside.

"Thank you," I said.

She smiled, a small gesture that sent an arrow straight to the bull's-eye of my heart. "Happy birthday, Lachlan. No one should be deprived of one of the best holiday traditions ever created."

I thought of my mother and the insane hours she'd worked, something I hadn't truly appreciated until I was out on my own. I wished I could go back and tell her it was okay, that I loved her and was so grateful for all she'd sacrificed. "My mom did the best she could, you know?"

"You bet she did." Olivia placed her hand in mine.

"I missed out on a lot growing up, but she missed out on more."

Her eyes softened. "She'd be very proud of you."

"I hope so." I glanced down at my tights. "Maybe not at this exact moment. But in a general sense."

"Every moment. You've accomplished so much, Lachlan. And you're just getting started."

"Olivia." I swallowed against a strange pressure, rearranging thoughts until they might come out right. "Why did you do this?"

"Your pants? They didn't carry your size. Did I try very hard to find another pair? Hm, maybe not."

"I mean all of this. Breakfast this morning. Giving me a childhood wish come true tonight."

"Because..." She paused, her gaze dropping to the console between us.

I slid a hand up the column of her neck, easing along the angle of her jaw and resting against her cheek. "Because why?"

Her pink tongue made a slow swipe across her top lip. "I wanted you to have a real birthday. I couldn't think of anything to get you that you couldn't buy yourself, so I created an event. That's what I do."

It was more than that. For her, for me.

I brushed my thumb across her velvet cheek. Saw her lips part and her eyes ignite. "I'm not sharing my candy," I told her.

Olivia leaned closer. "What's yours is mine and mine is yours. It's the law."

I was desperate to touch her, to taste the hope and possibility. "You can have ten percent."

"Twenty," she whispered.

I would've given Olivia everything I had. "Deal." Angling my head, I pulled her to me and lowered my mouth to hers.

Olivia's lips parted beneath mine, and relief and joy sang in my veins. Kissing Olivia was now my favorite thing. Forget game design. Who cared about movies and making money? All

I wanted to do was remain in the bubble that was this car and hold Olivia in my arms until my limbs gave out.

My hands cupped her face as she pressed against me. Olivia kissed like she meant it, and I cursed the console between us. I wanted to rip it out, pull her into my lap, and fog up these windows.

She sighed, a faint, satisfied sound that made me smile. Then she threaded her fingernails through my hair and gave my head a gentle tilt.

"Stop taking over," I said as I worshipped the curve of Olivia's top lip.

"I'm not." Laughing, she trailed a path from my cheek to my neck.

"I only have so much oxygen left before these pants kill me." I coaxed her mouth back to mine. "These last few moments of life should not be wasted."

"We're keeping those pants forever."

I'd just found the spot beneath her ear that made Olivia's breath catch when I heard the off-key blare of an air horn.

"Yoo-hoo!" The very familiar voice of Sylvie Sutton broke the atmosphere and crushed all my birthday wishes and dreams.

"Can we ignore her?" I asked as Olivia pulled away and straightened in her seat.

"Trick or treat, you lovebirds!" Sylvie yelled from the porch. "Keep it Rated G in this driveway!"

I scrubbed a hand over my face and counted backward from ten. "Let me guess. This is your grandmother's house?"

"You got it."

I ran my hand down her arm, making a thorough study of my disheveled wife. "Are we going to talk about what just happened?"

Suddenly the fair Guinevere couldn't quite meet my gaze. "You kissed me."

"You kissed me right back."

Her focus on the visor mirror, Olivia tidied her hair and straightened her regal crown. "I assumed it was for the sake of our audience." She snapped the visor shut. "Sylvie still needs plenty more convincing, so thank you."

The little liar. "Any time. Never let it be said I'm not a giver."

She flung open her door, peeled herself from the car, and brushed hostile hands against the crooked drape of her dress. "Let's go, Prince Spandex."

I smiled to myself. So far this marriage stuff wasn't half bad.

The Big Dipper winked between the magnolia trees as we walked up the driveway straight to where Sylvie stood with the door held open. She wore a platinum wig and a figure-hugging red dress. To everyone else, she probably looked just like Marilyn Monroe. All I saw was a saboteur.

"Hey, sugars." She patted her buoyant hair. "You got here just in time. Neighborhood intel reports Little Timmy Johnson's location is one block and three houses away. That boy makes candy disappear faster than Frannie escapes handcuffs."

I was learning sometimes it was best not to ask. "Hi, Sylvie," I said.

Her wig shifted as a strong breeze blew. "You have something to say to me?"

Of course she would take perverse pleasure in my discomfort. "Trick or treat."

Her pearly white teeth flashed in a grin. "I choose a trick."

Olivia threw out her hand, as if holding me back from a

crash. "Do not respond to that, Lachlan. It's too dangerous with this one. Sylvie, the man wants candy."

"Oh, I think he wants more than that." Olivia's grandma studied me, and not for the first time, I had the unnerving feeling she could read my mind. "Besides, it just so happens we're not giving out candy tonight."

Frannie poked her head out the door. "Only cupcakes."

I rolled my lace-covered shoulders and released some tension. "Even better."

"For goodness' sake." Frannie, dressed as a cowgirl, rested her hand on what I hoped was a fake holstered pistol. Brown eyes beneath unnaturally long lashes roamed across my form. "I see chest hair and the silhouette of a firm buttocks. Aren't you just the gift that keeps on giving?"

"She's harmless," Olivia said. "Aunt Frannie, please remember you have a boyfriend."

"Of course I do," Frannie said. "But a woman can still look. It's a free country. The Constitution protects my right to ogle."

Sylvie opened the door wider. "You know we're not going to let you two just grab cupcakes and leave. Come on in." She latched onto my hand and pulled me through the foyer. "Dark as sin in this house. Let me turn on some lights in my parlor."

At the click of a switch, light flooded the entire living room.

Revealing a houseful of familiar faces.

"Happy birthday!" they yelled in chorus.

Party horns blew off-key, confetti rained from the ceiling, balloons floated like clouds above us.

Miller, Hattie, Rosie, and many of the other folks I'd already met tonight. The remaining members of the book club. Paolo from the clothing store. A guy Olivia called Elton, who'd brought his dress-wearing poodle. John, the daytime security guard at the golf course. The two ladies who ran my favorite coffee shop downtown. Marvella Biggs, the woman who hit her golf balls into my backyard every Tuesday and Thursday morning.

The house was packed from seam to seam.

"Happy birthday, Lachlan." Olivia curved her arm around my waist and kissed my cheek. "Do you love the surprise?"

I looked down at my wife. "I think I do."

Music began to play, something soft and mellow, while people milled about. One by one, the visitors approached, offering me birthday greetings and the occasional comment on my attire.

"Are you hungry?" Olivia asked sometime later.

"Starved." My five Twix, four Reese's, and two Hershey's Kisses hadn't provided substantial sustenance. "But I'm afraid if I eat anything, I might bust out of these pants."

"That would make Frannie's year." Olivia jerked her chin toward the dining room. "Let's get in line."

She made a path through the crowd, and we only paused long enough to say hello to a few late arrivals. Olivia was a woman on a mission, and when it came to securing food, I couldn't say I minded.

"I had Giancarlo's Café cater." She handed me a plate. "I hope you like Italian."

Italian was my favorite, and I was certain Olivia knew that. "Sounds good to me."

Her phone must have vibrated from somewhere on her body, because she lifted the hem of her dress, then reached into her high-heeled boot. "Shoot, it's Celeste."

Celeste really needed to get a life. "Go ahead and take it."

Olivia stared at the screen while I grabbed a piece of hot, buttery bread. "No," she said. "Not tonight. This is the birthday boy's first Halloween." After a resolute nod, Olivia dropped the phone back into her boot and grabbed a plate. "Let's eat."

I spent the next hour mingling with the guests and going

back to the buffet table for seconds and thirds. Olivia and I had gotten separated three conversations ago, and I was more than content to watch her across the room. She could work a crowd better than anyone I'd ever known, and she sure knew how to throw a party.

Olivia now stood next to the fireplace talking to her sisters, both dressed as flappers. I'd spent the last decade obsessively studying people, and the good stuff was always in the nuance and details. Like an artist, I'd memorized every inch of Olivia's face and knew almost every mannerism. I loved how she often clapped her hands together twice when she laughed. I could get lost in the way she twirled her hair around one finger when she drifted in thought. I knew the difference in her genuine smile and the one she composed just to be polite.

And tonight, when Olivia's eyes scanned the room to find me, I nearly wept like a baby right in front of the remaining green beans and lasagna. (And yes, I was back for a fourth bite.) She'd done all this for me. On my birthday. As if it mattered. As if *I* mattered.

"You gonna take those last two pieces of bread or continue to hover over them in thoughtful consideration?"

I looked up to find Sylvie standing beside me. "I was just wishing for someone to share this other piece with."

She plucked the bread from my hand and took a buttery bite. "You're a pretty good liar. You know that, Lachlan Hayes?"

I thought of the lie that was my marriage. "I've suspected."

"You're over here looking a little forlorn. What's that about?"

"Just sad the Alfredo's all gone."

She pointed her bread crust in my direction. "You never suspected a thing, did you?"

"No." Had I guessed my wife would think of me on my birthday and plan an event so thoughtful it would take out my heart, wrap it in flowers, and hand it back to me? No, I hadn't guessed that. A birthday party this personalized was what people who loved each other did. Not two people who had been forced into a marriage. I knew my feelings for Olivia had crossed a line into full-on adoration. But the question was, what did she feel for me? "I assume you helped, Sylvie, so thank you."

"Olivia was the master planner. Worked her tail off. But all the family helped. Because that's what family does." Sylvie brushed some crumbs off the tablecloth, but her focus never strayed from my face.

"I'm very grateful."

"And you also look confused, hesitant, and like you're possibly losing feeling in your lower extremities."

At least two of those were correct.

"Let me tell you something, Lachlan." Sylvie stepped closer and put her hand on my shoulder. "You're family now, so you're one of us."

My eyes stung, and I had to blink and look away. What was wrong with me tonight? One mention of the word *family*, and I wanted to throw my arms around Sylvie and beg her to let me stay forever.

"It's an honor to be welcomed," I finally said.

Sylvie's eyes narrowed a fraction, and I knew she was holding up each word to the light and giving it a good study. "Sometimes it's hard to let yourself be loved, isn't it?" She didn't wait for my reply. "But it's there anyway—yours for the taking. Maybe it doesn't look like we think it will or happen the way we thought it would." She watched the room for a moment. "And sometimes the chance is offered to us only for a little while. So you have to be brave enough to take it. Else you'll risk losing what could be the best thing you never even knew you wanted."

I could hear my own heartbeat. Feel sweat bead at my brow.

"You're part of this family now, Lachlan." Sylvie patted my back. "You're good for our girl, and I do hope you'll stick around."

Thoughts heavy, my gaze drifted over the living room and foyer.

"Olivia snuck outside." With a long red nail, Sylvie pointed to my left. "Back door. Dollars to diamonds, you'll find her on the porch. She's always been a stargazer, our Olivia."

The woman had eyes in the back of her head. "Thank you."

"No, my dear." Sylvie curved her hand against my rough cheek. "Thank you."

I wove through the crowd, ignoring Miller's offer of a drink and pretending not to hear Frannie's catcall to dance. Exiting the living room, I made a beeline for the kitchen, as my man-leggings and I strode out the back door.

Then I saw her.

Standing at the edge of the porch, staring up at the stars. She was the light in the dark, my Olivia.

The storm door slammed behind me, and she turned.

"Lachlan. Hey." The corners of her mouth lifted in a tired smile. "How do you like the party?"

I was by her side in four strides.

Four steps to get to Olivia, lay my hands on her like I'd wanted to since we left her car, and pull her taut against my body. I'd intended to draw her to me and kiss her until we both couldn't breathe.

So how to explain what happened instead?

Somehow I just...hugged her. I wrapped my arms around my wife and held her like she was the only thing that could steady all that was shaky and unstable within me. My cheek found a place to rest on the top of her head, and I breathed in the scent of candy, a distant neighbor's bonfire, and the essence that was Olivia. She felt so right in my arms. Even with our height difference, she was still the perfect fit.

"Thank you," I managed to say. "Thank you, Olivia."

Delicate hands that commandeered a thousand tasks a day curved around my waist. Olivia melted against me, and I closed my eyes, letting myself be in the moment and absorb the new sensations of safety and...wholeness. This might not be love, but it could be the closest I ever got, and I wanted it to seep into my every pore.

Words failed me, as they often did. I wasn't the eloquent one between us. Olivia had provided a Halloween night that ten-year-old Lachlan never got to experience. I had friends inside the house and a table of wrapped presents bearing tags with my name. Yet what mattered most—almost to the point of aching—was the heart and care behind it all. That was the greatest gift.

"Hey, Lachlan?" came Olivia's voice.

I sighed against her hair. "We have to go in, don't we?"

One hand took a slow path from my back to my hip. "There's cake in there. If Frannie and Sylvie don't get to sing happy birthday to you, they'll ignore us for a week."

"And that's a bad thing?"

Olivia leaned back and smiled, and when she did, the air shifted. The wind changed.

It now blew in a direction that pushed Olivia and me together, instead of apart. The atmosphere no longer swirled with animosity and bitterness. Gone was the old anger and sharp-edged annoyance.

What was in its place frightened me to my battered core.

I loved her.

I loved Olivia.

This was...unexpected. And a bit terrible.

"Let's go inside," she said, finally stepping out of arms reluctant to release her.

"You go ahead." I took her fingers in mine and kissed the hand that carried her wedding band. "I'll be inside in a bit." I needed a second to get it together, to possibly convince myself I'd confused love with sentimentality. To relish the kind of moment I might never have again.

Olivia hesitated, but with a squeeze of her hand, let me go.

I watched my medieval princess walk inside, her dress billowing and her hair wild against the breeze.

I knew I was in trouble.

I had fallen for my wife.

And that game could never end well for someone like me.

FORTY-TWO

OLIVIA

OLIVIA

This afternoon we meet Paolo and try on tuxes.

LACHLAN

I already bought a tux.

OLIVIA:

This one's for the movie premiere.

LACHLAN

Tuxedos are all the same.

OLIVIA

Like video games are all the same?

LACHLAN

My divorce attorney will be contacting you immediately.

"She's smiling again, Rosie."

"You're right, Hattie. Lots of teeth. Cheeks engaged. Major smile." After flipping the store sign to closed, Rosie eased herself into a seat beside Hattie at the Lost Story Bookshop one week later.

"I smile all the time." Sitting in my favorite green chair, I sipped my coffee and tossed my phone into my bag. I had one hour until I was supposed to meet Lachlan at Paolo's.

Hattie observed me with those therapist's eyes. "Yes," she agreed. "Lately you do."

I did not want to dig into that with my sisters. Had I enjoyed the last few months with Lachlan? Yes. Had something shifted between us since his birthday? Oh, my goodness, yes. It seemed every time we'd been together, some Jenga puzzle piece of old assumptions fell away, and I feared soon that tower would crash and leave me with a broken heart. "Can we get back to how awesome Lachlan's interview with Anderson Cooper was?" I set my mug down on the dark oak table that squatted between me and my sisters like a boundary line. "Hattie, I've bragged on your new therapy initiative at the farm. Rosie, I've praised your Thanksgiving romance novel display." It really was a clever combination of cleavage and feathers. "I do believe I deserve more attagirls for his recent triumphs." Grinning, I propped my heels on the coffee table. "Please commence with bragging."

"Lachlan's birthday party went well too," Hattie said.

I opened my laptop and clicked on a document. "I think so. Thank you for all the help. Now, can we get to next month's store events?" Rosie had three young adult authors doing a book signing and writing workshop for teens, and we needed to decide on promotion.

Rosie peeled the wrapper off one of Frannie's cupcakes. "I'll post on my socials and in my newsletter. We'll call the paper and put some flyers in town. But back to you, Olivia. Lachlan couldn't take his eyes off you at his party."

I'd noticed his gaze on me often that night, and every moment we'd been together since. While I'd often found Taylor rolling his eyes at my extremes, Lachlan made me feel like I could be myself around him, and not only did he like it, but maybe I even made him happy. "We are married," I reminded them. "Crazy about each other and all that."

"Lachlan was clearly touched by the trick-or-treating idea," Hattie said. "Appealing to a wounded inner child is a thoughtful, loving choice, Olivia."

My sister's pointed scrutiny made me squirm. "And I got a bag of candy to boot, right?"

"Joke about it all you want," Rosie scolded, "but it was a really special moment for all of us to witness. You two totally get each other, you know? Your rushed relationship might've been quite unconventional—especially for you—but don't waste a single second of it. Take it from me, life is short, and you're lucky to have someone to share it with."

"Look, Olivia," Hattie said, "we had our doubts about you two, but seeing you and Lachlan together on Halloween made me realize he really does love you."

Love me?

No.

How on earth would Hattie get that impression? Surely it was just the façade we'd carefully crafted. Did I think he liked me quite a bit? Yes. But love? Surely not.

The very idea both thrilled and frightened. I'd been fooled by the illusion of love once before, and I couldn't make that mistake again.

"I'm glad you feel better about my...*unconventional* marriage," I finally managed.

"We both do," Rosie said. "It's clear you're crazy about Lachlan as well."

My smile froze on my face.

A retrospective of my time with Lachlan played in front of my eyes. Waking up in his arms in Vegas, our kiss in the bookshop, dancing with him at the governor's gala. Lachlan's laugh, his creative, sharp mind. The way my hand so easily sought his out, and the perfect fit of my fingers against his. His scent and his wry, boyish grin. The way he played the part of a loving husband unexpectedly well.

So well that I'd accidentally tumbled down a path paved with hearts and cupid bows.

But I swore to get back to my timeline. My Ten-Year Plan had never steered me wrong, no matter how many times I'd failed it. The plan was solid. It was well thought out. It had proven that love was a detour I couldn't afford until I reached my goals.

Maybe I did have it bad for my husband. Wonderful, silly, kissable Lachlan.

But Lachlan wasn't on my schedule.

And I couldn't fall for the man I would soon have to divorce.

CHAPTER
FORTY-THREE
OLIVIA

LACHLAN

The tux fitting is really just an excuse to see me in my underwear, isn't it?

OLIVIA

You do know the expectation is that you wear pants with this tux, right?

LACHLAN

What I know is that you sneak peeks of me in my boxers at home.

OLIVIA

Your Fortnight boxers glow in the dark. It's not like I meant to look.

LACHLAN

You keep telling yourself that, Mrs. Hayes. My undergarments and I will see you at Paolo's at eight.

PAOLO'S DRESSING rooms were chic and small.

Lachlan was not.

He had four tuxedos to try on, and the last five minutes had been nothing but the moans and groans of a man bumping elbows and knees into the walls.

Meanwhile I sat perched at the edge of a chair outside the dressing rooms, trying not to think about the fact that I madly adored my husband. Customers milled about, making their final selections before Paolo's closed for the evening.

"I can't get this shirt unbuttoned," I heard him mutter. "Who made this thing? The buttons are the size of Tic Tacs. Man-hands can't maneuver these."

Next came more sounds of body parts thudding against the cramped space, punctuated by a curse. "Do not rip that shirt, Lachlan," I warned him. "It costs more than my last paycheck."

All six-foot-something of Lachlan stood in that dressing room. Naked.

I needed to clear this visual from my head, so I thought of some distractions. Lachlan's article in *Fast Company*. Morgan landing a B list movie star influencer for Elite Matches. Celeste's son's robotics competition Saturday. Lachlan's bare chest and my hands running up his ribcage.

Not working!

Not. Working.

"Ouch." The dressing room door shook with the impact of a hit. "Just lost a button. I'll pay for it. The rest have to go, Olivia. I'm trapped in this straitjacket of a shirt. Seriously"—a grunt sounded from the dressing room—"can't get out. Remember me fondly."

"Don't pull on those buttons." I leapt from my chair and charged toward the dressing room.

"Is this how I die?" Lachlan groused. "Forever stuck in a

shirt and wasting away? I'm tearing this thing off. Going full-on Hulk in here, Olivia."

"No!" I flung open the door and it closed behind me with a thundering slam. "Hands off that shirt."

Lachlan looked down at the garment with disgust. "It's silk."

"I see that." He wore a shirt that was, indeed, quite ridiculous—and boxers. "It's very elegant." In the small dressing room, I stood toe to toe with Lachlan, wondering if I was pathetically deprived to be feeling light-headed at the sight of his bare legs.

They were legs. Everyone had them.

Still. Lachlan's were quite shapely. Long, with reddish hair dusted over his skin.

"Do you know who wears silk?" Lachlan growled. "People who are not me."

His fingers attacked the top row of buttons, and I smacked his hands. "Back away from the buttons and let me do this. What are you, a Neanderthal? We do not rip clothes. Especially Paolo's." I set to the task, and my palms made contact with Lachlan's chest. Spikes of heat and electricity jolted through my fingers and up my arms, as if I'd touched a live wire. Daring a look, I glanced up at Lachlan to see if he'd felt that, but his face gave nothing away.

"The tiny devil buttons, Olivia," he directed.

"Right." *Focus. Ignore the moderately firm muscle beneath your hands.* "Just forming my strategy."

"Mine would involve a sharp pair of scissors."

As shop chatter swelled outside, it felt like Lachlan and I were enclosed in our own little world. I popped one little button free from its hold, then another.

"Are your hands shaking?" Lachlan's voice near my ear went soft as the shirt's silk.

He smelled like spicy shampoo and man. "It's been a few hours since my last Red Bull. Probably need another hit." I willed my hands to cease their quivering while I slipped another button loose. Then another. It was hard to remain steady when I'd just realized I adored my soon-to-be-ex-husband, yet could not, should not have him.

In a matter of four shallow breaths, I finally finagled that silk shirt halfway undone. Lachlan's hair-speckled chest was on display, and I couldn't recall my own name.

"Olivia?"

That name sounded familiar. Probably mine.

Not removing my hands from the planes of Lachlan's chest, I slowly...slowly...raised my eyes to his.

And instantly noticed he didn't look so impassive now.

The gold flecks in Lachlan's eyes burned bright against the backdrop of green, and the intensity there would've knocked me back a step if there had been room. "Yes?" My voice came out parched, as if I'd been walking the desert in search of an oasis.

Lachlan's palm skimmed down the back of my head and trailed lightly against the length of my hair. "I've been wanting to say something to you for a while."

Did he know? Did Lachlan know I had ocean-deep feelings for him I must deny? "Go ahead." My eyes dipped back to his torso, but I quickly recovered. "I'm listening."

"I know I should've said something sooner, but...what you did for me on my birthday meant the world to me." Now Lachlan's knuckles traced a bold line above the neckline of my dress, skimming across bare skin and leaving a trail of shuddering awareness. "It was thoughtful and generous—the best present I've ever gotten."

"I'm..." Sometimes it was hard to tell if you were looking at the best thing ever or your next big regret. "I'm glad."

Lachlan's voice softened. "I wanted to tell you that night at home, but when I went to your room, you were asleep. And then with all my interviews and appearances, we haven't had a chance to talk much this week."

I released one more button and kept my grip on the opening of Lachlan's shirt. "You'd already thanked me."

"But it wasn't enough. Words couldn't adequately convey what that night meant."

My next line was "Then what could?" but I found myself unable to utter it. We were headed somewhere in this moment, two people in a canoe racing toward the waterfall. If we pitched over, it would either be the greatest thrill...or our demise.

"I think about you in that bedroom beside me." Lachlan stepped into what was left of the meager space between us. His body bumped mine, sending shock waves along my limbs. "I think about you all day, actually. Wonder if you're chewing on your pen like you often do. Or if you've wound your hair in a bun using that elastic thing you keep on your wrist."

When Lachlan reached for that wrist and pressed a kiss to the pulse that thudded beneath my hair tie, the bones in my legs dissolved. I was no longer a solid. I was a mass of gelatinous want and feeling. The only thing that could hold me up, the only one who could save me was Lachlan.

"I need you to know that you've come to mean a lot to me," he said beside my ear, before grazing the same spot with his lips. "So much that I'm consumed. On fire with it. I can hardly work for thinking of you. And wondering"—lips hovered over mine, taunting, teasing, and daring me to accept—"if you feel the same."

This man was a risk greater than any I'd ever faced. He held the power to ruin my career and crush my heart. Yet in this moment, closer than two bodies could be without combusting, I could only say, "Yes. I think I might."

He considered this. "I'll take it."

I wanted to trace his smile and memorize it with my hands. But mostly, I wanted to kiss it and go right over the edge, risking the fall.

Lachlan rested a hand over my head, his palm flat against the wall. Trying that again, were we?

"It's almost nine o'clock," he said. "I checked your schedule, and do you know what happens now?"

"I can't even tell you who the president is right now." I needed Lachlan's lips on mine and soon.

His head dipped, and his nose trailed against my cheek. "It says I kiss you."

"Does it?" My heart presently floated somewhere in the stratosphere, and I wondered if it would ever come back down. "I don't recall penciling that into the itinerary."

"I'm working off the edited version." Lachlan slid his hand into my hair before his fingers gently traced a silky strand. "Yes or no on this calendar amendment?"

There was really only one answer here. "Yes," I whispered. Not one to let opportunity pass me by, I rose on tiptoe and pressed my lips to his.

But then Lachlan pulled back, a slight lean of retreat. "I'm not kissing you as your fake husband." His eyes held not one trace of humor. "It's just you and me, Olivia. No pretense." Taking my hand, he placed it on his bare chest, right over his heart. "I'm going to ask you one more time. Yes...or no?"

Laughter peeled from inside the store. A cash register printed and spit out a ticket. Conversations blurred and blended outside our door.

But everything I wanted was right there in my arms.

My hand itched to move over his skin. I would worry about

my life plan tomorrow. "Lachlan, if you don't kiss me, we're buying this shirt for your premiere."

The taut clench of his jaw lessened, and his gaze went tender. "Then we better get to it. Because this thing is an abomination."

I rather thought the garment had served a purpose.

Lachlan took the hand over his heart, turned it over, and placed a kiss in the center of my palm, lingering there for a moment.

I couldn't take any more. Make fun of me and my schedules all day long, but time was meant to be used and the day meant to be captured.

And time for talking was over.

I threaded my hands through hair I had itched to touch again and pulled Lachlan's face to mine. Before I could take lead, Lachlan's mouth closed over mine, a laugh vibrating in his throat.

Holy day planners. This was perfection.

Angels could keep their pearly gates and their harp-threaded songs. Lachlan's emotion-fueled kiss was all the heaven I'd need. It was danger and safety, exhilaration and calm.

I sank into that kiss and let it pull me under. The world disappeared, leaving only two people on the planet. We were an island, and Lachlan was a marooned man in need of saving.

A nip here, a slow drag of lips there. Everything in me was on fire, and I couldn't get enough of this unexpected husband of mine. His mouth trailed a path from my cheek, then along the line of my jaw. That sensitive spot beneath my ear called Lachlan's name, and as if reading my mind, he obediently answered. Did he taste the salt of my skin or feel the beat of my pulse against his mouth?

Lachlan returned his attention to my lips as I finally gave

into the temptation to skim my hands beneath the shirt he detested. Warm, soft skin was my reward, and I let my fingers learn the terrain.

Yes, we'd kissed before, but not like this. It had never felt like this.

This was surrender and solace, with zero artifice, and I couldn't get enough.

"Everything going okay in there?" Paolo called.

My heart pounding, I somehow found the will to break the kiss.

Lachlan ran his knuckles down my flushed cheek. "Better than expected."

"Let me know if you need anything!" Paolo walked away, leaving Lachlan and me entwined like a mall pretzel.

"You and I need to talk," Lachlan said. "Things have changed."

Feeling too much at once, I could only nod.

His hand still planted over my head, he dipped his head and kissed me again.

Things had changed.

Like my odds of another heartbreak, my complications in moving to New York, and the expectation that I hold up all my carefully crafted plans and light them on fire.

I'd lost myself in a relationship before and vowed to never do that again.

Could I risk it all once more—for Lachlan?

CHAPTER
FORTY-FOUR
LACHLAN

I'D ONLY WAITED a lifetime for this weekend.

Yet here I was, cutting it close for boarding a ridiculously small plane to San Francisco for TechieCon, and all I could think about was how much I'd miss my wife.

Olivia stood beside me in the lobby of the regional airport Friday morning, and I pulled her to me, wrapping my arms around her fancy clothes, not caring a whit that I was surely wrinkling them. "Come with me to California."

"Lachlan, go find your gate before they leave you."

We'd gotten stalled on the interstate thanks to a wreck, leaving us minutes to spare. "Then we could drive. Together. I'll let you have control of the music for at least twenty percent of the time, and I'll fill the long, boring hours with detailed descriptions of my favorite moments in gaming."

Olivia laughed, a sound I loved more than the *Mars Wars* movie soundtrack I'd just heard last week. "I can't," she said. "I need to stay close to home for work." She rested her cheek against my sweater, one of those fussy wool things Paolo had selected. "But I'll pick you up when you get back."

"Then we sit down and talk. I have some things I want you to hear."

"What sorts of things?" Uncertainty flashed in her eyes, but I ignored it.

"Life decision things." Then before Olivia could utter another question, I leaned down and kissed her, wanting to leave her with another reminder of where my intentions clearly were now.

My lips gently teased hers, a whisper of touch and a preview of what we'd build on later. As she sighed into the kiss, I smiled, wishing we could stay there in that spot forever. Because the old anxiety whorled through my thoughts, telling me that what I had with Olivia was merely a mirage of what I wanted. But love could be more than an evaporating mist in my life.

The remnants of fear tried to squeeze between us, and I fought to shut out the foreboding feelings. I deserved love and a family. Those things that had been so easy for everyone else and so elusive for me. It was my turn. I wanted it all—Olivia, a thriving company, and, yes, maybe a little bit of payback.

I'd waited long enough. I just needed to talk to her and make sure we were on the same page, that she wanted to continue our relationship, and toss out any ideas of a divorce. But that would have to wait until I returned.

"You need to go." Olivia's hands held my face as she opened her lips against mine one more time. "The security lines here can be brutal."

I sighed and breathed her in, wanting to record this moment, her scent, and the feel of her in my arms. "Don't let Celeste harass you while I'm gone."

"Harassment is my husband's job," she said.

"He sounds terrible." My brain worked overtime analyzing her smile. Was it genuine? Strained?

"That's what I tell him."

"Wait, I almost forgot." As fight update announcements blared overhead, I dug into the pocket of my bag and pulled out a small box.

"What's this?" Olivia asked.

The lid opened with a dramatic click, and I held the box up for her inspection. Nestled in velvet, a shiny ring blinked in greeting. Two rows of rubies encircled a bold cushion-cut diamond, all set in an engraved band of floral and scrollwork.

"Is...is that for me?" she asked, her eyes wide on mine.

I didn't expect to feel self-conscious, but if this moment were a game sequence, it would be a frozen screen where every pixel was afraid to move. "Uh, yeah," I said. "It's occurred to me more than once that you never got an engagement ring. I finally did something about it." Olivia's face registered something akin to shock, but was that good shock? A bad, get-this-ring-out-of-my-face shock? "We've been photographed so much, I thought you needed to wear more than your band from the Vegas chapel, that according to my credit card statement, cost me a whopping ninety-nine dollars."

She held her left hand to her chest. "I kind of love our cheap bands."

"So you don't want this?" *This ring? My heart? My pride and shredded confidence?*

Olivia stared at the jewelry box, and one TSA agent and two families passed by before she finally spoke. "Of course I want it. Lachlan, it's beautiful."

She wanted the ring. I would not suffer utter and complete humiliation downwind of an Auntie Anne's pretzel shop. "I'm glad."

In my head, I'd practiced this a few times, and I'd said some really profound and moving sentiments. But now I could only watch Olivia, scanning her face and body language for all possible signals. Something was off; I was certain.

"Allow me." I plucked the ring from the box, then reached for Olivia's hand. "It matches very nicely with the gold-plated band blessed by Celine Dion." Then I slipped it over her finger, briefly bringing her hand to my lips for a quick kiss. "I guess we're going steady now." She said nothing, and the doubts began to stack in my head. "I wanted you to have it for the movie premiere. Red Carpet and all that."

Olivia stared at the ring glinting beneath the harsh airport lights. "Thank you."

I felt a scene change—as if we transitioned to a different level when I slipped that ring on Olivia's finger. Yes, I could be paranoid about anything that had to do with a relationship, but I swear her posture straightened, her eyes lost a fraction of warmth, and a hint of that old reserve returned.

Somewhere behind me a camera flashed.

Olivia glanced beyond my shoulder, then her gaze drifted back to me. "Good luck on the announcement. Keep me posted."

I leaned in and kissed her, hating that we didn't have time to have our big state-of-the matrimonial-union talk right then. "I'll text you every hour."

"That's not what I meant." She laughed against my lips, giving me a small measure of relief.

"Fine." I pressed my mouth to her cheek. "Every fifteen minutes, but any more than that, and I run out of quality content."

"Go, Lachlan. Catch your plane." Olivia gave me one last hug. "I'll see you soon."

"You know you're going to miss me," I said as I began to inch toward the check-in kiosk.

"I'll cry in my pillow every night."

"You can dry your tears on that bedspread you call a nightgown."

She gave a small wave. "Goodbye, Mr. Hayes."

"Goodbye, Mrs. Hayes."

I made quick work of the check-in kiosk and thought I might find Olivia still standing in the lobby, waiting for one last goodbye before I took the escalator upstairs.

But when I turned around, I realized there wouldn't be one more kiss or another chance to hug my wife.

Olivia was already gone.

FORTY-FIVE

OLIVIA

OLIVIA

I'm going to have to break up with you.

LACHLAN

Oh, really? Why is that?

OLIVIA

I now have a crush on the most famous tech entrepreneur in the world.

LACHLAN

Anyone I know?

OLIVIA

The CEO of Star Gazer Corp. just announced a new sound card that blew the industry away. The internet is aflutter, positively fanning itself and suffering hot flashes.

LACHLAN

Saw that did you?

OLIVIA

Watched it on the TechieCon live stream.
Lachlan, I'm so happy for you. You've worked
hard for this moment.

LACHLAN

It means a lot that you watched. I wish you
were here.

OLIVIA

Me too.

LACHLAN

We'll celebrate when I get back.

OLIVIA

BOGO night at the Dairy Barn?

LACHLAN

Babe, I think we're both worth full price.

"SHE'S LOOKING at her new ring again."

"But she's frowning. Why is she frowning?"

"Maybe it's indigestion...No? Just me?"

Sitting in my grandmother's living room Sunday afternoon, I pulled my attention from the diamond on my left hand
and to the circle of women around me. Who needed to pay a
high-dollar counselor when you had Sylvie, Frannie, and my
overly attentive sisters? But I wasn't sure they could help me
now. So much conflict in my head and heart.

On Saturday, Celeste had offered me the job in New York.

It was still hush-hush, but she'd wanted me to be prepared
when she made the announcement Monday.

After a full weekend of work for both Rosie and me, we'd

gathered at Sylvie's to eat homemade peach cobbler and pick our next book club selection. Frannie had nominated a novel titled *The Merman Who Loved Me*, which would've been a nice break from the string of Whitney Nicole books we'd recently read, but Sylvie and Hattie overruled her. Looked like our next read would be *The Astronaut Who Melted Her Cryogenically Frozen Heart.* Sylvie had already ordered up a double batch of dry ice for the munchie table.

"I think the ring is beautiful, Olivia." Hattie wore a curious smile that usually indicated an analysis percolated in that head of hers.

"And very unique," Sylvie said from her spot beside me on the couch. "Have you ever seen anything like it, Frannie?"

"Don't think I have." Frannie wore her favorite Beyoncé wig tonight, and she touched her glittery nails to new honeyed highlights. "I once had to use a diamond ring to saw through rope handcuffs. Remember that, Sylvie?"

Sylvie gave a little hum of agreement. "Iran, 1984. A mission went wrong, and as usual, Frannie and I got sent in to fix what the male agents had screwed up."

"I probably should've known better than to marry one of them." Frannie reached for her glass of sweet tea. "But two days held captive, sitting back-to-back while trussed up like pigs ready for the spit kind of bonds a man and woman."

"Impulse marriages are such a wild card." Sylvie glanced over my way. "But can also be so worth it, don't you think, Olivia?"

What exactly did I think? I thought my own marriage had turned completely confusing. If my story were a romance novel, it would have so many one-star reviews that said "Too many unbelievable twists." Or "The slow burn doesn't make any sense." Or perhaps "Meandering plot that leaves more questions than answers." (But it *would* get a small bump for excellent kissing and smolder.)

"Tell us again about the moment Lachlan gave you the ring." Rosie returned from the kitchen, her bowl full of another scoop of ice cream on top of her cobbler.

"It wasn't really this big romantic thing," I said, feeling oddly defensive. "More of a goodbye gift."

When Lachlan had first given me the engagement ring at the airport, my initial reaction had been one of radiant, bursty joy. Like Pop Rocks of happiness and something maybe akin to love. *Snap! Pop! Snap!* My heart had teleported outside of my body to leap over the ticketing counter and run laps around everyone around us.

Then...panic set in. What did I do? What did I really want? I'd immediately flashed back to Tyler taking me window shopping for rings. That diamond solitaire we'd chosen had been a total harbinger of doom. And this year I'd sworn to stick to that life plan—again.

As if given a sign, Celeste had delivered the news of the promotion.

Sure, Lachlan and I could do a long-distance relationship, but I didn't see that working. Not with the hours we both kept.

"I think Olivia's upset she couldn't go with Lachlan to his conference," Hattie suggested. "This is a significant weekend for him, and it's hard not to be there to support him, right?"

"Right." I had initially wanted to go, but work had made that impossible. And when that ring came out, something shifted inside me. I had feelings so deep for Lachlan, I could swim toward the bottom and never touch ground. But we had an impending separation date, and everything was just all messed up, now more than ever. What would Lachlan say when I told him about the new job? If he even wanted to stay together in the first place, would he still, knowing we'd see each other about as often as Old Lachlan shaved?

For the second time in my life, I had a promotion dangling, and yet I was considering throwing it all away for a man. Shouldn't I learn from past mistakes? Celeste's voice took up a significant amount of space in my head, and I could hear her now telling me there was only one answer here. I knew what *she* would choose.

"I love Olivia's face in this photo from TMZ." Rosie held up her phone. "Look at that smile. And, admit it, Olivia. Those are tears in your eyes, aren't they?"

"Our stoic sister showing big emotions in public," Hattie said. "It's been such a long time since she's opened her heart to love." She put down her bowl of dessert to focus on me. "It's like Lachlan knew he'd have to handle you with care, and he has. Classic slow burn, right?"

Sylvie rested her hand on mine. "Sometimes when you've been hurt in the past, the old memories see opportunities to whisper lies in your ear."

"Yeah," said Frannie. "Last week a memory told me I could wear an old miniskirt. Lies."

"Olivia knows what I mean, don't you?" my grandmother asked.

There was no point in denying it. "Right now my relationship with Lachlan is just very...complicated."

"Then uncomplicate it," Sylvie said. "At the end of the day it's about do you love him and does he love you. The rest can fall away."

"It's not that easy," I told her, aware I had the entire room confused, myself included. "I have so many competing forces in my head."

Sylvie's fingers curled around mine, and her own wedding

ring sparkled beneath the dim lights. "It's as easy as you want it to be."

It was on the tip of my tongue to tell my family everything —from the disastrous Vegas wedding, my promotion, to the possibly lovesick woman that I had become. But in a moment of restraint I settled on, "Things have become confusing with Lachlan."

"Does he want you do to role-play?" Frannie's eyes lit with interest. "I have some costumes you can borrow. My Madame Supreme Court justice outfit is newly back from the dry cleaners. It's a fave."

"Not what I meant." At all.

Hattie stood and grabbed her bowl. "How about another round of dessert, then we break out some wine and help you process some things on your mind?"

It would be so good to tell my family everything, to have at least one burden lifted, and to gain their insight into what I should do with my life.

"Hattie, maybe you should bring back the whole pan of cobbler." This was it. I was ready to stop living the lies in front of my family. I, Olivia Sutton, needed help. "I have something I need to tell you all."

Just as I was about to spill every salacious detail, my phone dinged with the unmistakable sounds of five different breaking news notifications.

"Don't pick up that phone!" Rosie yelled.

"Resist the temptation!" Frannie made a grab for my cell, but I moved quicker.

I snatched my phone and checked the screen. "Oh, no." I clicked the first notification, a news blast from *Wall Street Journal,* and felt my jaw go slack.

This was bad. Very bad.

"What is it?" Sylvie asked. "Did your boss forget the name of her first born again?"

"No, worse." I scrolled, scrolled, scrolled, speed-reading each article. "Lachlan's CFO was just arrested in San Francisco on fraud charges."

Sylvie scooted next to me on the couch and leaned over to get a look while I clicked on a second article. She read the headline out loud. "Maxwell Barclay, CFO of Star Gazer Corporation, arrested in the lobby of Ritz-Carlton on multiple charges of fraud." She gave a low whistle. "That's a lot of FBI agents in that photo for white collar crime. Must be *very* big."

I read the rest and felt my stomach sink. Maxwell was suspected of defrauding a large list of investors in an elaborate crypto scheme. According to the headlines, he'd created a private fund for digital investments that never existed, bilking people out of millions.

"Star Gazer stock is going to plummet," I said. "Investor confidence will totally nosedive. Lachlan has to be a wreck."

"Like in this photo?" Sylvie handed me her phone where another photo showed a different angle of the arrest. The FBI escorted Maxwell out with Lachlan in the background, his forehead pinched taut in anger.

When my phone rang, I didn't even bother checking to see who it was. "Hi, Celeste."

"Get to Flair now," my boss said. "War room meeting in an hour."

"I want to talk to Lachlan first," I told her. "I might need to fly out to California."

"I'll assemble the team," Celeste snapped. "If you're not there, I'll handle this disaster and you can kiss your promotion goodbye."

FORTY-SIX

OLIVIA

> **OLIVIA**
> I've left you eight voicemails. Please call me.

> **LACHLAN**
> Not free to talk now.

> **OLIVIA**
> Lachlan, I need to know you're okay. I can't imagine how you're feeling.

> **LACHLAN**
> I'm fine.

> **OLIVIA**
> Then answer your phone.

THE WAR ROOM at Flair sounded a lot sexier than it was.

I'd like to say it was an underground location Celeste accessed by way of retinal scans and cobwebbed passageways.

In reality, the War Room was nothing but an urgent, mandatory team meeting at some wildly inconvenient hour in the green conference room with snacks. Celeste did know if she was asking her people to be there on the weekend, she better provide quality noshings. And did she usually make me pick the food up on my way in? Of course.

But not this time. I set my boundary tonight and told her no.

Okay, I might've stuffed a box of Frannie's cupcakes in my messenger bag, but that was it. That was all I was contributing.

Time standing still felt like time wasted, so when I flew into the office, I skipped the elevator and took the stairs straight to the third floor. Elton sat at his usual spot, and his eyes went comically wide as soon as I entered the room.

"You're late." Celeste set down a charcuterie tray on the table.

I'd blown through two yellow lights and driven ten over the speed limit, making it in record time. We both knew I was not late. "Sorry."

She checked the time on her gold watch. "Gunnar is with a client in Dallas and will call in. Morgan was at the hospital with her father, so she won't be able to—"

"Here I am!" Morgan raced through the doorway and all but pole-vaulted across the table to her seat. "I apologize for being late, Celeste. I wasted ten minutes asking the surgeon to delay my father's triple by-pass."

Morgan could've been bleeding out, lying on the operating table herself, and by sheer force of her need to overachieve for Celeste, she would've stuffed some gauze in her wound and driven to Flair.

Celeste, ever professional in a black Prada mohair skirt and matching fitted blazer, punched a few buttons on a device that brought up Gunnar on the screen. She crossed her arms over her chest and gave a sigh that I felt to the bottom of my worried soul. "I'll skip the review of why we're all here. The goal is to pool our collective brain power and problem-solve for our biggest client. Olivia, do you have any updates from your husband?"

I wanted to lie here so badly. Morgan's eyes bore into me with lasering twin beams of condescension and vibrant distaste, while Celeste regarded me with an intensity that had me twirling my new engagement ring around my finger as if it would conjure miraculous ideas.

One rule of PR was to project the tone you wanted your audience to receive, despite words to the contrary. Clearing my throat, I sat up straighter and spoke with a calm I did not feel in the least. "Understandably, things are very chaotic for Lachlan and his team right now." Did he have a team? *Were* people there with him? I had no idea. And why did I not know? Because my husband hadn't communicated so much as a single emoji. "He's not able to share much at this time, but I'm waiting for an update any moment."

"Are you telling us you haven't heard from your own husband?" Morgan asked this as one would ask, *"So you forgot to wear pants?"*

"As I just said"—*you groveling twit*—"Lachlan and I have not had time for a lengthy conversation. My first concern was if he was okay or if he needed me to fly in to join him." Not that Lachlan had responded to any of those queries. "I couldn't attack my husband with immediate strategy and harass him with things he doesn't currently care about." I let my eyes travel the room, a woman taking control of the narrative. Or drowning in it. Whatever. "Please keep in mind my husband has just been betrayed by not only a trusted employee, but a close friend. Lachlan is reeling. This is more than a news headline, and it's more than business. He's upset and trying to make sense of what's happening, and for that we need to give Lachlan some space." My finale ended with an authoritative rise of volume and an extended pause to once again let my gaze rest on every person occupying a stinky cardboard chair.

Celeste blinked twice behind the lenses of her new red reading glasses. "Well, he doesn't have time!" She flailed a hand toward the ceiling. "His image is your job, Olivia, and his success is Flair's success."

"Completely agree," Morgan chimed in like a two-bit backup singer. "Let's get a plan and execute it." She opened the lid of her laptop. "I'm ready to stay as late as it takes, Celeste."

Elton gave a quiet whine. "I canceled a techno bubble rave for this."

"I'm sorry," I whispered, then turned back to Celeste. "I should be hearing from Lachlan any moment. In the meantime, I agree that we could go ahead and launch press releases on his behalf. Let's contact some news sources to leak some well-placed mentions of Lachlan's complete innocence and disconnect from Maxwell and his crimes. I've already locked down comments on Lachlan's social media, and working in tandem with the Star Gazer marketing department, I've drafted a statement for his website."

Two hours later, I downed the last dregs of the energy drink I'd later regret and hit send on the final email to a reporter Celeste knew at ABC News. My head ached, my brain felt gelatinous, and I just wanted to see Lachlan and wrap him in a hug. What must be going through his head right now? I couldn't imagine the pain and feelings of betrayal.

Celeste caught me checking my phone again. "Any word from your husband?"

I shook my head. "Sorry. I know he's very busy though, so I might not hear until late." Or not at all, a thought that stung.

Yes, I was in charge of his PR, but more importantly, I was his wife and his friend, darn it. Why was Lachlan shutting me out of this? He had to know that I was wrecked with worry.

Morgan plucked a cube of cheddar from the meat and cheese tray. "Maybe he can't contact you because his attorney has advised him not to. We basically know nothing more than what the news reported, which is very little. It's entirely possible there's significantly more to the story."

"That's enough, Morgan," Elton warned.

"What I'm saying is there could be a very big reason why Lachlan hasn't so much as texted his own wife since we've been here." Morgan's face of false concern fooled no one. "Surely he isn't involved in this criminal activity too." She sighed prettily and shook her head. "I sure hope not. Otherwise, we'll look like even bigger fools."

"We won't." I wanted to rip off Morgan's perky ponytail and stomp it on the ground. "Because I can assure you Lachlan not only had nothing to do with his CFO's crimes, but he had no idea. And if you so much as hint that my husband could be involved in something illegal again, I will—"

"Enough." Celeste stood and pushed her chair behind her with a squeak. "We don't have time for you two to come to blows and mess up this conference room."

"Couldn't make it worse," Elton muttered.

"I think we've done all we can tonight," Celeste said. "Go home, get a good night's sleep, and if we must, we'll reconvene in the morning if there is new information. Solid work, everyone. Goodnight."

"I could stay and continue to monitor news outlets," Morgan offered. "Reach out to some of my sources."

"Not your client and not necessary." Celeste inclined her head toward the door. "Off you go."

I slid my MacBook into my bag, wishing I could click my heels and be home. Wishing Lachlan would be there waiting.

"Don't pack up just yet, Olivia." Celeste adjusted the chunky necklace at her throat, her voice authoritative as a drill sergeant. "You and I need to have a chat."

FORTY-SEVEN

OLIVIA

IT WAS with no small amount of envy I resumed my seat and watched Elton and Morgan leave. If I hadn't married a millionaire gaming mogul, I could've gone home too. These were the burdens of being Lachlan's wife. That and finding his *Fortnite* boxers mixed with my unmentionables in the dryer.

My boss sat down beside me, pulling her chair close as if we were the best of friends. "Olivia, sweetie."

Wow, things must be worse than I thought if Celeste was breaking out the endearments. "Yes, ma'am?"

"I want you to know that I realize this situation has put you in a very difficult position."

"It has." I appreciated that Celeste understood. "I'm playing two important roles here—wife and a public relations manager." These roles had separated and blended in new ways, and I felt completely off-kilter. "Things are...complicated."

"I know, dear." Her head angled with such compassion that tears sprang to my eyes. "And of course as Lachlan's wife you should be his support system and confidant."

I sniffed and nodded. "Believe me, I'm trying."

"I know you are. You're our Olivia who never, ever gives up."

"Thank you."

"But your job hinges on turning this disaster around." Celeste handed me a napkin. "Not just the pending promotion, but your very job."

I recognized that tone in her voice and knew the prelude to a Celeste Coulson threat. "I'm doing everything I can think of to get ahead of this. I know Lachlan is an innocent bystander, and we'll make that clear to the public and his investors."

Her hand covered mine, making my engagement ring disappear. "Olivia, when things went bottom-up for you in college, I stepped in to offer you an internship and my assistance without hesitation. Do you know why?"

"You needed a babysitter." Apparently I was now too tired to filter.

"No." Celeste grimaced. "Well, yes, true, but also because I saw a fighter in you. And I saw myself. You were a hard worker, determined, and always operated from a place of discipline and maybe a tiny bit of anger. My instincts were spot-on, weren't they?" An answer wasn't required, and she didn't wait for one. "Now my instincts are telling me that you might know more than you're letting on."

"Celeste, nobody wants to hear from Lachlan more than I do, and as soon as he contacts me, you will be the first person I call."

Her hand gave my fingers a little squeeze. "Think long and hard, Olivia. I've always taught you the importance of having an ace up your sleeve to save for emergencies. Surely my New York-bound senior brand manager has *something* else to give me?"

This was dangerous territory, and I wanted to escape before Celeste wore me down. "Nothing."

She pulled off her glasses, giving me the unfiltered wattage of her stare. "This is your husband we're talking about. You live with the man. You don't have anything to bring to the table we could use to turn this around? A personal story he's shared? A business detail that would be industry news? A tidbit that could drum up sympathy or relatability? My dear, a never-released, personal interest nugget could restore all doubt and save Lachlan's reputation."

"Lachlan donated a hundred thousand dollars to create a STEM scholarship fund at the high school last week."

She tossed up her hands. "Who cares? People could still think he's as crooked as his Chief Financial Officer."

"He paid for dinner for the whole restaurant when we went out a few nights ago."

Celeste pinched the bridge of her nose. "You're deliberately offering crumbs, when what I need is the loaf of bread. Now start talking, or I will need to seriously reconsider my choice for New York." When that didn't register the response Celeste expected, she tried again. "Think of Lachlan. It's not that his dream will die a horrible, painful death. It won't. What it will do is flounder in mediocrity, which to him—or anyone with a dream—is a fate worse than failure. You and Lachlan both have everything on the line, and now so does Flair. If Lachlan or his company goes down, even for a season, then so do we." She clutched my hand in hers. "If you have the power to save Lachlan, you must do it."

The guilt of withholding information—it was too much. I wanted to be the brand manager Celeste dreamed of, the one I'd worked so hard to become. But mostly, I wanted to help my husband. There was no chance Lachlan was affiliated with Maxwell's fraud, and it killed me to think anyone would think for a moment he was. Lachlan was brave, kind, and he'd worked too hard for his reputation to go up in flames in one weekend. "There are some things about Lachlan's life I wish I could tell the world."

"Yes?"

"But he has a right to his privacy." Lachlan had sworn me to silence, and he'd meant business.

It's just that if the world knew that Benjamin Emmerich was Lachlan's father and how the man had cast his son away, only for Lachlan to rise from the ashes and overcome, wouldn't they love and respect Lachlan all the more? Everyone rallied behind an underdog. Lachlan was a self-made success who had defied incredible odds, only to enter the boxing ring with the man who had hurt him most. I'd mentally written this narrative until it was worth an Oscar.

But I could never share it, and I wouldn't. "It's not my story to tell, Celeste."

"Honey." Celeste placed her glasses on the table, her voice softening to almost a motherly coo. "We've known each other a long time. In those years we've gone through a lot together, haven't we?"

"We have."

"You saw me at my worst when my husband walked out. You supported me when my mother passed away. I'd like to think I was there for you when a certain Flair employee broke your heart."

Celeste had given me half a day off and instructions on how to build a bonfire with the things Taylor had left at my apartment.

My boss took a slow inhale and let her posture slacken ever so slightly, a rare sign of her own weariness. "Let's forget business. Forget all about the demands of Flair—your role, my role, our mutual drive to squash every single opponent and be number one."

"I'm not sure how to even occupy that headspace."

With a breathy laugh, Celeste rubbed her temple. "Admittedly, it hurts a bit, but push through the brain cramp and forget our work titles. Right now it's just you and me sitting here. Celeste and Olivia. Friend to friend. Fellow women who toil long and hard and need a safe place to vent." She got up and refilled her water glass, then slid a glass over for me. "Here's a confession for you. On Saturday nights I often wake up in a dead panic, reviewing all the ways I've failed my kids that week. To make up for it, I buy them expensive things they don't even need. I'm never home, I can't keep their calendars straight, and I've missed way too much of their lives in my pursuit of success. It's a hamster wheel I don't know how to exit."

I sat with that a moment. "Wow." So Celeste did know she was phoning it in as a parent—and she did care. That gave me a little hope for her and her children.

"I trust you to keep that to yourself." She tipped back the glass and took a quick sip. "You blab that, and I'll demote you to assistant to the interns. The ones working on the account for plant-based pimple cream."

A grin tugged at my lips, even as I checked my texts one more time. "I won't tell anyone."

Popping a block of cheese in her mouth, Celeste resumed her seat. "That felt good to share. Now, is there anything you'd like to confide? You have my word I won't pass it on to anyone else at Flair."

The desire to tell Celeste absolutely everything pulsed so strongly. I wanted to unzip my lips and let it all gurgle out— the drug-induced marriage, the bargain I'd struck with Lachlan thanks to my insane need to win that promotion, and even the very real chance I'd fallen in love with the man who was now shutting me out. And, let's not forget the personal details of Lachlan's that could shut off the open valve of public distrust for him and his company.

"If you want more to convince you this is a circle of trust," Celeste said, "I can tell you I went on my first date in years last weekend, and I spilled wine on the gentleman and twice called him by my ex-husband's name." She lifted her water glass in a mock salute. "Needless to say, I was not shocked when I didn't get a second date."

I really liked this side of my boss—vulnerable, human. Flawed and relatable. This was the version of Celeste who'd found me at the end of that terrible summer and given me new hope. This was the woman who'd taken me under her wing and saved me. "Please understand no matter how much I'd like to share, I have to honor Lachlan's boundaries."

Celeste twisted an invisible key over her sealed lips. "I understand. But right now we're just two girls doing some unburdening. In a bit, we'll walk out of this office like our conversation never even happened. Now, we know Lachlan was raised by his sweet mother. I'd love to know if we can mine any of the known childhood details for sympathetic gold."

I envisioned myself walking onto a frozen pond, not quite certain which step would make the ice break. I needed to tread very carefully, revealing nothing Lachlan wanted locked down. Yet there had to be something I could safely offer—to satisfy journalists *and* Celeste. "My husband had a challenging childhood," I finally said. "His mother worked her fingers to the bone, raising him on her own." I quickly told her about Lachlan's hard years growing up, the loss of a mother, how he basically took care of himself. The marriage details remained off-limits, but in no time Celeste had a much clearer picture of the person Lachlan really was—his character, his heart, and his determination that had shaped a man and an empire.

Now it was Celeste's turn to grab a compostable napkin and blot her eyes. "Oh, Olivia. I had no idea. What a story. It absolutely breaks the heart, doesn't it?"

"Yes," I agreed. "But despite all that, Lachlan is wonderfully kind and generous. I'd love the press to know how deeply principled he is, yet also humble and compassionate. Our core message should focus on the fact that Lachlan is not some spoiled rich man nor some stereotypical bad boy executive. He's deeply principled and relatable."

"Yes, relatability is so important," Celeste said. "Tell me, is his father is still alive?"

I gave a vague shrug. "His father is out of the picture. Lachlan's created his own family over the years, and his CFO was an important part. If I know my husband, he's reeling over the hits his business will take, but it's the devastation of Maxwell's betrayal that's hurt him most."

"Of course," Celeste said. "The poor man. He's gone through so much. How lucky is he to have you now? And I know when Lachlan's ready, he'll reach out to you and let you in. Because, like me, he'll sense he has a trustworthy, capable ally in you."

I sniffed at her words. "Thank you. I'm very worried about him."

"He'll call." Celeste enveloped me in a hug. "And when he does, you'll be there for him in whatever capacity he needs."

Inhaling the familiar scent of her expensive perfume, I blinked back tears. "Thank you for listening."

"That's what friends are for." Celeste chuckled as she stood. "But tomorrow? I'm back to being your boss. Back to forgetting where my son's practice is and giving way too much of my life to Flair." She walked with me to the door and held it open. "Let's think about how we can play up Lachlan's humble beginnings and exceptional character—without crossing any lines, okay? We have plenty to work with without disclosing any sacred facts."

"I'll work on that," I promised.

"I know you will." She looked so certain in my success. "Get in contact with your husband, compile a list of ideas to send me, then get some sleep, Olivia."

That last command was absolutely impossible.

"You're not alone in this." Celeste's assurance provided a much-needed measure of comfort. "And if you do everything you can"—She flicked off the lights, throwing the conference room into darkness—"things will work out as they should."

FORTY-EIGHT

LACHLAN

TWELVE HOURS ago I'd stood on top of the world.

Speaking to a packed auditorium of hundreds of tech rivals and aficionados, I'd presented the ZeusXL, the sound card that would launch the product arm of Star Gazer Corp into the stratosphere.

The visuals my team had created? Perfection.

The video game simulation I'd conducted? Flawless.

Seeing my bio-dad on row ten, scowling with his hands balled into fists? Surprisingly...hollow. Yes, I'd enjoyed it for a few seconds, but it hadn't been the soul-cleansing event I'd thought it would be. Very anti-climactic, as far as grand schemes of revenge went.

I'd been the king holding court in that moment. The crowd responded with thunderous applause, cameras flashing, reporters shouted questions. All I could think was that I wished Olivia had been by my side.

But sometimes kings get reminded they're just one mistake away from losing their crown.

At three a.m., I sat in the hotel bar, nursing a beer I didn't want and a half-eaten cheeseburger.

The bartender walked over drying a glass. "Sorry to nudge you again, sir, but we did close an hour ago. I'll be locking up in ten minutes."

This guy and I both knew I'd be leaving a tip large enough to make his car payment, as I was pretty much renting my barstool where I sat alone in the dimmed lights. The bartender had stopped asking if I needed anything some time ago, somewhere between a text from Maxwell's wife and my attorney's call demanding I check news sites on the internet for one final ambush.

"I know what they say," I'd told her half an hour ago. "Maxwell took money from a lot of people, he got escorted away by men in suits, and everyone questions my leadership and the stability of the company. I experienced it in real time, so I don't need to see it again."

High off my presentation, I'd been right there in the hotel lobby when they'd come for Maxwell. And before the FBI had got to us, Maxwell had already begun to make his way toward them, as if he knew. The look on his face when I'd ran their way, demanding to know what was going on, ready to defend my friend against any accusation—that look held resignation, regret, and almost relief. Like maybe he'd been glad it was finally over.

I knew when our eyes met that Maxwell was guilty of everything they threw at him.

I'd trusted that guy with my company and my life. I'd been best man at his lame vow renewal last year. I'd spent holidays with him and his family. Hadn't I more than compensated Max for his work? His bonuses alone could've funded the average American family for a decade. And this was how he thanked me? By running some sham Bitcoin investment scheme?

Besides the personal loss, I couldn't even begin to wrap my mind around the fallout for Star Gazer. The IRS would probably be on my doorstep tomorrow demanding an audit, and I couldn't even think about what this would do to our stock. For some reason, investors didn't like pouring money into a company built on shifting sand.

I'd wanted to call Olivia, but there hadn't been time, and my legal counsel had advised against speaking to anyone but them.

Fine. Maybe there had been time to reach out to Olivia, but I'd hesitated. Okay, avoided would be a more accurate word. But I needed to process the failure that was Maxwell, come up with an action plan for Star Gazer, and spend some time wallowing in the mire of embarrassment and anger. So, yes, I'd let Olivia's calls go to voicemail.

Then things got worse a half hour ago.

Much worse.

Because when Janet Paulsen of Paulsen, Reinhold, and Hassan called you, it wasn't because she brought glad tidings.

"Lachlan, you're not going to like the direction things have taken," my attorney had said. "The press found out Benjamin Emmerich is your father."

My hand had frozen over a nearly empty bowl of pretzels. "What?"

"Check the internet. See for yourself. I've got another call. If you need me to sue someone, let me know." Janet had then yawned into the phone. "Apparently I'll be up all night. Don't forget my fee doubles when I miss my beauty sleep. Triple if I have to skip my ten o'clock brunch."

"I'll FedEx you some pancakes." I ended the call, and even though I didn't want to, I pulled up a favorite news site.

And considered throwing up.

Un-freaking-real.

Second story beneath the headline showed a photo of me and one of dear old dad. "In Epic Move of Revenge, Lachlan Hayes Reveals Tech that Will Shut Down Benjamin Emmerich —His Father." Another site gave me top billing in the news proclaiming, "Abandoned by Father, Lachlan Hayes Defies Odds and Creates a Tech Empire."

It only got more soap-opera dramatic from there.

I'd never wanted to be connected to Benjamin. I was happy denying our biological ties, just as he was. If we ignored it, then the DNA couldn't speak. But now it was out there, and I was once again Emmerich's son. Specifically, I was his *unwanted* son.

This story leak might've boosted some investor confidence, but I would've chosen bankruptcy over pity. The world could keep their sympathy. I didn't need it then, and I sure didn't want it now. The next article I pulled up on CNN cited the information source as "a representative of Lachlan Hayes."

Olivia had gone to the press. In the middle of the night, my wife had reached out to reporters with a breaking news scoop.

I sat with that hurt for another half hour, eating a burger I didn't want and watching the captions scroll on the TV hanging on the back wall of the bar.

Maxwell's actions cut me to the quick, but Olivia's story leak ripped out my heart.

Now, as I laid down my Mastercard, a shadow fell across my plate.

Good Lord, I couldn't have sketched out a plot this bad if I'd tried.

"Hello, Lachlan." Benjamin Emmerich leaned an aging hip against the bar. "Or I guess I should say—son."

Of course he'd be haunting the halls of the hotel. Like a vampire. Dude probably melted in the sun.

"I was just leaving." The hotel and the entire state. I'd find a plane out of there at daybreak if I had to fly it myself.

"What's your rush?" Benjamin sat his tall self on the stool beside me, as if we were friends. "Congratulations on the sound card technology. How innovative to invent something and attempt to ruin my company all in one product."

"I thought so." My days of cowering to this man over, I faced him head on. "Be sure and tell your employees they all have jobs with Star Gazer anytime they want. They don't need to be collateral."

"How kind." Benjamin's white hair looked slightly disheveled, as if he'd run his hand through it once or twice. "But I take care of my own."

His smile was so mustache-twirly I had to laugh. "Right. Forgot you were such a family guy."

"I guess your PR wife didn't."

"My wife is none of your concern, *Dad*."

"I knew you'd cash in on my name sometime. Guess you wanted to wait for the right time. Like when your own company begins its first revolution around the drain." His large hand circled once, then twice.

"Star Gazer will be fine. And do you know why? Because we make more than one product."

"You're too diverse."

"Says the man picking out tombstones for his dying technology."

His green eyes flashed. "You think you know it all. You designed a little game that took off with all the hard work of a YouTuber unboxing a toy, and then you thought you could play entrepreneur. How's that working out for you?"

"I guess we've both had better days."

"I've been in this business long enough to see hundreds of

start-ups like yours come and go overnight," he said. "But I'm still here, and I'll be here next year and the next."

"Thanks for the warning." Where was that bartender? "Maybe you and my brothers can make new widgets and get back in the game. I wish you well." With that, I pulled out what cash I had and laid it over my ticket.

"You're reaching for things you can't have," Emmerich said. "Out of your league—with your business, your little movie, and maybe even your family. The things you've wanted have always been elusive, haven't they, son?"

I forced myself to unclench my teeth and put on that old *Who cares?* face I'd worn most of my life. "The last person I'm going to take career and marriage advice from is you."

"Your friend Maxwell betrayed you." Benjamin stood, his height no longer equal to mine. "Given your disdain for any connection to me, I'm wondering if your wife did too. You might not want my advice, Lachlan, but I'll leave you with some anyway."

"Make it quick, one of us still has a functioning company to run."

Benjamin Emmerich's veneers shined as he smiled. "I've had a handful of wives and business partners. But in the end, the only person I could ever depend on was myself. You put your trust in others, they're just going to let you down. I've worked my butt off to stay in this tech game for decades, and I won't be taken out by one single upgrade."

I was too tired to argue with a narcissistic blowhard. "Got it, Dad."

"I have other products in the works, other options. Your big reveal didn't catch me completely by surprise. My point is, you have to prepare for failure as much as the success. You sit here moping like you've lost your world, but what you should do is go back to your hotel room and get busy figuring out how to navigate your losses. That's what a CEO does. Because moments like tonight? You haven't seen the last of them."

"Very encouraging." I kept my face impassive, as if his words barely penetrated. "Got it."

"Yes, you have it now. But will you five years from now? Ten?" Benjamin's questions hung in the air like bubbles in need of popping. "Decide what matters to you and fight for it. That's how you stay in the game." His fuzzy eyebrows rose as Benjamin clapped a large hand to my shoulder. "Watch your back, boy. Because I'll return better than ever, and I won't hesitate to take you and your company down."

With that parting shot, Benjamin Emmerich, longtime tech magnate and worst father of the year, walked away, leaving me alone in the bar.

My dad was only partly right. Sometimes you did have to fight for what mattered to you. But other times, you had to know when to let go.

My business needed me now more than ever, and I'd work hard to keep it on level ground.

But my marriage?

Olivia had walked away from that last night, and it was time I did the same.

Just like we'd planned.

CHAPTER
FORTY-NINE
OLIVIA

OLIVIA

Lachlan, I can explain. Please call me.

OLIVIA

I had nothing to do with this. I need you to believe me. When are you coming home?

OLIVIA

TALK TO ME.

OLIVIA

I'm begging you to pick up the phone.

AT ONE O'CLOCK THE next afternoon, I stood in front of my TV and watched the news. I wasn't sure I'd moved from the spot since breakfast. Did I think if I changed networks, the headlines would be different? In all this time I'd become horribly aware of two things. One, my boss was a manipulative liar who would sacrifice anyone and anything on the altar of Flair. And

366

two, I had been such a fool to confide in her. For a bonus, we could throw in one more certainty, and that would be that Lachlan probably wanted to strangle me.

No matter the channel, the news was all the same. Unrest in the Middle East, inflation expected to climb, and Lachlan Hayes, CEO of Star Gazer Corporation, was the biological son of tech magnate Benjamin Emmerich.

A clammy sweat beaded at the back of my neck, and my heart thudded an unsteady pattern. I'd called Lachlan exactly fifteen times in the last hour with no response.

Because my husband thought I'd betrayed him.

So much was uncertain in my life, but one thing wasn't— the knowledge that Celeste was responsible for the leak to the press. It only took three texts to a few of my connections in network news to confirm. I didn't know how Celeste had uncovered who Lachlan's dad was, especially in record time, but I shouldn't have been surprised she'd gone digging for that information. Perhaps I'd confided too many personal details of Lachlan's childhood. As if the poor man needed one more thing to deal with.

Ten minutes later I stood in the kitchen and poured my fourth cup of coffee. I'd composed an entire monologue of what I'd say to Celeste when I finally calmed down enough to go into the office. How dare she? The unmitigated gall. I'd seen her act ruthlessly before, but this defied the boundaries of ethics.

I would *never* taxi that woman's kids again.

I picked up my phone and hit redial once more. "Lachlan, I know you're mad, and you have every right to be. But at least let me explain. Please, talk to me. I—"

"And what could I possibly have to say?"

I spun around and there, standing in our kitchen wearing jeans, a wrinkled sweatshirt, and a dark scowl was Lachlan.

Handsome, beautiful, Lachlan. I had to blink a few times to make sure my overwrought mind hadn't conjured him.

"Lachlan." Rushing to him, I threw my arms wide and hugged my husband with what was left of my strength.

He did not hug me back.

Noticing the distinct chill in the room and his stiffened posture, I took a step back. "How are you here?"

"Chartered a plane at an ungodly hour, then drove home to my loving wife." His eyes didn't quite meet mine.

I hated the flat, lifeless tone in his voice. "I have so much to tell you. You have to know I didn't—"

"What, Olivia?" Lachlan set down his travel backpack with an angry thud. "You didn't mean to go to the press with your knowledge of my dad? You didn't mean to betray my confidence—information I'd shared with you as someone I cared about? Do you know how many people knew about Emmerich? You, Miller, two attorneys, and my CFO who may have just booked an extended stay in a federal prison."

"I didn't go to the press. I would never have hurt you like that." He had to believe me.

Lachlan looked so tired—eyes bloodshot and puffy, a few days' worth of stubble on his face, and his expression resigned and distant. "I knew from the start I was business to you, a way to get that promotion. I guess you did what you had to do."

"It wasn't me." I needed him to believe me.

"Then who?" He watched my face for two heavy heartbeats before understanding dawned. "Let me guess—Celeste. Right?"

"Yes, but—"

"Seriously, Olivia?" Lachlan shook his head before stalking to the coffee pot and pouring himself a cup. "You had to know what she'd do with that information."

"I didn't tell her about Emmerich. I swear to you."

His hard stare felt like a slap. "I don't buy that."

"I did share how difficult you had it growing up—that I admit to. I told her about your mother and the challenges the two of you faced together. But when Celeste asked about your dad, I shut her down, Lachlan. I never said Emmerich's name or anything that would ever give her any hints who your father was."

"Then how did she know?"

"I was about to head to Flair and ask her that very question." I'd only stalled all day, mentally scripting how the scene would go. Most of the versions involved lots of screaming. Mine, mostly. "I would never intentionally betray you. Please say you believe me."

"I know you wanted that promotion badly."

"Not at the price of hurting you." And I meant that. The way Lachlan looked at me now spun webs of fear in the darkest corners of my conscience. I wanted to hit rewind and fix every broken thing. "I wished I'd gotten on a plane to you instead of spending one second at Flair."

Lachlan closed his eyes and drank deeply from his mug. I saw the situation through his eyes—the betrayal, the hurt, the ruin. So much ruined. Would Lachlan ever trust me again? He probably thought I was one more loved one who'd let him down. "Say something, Lachlan. Please."

Leaning against the counter, Lachlan scrubbed a hand over his face. "The good news is my stock will recover, if not surpass last week's high. You made me into a sympathetic, if not pitiful hero while generating interest in Star Gazer and all its drama."

Defeat elbowed me right in the heart. "You don't believe me."

Lachlan didn't deny it. "I've been assured big investors might pause, but every small investor wanting a piece of the next big tech company will probably call their brokers today. That should bring you and Flair some relief."

"All I care about is you."

His head raised sharply and his eyes locked on mine. "Me?"

"Yes. It kills me to see you hurt." I braved a few steps toward Lachlan, wishing I could touch him, but knowing it wasn't yet welcome. "I thought you knew me by now. Do you really think I'd be so heartless that I'd sacrifice you for the sake of a promotion?"

Lachlan gave a mirthless laugh and stared into his coffee cup. "You were just doing your job, right?"

"You're not a job. You're my..." This was surely the wrong moment to tell Lachlan how I felt about him. But how did I feel? I was crazy about this man, but also scared to death of where we went from here.

Lachlan finally looked at me, one eyebrow curved in challenge. "Your *what*, Olivia?"

Anxiety crept into my throat and strangled half the words I wanted to say. "I care about you."

"You care. Well, cool." The anger left Lachlan's face, replaced by that old familiar expression of boredom and bland disbelief. "Right. Well, no matter who gets the blame, the damage is done now."

"I can fix this," I said, feeling him slip away. "Somehow I'll make this right."

Lachlan deposited his coffee mug into the sink, then walked right past me and out of the room.

"Where are you going?" I asked as I followed him up the staircase. I was stalking my own husband, begging Lachlan to hear me out, rehashing details of my conversation with Celeste, desperate for him to tell me I wasn't to blame.

Lachlan's shoes fell heavy on the wood floor as he crossed the hallway and ambled into his bedroom. With a large amount of clatter, he retrieved a suitcase from the closet and began to fill it, pulling shirts and pants from hangers with no regard for care.

"What are you doing?" Was he leaving? "You just got here."

Lachlan paused. "Did you organize my closet?" Then he continued the pillage. "Of course you did. You handle everything."

Add closet organization to my long list of regrets. "Why are you leaving?"

"As long as my home base is still in San Francisco, that's where I'm needed." Lachlan moved on to his tie rack. "Losing Maxwell means my company is without half its leadership. I need to meet with attorneys, auditors, accountants, and my new buddies at the FBI."

Tears clouded my eyes, and I turned my head so Lachlan wouldn't see. "I could go with you," I said as I inspected a color-coordinated row of sweaters. "I could help out." *Beg you to forgive me and not let us go.*

"I don't think that's a good idea." Lachlan dropped a pair of Nikes into the suitcase. "You have work."

No. "Lachlan—"

"I'll be in California for at least a few weeks." He closed the lid and yanked the zipper with horrible finality.

I sniffed, pretty much not caring now that tears free-fell down my cheeks. "I'll come a few days early for the movie premiere."

"The day of the event will be fine." Lachlan's lips thinned into a small smile. "I should go. I have a plane waiting."

"Let me drive you to the airport."

"Not necessary."

This couldn't be how it ended. I knew if Lachlan walked out of this house, we were done. "After you kissed me in the dressing room at Paolo's, you said things had changed between us. We were going to talk—about us."

He grabbed a stocking cap and pulled it on his head. "I think I spoke in haste. You were pretty clear when we said goodbye at the airport you didn't feel the same."

Tears caught on the mascara Celeste had once recommended. "You didn't speak in haste. I—"

"Olivia, we were a business arrangement, right? Two people in a terrible situation who stayed married to satisfy our individual goals. And we succeeded, don't you think? Our relationship has run its course. In fact...I think I'd like to attend the premiere solo."

This had to be his rejection talking. How did I get through to my own husband? "We've planned for your premiere for months. I'm your publicist—and your date." Forget my usual need to control a client's outcome; I just wanted to be with Lachlan on his big night, to see his face as he watched his movie for the first time, and to share in his moment.

Lachlan reached for my hand, his touch achingly gentle. "It's time to go our separate ways." He sounded so terribly polite. "It's what I want."

I swiped at the tears, simultaneously hurting for the both of us. "What if *I* don't want to?"

His hardened features softened. "We've had a great time... and now it's over. I think we both let the pretend roles go to our heads, but the last few days have given me a much-needed shot of reality."

"I know you're mad, but—"

"I'm not mad." With a deep sigh, Lachlan leaned down and pressed a kiss to my forehead, his scent achingly beautiful and familiar. "I've got to go."

I wanted to cling to him, grab his arms and never let go. "Please don't leave yet." *Please don't leave me.*

"I'll call in a few days."

He wouldn't. We both knew he wouldn't.

Lachlan wrangled his suitcase down the stairs, as I trailed behind him, still waiting for the right words to turn back time and make all the wrong go away. But I had nothing.

This was what I'd once wanted wasn't it? An easy break from Lachlan and a tidy divorce to clear the way for my new job.

But everything felt so wrong.

I followed him out the garage door and into the driveway where November had painted the sky as gray as my heart, and the wind blew just as frigid. Leaves that had held bravely onto branches now fell one by one, fluttering to the ground in surrender.

Lachlan tossed his suitcase in the backseat and opened his car door. He jangled the keys in his hand as he regarded me, the warmth gone from his gaze. This was the same man who had kissed me senseless and made me feel things no one else had. And now we were just done. Somehow this calm, quiet goodbye hurt more than my last dramatic, cheating breakup.

"I'm sorry," I whispered.

"Me too." Lachlan reached out and tucked a windblown piece of hair behind my ear, his fingers tracing the arc of my skin.

"I've told no one about Benjamin. Not one person."

His hand fell away and tucked into the pocket of his pants. Lachlan said nothing, but his face made it clear he didn't believe me.

"We still have work to do," I reminded him.

"No." Lachlan said it so resolutely, like he no longer trusted me with his career. Or his heart. "I'm done. And now you can get back to your regularly scheduled life plan, right?"

I could. And that should make me happy. But why didn't it make me happy?

It was over. Our fake marriage had crashed just like that ill-fated boat in the Italian grotto. "I'll miss you." My quiet confession quivered with every syllable.

"Stay in the house as long as you need. My attorney will contact you with the next steps."

That sounded so final. We were back to being cordial acquaintances, former associates. "Goodbye, Lachlan."

He took my face in his hands one last time and brushed his lips over mine. "Goodbye, Livvy."

I don't know how long I stood there in the driveway, quietly weeping for Lachlan's trench-deep hurt and the confusion flooding my own bereft heart. But after some time, I became aware of the bitter air against my skin and the golf carts cruising by for their frigid afternoon games. Life carried on as if completely unaffected by the seismic shift in my world.

I had very little figured out when I finally found the energy to return inside.

What I did know was that I would see Lachlan in a few weeks.

But my husband?

I was certain he was gone.

CHAPTER
FIFTY

OLIVIA

ONE HOUR later the elevator doors of Flair swooshed apart, safely spitting me out to the third floor. My feet ached in my heels and words swirled in a vortex in my head. My blood pumped with nothing but coffee and anger, and anyone who got in my way had better be prepared for a stand-off. I was a hurting person who had hurt someone, a starting player in a chain of back-stabbing that had gone too far.

I'd received so many texts from Celeste and Elton, I was surprised my phone hadn't combusted.

Lachlan was gone. He'd driven away from his house and from me. I'd stood outside, halfway expecting him to circle the block and return, ready to talk. But that hadn't happened. And why? Because he still thought I'd betrayed his confidence and shared his biggest secret with my blabbermouth of a boss.

I guess he was right about one thing—I would now reset my life and get back to the Olivia Sutton Life Plan. Lachlan had been a detour I'd never planned on taking, and now that I could steer this life back in the right direction, my internal GPS didn't want to comply.

"Olivia." Celeste's assistant jumped from her desk, wearing joggers and running shoes. "The brand manager meeting started fifteen minutes ago. You're outrageously late."

"I'm aware."

Berta followed me down the hall, as if I were a flight risk. "They're in the green conference room. It's National Health and Fitness Day."

Stupid holidays! "Do you know what day it is for me today, Berta?"

She eyed my windblown hair. "A sleep in late day?"

"A get my heart stomped on and wake up betrayed by my boss day."

Berta's short legs struggled to keep up with me. "Sounds about as fun as the rest of them."

I flung open the conference room door, and the assistant shuffled in behind me, as if anticipating a scene.

"...and that's how I increased sales by thirty percent last month." Morgan's eyes widened as she caught sight of me. "Well, hey, Olivia. Nice of you to join us."

The room was full, but I only had eyes for Celeste, who stood there at the head of the table, wearing a Dior shift dress that clashed with her guilty expression. "Olivia...do come sit down."

"I'd rather stand." On a scale of one to ten, my anxiety registered about a fifteen as I walked toward my boss. "I'd like to talk to you, Celeste."

"We're obviously in a staff meeting." Her fingers clutched at her necklace. "It will have to wait until we're done."

"Then I'll start talking now." I glanced at my coworkers, who all looked equal parts frightened and enthralled. "I think everyone should hear how you overstepped your bounds with my client, somehow dug up and shared hurtful, private information, and basically punched ethics right in the face."

Elton picked up his coffee. "I'm all ears."

"You and I can speak in private," Celeste said tightly.

"After all I've done for you." That list could provide building materials for at least three more chairs in this biodegradable mess of a space. "I've chauffeured your children. I've been their part-time nanny and done the work of two brand managers. I've given up my nights, my weekends, my family time, and any semblance of a personal life."

"I do believe I've done plenty for you," Celeste clapped back. "Shall we revisit your last year of college when your university tossed you out?"

"That was seven years ago!" Man, did that feel great to raise my voice at my boss. "My debt is paid. I've been more than a good return on your investment. Let's talk about what happened last night."

Celeste glared at me over her glasses. "Not here."

"Oh, yes, right here." I wasn't going anywhere until we had this out. "Right here in this room that smells like patchouli and wet pizza boxes. Last night I shared details with you about Lachlan's life, and you assured me it would stay between us. What was it you'd said? We were just two girls doing some unburdening, right?"

Celeste sniffed in disgust. "You obviously had put personal feelings over the success of your client and of Flair, and I needed to take charge."

"What you did was betray Lachlan and me." How had I ever thought Celeste was worthy of hero status? "My priority was my husband, and you knew I was feverishly working on his PR. I could've managed that just fine without exposing his paternity to the entire world."

Elton gasped. "You did that?" He pointed a scone toward Celeste. "Girl, no."

"Tell me how you discovered the truth about Emmerich," I

demanded. "Did you hire a private investigator to work overnight?"

"No," Celeste said hotly. "I dug around myself. It wasn't hard, so when you're aiming that blame, keep in mind anyone could've uncovered who Lachlan's dad was, and soon someone would have. I scanned the internet for paparazzi photos and easily found a dozen of Lachlan and Benjamin at a restaurant in New York. Their resemblance is unmistakable. My son showed me Lachlan's old gaming YouTube account from his college days, and wouldn't you know it, his half-brothers, who he called by name, made appearances in a few of his videos. All that took me less than three hours. If Emmerich and Lachlan wanted their connection kept private, they should've worked harder to make that happen."

"People matter, Celeste." My skin burned with heat, and it was all I could do not to bellow. "The lives of a father and son matter. *I* should've mattered."

"I will not tolerate failure on my watch, Olivia." Celeste was not a woman accustomed to being challenged, and she didn't seem to know what posture to strike while enduring it. "You had an ace up your sleeve, and you refused to use it. You knew what you needed to do for your client, and you wouldn't pull the trigger."

"What about the right thing to do as a human being?" I asked. "Do you have any idea how much I've looked up to you all these years? I wanted to dress like you, talk like you, command a room like only you can. But now?" Good heavens, I'd been so blind. "Now I realize how hollow your success is. You'd sell out your own kids if it meant a win for Flair."

"It's time you left." Celeste stabbed a finger toward the door. "I'll have Berta pack up your desk."

"You can't fire me, Celeste." These next words frightened as much as they satisfied. "I quit."

Celeste gave a bitter laugh, her smile saying *oh, you simple little girl.* "That promotion was all yours, Olivia. You're going to throw it away now?"

"No." I saw the truth in her face and knew she'd played me for a fool for the last time. "You've passed me over before, and you would've done it once more. You need me here too much— for Flair and for your children. I've been your Yes Girl for years. But today? Today I'm telling *you* no. I'm done."

"Fine!" Celeste yelled. "I don't want someone this sensitive and immature anyway."

"And another thing?" If I was going down, I might as well torch this job beyond all recovery. "I despise theme days. We all do. I hate wearing costumes to work. Nobody thinks they're fun, and the only thing they inspire is stress."

Elton lifted a hand to testify. "They make me chew Prozac like bubble gum."

"Goodbye." I gave a room-sweeping wave. "I've learned a lot during my time here, I'll miss most of you, and I wish you all the best. Oh, and Morgan, Celeste's kids have to be at school by 7:45. You should probably learn the route."

"You're making a huge mistake," Celeste called out as I walked to the door.

"I've made a lot of mistakes lately." I glanced back, taking a mental snapshot of my old life. "But this isn't one of them."

CHAPTER
FIFTY-ONE
OLIVIA

SYLVIE

Olivia, open your door or I break it down with nothing but my bare hands.

ROSIE

Answer the phone, Olivia.

HATTIE

If you need to talk, I'm here.

SYLVIE

Of course she needs to talk. And even if she doesn't, I DO.

HATTIE

I have a listening ear.

SYLVIE

I have sweet tea.

FRANNIE

I have cupcakes.

ROSIE

I have books.

You could run from my family, but you couldn't hide.

Believe me, I'd tried.

So on Friday afternoon when a window in Lachlan's living room eased open as if by magic and Sylvie threw a leg over and fell inside, I didn't even bother getting up from my cocoon of blankets and misery on the couch. Sure, Lachlan's house was armed to the very last shingle with the best security system money could buy, but of course that didn't stop my retired CIA granny.

It was a waste of breath to ask, but I did it anyway. "What are you doing?"

"Young lady"—Sylvie dusted off her pants and stood. "—I'd like to talk to you about your car's extended warranty."

My head lolled to the pillow behind me. "Is there anything I can do to convince you to go away?"

"No."

I closed my eyes and accepted my fate. "Then go let the others in."

Exactly thirty-four seconds later, the Sutton clan and Frannie stood in my living room, bearing snacks, two gallons of tea, and a bag of paperbacks from the Lost Story.

"Wow." Frannie walked around the couch, taking a 360 view of my condition. "It's worse than I thought. When's the last time you showered?"

"I don't remember." Wednesday? Thursday? My days no longer consisted of work and Lachlan. Turns out it was harder to keep tabs on nebulous things like time when you whiled away the hours with Netflix and snot-crying.

"You missed Sexy Book Club on Tuesday," Sylvie said, "So we knew something was amiss."

"I thought maybe you'd been kidnapped." Frannie parked it on a leather chair and unboxed the cupcakes. "Sylvie and I haven't had to retrieve someone from the clutches of evil in a long time, so I was a little bummed when we learned you were most likely home."

"Sorry to disappoint." I still had one season of *Grey's Anatomy* to watch, and I really needed the ladies to move it along. "What can I do for you? I'm very busy."

"We can tell." Rosie sat at the end of the couch, giving my feet the once-over. "Are those Pac-Man socks?"

I adjusted the blanket with a huff. "Maybe."

Hattie eased herself to the floor beside me. "And is this really my fashion-obsessed sister wearing Lachlan's vintage Donkey Kong sweatshirt?"

"I found it in the dryer." Because I'd looked for it three days ago during an especially bad crying jag. Even laundered, it somehow smelled like Lachlan. "My silk blouses are indisposed."

"Sugar, Miller talked to Lachlan," Sylvie said. "We know your husband's in California...for a while."

"Elton stopped by the shop." Rosie pulled off the lid on a gallon jug of tea. "He told us you quit Flair."

"About darn time." Sylvie held up her hand for an air high-five, but I couldn't dredge up the energy to lift my arm or my spirits. "To use the words Hattie says way too much, would you like to talk?"

Hattie grabbed a cupcake from Frannie. "I don't say that a lot."

"Like daily," Rosie countered. "But we love you for it. Now spill, Olivia. Tell us what's going on."

Where to even begin? "You know how in a romance novel

when secrets are spilled, the book gets better?" I sniffed indelicately. "Turns out in real life, you pretty much get the opposite effect."

"Ohhh, we're gonna need more cupcakes." Frannie picked up her phone and punched some buttons. "I'll have my sweetie Ernie deliver."

I wasn't sure there were enough cupcakes in the city to make my problems any better. "I made the mistake of talking to Celeste about Lachlan's childhood. She did some research, discovered who his biological father is, and she went right to the media." I accepted a glass of tea from Rosie and unfurled the story that I'd kept wound around my heart all week. I told the ladies everything from Celeste's betrayal to the moment Lachlan told me goodbye and left his house and me in his rearview mirror. "But it's okay." Ever prepared, Hattie handed me a box of tissues, which I used with a loud series of blows. "Because now I can get back on track with my timeline. I still have two years before I'm supposed to fall in love and etch out a little time from my bustling career to dedicate to a relationship." My nose continued to run as the tears returned. "Not that I have a job to sacrifice or anything."

Oh, gosh, my life was a toilet bowl, and I now swam circles in its murky depths.

"Everything is terrible, girls." I held up my glass for a refill. "Lachlan answers my texts, but they're all ridiculously polite and impersonal."

"Have you tried sexting?" Frannie chewed a large bite of cupcake. "Worked for me and Ernie. Would you like some pointers?"

Ew. "No, but thank you."

"Offer doesn't expire, dear."

I grabbed a pillow and hugged it to my chest. "I have no job prospects, and my husband just left me."

"But you'll see Lachlan at the movie premiere, right?" Hattie asked.

I swung my legs over the side of the couch, my unused muscles numb and tingling—much like my heart. How did I explain the premiere—that it was just the final job in an agreement made by two desperate people who'd been victimized in Vegas? "Lachlan doesn't want me there."

"You're still his wife," Hattie said. "Olivia, this doesn't have to be the end of you two. So you had one big fight, that doesn't—"

"We didn't really fight," I told her. "I wish he would've gotten mad, but he didn't. Lachlan was very calm and kind about the fact that my boss let the world know who his father is, even when he thought I was responsible."

"Then what's the problem?" Hattie asked.

The problem was that Lachlan thought I didn't love him, but how did I explain that to my family? "So many people have let Lachlan down in his life. Now he thinks I'm one of them."

"But if your marriage can't survive one hiccup," Rosie said, "then something's incredibly wrong. Marriage is something you fight for. Love is too important to walk away that easily. Maybe he's running scared."

I was going to have to tell them, wasn't I? I'd kept it to myself long enough and the lie of my fake marriage had weighed me down ever since we'd left Vegas. "I have something else you should probably hear."

"Wait." Frannie pulled a piping bag of icing from her coat pocket and squirted it directly into her mouth. "Okay. I'm ready."

I'd disappointed so many people lately, what was four more? I couldn't sink any lower. These people were my family and *had* to love me no matter what. "Lachlan and I didn't mean to get married. I'd never dated him and our relationship wasn't real."

A dog barked somewhere outside.

The heater kicked on and hummed a monotone tune.

The TV screen stared back at me in a paused tableau.

Finally Sylvie spoke first, her voice dry as the magnolia leaves in the backyard. "What? No way."

"I'm so incredibly shocked," Hattie drolled.

Rosie considered her manicure and matched Hattie's flat-lined tone. "But you two were so convincing."

"Nobody's ever fooled me like you two." Frannie squeezed out more icing. "Such acting skills. You should be an actress. Or join the CIA."

I sat up straighter, my back cramping with the effort. "You guys knew?"

"Do you think we're completely crazy?" Sylvie held up her hands. "Don't answer that. But yes, we knew."

"Why didn't you say anything?"

"Because we got a front row seat to a romance novel in real time," Rosie said. "Two opposites. Enemies to lovers. A tumultuous past. Forced proximity. You two have it all."

"Except a real relationship." Such a dismal thought required more sugar.

"We didn't know what we were watching," Hattie added. "But it was fascinating."

"From anyone else, we would've challenged the quickie wedding." Rosie propped her feet on the ottoman. "But you've never made a decision that wasn't thoroughly analyzed to death, so we assumed you had your reasons."

I clutched a blanket to my chin and eyed the box of baked goods. "I don't analyze everything."

"I've seen you make a spreadsheet before buying toilet paper," Frannie said.

So maybe I was typically an over-thinker. "Lachlan and I were roofied in Vegas." I let the ladies process that one, receiving all sorts of cries of dismay from my sisters and promises to mete out justice from Sylvie and Frannie.

"Oh, Olivia," Hattie said. "I wish you would've confided in us. That's terrible."

"Lachlan hired a private detective," I told them, "but it ended in a dead-end." Kind of like my sham marriage. "The last few months have been head-spinning."

"Are you saying you didn't mean to fall in love with your husband?" Frannie asked. "This is just like in *Wrap Me in Your Fins*, the Victorian merman romance we read last year. The couple wed for convenience and fell in love, despite their class differences—*and* his inability to breathe more than ten minutes on land."

"I'm not in love with Lachlan." Nor was I in an amphibious relationship.

"Then why do you look dehydrated from crying?" Sylvie asked.

"Because I didn't have anything better to do after I quit my job."

"What *do* you feel for Lachlan?" There Hattie went with that therapist voice and her *tell me everything* eyes.

Last night my heart asked me if I loved Lachlan, and I pleaded the fifth. No comments at this time. "I hate that I hurt him—or that he thinks I hurt him." I could still see Lachlan's face when he walked into the kitchen that morning he returned home. "He left believing I outed him to the press and regarded him as nothing more than a business arrangement."

"Is he important to you, sugar?" Sylvie asked.

The answer was so simple...yet so complicated. "Yes."

"I know a big *but* when I hear one," Frannie said, "and I hear a big but."

"But my goals don't allow for a real relationship right now."

"Because of the life plan," Sylvie asked, "or because you have an ex-boyfriend who left so much scar tissue there isn't space?"

"The plan works," I said. "I need to remember that. Deviating from the timeline has never, ever served me well."

Rosie stood and brushed crumbs from her dress. "I hate to break this up just when I'm about to argue with you, Olivia, but three of us have a shift at the bookshop that starts in thirty minutes."

"We're helping with an author event." Hattie pulled me in for a hug. "But we'll be back."

"I know, I know," I said into her flannel shirt. "Because this conversation isn't over."

"No." She squeezed me extra hard. "Because we're not letting you go through this alone. Pizza tonight at your place, so shower and run a brush through your hair before we return."

"Fine." I ignored her smack to my backside and walked with her to the foyer. "But I'm not putting on a bra."

"Pretty much my life motto." Frannie grabbed her purse and hoisted over her shoulder. "Bye, baby. And if you want, me and Sylvie can take care of that dragon ex-boss of yours."

"No, leave Celeste alone."

Frannie opened the front door and stepped outside into the gray day. "Maybe a teensy-weensy relocation to Bermuda? Oh! I bet she has a fancy car. What if it disappeared?"

"Not necessary," I said, "but I appreciate the thought. I love you guys."

"We love you too." Rosie hugged me tightly then joined the others on the sidewalk. "See you later, sis."

I shut the door behind me, turned around, and pressed my aching back to the cool hard wood.

"Now that they're gone, let's really talk."

With a startle, my eyes popped open. "Sylvie!" There my grandmother stood, stealthy as ever in the doorway to the living room. "Didn't I just usher you outside?"

"Nope." She sashayed back into the living room and sat down next to my pile of cozy blankets. "Have a seat, Mrs. Hayes." She patted the space beside her.

That might be the last time anyone referred to me as Mrs. Hayes. Why was that thought such a landslide of sadness? "I'm all talked out, Sylvie." I flopped down beside her. "Do you hear that? It's Netflix calling my name."

Sylvie rested her hand on my leg. "Why haven't you gone after Lachlan?"

So many reasons, all of which I'd listed in triplicate in my head. "Why would I? We said we'd end it after the premiere, and we are. Lachlan just got a jumpstart on the separation."

"You know what I think?"

"That's a rhetorical question, isn't it?"

"I think when Taylor ended it, it wasn't the loss of a great love that broke your heart. It was that you took a chance and failed—that's what really messed you up. You stepped off that neurotic schedule of yours and it didn't pay off. You've been carrying hurt and shame over that ever since."

"Taylor stole my client, my ideas, and my promotion. There's plenty there to jack a girl up."

"But losing him doesn't compare to Lachlan walking out, does it? Because when it's that grand love of a lifetime, it wrecks you like nothing else can."

My mask of annoyance slipped and my bottom lip quivered. Hot tears escaped down my cheeks, and I furiously dashed them away. Because if I gave into the tears again, I wouldn't be able to stop. "Sylvie..."

"Yes, sugar?"

"I didn't mean to fall in love with Lachlan."

"Oh, hon." She wrapped an arm around me and folded me into her side. "We all fell for the boy."

"Why did he have to be so great?"

"Same thing people say about me, sweetie. Lachlan and I can't help it. We are who we are."

"Breaking up is the right thing to do." I said the thought aloud because both of us needed to hear it. "Lachlan and I are so very different, and I have things I need to accomplish first."

"Different can be good," Sylvie said. "And what's stopping you from knocking out goals just because Lachlan's in your life?"

"Do you realize what happens when I deviate from the plan?'

Sylvie perched at the edge of the couch and angled her petite body toward me. "Honey, life is messy and crazy. That's the beauty of it all. If you avoid the messy and the mystery, you avoid some of what this world wants to offer. Bees don't fly in straight lines. Birds don't. Neither does a canister of tear gas. Just ask the Sultan of Brunei who tried to cop a feel in 1998 and hopefully still cries every time he thinks about it. You keep drawing your straight lines from point to point, but this crazy journey is a squiggly path with highs and lows and curves and swerves."

I thought of Italy, of Taylor, and the morning I woke up wearing a wedding ring. "It's also where things hurt."

"It can be." Sylvie reached out and swiped a tear from my cheek. "But you know what else hurts? Missing out on living. Missing out on saying 'yes' and 'maybe' and 'let's see where this goes.' Honey, do you love Lachlan?"

Lachlan.

The man who made me laugh, who filled out a Minecraft t-shirt better than anyone had a right to, and the guy who danced like a dream. He was hallway conversations when I was sick and early morning debates over strong coffee. Lachlan was the man who waited up for me every evening with dinner warming, while filling my days with funny texts that caused heart emojis to float overhead. I'd never forget how he'd hugged me on his birthday, as if he'd never received a greater gift. We'd made so many memories in the short amount of time we'd been together, and they'd kept me company every minute since Lachlan had left.

"I do love him." There. I'd said it. I waited for the rush of freedom to come with the declaration—but it didn't. "If Lachlan ever felt anything for me, it's gone."

"Go to the movie premiere." Sylvie held my shoulders in a firm grip. "Take that chance and tell Lachlan what's in your heart."

"He doesn't love me." I clearly felt more for him than he did for me. Because reoccurring themes and all that. "If he did, he wouldn't have ended things the way he did."

"But my dear...what if you're wrong?" Sylvie pushed to her feet, as if that settled it all. "You have twenty hours before your plane leaves tomorrow morning."

"What?"

"You and I leave at ten." My grandma waved a hand in my general direction. "I'll pick you up, so put some makeup on, for crying out loud. You have one final act as Lachlan's public relations manager, and you're gonna do it." She gave my cheek a smacking kiss. "We'll be back with dinner, but in the meantime shower and do something constructive with your time."

"Like job hunt?"

"That can wait." Sylvie's lips curved into a sly smile. "Say, have you ever played a game called *Mars Wars*?"

"You know I don't play video games."

"Maybe you should start. Besides pack, what else do you have to do?" My grandmother hugged me again. "And maybe get Lachlan a new security system."

CHAPTER
FIFTY-TWO
OLIVIA

How hard could a video game be?

That was exactly the question I'd asked myself after another crying jag and two slices of cold pizza.

At two-thirty in the morning, I put my plate in the sink, then made my way to Lachlan's office wearing Lachlan's sweatshirt so I could sit in Lachlan's monstrous gaming chair. For the record, he was right. The sci-fi prop of a chair *was* like sitting on a pillow of clouds. Would he notice if I took it with me when I moved out?

Just the thought of leaving made my stomach churn. I'd begun to think of his house as ours, silly as it was. My family had brought me dinner just like they'd promised, and they'd sat with me until late. The ladies had filled the living room with laughter and conversation, and when I burst into tears twice, they plied me with hugs and homemade cookies.

On Monday I'd update my resume and LinkedIn profile, then scour the internet looking for a new job. But not this weekend. No, this weekend was for feeling sorry for myself and wondering if I needed to rework my life plan too. Instead of a serious relationship by thirty, maybe I just needed to plan on getting a dog. I missed Lachlan so much I ached with it, and I wondered if the feeling would ever pass. Would I walk through the rest of my life thinking of him, hearing his voice in my sleep, and reliving every moment we had together? I kept waiting for the storm of sadness to subside, but it had only amped up like a big old emotional hurricane.

Part of me thought Lachlan's reaction was a bit extreme. To just walk out on us because the world now knew who his father was? Yes, I had shared more than I should have with Celeste, but she was the one who had taken it way too far.

But maybe it didn't matter because the end result was the same—Lachlan felt betrayed by someone he cared about, someone he'd trusted and shared part of his heart and life with. He'd been hurt a lot in his life, and he'd been rejected by those he loved too often.

Not that he loved me.

Probably didn't.

But what if he did?

"All right, *Mars Wars*." Sniffing, I logged into Lachlan's computer, clicked his game app, and with a little finagling, the mammoth screen dangling above the chair came to life.

Skipping the cinematic intro, I cut right to the chase. I'd played a few games on Elton's PlayStation, but I had no idea what I was doing with Lachlan's game.

Still, I could appreciate the graphics, the incredible scenery of his imaginary space world, and the phenomenal biceps on my character, who went by the name of Captain Triton. Apparently the goal was to get through exactly one million levels in order to rescue the fair Princess Serafina.

And maybe I was punch drunk on carbs and self-inflicted misery, but the baddie on level two kind of looked like me. I would swear I heard Captain Triton call this snake-haired woman Bolivia Dutton, so obviously not me. Though before I finally stepped into the shower in the mornings, there was at least a passing resemblance.

Awkwardly navigating the keyboard, I made my Captain Triton shoot a laser gun at aliens, crash a space craft, and jump over obstacles during a downpour of acid rain. Who knew Mars was so violent and ecologically unstable?

It was like Lachlan said—each time I messed up, I took what I learned and got a little further the next time. I could see how this game was so addictive, especially when played on a screen larger than a football field and so bright it could burn my retinas. Every time my character died, I immediately jumped back in and returned to kicking alien butt and trying to save a princess.

Did I check my phone a dozen times during the game? Yes. But I thought Captain Triton, who seemed to be the romantic sort, would understand.

Two hours later, high on the success of finally reaching level ten, I pressed pause on the app and ran to the kitchen for a water refill and another slice of pepperoni.

I startled upon my return, hearing voices from the office.

"The love of Captain Triton and Princess Serafina could not be denied. He would cross galaxies, jump worm holes, and fight every evil beast to find the lady who'd stolen his heart."

Was that the introduction of the game playing? Returning to my plush seat, I fixed my gaze back on the screen where something as intricate as a movie played. Settling in, I took a bite of pizza I didn't really need and watched the *Mars Wars* origin story unfold.

"An unlikely hero is our Captain Triton," a male voice narrated. I'd heard that deep voice in my dreams and smiled at the thought of Lachlan telling the story he'd created. "Many men have tried to save Serafina, but all failed. Time is running out to rescue the princess. The Ring of Hope, a promise of fierce courage and abiding love, unlocks Princess Serafina's gilded cage. Can Captain Triton find it in time...or will he lose the princess forever?"

I leaned forward in a rush, all but smashing my nose to the monitor.

There in high-definition graphics so real I could almost reach out and touch it was the very ring I wore beside my wedding band. Pressing pause, I studied the ring Captain Triton must find, a symbol of courage and love. Two rows of rubies encircling a cushion-cut diamond? Just like mine. An engraved band of florals and scrollwork? The same.

For the first time in days, my sluggish heart beat a new rhythm, one of hope and possibility.

Lachlan *did* love me.

Didn't the proof sit sparkling on my left hand?

If he loved me, then we had something to work with—we had a chance. Lachlan couldn't turn off those feelings that quickly, hurt or not.

I'd spent my career turning bad situations around, and my PR analysis said our relationship could definitely be restored. It just needed a little communication, some finessing, and a special kind of brand management.

And kissing. Lots and lots of kissing.

Because I loved Lachlan Hayes.

I loved his beautiful, scratchy face, his big hands, and the way his eyes sparkled when he fired off a bit of sass in my direction. I loved his deep laugh, his easy smile, and the way his hand sought mine like I was his safe place. Which I was. And would be again.

I adored how Lachlan's mind worked, so differently from mine. He was an innovator, a creator, and a natural storyteller. I prayed he hadn't written our ending just yet.

Grabbing my phone on the desk beside me, I punched a few buttons and pressed it to my ear.

Finally, I got an answer on the fifth ring. "This better be good, Olivia Sutton."

"Sylvie?" I smiled at her craggy voice. "Let's go to a movie premiere."

My grandmother yawned on the other end. "My bag's already packed."

CHAPTER
FIFTY-THREE
LACHLAN

I'D JUST STEPPED AWAY from Ryan Seacrest when I saw her.

Olivia.

On Saturday night, the red carpet felt about as comfortable for me as a nudist colony in winter. Cameras flashed, people scurried everywhere, reporters shouted questions. I watched actors and actresses strike poses just like Olivia had taught me. Designer dresses, tuxes more expensive than a year of college.

I stood by a backdrop of *Mars Wars* and watched Olivia step from a limousine, a vision in a gold glittery gown that fit so well it looked like she'd poured herself into it. She wore her hair in waves that once again reminded me of old Hollywood, but her black stilettos were pulled straight from my fantasies. My gosh, she was a vision. All these plumped, tucked, and filled actresses, and none compared to the woman I'd briefly called my wife.

The red carpet area swarmed with cast and crew, while assistants and press buzzed about. But that crowd parted when Olivia walked my way. Make room for the starlet.

"Lachlan, we need some shots of you and the lead cast members," the executive producer said as he checked a message on his beeping phone. "Join us in five?"

"Got it, Ken," I told him, my eyes tracking every step Olivia took. What was she doing here?

The producer followed my line of focus and grinned. "Maybe we better make that ten." And with that, Ken disappeared into the crowd, intercepted by reporters and well-wishers desperate for a moment of his time.

It had taken everything in me to ignore Olivia's calls and texts. I'd spent months talking to her daily, texting sometimes hourly, and I'd felt her absence this week like a lost limb. To need someone you couldn't have was almost unbearable—yet nothing new in the course of my life.

A photographer snapped rapid-fire shots of Olivia as she approached, and I couldn't help but notice she didn't wear that practiced, perfectly angled smile she'd taught me. Nor did she even look at the photographer. I was pretty sure that uncertainty I saw on her tired face was not the look she was going for, and it made me both curious and unsettled. I'd told her I didn't need her here. Not because I'd mastered the necessary skills to pull off a stylish evening among Hollywood elite, but because I simply couldn't handle pretending to be married to Olivia one more second.

That apprehensive beauty of a woman sidestepped one of the highest paid actresses in Hollywood and stopped right in front of me.

Olivia looked at me.

I looked at her.

"Hi," she finally said.

"In the neighborhood?" I inquired.

"Yes." She licked her red, glossy lips. "My husband is here somewhere."

"Is he now?"

Olivia leaned closer, her voice dropping to a stage whisper. "You might've seen him. He's a very big deal."

"Really?"

"Really." Her smoky eyelids blinked rapidly, an interesting sign of nerves. "He, um, told me not to come here, but I couldn't help it."

"You must be his PR manager."

"No." Blue eyes locked onto mine. "I'm his wife."

There wasn't a single weapon in *Mars Wars* that could devastate more than Olivia could. My blood roared in my head, and my bowtie constricted the very neck that now seemed devoid of oxygen.

I just couldn't do this. "What are you doing here, Olivia?"

The warm night air blew her dangling earrings. "I'm Princess Serafina."

A flash lit the space beside us. "I'm quite certain you're not."

"I saw the Bolivia Snake Hair woman." She gave a dismissive shrug. "Rude, but I get it. That was another time, another me. I'm definitely Serafina now."

"This is a bold statement." *Hey, let's rip out Lachlan's heart in front of a hundred cameras, shall we?*

"I'm that woman waiting for you. Except you won't answer calls or texts or the thousands of messages I've sent using nothing but telepathy and really bad renditions of Celine Dion songs."

"Don't do this here, Olivia." I had so much riding on tonight, and after the hits I'd taken recently, I couldn't endure one more public disaster. "I get that you needed to see our deal to the end and claim your success, but after the premiere, you and I have to go our separate ways." The urge to reach out and touch Olivia raged. I'd missed her more than I thought possible, and seeing her tonight poleaxed what was left of my heart.

"I quit Flair," she said. "I'm currently unemployed."

That was... unexpected. "I'm sure you're very hurt and confused right now."

"Nope. Things are pretty clear. Like the fact that I'm still so enormously sorry Celeste went to the press and you think I was responsible."

"I've had some time to reconsider." Because Olivia had been right—I did know her. And, okay, I'd done a little investigating of my own, but my trust issues had been sorely tested of late.

Olivia's posture slackened in relief. "You must believe I'd pick you over my job any day."

It was hard not be charmed by her fervor. "Would you now?"

"Something else that's clear is that you and I belong together, and I'm sorry I didn't tell you that when you left. Face it—we're hot stuff, Hayes. A couple for the ages. The ultimate hero and heroine. Swoon and Swagger. Trope-tastic."

"It's not going to work, Olivia." We were done. I'd ripped off that Band-Aid when I'd left Olivia standing in my driveway. "That's not how the plan goes."

"Plans change."

That declaration had my attention. "Yours don't."

"I should've told you how I felt sooner, but I have some baggage. Tunnel vision. Possibly a neurotic tendency or two." Olivia brushed some lint from my tuxedo jacket. "I had a long talk with Sylvie—she sends you her love, by the way."

Another arrow to pierce my soul. Sylvie was part of a family like I'd always wanted.

Olivia took a deep breath, then plodded on. "My grandmother reminded me that the people who were supposed to love you left. I know that's shaped who you are—and maybe made you scared to give your heart and trust me. And while my favorite romance novels have the hero going after the heroine with some grand gesture, your heroine came for you, Lachlan. And do you know why?"

Nope. I was not gonna let myself hope. "Because you need one final big PR event for your resume?"

"Because it's time someone showed up for you and gave *you* the grand gesture." Olivia reached out and rested a soft hand against my cheek, her thumb sweeping against the stubble I'd rebelliously allowed. "And because I love you, Lachlan Hayes."

As far as events went, this one between us was a big one. Seven simple words, yet they could unlock so many levels. My pulse doubled in pace, and I struggled to think of an adequate response.

"Hayes!" Ken, the producer called mere feet away. "Picture time, dude."

"I need to go," I told Olivia. "Surely you don't want me to miss a photo opp."

But Olivia didn't budge. Instead she removed all space between us and clasped my forearms. "I said I love you."

"I...I heard you."

"Lachlan, I've been determined to follow my life plan, but none of it matters if you're not part of it. I thought my last relationship was doomed because I'd strayed from the timeline, but it failed because I was with the wrong person." She squeezed my arms. "You're my person."

To our left the cast and grew gathered in front of an intricate *Mars Wars* backdrop. That was where I needed to be, but I couldn't seem to make my feet move. "Olivia, it's probably natural that we felt some connection. We lived together and pretended to be in love."

"Can you tell me what you felt for me in the last few weeks wasn't real?"

I wouldn't lie to her. "No."

"Do you love me Lachlan?" When I didn't respond Olivia held up her left hand, the lights around us glinting across the facets of her diamond. "I'd also like you to tell me if anyone can buy these rings?"

I blinked against more flashes of light. "What are you talking about?"

"Is my ring a mass-market product from the movie merchandising?" Olivia asked.

This felt like dangerous territory, a black hole of conversational topics. "Pretty sure there's no merch like that."

She swept the windblown hair from her eyes, her gaze steadfast on mine. "You had this ring made, didn't you?"

"I'm not sure it matters." Everything. It actually meant everything.

"Tell me what it means," she demanded because my wife was bossy like that.

"I really have to go," I said. "We'll talk about this when the after-party's over." I took three steps away from Olivia when I heard her call above the noise.

"I know you love me, Lachlan Hayes!" I turned to see her hold up her hand again. "I sat in your big ugly chair and played *Mars Wars*. This is the Ring of Hope, sitting right next to my wedding band, and I'm pretty sure it's a promise of fierce courage and—"

"And abiding love," I finished, walking back toward her. Maybe I was a glutton for further punishment, but I never quit on a level when it got good. I stood before Olivia, feeling the stiches of old wounds itch. Faded wishes whispered prayers I hadn't uttered in years. I'd been denied love so many times, but this sure resembled the real thing. "So," I said, afraid if I blinked Olivia would disappear, "you played *Mars Wars*."

She smiled. "Till four in the morning."

"My high score is two million and seven."

"Mine is two hundred and seven," she said just as arrogantly.

I was out of my mind crazy about this woman. "Then you didn't get far enough to know that after the Big Bad is defeated, there's a hidden bonus scene. Once the princess is freed, she has to rescue Captain Triton from a dragon."

Olivia's hand slipped into mine. "I'll slay dragons for you, Lachlan Hayes."

If she didn't stop talking, I would bawl right in front of the Who's Who of Hollywood. "People think Captain Triton saves Serafina," I said roughly, "but what they don't realize is she saves him—from darkness, from himself. You think you can save me, Olivia?"

"I'm really trying." Her gaze went warm on mine as she captured my other hand. "You told me at the airport this ring was just a piece of jewelry, but it's not, is it?"

"It was for my wife."

"I'm your wife."

Not one molecule in my body moved. "Are you?"

She removed all space between us, then looked up at me with eyes as fierce and certain as that first day I'd walked into Flair. "Yes."

Then I kissed her. Grabbed Olivia with zero finesse and kissed the sass right out of her.

In the last few months I'd learned an endless list of ways to be dignified and diplomatic, but that training never covered what to do if the woman you loved followed you to California and promised to slay your dragons. I knew people were watching, photographing even, but I didn't care. All these days without Olivia in my arms had been too much, and I showed her exactly how I'd missed her. My mouth held hers while my hands got lost in the soft waves of her hair. I captured her sigh, my fears abating with every exquisite brush of lips and breath.

"I love you, Olivia," I told her. "I didn't mean to, but it happened."

"I accidentally love you too." She rested her forehead against mine. "What are we going to do, Lachlan? I need a plan."

"Fail forward—together."

Olivia looked up at me, a ghost of a smile on her lips. "I've had some practice at that lately."

"How's it feel?"

"Kind of terrible." She rose on tiptoes and kissed my chin. "But I know it's taking me where the good stuff is."

"And that includes me?"

"It has to," Olivia told me. "You and that awful gaming chair and the sweatshirts of yours I've been sleeping in and the breakfast you're going to fix me every morning."

"See, you have part of a plan already."

She sealed her lips over mine while the *Mars Wars* theme song began to play. "Let's go watch a movie, Lachlan."

Inside that theater was a realized dream, a miracle so big I couldn't fathom the odds. But the movie and gaming success meant nothing without Olivia by my side. Life hadn't always dealt me the best hands, and there would be days ahead where I'd worry that abiding love would disappear. I hadn't freed Olivia from a gilded cage, but maybe I'd help release her from the bonds of her past too. Like my good friend Captain Triton, maybe we could push through with fierce courage—together.

"We'll have quite the story to tell our children," I said as we walked hand in hand toward the theater.

Olivia leaned against my side, her dress billowing behind her. "Worthy of a romance novel."

"Or a video game," I said.

My wife stopped and wrapped her arms around my neck, pulling me in for one more kiss. "Or just a really wonderful life."

EPILOGUE
OLIVIA

One Month Later...

LACHLAN

Lunch at the Lost Story? I'll swing by that
taco truck you love.

OLIVIA

I'm very busy not working. Do you realize how
much quality TV I've missed over the years?

LACHLAN

Tear yourself away and meet me at the shop.
I'll buy you a cupcake.

OLIVIA

Can't. After TV time is over, then it's a three-
hour block of Mars Wars.

LACHLAN

I've created a monster.

OLIVIA

You're just bothered because I've systematically and strategically raised my score by 60%.

LACHLAN

I still think Sylvie slipped you some cheat codes.

OLIVIA

Not true, but I am sleeping with the game designer.

LACHLAN

The perks to that must be endless.

OLIVIA

That's what he tells me...

FOUR WEEKS after the world's best movie premiere, I inspected myself in our bathroom mirror as I applied makeup for the first time in weeks.

Coffee-stained leggings? Check.

Mars Wars sweatshirt stolen from Lachlan's closet? Check.

Hair in a disastrously disarrayed bun on my head? Check.

High heels? Nope.

Designer outfit I'm still paying for? No way.

Weighty expectations to overachieve and follow a meticulously created life plan? Never again.

Because plans were great—and don't get me wrong, I was still making them—but my days were just as sweet in all the side roads and detours that life took me down. Like now, for instance. I'd *planned* on watching two hours of a reality show, grabbing a snack, then committing to two more hours of *Mars Wars*. But instead, I was meeting my husband at the Lost Story.

And I hoped *his* plan included queso, extra salsa, and his lips on mine.

Fifteen minutes later, I parked the car near Rosie's store and burrowed deeper into my coat. Light flurries spit and spun in the crisp air, and I could smell snow on the breeze. The sky above me might've been gray, but my heart was as bright as the sunshine in June. In a few days it would be Christmas, and I couldn't wait to share it with Lachlan.

Mars Wars the movie earned blockbuster status right out of the gate. It still played in sold out theaters across the globe, and there was buzz already for the screenwriter and lead actor. I was so proud of Lachlan, I could hardly stand it.

As I opened the front door of the Lost Story, a bell tinkled overhead and warm air whooshed out to welcome me.

"Hey, Rosie." I waved to my sister, who stood behind the cash register, ringing up a sale to Sylvie. "Do not let her buy any more Harry Styles photo biographies," I called out.

The store was sadly empty for the noon hour, but I knew Rosie had been crazy busy for the holidays. And maybe I'd just missed the rush, because Hattie stood in the mystery section, unboxing books. That was so like her to help on her lunch break. We Suttons liked to pitch in.

"Another date with your sweetie?" Sylvie asked as she slipped her receipt in her bag and made her way to me.

I tugged off my gloves and stuffed them in my coat. "Tacos and books. What more could a girl ask for?'

"Hm." Her lips curved into a smile. "Indeed." Then my grandmother threw her arms around me and yanked me into a hug that would've done rib damage to someone who *hadn't* put on ten pounds from near-constant gaming. "I do love you, Olivia."

"I love you too." I awkwardly patted her back. "Have you seen Lachlan?"

She straightened and smoothed her flawless hair. "I believe he's around here somewhere. Rosie, have you seen Lachlan?" she called.

Rosie pointed toward the middle of the store as she slapped some wrapping paper on a trio of books. "Last spotted in the romance section. Follow the scent of nachos."

"I'll see you at book club tonight." I kissed my grandmother's cheek, then wove in between shelves and beautifully decorated displays. The holiday cozy novel section was a personal favorite. I thought Rosie's miniature Christmas tree adorned with poison bottles and faux murder weapons qualified as borderline genius.

Now that Celeste and Flair no longer controlled my life, I'd dedicated more time to helping at the Lost Story, turning Rosie's marketing plan up a few decibels until it blasted even more fun and community, luring in customers and book lovers like never before. Rosie had hired extra staff last week and was currently interviewing for a store manager.

I spotted the top of Lachlan's head over a bookshelf and smiled. That handsome fellow was my husband. And my boss.

Starting next week I'd be the new senior brand manager for Star Gazer Corporation. We'd recruited Elton as well. His sign-on perks included a bonus, the freedom to bring FeeFee to the office anytime he wanted, and the assurance our conference rooms wouldn't smell like sawdust and well water. New York and big city PR firms no longer held the same appeal that they once had. But Lachlan and the life we'd build in Sugar Creek? This was what my new dreams were made of.

Lachlan stood in the romance section, studying the colorful spines. I snuck up behind him, wrapped my arms around his waist, and pressed my cheek to his back. "The new Whitney Nicole book is a good one. It's set on a dude ranch, if you're into cowboys."

With a quiet laugh, Lachlan turned and held me in a warm, flannel embrace. "I'll just borrow your copy." He kissed me right in the store, as if he didn't care to scandalize books and patrons. They were all used to it by now anyway. "I'm more into the sexy public relations type. The kind who end up with tall, devastatingly handsome tech nerds."

"What a coincidence," I said. "That's my new favorite too."

He released me and pulled a list from his pocket. "I'm shopping for Sylvie. Come help me find the book she requested."

I peered closer at the massive list. "She asked you for seventy-one things?"

Lachlan nodded. "That was after a deep edit." He pointed to item number forty-two. "Rosie swears this book is here, but it's hiding."

"Fine." I sighed dramatically. "But then you ply me with tacos. The urban fantasy romance is on the next aisle. Let's go."

With my husband's hand in mine, I tugged him around the shelf and into the next aisle where...

Where a blanket sat anchored by a picnic basket, candles, and a bottle of wine?

"What's going on?" I heard myself ask. "Lachlan?" Receiving no answer, I turned around.

And found Lachlan kneeling on one knee in the Lost Story, while my entire family stood behind him. There was Sylvie, Frannie in a new wig, my parents, my sisters, and even my brother Colin.

"Oh." Tears immediately welled. "I don't think this book-shop event was cleared by marketing."

"I have the owner's permission." Lachlan reached for my hand and clasped it in his. "Olivia, you came into my life in the most unexpected, life-changing, and highly illegal way." His grin would still melt my heart sixty years from now when my hair was white and our grandchildren forgot to call. "You became my best friend in a short time, filling a space in my heart I'd assumed was forever off-limits. You challenged me, you encouraged me, and you made me laugh. You also made me want to kiss you the first day I moved you home."

I probably would've punched him if he had.

With a laugh, Lachlan sniffed and swiped at the tears now glimmering in his green eyes. Heavens, I loved this man.

"I once thought love was for movies and games," Lachlan said. "But you came along and taught me love really could be for me too. Olivia, I want to spend forever with you. You, and your bossiness, your constant planning to the last detail—"

"I've backed off a lot," I said toward my family. "I need that noted."

"Your occasional planning to the last detail," Lachlan amended. "I love the way you take lead when we dance in the kitchen, the way you hog the TV remote, and I've even come to appreciate the way you steal my gaming sweatshirts when you think I don't notice. But I do." He kissed the top of my hand. "Because I notice everything about you, wife. It's my new favorite pastime. Well, that and beating you at *Mars Wars*."

"I'm closing in on his score," I told our audience. "And he's scared."

Lachlan smiled. "What I love about you most, Olivia, is your heart. You love fiercely and your loyalty is unmatched. You work hard at everything you put your intentions to, and the very thought that you're mine still takes my breath away every day."

Oh, goodness. This was better than any novel I'd ever read. And it was all mine.

"So, Olivia Sutton Hayes." Lachlan clasped my fingers even tighter. "Will you marry me?"

I gave a watery nod. "But we are married."

"I'm so confused," I heard Colin say.

"I was told there'd be tacos?" from Frannie.

Lachlan's eyes, full of love and happiness and a lifetime of wishes, held mine. "You and me, Olivia. This time we do it right. In a church. With a pastor who doesn't belt out "My Heart Will Go On" during the nuptials. Your family, our friends, and a bride and groom who are of sound mind and so much love we make the whole chapel slightly nauseous."

"And cake!" Frannie yelled.

"Sounds about perfect." Just when I thought I couldn't love Lachlan more. "Now stand up and kiss me."

Ignoring the squeak of the old hardwood floor, Lachlan ascended, drawing himself up like the handsome Captain Triton he was. This guy was my future and my everything. And to think, I'd almost missed it all—just because he wasn't written in ink on my life plan. Wild detours would always kick up my anxiety, but with Lachlan by my side, I'd be okay. And if not okay, then we'd just kiss a lot while we rode out the storm.

Lachlan's mouth covered mine, while my hand slid up his chest and rested right over his heart. Beneath my fingers was a beat that thudded steady and true. Just like my Lachlan. He was comfort and excitement, thrill and safety. He'd been let down and left behind enough times to ink lasting tattoos of pain, but that ended with us. It stopped with me. Because I was never letting this six-foot-two stud muffin of gorgeousness go.

Not that Lachlan wasn't getting a heck of a deal by marrying me. He certainly was. PR whiz, expert problem-solver, and a formidable wingman in *Mars Wars*. Plus, I came with a giant family of delightful crazies.

Sylvie stepped into the aisle. "Do you have another ring for Olivia?" Sylvie asked.

"No need." I held up my left hand. "Totally covered."

"Actually," Lachlan said, "I have something better." He reached into the shelf next to him and pulled out a Tiffany blue bag. "For you, Mrs. Hayes."

A hush fell over the shop as I dug into the famous bag.

Then pulled out...a customized game controller. The tears returned again. "My very own?" I asked.

"Because I love you so much. And because I want you to leave mine alone." Lachlan pressed his lips to my cheek. "I scraped cheese dip off of it last week."

"I love you, Lachlan," I said for his ears only.

"You haven't given the poor man an answer!" Sylvie yelled.

"Yes," I said with zero hesitation, holding my husband in my arms. "My answer is yes."

Lachlan kissed me again, his touch sweet, gentle, and a promise of what was to come. "To happiness," he said, repeating the famous *Mars Wars* otto. "May be both find it."

I snuggled into this man of mine, smiling against his awful pink plaid shirt. "And let it lead us where we need to go."

"Together," he said.

Now that was a plan I could count on. "Together."

ALSO BY JENNY B. JONES

SWEET ROMANTIC COMEDY

Lost Story Bookshop Series

Wild Heart Summer

A Katie Parker Production (Books 5 & 6)

Enchanted Events Mystery Series

His Mistletoe Miracle

A Sugar Creek Christmas

The Holiday Husband

Save the Date

Just Between You and Me

YOUNG ADULT

A Charmed Life series

A Katie Parker Production series (Books 1-4)

I'll Be Yours

There You'll Find Me

About the Author

Get a free book from Jenny by signing up for her newsletter at **www.jennybjones.com/news**.

Award-winning author Jenny B. Jones writes rom-com with sass and Southern charm. Since she has very little free time, Jenny believes in spending her spare hours in meaningful, intellectual pursuits, such as checking celebrity gossip and pursuing her honorary PhD in queso. Jenny digs foster care, animal rescues, and her adorable son. She lives in the great state of Arkansas, where she's currently at work on her next novel and loves to hear from readers. Check out *Finding You*, the movie adaptation of her novel *There You'll Find Me*.

www.jennybjones.com

 facebook.com/jennybjones

 twitter.com/JenBJones

 instagram.com/jennybjonesauthor

ACKNOWLEDGMENTS

This book would not have been possible without the help of people I love and appreciate in squeezy, huggy, grateful amounts.

With profound thanks to:

Erin Valentine— dear friend, incredible proof editor, and one of my favorite librarians.

Judy Christie— comma genius, brilliant writer, and one of the most intentional encouragers I'm blessed to know.

Christa Allan— sassy friend, tolerant and wise grammarian, and woman who writes lines I highlight and wish were mine.

Jocelyn Bailey— editor extraordinaire, tolerant of my million texts on writing and Royal watching, and one of the kindest, smartest, classiest gals I'm blessed to call friend.

A big thank you to all readers, whether you got the book for review or for fun, I appreciate your love for books and authors.

www.ingramcontent.com/pod-product-compliance
Lightning Source LLC
Chambersburg PA
CBHW020504260626
47156CB00006B/1856